About the author

Joan Brady is an author and freelance writer. She has worked in Irish journalism for most of her life but has in the past found gainful employment as a waitress, a secretary, an agony aunt and a bartender. She is a self-help aficionado, which is where the inspiration for *Reinventing Susannah* came from. Her first novel, *The Cinderella Reflex*, is also published by Poolbeg.

Find out more at www.joanbradywrites.com

Acknowledgements

If it takes a village to raise a child, it takes a team to publish a book.

Sincere thanks are due to:

My publisher Paula Campbell for all the encouragement during the last year.

My editor Gaye Shortland, whose valuable input has made *Reinventing Susannah* into a bigger and better book than it would have otherwise been.

My agent Tracy Brennan of the Trace Literary Agency for all her enthusiasm.

Tara Sparling for reading the manuscript early and often and managing to sound enthusiastic *every single time!*

Carolann Copland and Bernadette Kearns for all their support in the ups and downs of the writing life.

The team at the Wexford Literary Festival, especially fellow scribes Carmel Harrington, Caroline Busher and Cat Hogan.

The readers of *The Cinderella Reflex*, especially those who expressed how much they liked it. That means more than I can say.

Susannah, the heroine of this book, who reminded me of the words of one of my favourite writers, the late Nora Ephron: "*Above all, be the heroine of your life, not the victim.*"

All the friends who had my back when I needed them to. You are too numerous to mention here but you know who you are.

The Saturday walkers – for making my weekends brighter.

Jane and Darren Kelly, for bringing the sunshine back into my life.

And, finally, to Dave. Sometimes courage is not about one big gesture, but simply doing the right thing day after day.

"*When the first baby laughed for the first time, its laugh broke into a thousand pieces, and they all went skipping about, and that was the beginning of fairies.*" J.M. Barrie

For Jane O'Connor Kelly

CHAPTER 1

When the phone rang, Susannah deliberately rejected the idea that it might be more bad news. It was nine months now since her mother had died, nine months since every time the phone rang she leapt up from whatever she was doing, her heart hammering as she snatched up the receiver.

"Susannah — can you get away?"

"Rob?"

Susannah was surprised to hear her husband's voice. According to him, he rarely had time to do *anything* apart from the mountains of work which had built up since the bank let half their staff go under a redundancy scheme, meaning the remaining "lucky" ones got to do two jobs instead of one.

"Is there anything wrong?" she asked.

"Wrong? Why should there be something wrong?"

"No reason." Susannah put her hand on her chest, aware that her breathing had speeded up and her muscles had tensed at the sound of the phone.

"Are you busy?" he asked.

She glanced out at the black plastic bags lined up like sentries along one wall of the conservatory, destined for the dump or the charity shop. She had just finished a marathon clear-out, with the twins' permission and certain strictures, ruthlessly culling anything to do with the past.

"Not especially. Why?"

"I wondered if you could come into town – meet me for lunch?"

"*Lunch?*"

"Yes – what's so strange about that?" Rob's voice had a definite edge.

Apart from the fact that you haven't asked me for lunch since the girls were about twelve? Susannah wondered silently. Plus, she remembered Rob making his sandwiches last night, slapping on the butter with a lot more force than was necessary. Or had that been the night before? All the days seemed to run into each other nowadays.

"How come you have time for lunch?"

"It's Dress-down Friday," Rob said aggrievedly.

"Oh right … I forgot."

Dress-down Friday was a new policy the bank had initiated for staff who weren't working directly with the public – a misguided attempt to soothe the simmering outrage among them as their terms and conditions were quietly eroded. They got to leave their career suits at home and got an extra half-hour for lunch in the hope that morale might improve.

"So I'll see you at one," Rob said brusquely. "In that restaurant near the office – you know the one. It does pasta and pizza."

"Oh yes." Susannah felt a flicker of optimism. "I like it there. I haven't been in years. I can walk down the canal from the train station."

Silence.

"Rob?"

Susannah stared at the phone. He'd hung up on her.

She shrugged. At least it meant a reprieve now from getting rid of the bags.

She couldn't look at them without an ache in her heart. They contained over twenty years of twin paraphernalia. Susannah tried to appreciate the benefits of a household that looked as if nobody lived in it. No cups scattered in every room, no mascara and make-up caked into every available surface, no trying to unplug Good Hair Day instruments from the most awkward places.

She had what she'd said she wanted for years – a house that stayed that way when she cleaned it – but she'd have given up the neatness in a heartbeat to have them back.

But no matter how long or how little a time Jess and Orlaith stayed in New York, even if they moved back home for a time, Susannah knew things would never be the same again.

They had moved on, and she had to find a way to move on too. But how? Before Rob had phoned unexpectedly, her day had been empty, apart from the run to the charity shop.

Now, though, her husband wanted to have an impromptu lunch with her, so she pushed down the thought that she was in an almighty rut and got ready for the trip into the city.

She swapped her jeans and sweatshirt for a brown skirt and sparkly top she'd bought for Christmas, pulled on her winter boots and coat and started off for the train station.

The wind was icy and she pulled up her collar. All the festive decorations had been taken down but the village still had a lovely, bustling feel to it. It was a seaside, middle-class suburb with lots of shops, bars and restaurants. A big proportion of the young people had moved abroad, for work or for adventure, and sometimes because they married someone from another country, or even continent, a fear that haunted Susannah whenever she thought about her daughters living in New York.

Orlaith and Jess were only twenty-one, on an internship at an international fashion-and-style magazine in Manhattan, and were due back within a year. But a year was a long time when anything could happen.

Or nothing, if you were living her life, Susannah admitted. She thought back to the tense exchange between her and Rob earlier and felt a flutter of anxiety. They hadn't adapted well to being empty-nesters, but it was nice of him to try and cheer her up, to share his Dress-down Friday with her.

She pressed her forehead against the train window, watching the green fields give way to a more urban landscape. Soon enough the train was crossing the Liffey, the river that divided Dublin's north and south sides. Susannah watched the tugboats and cargo transporters on the water, a sight that never failed to cheer her up. When she saw that a huge cruise ship was docked today, an unexpected spark of optimism flashed through her. Maybe she would suggest to Rob that they should go on a cruise. They could visit the girls in New York and then fly down to Fort Lauderdale and board a ship bound for the Caribbean. That's what they needed now. New adventures for just the two of them.

Out of nowhere, a memory came to her. The twins had been tiny, and first one of them had caught a bug and then the other. She was working as a newspaper reporter on a big High Court case while Rob was struggling with his long hours at the bank.

They had spent the evening changing puke-filled clothes, sponging down hot little foreheads and calling in favours from friends so they could both go to work the next day. At one o'clock they were still awake, lying on top of the bedclothes, wondering if it was safe to finally go to sleep or if one of the girls was going to be sick again, when Rob had suddenly leapt out of bed.

"Hang on, I've just thought of something." He hurried out of the room.

Ten minutes later he arrived back with steaming mugs of hot chocolate. He placed them on the bedside locker and went away again, this time returning with a big notebook, an atlas and some coloured pens which he spread out across the bed.

"One day we'll look back on this night with fondness," he told her.

"Why's that?" Susannah asked half-heartedly. She was desperate for sleep, but she still had one ear cocked in case one of the children stirred. She sipped the hot chocolate, trying not to think about how overwhelmed she felt lately, caring for two toddlers and trying to keep on top of her career.

"Because we'll remember it was the day we planned our Big Adventure," he said happily.

And he had sat there with his map and his foolscap pages and fancy pens and brought her all around the world with his imagination. They would travel in a camper van, he explained, sketching it out on a page. They would stay in each place until they tired of it, and then they'd set off for somewhere new.

"The girls will love it!" She was sitting up now, and wide awake, carried away by his enthusiasm.

"All my girls will love it!" He reached over and kissed her.

"The twins might be little nerds who won't want to take the time off school," she warned him.

"It will be educational," he said airily. "And it will be so *exciting*. Who could resist it?"

The girls, as it turned out.

Susannah smiled ruefully as she thought about how they had turned out to be two lovable social butterflies who enjoyed getting a suntan and shopping in the Mediterranean resorts where they spent their summer holidays.

The idea of touring remote Eastern European caravan sites had been greeted with horror each and every year, and gradually Rob had stopped mentioning it. Susannah spent the holidays reading on a sun-lounger while the girls amused themselves, and Rob exercised his itchy feet by heading off on his own to visit an ancient ruin or the next village or whatever, really, was around the next corner. She used to tease him that he was like the bear in the song who always wanted to see what was on the other side of the mountain.

And now there was nothing to stop them going on their Big Adventure. They could do more than just seeing the girls and a cruise. Rob could probably swing an extra couple of weeks' unpaid holidays. That would give him almost two months. They could plan it all out together, and while they were away maybe she'd even figure out what it was she wanted to do with the rest of her life.

The small fantasy made her so happy she was smiling to herself by the time she reached the restaurant.

She looked around curiously. It was already filling up with people on their lunch-breaks and Susannah knew a lot of Rob's colleagues dined here.

The Dress-down Friday girls were wearing short skirts and high heels, glittering jewellery and sexy, fitted jackets. It hadn't been like that in her day. With women's equality in the workplace still in its infancy you walked a fine political line between looking too much like a ball-breaker (shoulder-pads) or being accused of using your feminine charms to get ahead (low necklines).

She smiled at the memory as a waiter led her to a table near the back of the restaurant.

She chose the seat facing the door, so she could watch for Rob arriving, absorbing the buzz of conversation rising and falling around her. This is what her life would be like now if she hadn't given up work to look after the girls, she reckoned. Her days would be filled with colleagues and conversation and getting things done, instead of the empty suburban existence she had now.

She'd have been promoted by now, for sure, she decided. Probably several times. She'd loved her job and had been very good at it.

But the decision to quit had been made for her, not long after the Big Adventure night when another child-care crisis had finally finished her and Rob off as a working couple.

They couldn't go on the way they were, feeling exhausted all the time. Susannah felt she was doing neither job properly, so she'd left without giving it too much thought, assuming she could pick her career back up again after a few years, after the hard bit of the child-rearing was over.

But she hadn't predicted how much she would love spending time with two chubby cheeked little girls who had grown up to be her constant companions. Except when they were teenagers and they didn't want to know her for – oh, about ten minutes.

She'd discussed going back to work with Rob then and a few more times since, but he always pointed out how work had changed since she'd been at the coal-front. Now it was all backstabbing and cut-throaty apparently and he told her she'd be mad to even consider it.

But, she noticed, the Dress-down Friday girls didn't look like they were backstabbing each other. They were all on that high of a week's work well done, a feeling Susannah still remembered and hadn't ever got during all her years of housekeeping.

The waiter arrived with the menus and a basket of warm bread. Susannah ordered a bottle of white wine and took out her reading glasses to peruse the menu.

But then she saw Rob pushing open the restaurant door. He hadn't spotted her and for a few seconds she watched him as if he were a stranger. His Dress-down Friday clothes consisted of neatly pressed blue jeans, a flannel checked shirt and polished, brown boots. His hair needed a cut – it was curling over the top of his shirt-collar – and he looked more like a cowboy than a stressed-out banker.

He caught sight of her and gave a small wave, weaving his way through the crowded tables to slide onto the chair opposite her.

"I'm loving the dress-down policy." Susannah leaned over to brush his hair out of his eyes but he pulled his head back a fraction, out of her reach. "You okay?" She raised her eyebrows.

"Sorry. Stressful morning." He opened the menu and studied it intently.

Susannah's spirits dipped. This was starting to feel less like an impromptu lunch to cheer her up and more like an opportunity for Rob to tell her something bad had happened.

"Is there talk of more redundancies?" She knew this was one of his recurring nightmares. A lot of his colleagues had lost their jobs in the last few years as the banks shed staff in an effort to absorb some of the losses of the economic crash.

"There's always talk of more redundancies."

The waiter arrived with the wine and Rob nodded at him tersely to fill his glass. He'd knocked back half of it before the waiter had even filled hers.

"Well, you know what they say," she quipped. "The beatings will continue until morale improves."

"Is that supposed to be funny?" His head jerked up to look at her.

"No. Well, yes, actually, it was." She dropped her bread roll back onto the plate. "Look, Rob. I don't want to have to keep on asking you. So just tell me. What is going on with you?"

He coughed, his brown eyes blinking nervously behind his glasses.

"It's not you," he said finally. "It's me."

"I know that. That's what I'm asking you – what's going on with *you*?"

"I've done something – significant. Without discussing it with you." He lifted his chin in a gesture of defiance.

Susanna pushed her plate away.

"What? What have you done?"

"I … I've applied for a career break. It's for one year. I didn't tell you because I didn't think they'd let me go. But … er …" Rob faltered a bit at this point and took another gulp of wine. "But … they did. I got the email this morning."

His features darkened and Susannah knew he was mortified that he hadn't been as indispensable to the bank as he'd thought.

"I've been accepted for it, Susannah. I'm free."

Susannah swallowed. Questions shot through her mind. Why didn't you tell me you were going to do this? What are you planning to do with the time? Can we afford it? Why are you talking to me as if I'm a work colleague?

But when she went to speak she felt like something was stuck in her throat. Maybe a piece of that crusty bread had gone down the wrong way. She poured herself some water from the pitcher and sipped it cautiously. No crust in her throat. Just an uneasy feeling there was more to come.

"So ... what's the plan? For this career break?" she finally managed to ask.

"I'm going away for the year. In a camper van."

Susannah laughed out loud. "Really?"

"Well, that's what I'm thinking." He sounded vaguely defensive.

"I must be psychic!" Susannah felt relief surge through her. It was their Big Adventure! Rob had remembered.

"What?" He sounded irritated.

"I was just thinking of that night on the train over here," she said excitedly. "The night both the girls were sick and you said we'd look back on it fondly one day because we'd be having such adventures. How we'd get a camper van and go travelling. We'd stay in each place until we got tired of it ..." Her voice trailed off as she noticed how puzzled Rob looked.

"I don't remember any of that," he said flatly.

"You said it would be the dream that would keep us going through the hard times," she prompted him again.

But he just shook his head and picked up his wineglass. "I don't. And, Susannah, this has nothing to do with your dream."

"It was *your* dream, not mine," she reminded him stubbornly. "And I know it won't be the same without the girls. I suppose we should have done it years ago while we still had the chance to have them come with us. But we can still have fun, just the two of us."

"I'm going on my own."

"*Hah!*" Susannah choked on her wine, grabbed her napkin and pressed it to her mouth.

"Are you okay?" He was watching her cautiously.

She didn't answer him. She wanted the lunch to stop now, for neither of them to say anything they would regret later.

"So," he queried, "what do you think?"

Susannah chose her words carefully. "I think all the stress of work is getting to you. I think you should go back to work and explain you made a mistake about the career break and that what you really want is a few weeks of unpaid leave."

"But that's *not* what I want!" He was suddenly belligerent.

"But you can't actually be considering going away for a year on your own. In a camper van? Really?"

"I want to find my smile." He bit his lip.

Susannah laughed out loud. "That's out of that Billy Crystal movie – about men going off to be cowboys!"

"Actually, the line came from the female character telling her husband to go and do what he had to do to find his smile," Rob challenged her.

Susannah blinked. "Why are you quoting from that film now? It's ancient."

"I watched it again recently."

"So you think I should be encouraging you to leave me?"

"I'm not leaving you. Not forever." He paused. "And not for a twenty-five-year-old intern," he added meaningfully.

The waiter arrived to refill their glasses, overheard Rob's side of the conversation and walked straight past their table.

Susannah raised her eyebrows. Rob was referring to his ex-colleague Kevin who had done exactly that – left his wife and three teenage children for some young one who had come to work at the bank under a government scheme to give graduates experience of the working world. But it was Kevin who got an experience nobody had been banking on.

And now here was Rob comparing himself to Kevin – as if it was inevitable that all the middle-aged men at the bank were going to do something crazy and it was just a question of degree and timing.

"Rob. Listen to me." Susannah addressed him kindly. "You're not Kevin. And you're not someone in a movie. You're just … a guy who works in a bank. You're probably suffering from work-related stress – and missing the girls as much as I do but not admitting it."

"I do miss them." He looked relieved. "Do you think that's what it is? This awful miserable feeling I wake up with every day?"

"Of course it is." She reached over and took his hand in hers. "You just need a break. It's *normal* to be feeling the pressures of mid-life at our age."

Rob snatched his hand back. "Thanks for the analysis. But you can't treat me like I'm a child you can coax out of a tantrum." He sniffed. "I have *dreams*, Susannah."

"We all have dreams," she said softly. "Don't you think I have things I want to do too?"

"Well, the difference between you and me is that I'm doing something about mine!" His voice rose. "Whereas all you do is walk around the house like a ghost."

She flinched, aware of the curious stares of other diners. She offered him the wicker basket of bread. "Here, eat something."

He pushed his glasses back from where they'd slipped down his nose and glared at her. "You're doing it again. Treating me like a child. Well, do you know what – I'm not very hungry any more."

He stood up, bristling with anger, nearly toppling over his chair in his haste to get away.

Susannah stared after him as he stomped off in his boots, swinging through the restaurant doors like he was John Wayne in a western instead of a banker in an upmarket bistro in Dublin.

The waiter reappeared out of nowhere and refilled Susannah's glass.

"Thank you." Susannah was mortified. She sat there, paralysed, trying to figure out what the hell had just happened while the Dress-down Friday girls threw pitying glances her way.

Her husband had just told her he was leaving her. Not in the catastrophic way of having a terminal illness. Or even, as he'd put it himself, for a twenty-five-year-old intern. But he was leaving her nevertheless.

For a *camper van*.

She drummed her fingers on the tablecloth, wondering how the hell she hadn't seen this coming. How many times in the years gone by had she wished her husband would do something to surprise her? Something out of the ordinary to lift them both out of the humdrum routine of rearing a family? Or to take her out of the depths she'd fallen into after her mother died last year?

Something to make her remember the man she'd fallen in love with, the man who'd beaten off the exhaustion and stress all those years ago to keep her enthralled with tales of the Big Adventure they would have one day.

Well, he'd surprised her today, she thought, the irony not lost on her. Because he'd just told he was going on their Big Adventure without her.

CHAPTER 2

"It's a mid-life crisis. Clearly." Cara sounded as if she didn't know whether to laugh or cry.

Susannah tightened her grip on the phone. This had been her sister's mantra for the last week, ever since Susannah had told her about the disastrous Dress-down Friday lunch with Rob.

"He's *leaving* me, Cara. All that stuff about going off to find his smile and dressing up like a cowboy? Simple code for 'I'm sick of the sight of you and I want out'!" A pulse fluttered in Susannah's throat as a thought occurred to her. "Maybe he's met an intern too, and he's going to tailgate on her gap year."

"No," Cara said firmly. "Look, it's what you said. Everything's getting on top of him with the girls gone and the stress of the redundancies and –"

"So he gets a bit of stress in his job and decides to throw everything away? That doesn't make any sense. If I'd done that every time I've had a stressful day ... well ..."

Cara was silent. She didn't have to be reminded that the last couple of years hadn't been easy for her sister.

"All he had to do was to keep his head down at work," Susannah said bitterly.

"Look, if you want to skip tonight, I could come over ..."

"No. I want to go."

Susannah always looked forward to the book-club night. And she didn't have to contribute too much – she could listen to what the others had to say about the story. Or she could tell them all about her errant husband and watch them lose all interest in their book of the month in favour of this much-nearer-to-home drama. Stranger than fiction, someone was bound to say.

"I think you're working yourself into a panic over nothing, Susie. I don't think he's going to go." Cara paused before adding helpfully, "Do you want me to pick you up? You could have a few glasses of wine?"

Susannah stared through the conservatory window, considering. Get absolutely hammered? Or not? The garden looked the way she felt, the branches of the trees stripped bare and mournful. It was late afternoon and almost dark already, with a persistent drizzle of rain obscuring the view. What she could see looked dead and brittle.

"No. I'll drive. I need to keep my wits about me."

"See you at eight so," Cara said in a small voice.

Susannah sat in the cane armchair and shivered. The bags of clutter had finally been carted off to the charity shop and everywhere felt eerily empty. She had her heat on the highest setting but it was doing nothing to warm up the frigid atmosphere that seemed to have enveloped 18 Pine Close since Rob had dropped his bombshell.

All week she had tried to continue the conversation he'd begun in the restaurant but Rob had refused to discuss it. In fact, he'd barely spoken to her since. Each evening he bolted down his dinner and made a dash for his tiny office in the box-bedroom, where he holed himself up each night, even sleeping in the tiny single bed that was reserved for the very infrequent guests they had.

Susannah hadn't been in that room in months – not because there was any privacy arrangement between them but because she assumed everything in the office was related to his boring bank work. But spreadsheets were just not that fascinating, she suddenly realised. Not even to Rob.

She stood up and walked slowly up the stairs. She hesitated outside the box-room, her hand on the doorknob, wondering whether she wanted to go in at all, trying to figure out what she might find on the other side of the door. Finally, she turned the handle firmly and stepped into the room. And blinked.

Rob Stevens was a neat man. Organised. Like clockwork, her mother had described him, when he used to collect Susannah in the early days. His wardrobe was OCD tidy – four black suits and fourteen white shirts for work, folded navy jumpers and blue jeans for weekends. A black Crombie for winter, belted beige trench for Spring/Summer. It was uncomplicated attire, which didn't give him any confusing choices, was how he'd explained it to her once. Susannah, whose wardrobe was an eclectic mess of clothes in different sizes depending on whether she was on a diet or not, hadn't a clue what he was talking about but she'd smiled encouragingly because it seemed very important to him that she understood.

But now the box-room was in chaos. Piles of travel books and atlases covered every available surface: the desk, the chair, the single bed with the duvet not even smoothed over.

Susannah moved towards the desk and scanned the books. *1000 Places To See Before You Die*, *Gap Year for Grown-Ups*, *The Australian Bush*. He was going to the Australian *bush?* Heart hammering, Susannah noticed that a large, colourful atlas was opened on the South-East Asia page. But then there was a map of the world on the wall, with yellow pins stuck on various places there. Belize. Chile. The Galapagos.

Two journals – *The Travel Planner* and *The Travel Diaries* – were stacked beside his laptop. She picked them up and flicked through them for clues. But both had virgin, blank pages. She tossed them back onto the desk, and pulled open the desk drawer. She rifled through the pens, highlighter markers, more maps and brochures until she finally found something she could make sense of. It was a spreadsheet. Hah! This was more like Rob.

She pulled it out and squinted at the columns, the meticulous calculations in their neat printed rows. Rob had worked out that if he saved X amount a month on A, B and C he'd have Y amount in three years. The interest generated by his saving deposits in a high-interest account would net him a not insignificant amount – a small cushion for "emergencies".

Susannah frowned at the document. He'd been secretly saving for three years? From long before the girls had left for New York? From before her mother had died? Her mind roamed back over the weeks and months, trying to pinpoint what she'd missed, what clue she hadn't picked up on. But she could think of no defining moment that revealed just when – or why – her husband had started cutting her out of his hopes and dreams.

She sat down on the second-hand swivel-chair Rob had picked up at work when the bank was investing in super-ergonomic seats for their employees – "So we can't sue them for keeping us super-glued onto the chairs for hours on end," he'd declared bitterly at the time.

She opened up the laptop and tapped in Rob's password. They had no secrets from each other – or so she'd thought, before she discovered this little den of plot and intrigue. A screensaver of a red VW Beetle camper van with stickers plastered over the bodywork flashed at her. Susannah moved closer to read the messages. Stupid slogans like *Surf's Up!* and *Life Begins at the End of Your Comfort Zone* assaulted her. She stared at the screen, wanting to find out more, but she'd be late for the book club if she didn't get a move on.

Reluctantly, she closed down the computer and left the room.

She walked into her own room – her and Rob's room – and stood under the shower in the en-suite, her mind buzzing as the water scalded her skin, drumming a rhythm on her neck and shoulders, one thought after another whizzing around in her brain.

It was clear now that Cara was wrong. Rob's travel plans were less of a Walter Mitty fantasy and more the advanced stage of an organised escape plan. She was going to have to think up a way to talk him out of it. Or talk him into going somewhere with her instead.

She stepped out of the shower and dressed quickly – new denim jeans, stripy top, trainers – trying to keep her mind in the present, not allowing it to fly through all the scenarios it kept creating.

She looked in the mirror doubtfully – as if she might find the answers to her questions there instead of in the garden she'd looked out on earlier.

But nope. Nothing had changed. She was still tall, with a mane of tousled red hair and a smattering of freckles across her nose. She was going through a fat phase – Christmas and a few months of comfort-eating after the girls left meant she was in her bigger clothes. But she was healthy and fit. Fit enough to do a thousand things with her life – except she couldn't think of one of them at the moment.

Sighing, she turned to grab her bag and jacket, checking the pocket for her keys. She took the stairs two at a time, anxious to get away, feeling claustrophobic in her own home. She was reaching to open the hall door when it was pushed in from the outside and Rob stepped into the hall. He was drenched, his hair plastered into his head, the jacket of his suit sodden with rain.

"What you doing home so early?" Susannah peered out behind him, puzzled. The drizzly rain hadn't got any worse. "How did you get soaked just coming in from the car?"

Rob looked to the side of her and a nervous tic flickered under his eye.

"I, er … got the bus home."

"Oh. Did the car break down? Where is it?"

"It's not broken down."

"You ran out of petrol?" Susannah was becoming more confused. Rob never ran out of petrol. "Do you need me to take you to the garage?"

"No. I – er – sold it."

"You sold your car?" She took a step backwards. "Why?"

"Well, there's no sense in letting it sit outside in the drive for twelve months. And I need the money."

He took a step toward her.

"Susannah, we need to talk."

Susannah took another step back, afraid he'd try to touch her.

"I've been trying to talk to you for the past week and you just brushed me off. And I'm going out now."

"But you have to listen. Everything's moving faster than I thought. I've got a date for leaving work. It's in two weeks. And I want to go as soon as possible after that because everyone I've spoken to says the time just flies and I need to make the most of it."

"Everyone you've spoken to?" Susannah had a fleeting sense that a complete stranger, an imposter husband, was standing in her hall. "Who's everyone?"

He flushed. "People. Some of the young people in work who've done it. People on the forums who are already doing what I want to do."

"So why do you want to talk to me if other people know it all?"

He shrugged. "Stuff. Logistics. Finances."

Without warning, Susannah's sense of shock evaporated and a cold fury swept over her. Her hands curled into fists and she pushed them into her hips as she fought off a frightening urge to punch Rob in the face. She counted to ten. And then tried for twenty. She was proud that she got to sixteen before she spoke again.

"Well, here's what I have to say about it, Rob. *Stuff* your *logistics* where the sun doesn't shine. Now, get out of my way."

Rob reeled away from her, staring as if she had actually struck him instead of just imagining it. She walked as fast as she could to her car, flashing the fob to open the door as quickly as possible.

She jumped in, shaking the droplets of rain out of her hair and ramming her keys into the ignition. Then she screeched down the driveway, intent on putting as much distance as possible between them in the shortest amount of time.

But she'd only got a mile up the road when she pulled in to the side of the road. She couldn't drive in this state of rage. She'd end up under an articulated truck. She shook her head, scarcely able to believe what she knew so far.

Rob had sold his car. He was leaving work in two weeks. He was leaving *her* "as soon as possible after that". He was talking to people at work and on Internet forums instead of to her.

How in hell had she not seen this coming? There had been a few things niggling at her for sure. But they had been like distant bells. She hadn't liked that Rob was working ridiculous hours for instance. But she'd put that down to his increased workload after the bank had made so many people redundant.

And when the girls left and her crammed days had become empty overnight she could see a distance had sprung up between them. But she'd reckoned that was a consequence of the sadness they'd both felt after her mother died, and trying to adjust to life without Orlaith and Jess.

There'd been nothing she'd call significant. Nothing to warn her that she was facing disaster.

After almost a quarter of a century, Susannah had learned

that marriage was like life, with its ups and downs and miscommunications and disasters and compromises – all of that made acceptable and sometimes outweighed by the good times.

In fact, she'd even started to have odd flashes of optimism lately, as if the inconsolable grief was starting to abate at last. She'd reckoned that the worst might be over and that she and Rob were ready to start a new chapter in their lives.

She sighed. Rob was right. They needed to talk. She pulled her phone out of her bag and tapped out a text to Cara. **More stuff on Robgate. Won't make it after all. Give my apologies. Text u 2m.**

She pressed 'send', flung the phone onto the passenger seat, put the car into gear and did a U-turn.

She found Rob sitting on the bed in the box-bedroom, tucking a pair of bright-orange surfer shorts into the top of a stuffed gigantic rucksack.

"Can you just stop this charade?" she appealed, her hands flung wide. He went to say something but she stopped him: "Let me say this first. I've been in shock since that lunch in the restaurant. But, to be honest, I didn't take you seriously. Cara said it was probably some Walter Mitty fantasy and one evening you were going to walk through the door and tell me that. Instead, you came home to tell me you've sold your car. So you've got my attention. Talk to me. I deserve a proper explanation."

"I'm sorry." He kept his head bent, presumably so he wouldn't have to look at her. "I understand how you feel. I should have told you earlier. But, as I explained already, I never thought the bank would let me go. Until I got their email saying the career break had been approved it was just an idle fantasy, something to get me through the day. And then I had to pull out or pull the trigger." He looked up at her, a flash of defiance on his face. "And I pulled the trigger."

"Except I've looked through all this," Susannah gestured towards the cluttered desk laden with papers and documents, "and I can see that you've been planning and saving and scheming about this for three years. So you *didn't* just decide when the bank sent you an email."

"But I've just told you. It was Walter Mitty stuff. Cara was right about that. But now it's something different. It's real. And it's something I have to do, Susannah."

She sat down on the bed beside him. "So let's do it then." Sensible Susannah. Mrs Fixit. She'd fixed worse problems. And she could fix this. "Together. I'm not sure I want to go off for a full year but we could compromise. We could –"

"No, we couldn't. I'm going on my own."

"And what about me? And Orlaith and Jess?"

"They're adults, Susannah. We're all adults. Besides, the girls are living in New York now. It's not going to affect their lives. I'll explain it to them."

"No!" Her voice came out like a whip. "You won't. They'll worry and fret. Jess will probably want to get the next plane home."

"And how would we keep it from them, even if I wanted to?" His eyebrows drew together, puzzled.

"I'll figure something out." Susannah could be stubborn too, especially when it came to her children. "They're supposed to be carefree at this time of their life. We can't let your mid-life crisis ruin all of that."

"And when do *I* get to be carefree? To do something I've always wanted to do? Give me one reason why I shouldn't follow my dream."

She raised her eyes to heaven. It was like arguing with a teenager. "Because you're married?" she ventured.

"Marriage isn't a prison sentence." He was staring at a pair of beige sandals, his attention in the conversation waning.

21

"It was a life commitment last time I looked."

"Now you're just trying to lay a guilt trip on me." He flashed her a look of dislike.

"Meaning what?"

"Meaning you need to get a life, Susannah. Like I'm doing."

"So all this palaver is your way of saying you want out of our marriage?"

"No! Of course not."

"So what then? We're on a break?"

"Yes." He missed her sarcasm.

"I don't agree with any of this, Rob. I don't know anything about your plans, your destination, nothing."

"Well, that's easy. It's Dublin to Bangkok and from there wherever my North Star takes me."

He said "NORTH STAR" as if it was all in capital letters.

"Have you been watching reruns of Oprah? Reading *Eat, Pray, Love* maybe?" Susannah's nostrils flared.

"I wish!" he said plaintively. "You seem to be forgetting I've been rammed onto the 7.12 to Pearse Station every single weekday for over two decades now. Sitting at the same desk with the same people counting other people's money."

"Don't you think those shorts are a bit orange?" She raised her eyebrows at the offending garment and he stuffed it angrily out of sight.

After that the conversation got silly. Susannah issued ultimatums and Rob pretended he hadn't heard them. She asked how they would keep in touch and learned that they wouldn't – well, not in any way she knew of anyway – like emails or texts or phone calls.

A young colleague at work had apparently helped Rob set up a Facebook page – he was going to call himself "The Intrepid Traveller". And Susannah was welcome to befriend him and follow his news through his posts there. He'd have his mobile with him for "genuine emergencies" but he reckoned he'd never find himself if he was always ringing home. He sounded as if he was leaving on a space mission.

It turned out she'd be okay financially – all the overtime hadn't been at the behest of the bank bogeymen after all, but had been done of Rob's own free will. That, selling his car, and the fact that he'd barely been outside the door socially for nearly three years had allowed him to build up a considerable sum – enough to pay the bills at home for a year on top of his running-away money.

Susannah knew she should probably appreciate it more. She knew of lots of women who had been left in dire financial straits when their marriages broke up. Maybe that was why she offered to drive him to the airport.

Cara fought with her over that. "He's not going on a business trip," she snapped when she told her.

"I know that. It's just that, if I'm not going to see him for a year, I feel –"

"It doesn't matter how you feel." Cara was furious. "Taking him to the airport is like you're saying it's okay for him to do this – as if you're condoning his nonsense! You should tell him you'll be changing the locks on the hall door the minute he takes that ridiculous rucksack of his over the threshold – that might make him think about consequences!"

"Look, Cara, he's going whether I condone it or not."

She'd fought the good fight to save her marriage, and she'd lost. Nothing she came up with, including the suggestion of marriage counselling, had made any difference. She knew by the set of his chin and the distracted look in his eyes that his heart and mind were firmly set on a faraway horizon that didn't include her.

"I've done all I can," she told Cara simply.

"Well, I still think putting him on the plane is a mistake," her sister said.

And, as it turned out, she was right.

The tension inside Susannah's car as they drove to Dublin airport was frostier than the late January weather outside.

"At least you'll be leaving all of this behind," she said, gesturing to the frost-covered grass verge on the centre aisle of the motorway that would take them to the airport.

"Hmmm," Rob mumbled. He adjusted the black straps of the rucksack, which he had balanced between his legs as he sprawled beside her on the passenger seat.

"So what's the temperature in Bangkok now?" Susannah tried again, wincing because she sounded like an over-chatty taxi driver.

"Warmer than this anyhow," Rob replied, his eyes fixed on the car in front of them as Susannah maneuvered the car around a roundabout.

It's twenty-six degrees, Susannah wanted to scream at him. Twenty degrees higher than in Dublin. I know this because I looked it up. And I know you had to, too. Why won't you talk to me?

He tried to get her to leave him at the drop-off point at the departures doors but she insisted on driving into the short-term car park, locking the car and trailing after him into the airport terminal, hovering behind while he handed over his ticket and passport and checked in his luggage.

She wanted to stand there as long as possible, in his line of sight, making him notice her pale, sleep-deprived features, hunched shoulders and bewildered expression. She needed him to notice what all this was doing to her.

But if he did, he didn't seem to care. He kissed her briefly on the cheek and, as he made his way to the security-check queue, she thought she heard him whistling.

When he got to the corner where he would disappear from her life he stopped briefly to wave back at her and it seemed to

Susannah that his posture had already changed. He was standing straighter, more easily balanced on his skinny legs, the look of relief on his face erasing some of the perpetual crankiness she had become so used to looking at.

And then, just like that, he was gone.

Leaving Susannah all on her own for the first time in – well, ever actually. She'd married young, going from her parents' house to the first home she and Rob had set up together.

She drove the dark roads back from the airport, pondering with not a little trepidation on the fact that she was about to spend the first night of her life on her own.

CHAPTER 3

Katie Corrigan opened the newspaper and smiled at her horoscope.

Good things are taking place behind the scenes. Love and opportunity are yours for the taking. Don't let it slip through your fingers. The harder you work the luckier you get. See your ideas through.

She was most encouraged by the line 'the harder you work the luckier you get', because hard work was her super-power. Her job as features editor for the *Daily Post* meant long hours, daily deadlines and the stress of things never going quite the way they were supposed to but she wasn't complaining.

She could handle it. She was organized, sharp, and on time, always beating her own deadlines. She made lists about lists and ran her life on the Three D's: Do it, Dump it or Delegate it. And since she didn't actually have anyone to delegate to, it was just two categories she had to worry about.

She shrugged her shoulders and they crackled with tension, the result of four hours bent over her computer. It was far too long to be sitting in one position – but she was under serious deadline pressure to get her pages out.

"Hello, beautiful." Daniel Gilbert sauntered into her cubicle and parked himself on the corner of her desk, ready for a chat.

Katie quickly closed over the newspaper. Reading horoscopes was her guilty pleasure – far from the professional image she wanted to project. She intended to be editor of the *Post* one day and she needed to act the part.

"You filed your column yet?" She raised an eyebrow, still thinking of her deadline. Daniel's latest instalment of the *Footloose and Fancy-free* column, his diary of how hard it was to find the One and how disorientating that could be once you were in your thirties, even when you were male, was always funny. It would be one of the best things she had for the Valentine's Day supplement, she reckoned.

"Yep, it's all there." Daniel nodded at her computer.

He was a stereotypical tall, dark and handsome young man, an Orlando Bloom lookalike with a shock of dark curls, a great sense of humour and a killer smile. Katie didn't believe for a minute that he'd have any trouble at all finding the One if that was what he really wanted. She reckoned he was having too much fun looking, plus it gave him great material for his column.

"I'm here to give you a heads-up," he said. "Mike is looking for something novel for the Valentine's Day supplement."

"No!" Katie's eyes automatically flicked to the wall clock. It would be putting even her fastest, hungriest freelancers under considerable pressure to write something novel in under three hours. "Doesn't *Footloose and Fancy-free* qualify as novel? What's it about today anyhow?"

"Why a loved-up couple's day should be banned on the grounds of discrimination against singletons."

"And it's funny?"

"I think so. But probably not novel in fairness. And Mike is in a fouler. The figures might be down. Or he might have a hangover. It might be easier just to tell him you'll get something."

Or it might be quicker to just write something herself. Before she'd started her job as features editor she had been the go-to person to dash off a thousand words when Mike was looking for "something novel" for Valentine's Day. Or Christmas. The summer holidays. Halloween. She had lost count of the times she'd written variations of 'Spells to Bewitch Him With', or 'How to Tell if Your Holiday Romance Will Go the Distance', and 'How to Get Him to Give You a Ring – Not the Telephone Type'. Hah bloody Hah. It would be hilarious if it was so not.

When she'd started work at the *Daily Post* she'd imagined herself reporting on the stories behind the news headlines from all around the country. But she'd never been able to make the step away from lighthearted features. Probably because she hadn't got any political scoops, in fairness. But also because she was a bit of a magician at the lighthearted stuff and she'd got stuck with that.

"You're a victim of your own success," Mike had said, smiling thinly when she'd explained she wanted to branch out to writing about other issues.

When she'd let him know she was interested in politics, he told her to ring some female politicians and ask them what they kept in their handbags. When she'd said she'd like to get involved in foreign affairs, he'd got her to ring a high-profile female war correspondent to ask her where she was going on her holidays. The reporter had slammed the phone down on her, not that Katie blamed her.

That was the day she'd decided she was going to have to take her life into her own hands and go for promotion, not be bossed about by the likes of Mike for the rest of her life.

The big downside of her new role was that she missed reporting, going out on interviews and coming back to write her stories from a big open-plan office, full of the noise of people beating deadlines and shouting about the latest story about to break.

She had fondly imagined that as features editor she would

have the luxury of thinking-time – time she'd intended to use to plot her professional development – but she was still on a steep learning curve and working on a daily newspaper meant quiet time was always at a premium.

"Hey up, here comes Mike now," Daniel warned.

Katie looked up to see her boss loping down the corridor towards them. Everyone was always wondering if this would be the year that Mike finally hung up his boots at the *Post* but Katie doubted he would any time soon. He was a man possessed of a nervous energy which kept him on the move all the time – fidgeting, nattering, and thinking up ways to annoy people. She reckoned he had to be a not-very-healthy sixty-something. He had a pasty complexion, a belly straining over his trouser-belt and eyes permanently ringed with tiredness. All the alcohol in his system would explain that.

"Hey there." He reached Katie's cubicle and stopped, pushing his reading glasses on top of his bald head. "So what have you got for tomorrow?"

Katie passed across a white, foolscap sheet of paper with her list of feature articles itemised on it. He held it between his thumb and forefinger, squinting to read it because it appeared to be too much trouble for him to pull his bifocals down.

"Same old same old!" he announced, pulling on his earlobe absent-mindedly. "We need something different – new."

"We have Daniel's latest *Footloose and Fancy-free* piece as well – why Valentine's should be banned because it discriminates against singles."

"Something new?" Mike raised his eyebrows.

"It's the way Daniel writes it," Katie pointed out, as if she'd already read it.

But Mike wasn't listening. Daniel was right. Something was bothering him.

"Hey, I have an idea!" A familiar voice floated over the partition.

Katie's stomach clenched.

Jennifer Leslie was the paper's social diarist. She gossiped for a living and eavesdropped for a hobby and couldn't ever mind her own business.

"Katie could write a column about when Luke is going to put a ring on her finger!" Jennifer wheeled herself and her office chair around to Katie's cubicle and parked next to Mike.

Mike slapped the palm of his hand against his forehead. "That's what I'm talking about," he told Katie, jagging his thumb in Jennifer's direction. "Something novel."

"What's novel about that, Jennifer?" Daniel folded his arms, playing devil's advocate and taking up for Katie at the same time.

Jennifer was unperturbed. "It's asking the question – why should women have to wait on men to propose to them in this day and age?" She raised her hand so they could all see the giant diamond glittering on her ring finger. "I got this twelve months after I met my John."

"Which wasn't today or yesterday," Katie said. "It was a different era, in fairness."

"Exactly. Women couldn't pop the question then but there were a lot of things we couldn't do. Like keep our jobs in the Civil Service if we got married – we had to leave so a man could have it." She frowned at the memory. "But nowadays we're all supposed to be equal but women still wait for a proposal. It's an anomaly. Maybe it's because they're all living together and there's no incentive for the man to propose. Take my cousin's daughter –"

"Er, let's not," Katie said quickly.

Jennifer's job involved attending a lot of evening events and she always had time to fill in between her engagements. If she got started on one of her stories it would be hard to shut her up and Katie wanted to get home at some point tonight.

"Yes, but doesn't Jennifer have a point?" Mike's eyes narrowed. "Young women today are independent in their careers but when it comes to getting married they're all Waity Katies, like Prince William's missus was, having to wait on their fella to pop the big question. Why don't they propose, buy the ring, risk the rejection? Hmm?"

Katie stayed silent, praying the conversation might dry up from lack of oxygen.

"The reason Daniel's blog is so successful," Mike continued, "is because he has turned the playboy thing on its head – he's the needy one. So you could do the same thing by proposing for Valentine's Day."

"Excuse me?" Katie's eyebrows shot up.

"You have a fella, don't you?" Mike demanded.

"Er – yes, I do. But we don't have any plans for –" she coughed, "marriage."

Jennifer smiled at her understandingly.

"They all say that," she explained to Mike. She turned back to Katie. "Why don't you write about why women don't propose? I'd say there'll be very few women going down on one knee this Valentine's Day."

"Okay – but I don't want to write about my private life," Katie warned.

"But personal stories are exactly what our readers are interested in," Mike butted in. "We know this. That's why *Footloose and Fancy-free* is so popular. Because it's so personal."

Katie bit her lip. Daniel loved writing about his life, and the world loved reading about it. But that was because Daniel Gilbert had a very interesting life to write about. He travelled all over the country, interviewing ordinary people doing extraordinary things for his *Abiding Passions* slot. When stars arrived on European publicity tours that didn't include Ireland in their schedule, Daniel would be duly dispatched to London to interview them there. He'd covered the royal wedding of William and Kate and had even been invited to the Oscars one year when

Ireland had somebody nominated for a gong.

His personal life was no less interesting. In summer he took off late Friday afternoon so he could be hitting the waves at home in Sligo by six on Saturday morning with his surf buddies. In winter he went skiing. And in between he had all his *Footloose and Fancy-free* romantic adventures.

What Katie did was work, go home, chat to Luke on the phone if they weren't meeting up, hit the gym, watch the news-analysis programmes so she could be au fait with the current affairs for the next day, and go to bed, sometimes even managing to read a few pages of fiction to help her drop off.

Again, she wasn't complaining. In fact, after a chaotic childhood, she found the routine and regularity of her lifestyle soothing. She knew what to expect from day to day, from week to week.

But it meant she would struggle to write three hundred, very boring, words about her life. And she needed at least a thousand very interesting ones to fill this column.

"I think it's just what we need." Mike took a red pen from behind his ear and made a big circle around the feature she'd commissioned on 'The Hidden Meaning of Your Floral Bouquet'. "You can scrap this."

He moved away, breathing heavily as he lurched off the way he'd come.

Daniel shook his head at Katie's shocked expression. "I've told you before. You can't let him bully you like that."

"And yet somehow he just did," Katie sighed. With his decades of experience in the newspaper business and his rock-solid confidence in his journalistic hunches, Katie always felt herself floundering whenever Mike challenged her.

"You need to find a way to deal with him." Daniel glanced at the clock. "But I guess that's for another time. Now, you'd better get on with getting that feature out."

He gave her a sympathetic smile and went back to his own workspace.

"Thanks for that, Jennifer," Katie snapped as the older woman made to disappear back to her own cubicle.

"Ah look, I'm sorry." Jennifer stopped and swirled back around to face Katie. "I shouldn't have interfered. But Mike's right – people love to feel they're getting a little window into someone else's life. That's why I get paid for going to parties."

"But the people you write about in the social pages have exciting lives," Katie pointed out. "And I don't."

"Really?" Jennifer's eyebrows disappeared into her frosted-blonde fringe. "Surely you don't believe all that? It's the edited showreel. Or outright made-up stuff. You don't need to have an exciting life to write an opinion piece. And it doesn't have to be the gospel truth. Have a bit of fun with it."

Kate turned back to her computer, irritated. There was no sense in getting into an argument with Jennifer. She didn't have time, for one thing.

She opened up a new window on the computer, a frown creasing her forehead. Why didn't women propose, she wondered? She seriously didn't have a clue but she started typing anyway, letting her fingers fly over the keyboards, writing anything that came into her head. Her mind went back over her and Luke's romance – smiling at the memory of their first date four years ago.

They had met when she'd been interviewing his boss for a medical feature she was writing – Luke worked as a medical journalist on a large trade-paper. So far, the question of marriage had never come up between them and it suited Katie that way. She'd never been that little girl who played brides with her Barbies and she had enough going on in her life, trying to make progress in her career, without the distraction of marriage.

She frowned. She needed to put herself in the shoes of

someone who did want to get married. Her first cousin Brenda, for instance. Brenda had always wanted to play Bride Barbies. And now she had to deal with her overbearing mother who was always nagging her about giving her a grandchild even though Brenda hadn't had a date in twelve months.

Then she remembered an old school-friend who knew her partner was going to propose for ages but she still had to pretend it was all an amazing surprise and go through an entire 'Oh My God, I'm the luckiest woman in the world' routine.

She supposed, when she thought about it, she could see Mike's point. She didn't know why women still waited to be asked and, frankly, she couldn't have cared less. But that was beside the point. Her eyes darted to the clock again. She had barely ninety minutes to make Mike's point. She started to type again.

"So what's with women in the twenty-first century? While we have achieved equality in the boardroom, taken responsibility for our own destinies in the area of reproduction and damn near do it all, there is one big area where we may as well be back in Jane Austen's time.

And that's when it comes to popping the (Big) Question.

Whether you're dreaming of a big fat wedding with a church blessing, a flouncy dress and 200 guests, a cool civil ceremony, or a woodland hippy humanist affair, one thing hasn't changed: women still wait to be asked.

When the Duchess of Cambridge waited for Prince William to propose the media were spectacularly unkind, dubbing her Waity Katy, but what's so different about her and most other women wondering whether the wedding is on or not?

Of course, you can propose if it's Leap Year, but that's not for a while – time for your viable eggs to be deteriorating, time for Romeo to decide the whole

marriage thing isn't for him after all – well, not with you anyway. Time during which, instead of being the pro-active woman you are in every other area of your life, you'll be just – waiting.

Going down on one knee to your beau may not be what you imagined when you were playing Bride Barbie, but it could be the most romantic proposal you could dream of – because you'll be the one making it happen. You've always wanted say yes on top of the Eiffel Tower? Go ahead and book the flights and the fancy hotel room. You'd prefer it to happen driving through Rome – get on to a good concierge and get him book you a limo.

Yes, you run the risk that your man might turn you down, but then at least you'll know where you stand, won't you? Anyhow, my guess is that most men don't propose unless they're pretty certain the answer will be a yes, so women should aim to have the same sort of clarity in their heads before they start making their proposal plans ..."

She was flying now, thoughts and ideas effortlessly making the journey from her head to the page, and when she finally ended her column with a flourish, she smiled at the wall-clock facing her.

She'd finished with seconds to spare.

CHAPTER 4

Four weeks later

Susannah woke up, rigid with tension. A film of sweat covered her skin and her nightdress was damp and tangled. The pillow she'd put down the middle of the king-sized bed to make it seem not quite so king-sized was flung on the floor. Her breathing was coming in fast and shallow gasps.

Scraps of a nightmare flashed across her mind; she was being chased, running to get home, not quite making it. She sat up, groping around for the light-switch. Four o'clock.

She swung her feet out of bed and placed them flat on the floor, trying to ground herself. She'd had nightmares like this before and knew she needed to move her body to help the panic to subside. She forced herself to walk the twelve paces from her bed to the en-suite bathroom.

She splashed cold water on her face and buried her face in a towel, trying to get her breathing to slow down. When she looked up, her reflection in the mirror startled her. Dark shadows stained the skin beneath her eyes and her complexion looked pale and waxy.

She padded back into the bedroom and threw herself flat on her back on the bed. A crack in the ceiling crept almost across its entire width. The bedside lamp barely lit her side of the dark room. She got up and switched on the main light.

The first time she'd dreamt she was being chased was when she was a young teenager. It was after an older man from her neighbourhood had stalked her. For several months he seemed to be everywhere she was. Coming home from school, getting off the bus from town, walking home from a friend's house. She would turn and there he'd be. Loitering against a fence or lurking on a corner.

The stalking went on for months, the nightmares for years. Even now, whenever she felt pressured by life, the dreams would return. In the weeks since Rob had left, they had returned to haunt her.

She knew it was a warning signal, a sign she was letting her life get out of control and that she needed to take better care of herself. The vague sense of impending doom that had descended on her after her mother died had returned and sometimes it felt as if a grey creeping fog was enveloping her, slowing down her movements and speeding up her thoughts.

She'd looked up a dream-interpretation book once and learned that being chased meant you were giving away your power in real life. She looked at the vast space of the empty half of the bed, the one Rob used to sleep in. Could you give your power away to someone who wasn't even there?

She spent the day getting ready for her book club. She was delighted to be busy – scrubbing the house, organising the food and drink. She couldn't wait to hear the sound of voices in the house again, people to distract her from the shadowy corners and the eerie quiet and the too many rooms and her own frigging thoughts. If she had thought Pine Close had been quiet when her daughters went to New York, it was nothing compared to the emptiness of the house now and she'd learned she hated her own company with a vengeance.

She was ready and waiting a full hour before her guests were due to arrive. A fire crackled in the grate of her living room and a couple of purple hyacinths lent a splash of colour to the room, even if their distinctive scent was a bit overwhelming. A dozen tea-lights flickered in small glass holders on the mantelpiece.

She had white wine chilling in the fridge and a bottle of red opened on the coffee table, a good third of it already poured into her own glass.

The food was simple – a platter of antipasti – black juicy olives stuffed with slivers of garlic, four crumbly blocks of different cheeses, strips of Serrano ham and crusty bread she had drowned in her own home-made herb butter. Individual ramekin dishes of stewed apple and crumble finished off her offering.

If she were to go down with the ship that Rob had so inexplicably abandoned, it would not be because she'd resorted to sloppy hostessing. She had promised herself there would be no stabbing of plastic film on microwave meals for one and she was still making everything from scratch, even though it seemed like a monumental effort for just one person and she often ended up throwing out more food than she'd eaten.

She bought her groceries online, which saved her having to face inquisitive neighbours in the village and rarely left the house unless she had to.

She kept replaying the last time she'd seen Rob at the departures gate, waving him off as if he were a wayward teenager. Apart from an email to say he'd arrived safely in Bangkok, she'd heard nothing from him since.

She knocked back a large mouthful of wine and picked up her book again. It was a Douglas Kennedy title about a woman who was really a ghost. Susannah had tried to read it during the week – it wasn't as if she had anything else to do – but for the first time in her life she was finding reading a chore. Now she had to keep going back over previous paragraphs, trying to keep up with the story.

The doorbell broke through the silence of the house and she gave a silent prayer of thanks as she jumped up to answer it.

"Olivia! Come on in." She pulled the hall door open wider. Behind Olivia in her good camel coat and sturdy winter boots stood Phil, a new member of the book club. He was stomping his boots on the drive, and she could see his breath frosting in the night air. At the end of the drive, Cara was pressing her key fob at her car, locking the doors and setting the alarm.

The book club had started three years ago and, while they rarely had a full attendance, Susannah, Cara and Olivia were the stalwarts who almost always made it on the first Wednesday of the month.

Cara had only recently introduced Phil, explaining how he worked in a bookshop in the city and would be good at recommending new titles, but this was Susannah's first time to meet him. Olivia had met him the night Susannah had returned home to have the showdown with Rob.

As they all trooped in out of the cold night, Susannah focused on being a good hostess, depositing coats and scarves in the hall cupboard and retrieving the bottle of white wine from the fridge.

"I've been looking forward to tonight all week," Olivia remarked. Coming up to sixty, Olivia was a well-groomed strawberry-blonde with a sharp intellect which she'd used to earn herself a first-class degree in psychology after her marriage had broken down. "Thanks for having us, Susannah. Everything looks lovely."

"Yes, you'd never guess Rob has legged it, would you?" Cara said, flopping down beside Olivia.

Phil, whose six-foot frame dwarfed the armchair he was sitting in, raised a quizzical eyebrow.

"Susannah's husband," Cara told him. "He's gone off to find his smile. By the light of his North Star. Or some such gobbledygook.

He belongs to this Gap Year for Grown-ups forum. A bit of a misnomer, if you ask me, considering he's behaving like a teenager."

"They're people who never got the chance to follow their dreams when they were young and they want to make up for it now – something like that," Susannah explained weakly. She wasn't sure she wanted to talk about this in front of someone she'd just met.

"It sounds – adventurous," Phil said carefully.

Susannah smiled at his diplomacy. He looked to be in his late forties, skinny, with closely cropped black hair and the complexion of someone who spent a lot of time outdoors, which was odd, considering he worked in a bookshop. A silver stud earring glinted in his right ear.

"If you call running away from your responsibilities adventurous," Cara sniffed. She sipped her wine.

"So how are you coping, Susannah?" Olivia asked brightly.

"Sure with all the work he was doing she probably doesn't even notice he's gone," Cara said.

"I do notice." Susannah helped herself to some herb bread. "It's horrible. The house feels so empty." Herb bread was one of her favourite things, warm and dripping with butter, but she left it untouched on her plate.

"I still can't believe Rob did it." Cara looked at her thoughtfully. "It's just not like him. I wonder if it's a cover for something else?"

"Like what?" Susannah shot her a puzzled look.

"Like a travel dating site for married people? But they're trying to hide it behind this follow-your-dream guff?"

"Rob didn't have to take a twelve-hour plane journey to meet someone else," Olivia said quickly. "He could have done that at home."

"I can testify to that," Phil said.

There was an awkward silence. Olivia's ex was now married

to someone else and they had a child together, while Phil's wife had apparently run off with her personal trainer some years ago.

"It would be easier to understand if he had met someone else," Susannah said. "And maybe easier to cope with too. As it is, everything is too confusing – like living in limbo."

"That's because you let Rob go away believing he could walk back into your life whenever he felt like it!" Cara's nostrils flared.

"So what are you going to do?" Olivia asked.

"Do?" Susannah laughed. "Well, my window of time for locking Rob in the attic has closed. That was one of Cara's ideas."

"I didn't mean what are you going to do about Rob." Olivia traced a finger around the rim of her wineglass. "I mean what are you going to do for yourself – to help you adapt to this new phase of your life?"

Susannah thought for a moment. "Wait?" she said eventually.

Olivia's eyebrows almost disappeared into her fringe. "Really?"

"What else can I do?" Susannah pushed some cheese around her plate. "It's not like it was something I planned for. We were supposed to have this whole Golden Years thing going on by now – you know, mining all those cut-price mini-breaks for nifty fifties. Visiting the girls in New York."

"You could still visit the girls," Cara said quickly. "I'd never say no to a shopping trip to the Big Apple."

"But a trip to New York will be over in a week. What about the rest of the year?" Olivia persisted.

Sensing Susannah's bewilderment, Phil butted in. "I think what Olivia is getting at is this – what would you be doing now if you didn't know Rob?"

"If I didn't know Rob?" The words percolated through Susannah's mind. She couldn't imagine a world where she didn't know Rob. "I don't know. I always felt that we –"

"You're saying 'we'," Olivia pointed out. "But there is no 'we', is there? Not now."

Susannah looked at Olivia sharply. She felt like telling her to mind her own business. But then she thought of her empty mailbox, her silent house, her solitary dinners, and Rob suggesting she could keep in touch by 'friending' him on Facebook, when he knew she didn't even have a Facebook page.

Olivia was right. There was no we. She was living in a fantasy world, paralysed with shock and fear, fooling herself that she could somehow sit it out until Rob changed his mind and came back home.

She had somehow let a month go past and she still hadn't told their daughters that he'd gone. The truth was they didn't stay in touch with home as much as she'd thought they would — something which had disappointed her bitterly, but now she was grateful for it because it meant it had been easy to hide the truth about Rob.

On the couple of times they'd phoned she felt she'd been economical with the truth rather than an outright liar and that she was protecting them from the situation because she wanted this time of their life to be carefree, uncontaminated with worries about their parents. She'd worried so much about her own mother for the past few years. It had taken over her life and she didn't want that for Orlaith and Jess now.

"I often thought of going back to work," she said slowly. "That's if I could find anyone who'd want me in my fifties."

"What do you work at?" Phil asked.

Susannah smiled proudly. "I worked rearing a family. Hardest and most satisfying job in the world. Before that I was a political reporter."

"You should start looking," Cara rushed in eagerly. "I'll help you update your CV."

"And you need to get on Twitter," Olivia added.

"I do?" Susannah's stomach dipped. She had an email account of course and texted people on a daily basis like everyone else. But the first online supermarket order she'd placed had taken her two hours to complete. She would have been to the supermarket and back twice over in the time it took her to figure it all out.

And she was dreading the day when missing seeing the girls' faces overwhelmed her completely because that was the day she was going to have to learn how to Skype.

"Katie says Twitter has the news first these days, faster than the wires," Olivia said. "And all the politicians have accounts – especially the young, up-and-coming ones."

Katie was Olivia's daughter, who was a journalist with the *Daily Post.*

"And LinkedIn. You need to put your professional profile on that," Cara said. "Heh, why don't you do it now?" She was all excited. "We could help you. Go on, get your laptop!"

"This is a book club, not a jobs club, Cara!" Susannah smiled.

"I could ask Katie if they have any openings at the *Post*," Olivia said suddenly.

"That's really generous of you," Susannah said, "but I haven't been in the workforce for over twenty years and, according to Rob, it's very cutthroat now. And as for all that Twitter stuff and Facebook and the like – I'm not sure I'd be able for it. Besides, there must be young graduates queuing round the block to work for half nothing at the *Daily Post*. Like the interns at the bank. That's when all the trouble began," she added, half to herself. "When the interns arrived."

"Of course you'd be able to go back to work," Cara said. "Look at Martha O'Connor. She went back to work at sixty and now she's a millionaire!"

Susannah's neighbour had indeed carved a successful business out of supplying calorie-controlled meals, delivered to the offices of high-flying executives. Through that she'd met an overweight tycoon who lost three stone on her plan and then invested in her business so she was able to grow it on the international stage. At some stage along the way they'd become romantically involved and the last Susannah heard was that they were now happy and healthy and rich and living the good life in sunny California.

It was a feel-good story that had precisely nothing to do with Susannah's life. She didn't have anything like the entrepreneurial spirit of Martha O'Connor. She didn't even want to have to learn Twitter for God's sake. What she wanted was a time-machine which would take her back to her old life, back to the days before her mother, and then the girls, and now Rob, had all left her.

But she'd had enough of being the centre of attention, and she wasn't going to let the evening be hijacked any further.

She opened the book and cleared her throat. "As the host, it falls to me to declare the book-club discussion open," she announced.

They all somewhat reluctantly opened their books. They were easily sidetracked away from discussing the book of the month if someone had something more interesting going on in their lives. And Susannah's life certainly seemed more interesting at the moment than most of the books they'd read.

But soon enough there was a lively discussion flowing and by the time the evening was over Susannah felt uplifted by the food, drink and stimulating conversation.

After everyone had left, she felt relaxed and even though she still double-checked all her windows and doors before going to bed, for the first time in weeks she fell into a deep, dreamless sleep.

CHAPTER 5

Katie hunched over the newspaper, scanning through her column. It was only when she saw it, published in the paper with her picture byline above it that she realised people reading it wouldn't know she was just parroting the stuff Mike had said to her, putting his opinions into words so she could get out of the office on time.

Readers would think this was how she actually felt. She wasn't sure she liked that and she was glad when her mobile rang to save her thinking about it.

"Hello. Katie Corrigan here."

"So. I'll be buying a hat soon?"

"Hah! It's not what you think!" Katie's fingers crept around to the nape of her neck to massage the knot of tension which seemed to be a permanent fixture there.

"What do I think?" Her mother couldn't keep the mirth out of her voice.

"Probably that – ah, never mind. Look, the column was something Mike wanted – something novel for the Valentine's Day supplement. It's all top-of-the-head, tongue-in-cheek stuff. I dashed it off in a hurry."

"Hmm. I wonder will Luke see it like that?"

"Of course he will. And if he doesn't, I'll explain it to him. In words of two syllables if necessary."

"If you did decide to propose to him, he'd be mad to turn you down."

"I'm not proposing!" Katie's voice rose. "I've just explained it to you. It's a makey-up column I had to do under pressure."

"Well, that's okay then." Her mother backed off. "Anyhow, that's not why I rang. I met someone recently you might be interested in. It's Cara's sister – Susannah Stevens. She's a journalist and thinking of going back to work. Aren't you always looking for good freelancers?"

"Going back to work? Where has she been?"

"Rearing a family, I think. Now the family has flown – including the husband apparently – and she has to reinvent herself."

Katie stifled a sigh. Reinvention was her mother's favorite topic. Since Katie's dad had left them for the woman who was now his second wife, her mother had crammed more into that time than the whole of the rest of her life, or that's the way it sometimes seemed to Katie. She'd qualified as a psychologist, travelled the world on her own and had engaged in several unsuitable relationships – well, unsuitable to Katie anyway.

When she thought about her mother's life now, it made Katie wonder whether she had spent the other part of it – when there had been just the three of them – in such dire boredom that she felt compelled to make up for it now by attacking life with an energy that Katie found strangely unnerving.

"I'm not sure how I could use her. If she hasn't worked in years ..."

"But her husband's left her for a camper van!"

"Really?" Katie's antennae went up. That sounded novel enough, even for Mike. "How does that work?"

"He's fecked off to somewhere in Thailand. She found all this travel porn in the box-room and his computer screensaver was one of those old-fashioned Volkswagen camper vans that hippies used to go travelling in years ago. He'd been planning it for years apparently. In secret."

"And she's willing to write about it?" Katie was becoming more interested in this woman.

"I'm sure she will," Olivia said airily. "Haven't I just told you? She's a journalist. Isn't that what you do? Write about stuff that happens to you?"

"It depends on what sort of journalist you are." Katie scribbled down *camper van woman* on her jotter. "Let me think about it. So – what are you up to today?"

It was feasible that Olivia could be doing just about anything – she might have a client – she worked as a freelance therapist now. Or she might be attending a workshop, or plotting one of her travel excursions to somewhere far-flung and exotic. Or sitting in having tea and cake. Her mother was never predictable.

"Hmm – I've no plans. Maybe I'll have a look at some mother-of-the-bride outfits. Just in case."

"Not funny. Goodbye!"

Katie switched off the phone with a smile on her face. Even if she didn't always agree with her mother's choices over the last few years, at least she hadn't buckled under the acrimonious breakdown of her marriage. And her sheer joie-de-vivre was contagious – Katie felt cheered up already.

And one thing she could be sure of. Luke would know where she was coming from with the column. She was looking forward to explaining the back-story to him tonight. They were booked into Fredo's, an upmarket Italian restaurant that would be packed with other couples because it was Valentine's Night, the very essence of the loved-up couples soirée that Daniel Gilbert was taking tongue-in-cheek umbrage about in the paper today. But Fredo's had a great atmosphere and fantastic food and Katie was looking forward to it.

The desk phone rang.

"Katie Corrigan here."

"Katie!" It was Mike. "Congratulations on the column. You said exactly what was on my mind."

"Thanks!" Katie couldn't stop herself from smiling. Praise from Mike was rare indeed.

"Yes – it really works. Fair play to Jennifer for coming up with the idea."

Katie's shoulders hunched up around to her ears again. Really? Jennifer was getting the kudos for this, just for throwing an off-the-cuff idea at them – an idea that meant Katie had to work overtime to pull it off?

"And she's had another great idea. She emailed it to me last night."

That was probably when she came back to the office half-cut from the champagne reception she was attending, Katie thought sagely. Easy enough to have ideas in that state, especially when you didn't have to do anything about them.

"Yeah, she met someone at a gig who was saying we really need a 'Mind, Body, Spirit' strand – apparently all this self-help palaver is very on-trend now. Angels at your head, healing with universal energy, finding your inner child – all that nonsense. It could be a double-page spread. Weekly. Think about it."

And he put the phone down.

Katie hung up the receiver, wrestling with a mixture of emotions: anger at Jennifer for interfering yet again, annoyance at herself for falling for Mike's fickle praise so easily, apprehension because her boss had just landed her with another barrowful of work when she was already overextended.

She scribbled the initials MBS onto her jotter and switched the phone to voice mail. She didn't have time to think about all this now. She needed to focus, again, on getting her pages out on time. She switched her mobile off, blocked off the Internet and for the next three hours worked solidly on editing the features for the next day's paper.

By the time she'd finished, the small knots in her neck had solidified into rigid blocks of tension. She rolled her shoulders back, stretched and glanced at the clock.

Time for lunch. Good. She'd seize up altogether if she didn't start moving her body. She shrugged into her jacket. Her lunch-break was a bit of a misnomer, because the 'break' part of it hardly ever entered into the actual experience. Normally it involved eating something at her desk – a sandwich or a polystyrene container of soup and a cup of tea.

But today she had a work meeting set up with Daniel Gilbert. They met over lunch every week, in a coffee shop four doors up from the office. It was one of the highlights of her week. Listening to Daniel talk about his exploits was Katie's fix for the cabin-fever which frequently overcame her at work – times when she'd wonder whether she'd made a big mistake in not sticking with her writing job. But there was nothing she could do about it now: she'd made her bed and all that. And if she was serious about her ambition to be editor of the *Post* one day then she needed to get all this production experience on her résumé.

She spotted Daniel sitting at the back of the café at their regular table, tucked away out of view of the street.

"Hey!" She slid onto the bench opposite him, signalling for the waitress at the same time. Lunch would have to be quick.

Daniel had the latest edition of the *Post* spread out on the table.

"So," he said, grinning broadly. "Have you bought the ring? Will you give him roses?"

"Don't you start!" Katie scanned the menu. "I've had my mother on already, asking when she can buy a hat."

"And what about Luke? What does he think of it?"

Katie shrugged. "He hasn't read it yet. He's been in London at a conference for the last few days. He's back this evening." She pulled the newspaper towards her. "It's obvious it's written tongue-in-cheek, isn't it? Nobody would think I was serious, surely?"

"You wouldn't have done your job properly if people didn't think you were serious."

Katie raised her eyes to heaven. This was another reason why she never wanted to write about her personal life. It led to all sorts of misconceptions and miscommunications. "Lucky then that Luke knows me well enough not to fall for that."

The waitress arrived, a dark-haired woman with several colourful tattoos down both her arms. Katie had never seen her before but staff turnover at the coffee shop was high, because the owner mainly employed students or young people travelling or in transit in some way. It lent an international atmosphere to the venue and she avoided jaded staff who had been there too long. Katie ordered a goat's-cheese panini, Daniel opted for a steak roll and they both ordered strong coffees.

"So what are you doing for Valentine's then?" Katie asked.

"Writing a blog post about the pain of being a singleton in a crowd of happy couples," Daniel grinned. "What else?"

"Poor you. Luke's booked us into Fredo's."

"Swanky, but not my scene."

"You're very cynical for a young fella."

He flicked to a picture on his phone and showed it to Katie – a beautiful blonde girl she recognised as a young socialite who often appeared in Jennifer's pages. "I'm having Lucy over to discuss my blog. She wants to get into journalism."

Katie shook her head and laughed. "I'm disappointed in you."

"Why?"

"Because that's the first time you've been predictable."

"We're all looking for love, Katie." Daniel smiled and stuffed the phone back into his pocket. "So what else is up?"

"Well, Mike has just landed a new idea on me. Courtesy of Jennifer again. A 'Mind, Body, Spirit' strand – double-page spread, once a week."

"Ouch!" Daniel frowned. "That's going to be a ton of work.

You need to get an assistant, Katie."

"Yeah, I'll order one of those from the Assistants Fairy, shall I?" Katie gave him a look.

"I'm serious. You'll burn out if you keep taking on more work. What about an intern?"

Katie frowned. "Remember the intern from last year? Looked like a supermodel, turned her nose up at anything she deemed to be beneath her – which was everything apart from going out to shadow Jennifer – and spent all her time on Facebook? I don't think so. Managing her was a job in itself. "

"Maybe that was because of that control-freak thing you have going on. Things just have to get done, Katie, they don't have to get done perfectly. And they don't all have to get done by you."

Katie smiled. If anyone else had called her a control freak she would have had a fit, but Daniel had a way with him that could get him off a murder charge.

She took a notebook and pen out of her bag. "Let's get down what columns you have lined up for the next few weeks, okay?"

As usual the lunch-break flew by. Katie was late back to work and put her head down, intent on spending the rest of the day playing catch-up. But Mike wandered out in the mid-afternoon, asking her what ideas she had for the 'Mind, Body, Spirit' pages.

She took a deep breath. "I'll need to hire help, Mike. I am just so busy with everything –"

She was all ready to get into justifying herself but Mike raised a hand to cut her off.

"Do whatever you need to do. But hurry up about it."

"Oh. Okay. My mum rang earlier about some friend of a friend whose husband has just left her. She's keen to get back to work apparently. She used to be a journalist years ago and –"

"Whatever," Mike said tetchily. "Just handle it, Katie."

When he was gone Katie took a deep breath. She was astonished at how easily he had agreed with her. Maybe Daniel was right – maybe she needed to stop trying to do everything herself and learn to ask for help.

But, by late afternoon Katie was back in the default mode of playing catch-up. One of the freelance writers phoned to say she was having major problems using the paper's new system for filing copy and, as soon as she'd sorted that, Katie's own computer screen froze. She stared at it angrily, as if it had stopped working deliberately, just to spite her.

Of all the days, she thought wearily, punching out the phone number to the IT department. Her chances of getting out of the office on time had just dropped to zero. She couldn't do much until her computer was fixed but neither could she go home because the computer department worked on the basis of whoever shouted loudest and most often got attended to first – so she had to stay and make sure she was in that category.

She made herself a strong coffee and spent the time looking at her monthly planner, trying to find some time slots where she could work on the MBS pages.

By the time she finally got to squash herself into the crowded commuter train to go home, her fantasy of a two-hour pampering session before Fredo's had long since evaporated. She thought about what she would be missing as she clung grimly to one of the straps hanging out of the ceiling: a scented warm bath, a cold glass of wine and some chill-out music while she got dressed and did her make-up. She had a new outfit for the occasion and had been looking forward to the night for weeks. By the time she finally turned the key in her front door she'd already calculated she had six minutes for a shower, five to do her make-up and three to slip into her gorgeous black dress before the taxi was due to arrive. Even at that, she barely made it and was shoving her feet into black pumps when the cab pulled up outside her house.

She pulled her red winter coat over her shoulders, took the stairs two at a time and slipped with relief into the back of the cab. The driver was an unusually silent type, something she was grateful for as she sank back into the beige-leather seat and closed her eyes. She could use the car journey to clear her head of work before she met Luke.

Fredo's took its good name seriously and the owner had managed to create a pleasantly buzzy atmosphere as well as holding on to his extremely talented head chef.

When Katie arrived she saw the restaurant had been transformed into a romantic haven for the night that was in it. A dark-haired musician who looked like a gypsy was playing love songs in an alcove and the tables, all filled with couples, were each adorned with a single red rose. Katie thought fleetingly of Daniel and how he'd said everyone was looking for love. She wondered how he and Lucy were getting along. Good, she hoped. Daniel deserved to find someone wonderful.

She found Luke seated in a small, intimate alcove towards the back of the restaurant.

"Hi!" He stood up as she approached.

"Hi, yourself!" She kissed him. "I missed you."

He was dressed in an expensive dark suit and a light-blue shirt. He was, as he said himself, short, blond and handsome. When they met first he used to tell her it was lucky he made her laugh so much, so he could make up for the fact she could never wear heels with him.

"I missed you too. Medical conferences are so boring!"

Luke's job as a medical journalist was well paid but his big love was writing fiction. He always loved hearing about Katie's job, which he said was far more creative and fun than his own. Katie didn't quite see it like that, especially after a day like the one she'd just had, when trying to keep on top of her workload seemed like trying to hold back the tide, but she knew he loved the juicy titbits she fed him. He was always fascinated with it – what writers she was using, what celeb Jennifer had met, and what news stories might be breaking overnight.

The first part of the evening flew by as she filled him in on all the gossip.

They were on dessert before he even mentioned the column. Katie had drunk half a bottle of wine, kicked off her shoes and was wrapped up in listening to the musician who, now that she was paying attention, was actually really good.

"Just so you know," he said. "When you propose to me I don't care where it is – just so long as you do it."

Katie's attention snapped back to him.

"I'll keep that in mind," she said lightly.

He reached out and caught her hand. "But I'd prefer it to be sooner rather than later."

"Really?" Katie took her hand out of his and started pleating her napkin between her fingers. "What's brought all this on?"

"Your column, of course. It got me thinking. And, well – you're not getting any younger, are you?"

"Neither is anybody else." Katie felt a flicker of annoyance.

"That's true. But you're the one with the deteriorating eggs."

"Excuse me?" Katie was about to launch into an outraged response when she remembered that's what she had written in the column. Luke was only quoting her own words back to her. She shifted in her chair. "It was meant to be a joke."

"And I got an awful slagging about it from my colleagues in London."

Katie frowned. "How?"

"They do have the Internet in London, Katie. And we met up for dinner at night. So your column came up for discussion."

"Really? Didn't you have medical stuff to be talking about?" "Seriously?" He raised his eyebrows. "Your column was a thousand times more interesting. And now they're all waiting by their phones to see if I'll have anything to report tonight." He smiled and tried to hold her hand again but she quickly pushed it into her lap, out of his reach.

"The column was just something I wrote to keep Mike happy. He wanted something more novel than anything I had and Jennifer came up with the idea of why women don't propose – like it's the last bastion for feminism. Or something." Katie was starting to feel very hot.

"So you're going to propose to me to please Mike?" Luke's tone was still light-hearted, but she saw a muscle in his jaw twitching.

"I'm not going to propose to you at all."

He frowned. "But what you said in the column – no, don't tell me –" He shook his head as reality dawned. "You actually didn't mean a word of it."

"I'd never write about anything so personal."

"Except you just did." His voice sounded flat now.

"I've just told you. It was tongue-in-cheek."

"I understand. You're not going to propose to me."

"Sorry," Katie said, wondering why she felt she had to apologise.

"But I have a proposal for you." He pushed his hand into his pocket.

Katie stared at him, terrified he was going to produce a ring.

He held up a silver hall-door key, glinting in the candlelight. Katie recognised it. She had given it to him ages ago, a key to her apartment for the nights he stayed in her place. He placed it in the centre of the table, between them.

Was he giving it back? Breaking up?

"I'm tired of living in two places, Katie – and I want us to take the next step in our relationship. I understand you don't want to get married yet – so how about we move in together?"

Katie looked at the key, trying to figure out how she could get out of this dangerous territory they'd strayed into without insulting him.

"You do want to take the next step, don't you?" He was

nodding at her, a lock of blond hair falling into his eyes as his head moved up and down encouragingly.

Katie swallowed. "I want us to be together, of course I do. Eventually. But right now the new job is taking up so much of my time and energy. Honestly, I'm like a zombie by the time I get home some nights. Maybe when things have quietened down a bit?"

"But things never quieten down for you, Katie, do they?" He was disappointed. Hurt. "Because you're always chasing the next shiny thing."

Chasing the next shiny thing? Katie thought of her work-to-bed life and wondered whether she and Luke were living on the same planet. But she needed to shut down this Pandora's Box, not pull out more controversial stuff for discussion.

"Look, I don't think we should spoil Valentine's Night by arguing over a stupid column I was forced to write by my very bossy boss," she joked.

"It's not about the column, Katie."

She didn't want to ask him what it was about so she stayed silent. And so did Luke after that, and they sat there, surrounded by flickering candlelight, and the laughter of all the other diners around them and the singer, who seemed to be now singing some sort of lament, which was a bit ridiculous on the night that was in it.

She tried to remember something funny Jennifer had said so she could amuse Luke with it, get them both on to safer ground. But before she could think of anything, Luke had called for the bill.

As they got ready to leave, Katie noticed the closed expression on his face and she knew something had changed between them tonight. Changed irrevocably.

CHAPTER 6

Susannah spent her 25th wedding anniversary like a love-struck teenager waiting for something from her husband to mark the occasion. Her expectation of flowers faded as the day went on, but she still checked her phone every few minutes, waiting for a text or an email, an electronic thinking-of-you to bridge the gulf between Dublin and Thailand.

She even indulged in some mental gymnastics, calculating the time difference between Dublin and Bangkok. Maybe Rob was so disorientated that the date had somehow slipped his mind, she reasoned. He was living in a completely new culture now, and he might not have settled in yet.

But by two in the morning a sleepless Susannah realised it was actually the next day in Thailand and had to conclude that Rob had chosen to ignore their anniversary. Or maybe he was having such a good time he hadn't given it, or her, or home, a single thought.

Olivia was right, she thought, turning off the bedside lamp and thumping the pillows. She had to stop believing Rob was going to arrive at the front door any day now, sheepish and asking to be forgiven. She had to find a way to move on. But the trouble was she didn't know how to do that. It was like her mind was stuck in a rut of thinking in just one way, and when she asked it to come up with new ways of living, it just came up with a great big blank.

She finally fell into a fitful sleep but by six she was awake again, feeling stiff and tense, the remnants of another half-remembered dream flitting through her mind as she pulled on her dressing gown and went down to the kitchen.

She made herself eat breakfast – cereal, fruit and coffee – but after that she just mooned about the house, tidying in aimless fits and starts, staring out the window, not knowing what to do with herself, or the day.

By eleven she knew she had to take action. Anything would do, she reasoned, once it got her out of the torpor that was swallowing her up. She went up to the box-room and surveyed the desk: Rob's old command post where he'd hatched his running-away plan. She shoved all the travel books and notebooks to one side and switched on the computer. She needed to figure out how to get on to his Facebook page and see what was happening with him.

After that, she would phone New York and finally explain to the girls that their dad had left home. She couldn't keep it from them any longer. She was dreading their reaction. Orlaith might be philosophical. But Jess would worry. Jess worried about everything. Susannah wanted to frame the situation in as positive a light as possible for her sake. She shook her head slightly, still bewildered that Rob had found the chutzpah to do what he did while she could barely summon the courage to leave the house.

As she waited for the ancient computer to power up, she pulled out a pen and a notebook and began to scribble down her thoughts. Your father has gone on a bit of an adventure. That brought an unexpected lump to her throat so she crossed it out. Your father has taken a sabbatical from work. That was it. A sabbatical was an actual thing. Something grown-up people did all the time. But she could hear the clamour of questions already. But why? Where? Why aren't you with him? Questions she wished she knew the answers to.

The phone rang, shattering the silence of the house. Susannah stared at it for a second. Rob, she thought, with his belated Valentine's greeting. She exhaled a big breath of relief as she grabbed the receiver.

"Rob?" She could hear her own voice, high-pitched, too eager. But she didn't care. She just wanted to hear his voice again.

"Hello there. I'm looking to speak to Susannah Stevens."

Susannah frowned, trying to place the brusque, young female voice while fighting the disappointment that, once again, her husband had let her down.

"This is Susannah." It was probably someone trying to sell her something.

"Hi, this Katie Corrigan from the *Daily Post*. I got your name from my mother – Olivia."

"Oh!" Susannah's grip on the receiver tightened as she tried to focus.

"She said you're looking for work?"

The book-club night. Susannah had forgotten all about it. "Yes. Yes, I am."

"Good. Because I need a reliable freelancer and Olivia recommended you. She says you're experienced and keen. I'll need to see your CV, and some examples of your work. But all going well – would you be interested?"

Susannah's mind raced into overdrive, analysing all she'd have to do to get ready for this unexpected opportunity.

With luck she could be up to speed by the end of the week, she reckoned. She needed to look through all her old press cuttings, photocopy her best work, figure out how to plug the gaps in her CV. And look at the news to catch up on current affairs. She hadn't even read a newspaper in weeks. She'd need to buy something professional to wear. And, hell, maybe she could hire one of those life-coach people while she was at it, someone to help her jumpstart her plummeting motivation in less than a week, so she could present herself positively to this super-confident-sounding daughter of Olivia's.

"Yes. I would be. I am."

"Great. So I have a time slot this afternoon. Two thirty. Can you make that?"

Susannah's stomach dipped. "Today?"

"Yes – today. Is it not convenient?"

"It's – it's very short notice. And I need to –" Susannah stopped mid-sentence as the computer in front of her finally came to life and she found herself staring at Rob's screensaver. The image of the red-and-white camper van with the stupid slogans on it. Another slogan had been added. Rob must have done it before he'd left.

Don't Look Back – You're Not Going That Way.

Susannah's stomach clenched. What was wrong with her? If Rob could go halfway around the world on his own, leaving her, his job, their life on a whim, then she could get herself onto a train and meet Katie Corrigan this afternoon.

"Susannah?"

She took a deep, steadying breath. "I was just thinking that I can switch some appointments around – you know, this is pretty important to me. Where do you want to meet?"

Katie mentioned a hotel near Herbert Park, on the south of the city. Susannah knew it vaguely – as far as she could remember it was a ten-to-fifteen-minute walk from her train station. She tried to think up some questions, something to engage Katie in conversation so she could gauge what it was she was looking for. But she had already hung up.

Susannah stared at the receiver in her hands. What now, she wondered? She glanced at the clock. She had less than four hours to turn her life around.

Susannah spent the time wisely and, as she walked along the

canal on her way to the hotel, she glanced down at her old briefcase, worn now with age, but still holding up. It was stuffed with her CV, years-old examples of the work she had never been able to throw out, the book she was reading for the book club and the pens and notebooks she carried everywhere with her.

Far from the suited and booted look she'd like to be channeling, she was wearing the dress she'd bought for Christmas – a brown jersey frock teamed with brown boots and her beige, belted trench.

She was worried about meeting Katie. She wasn't sure how she could portray the gaps in her CV in a positive light and come across as confident and competent when she felt the opposite.

A TV chat show she'd seen recently flashed through her head. Daytime television was a lot more useful than its reputation suggested. This particular programme had featured a careers counsellor who suggested that women wanting to return to the workplace needed to see themselves in a different way. It was all about what he called transferable skills.

She could see him in her mind's eye now, a handsome, dark-haired young man who had written an entire book on the subject.

"Women returners need to remember they have effectively been the CEO of an organisation called 'Home' and need to pitch themselves as such to potential employers." He looked earnestly into the camera, switching his attention directly to the viewer at home. *"You have managed people, budgets, nutrition, psychological development and administration tasks. You have demonstrated high-level logistical skills. And it's these very skills you are now going to use to carve out a new, successful career for yourself."*

It was all very comforting until Susannah remembered that her particular organisation called Home was a spectacular fuck-up at the moment. She speeded up her walking pace, determined to outrun the sarcastic commentary in her head. She was overthinking it all, she decided. She may not have worked for years but the fact was she had a proven track record, as evidenced by her bulging briefcase. That had to count for something. And Olivia had recommended her and she was Katie's mother. That would count for even more, probably.

She was feeling better until she realised her route was bringing her straight past Rob's old office and the restaurant where she'd been given her marching orders.

She stopped outside it, peering through the window where they'd had that awful conversation.

She couldn't do this, she realised. She didn't have the nerve and she was way out of her depth. What was the point in adding to all the misery she was feeling by making a fool of herself? And of Olivia too for recommending her?

She was getting ready to retrace her route back to the train station, mentally rehearsing what excuse she would give to Katie, and Olivia and Cara, when out of nowhere the slogan on Rob's screensaver flashed through her mind like a neon sign. *Don't Look Back – You're Not Going That Way.*

It was clichéd but true. There was nothing at home for her. Nothing. Whatever lay ahead, it couldn't be worse than that. She took a deep breath, pushed her shoulders back and resumed her journey towards the hotel, her pace picking up into a fast power-walk.

By the time she reached the entrance, her cheeks were pink with the exertion and her blood was pumping with adrenaline. She could do it after all, she told herself triumphantly. She was doing it.

She marched through the revolving doors and chose a seat in the lobby, facing the entrance so she would see Katie when she arrived. She'd looked her up on the paper's website and knew she was an attractive young woman with blonde, wavy hair and a look of Olivia about her.

Susannah glanced down at her résumé. It looked good on paper, dynamic even. It was evidence of an ambitious woman with a steady belief in her own talents. But it felt as if it belonged to someone else. A stronger, better version of who Susannah was now. She closed the folder with a tiny sigh and looked up just as Katie Corrigan entered the hotel.

Olivia's daughter cut a striking figure, impeccably groomed in a cream cashmere coat and black, polished boots. But as she drew closer, Susannah could see she looked tired under the carefully applied make-up.

Katie stopped by her chair. "Susannah?"

"Yes." Susannah stood up to greet her.

Katie shrugged out of her coat, shook hands briefly and sat down in the chair opposite.

"Look, this is going to seem very rude. But I'm afraid I have to get straight down to business. Something's come up at the office. A mini-crisis." She frowned. "Sorry."

A waiter hovered nearby, waiting for their order, but Katie ignored him.

"So – have you brought your CV?"

"Sure." Susannah passed over her manila file, taken aback by Katie's abrupt manner. Surely she could spare a few minutes for them to get comfortable in each other's presence?

But Katie was already scanning through her résumé and Susannah turned her thoughts to how she could expand on it. She could talk about how she'd reported on national politics, and the award she'd got as part of the editorial team that had brought down a government back in the day. The time she'd travelled to Washington to cover a story of how the IRA was funded by wealthy US benefactors and the tour of the orphanages she'd done in Romania after the fall of Nicolae Ceausescu. That should be enough, she reckoned. She heaved a deep sigh as Katie closed the folder.

"So," Katie looked at her, "do you have any experience of covering MBS?"

"MB-what?" Susannah wrenched her mind away from the disturbing memories of what she'd witnessed in Bucharest.

"Mind, Body, Spirit. Wellbeing, Reiki, Random Acts of Kindness?" Katie waved a hand vaguely. "That sort of thing."

A tic pulsed in Susannah's throat. "I can't say I have. As you can see," she gestured towards the folder Katie was now handing back to her, "I covered hard news. Investigations. Social policy. Politics."

"Well, never mind – we get a ton of promotional material on MBS into the office. I can have it all sent on to your home address. You can mine it for the best ideas. But remember anything you write will have to be personalised – you'll need realistic case histories to illustrate the stories. Otherwise it will read like boring, woo-woo bullshit. By the way, how old are you?"

Susannah fleetingly wondered how the gentle, diplomatic Olivia could have spawned the blunt young woman sitting opposite her.

"I'm fifty-three, " she said quietly. She waited for Katie to take a mental step back in horror at her advancing years.

"Good," Katie said. "So, for example, you could write about fifty-two challenges for a fifty-two-year-old. One for each week of the year – that sort of thing."

"But I'm fifty-three," Susannah pointed out. "Never mind," she added quickly as she saw a frown darken Katie's pretty face. Obviously she could take artistic licence with her age. But she couldn't ignore the confused communication between them. She leaned forward in her chair. "What did Olivia tell you about me exactly?"

"That your husband left you for a camper van." Katie raised her eyebrows. "Sorry for your trouble."

"He took a career break," Susanna corrected her.

"A career break in a camper van?"

"I don't know if an actual camper van is in his plans."

Susannah was getting flustered. "He had a screensaver of a camper van on his computer and I told Olivia about it. So maybe that's why she thought —"

"Well, it's the camper-van angle which sold you to me. It's an unusual slant on the ho-hum story of a husband leaving the wife for someone younger and shinier who spends all her time telling him how wonderful he is. I mean, how clichéd is that?"

Susannah remembered Olivia's marriage had broken up after Katie's dad had met and married a much younger woman. As far as she knew, they had a son who would be about nine by now. Seán. Katie's half-brother.

"My husband hasn't left me," she insisted. "As I said, he's on a career-break."

"Where?" Katie asked.

"Thailand."

Katie threw her a sympathetic look. "Whatever. Anyway, MBS is the sort of stuff my paper is interested in promoting."

Susannah's fingers gripped the folder with her CV in it. She thought back to that morning, and the hours she had spent racking her brain trying to figure out the best way she could present herself, how she could impress Katie Corrigan.

And all she was interested in was that Rob had left her for a camper van. A sound bite that had piqued her interest.

With belated clarity, Susannah could see that Katie wasn't trying to fill a political-correspondent or a news-analysis role in the *Post*. And if she was, she wouldn't have come to someone who hadn't seen the inside of a newsroom for over two decades. She would pick someone who could file the copy and shoot a video for the paper's online edition and tweet about it too. All at the same time, probably.

"Well, are you interested?" Katie was looking impatient, drumming her nails on the arm of her chair.

"It's very different to my previous assignments," Susannah said uncertainly. That was the least of it. She mentally shuddered when she thought of the technological advances that had been made since she'd last held down a job. What would Katie say if she knew that when she'd phoned her this morning she had been staring at the computer as if it was a spaceship, trying to figure out a way to access her husband's Facebook page?

But it seemed that Rob had unwittingly done her a favour by leaving her. His uncharacteristic behaviour had somehow made her skills marketable again, given her a chance to get a tentative hold at the *Post*. She smiled at the irony of it.

"What's so funny?" Katie shifted in her seat.

"It's just that I've been worrying my head off all day about how I was going to sell myself to you after being out of work so long and – well, I didn't think you'd be so interested in my husband. That's all."

"In fairness, I don't think features on politics from twenty years ago would excite my readers. Or anybody, for that matter, apart from historians. My husband left me for a camper van? That, they would be interested in. I'm interested in it anyhow." Katie leaned forward. "The question is, are you interested in writing it?"

Susannah considered the question. No, was the clear-cut answer. But she knew enough to realise that opportunities like this didn't present themselves every day of the week. And she was so, so bored with her life.

"I'm interested," she said firmly.

"Good. I need a thousand words by this day next week. I'll pay you one way or the other and, if I like your writing style and you can meet a deadline, we can talk about the terms and conditions of regular freelance work at the *Post*. Is that okay?"

"It's great." Susannah had no idea how she was going to write and deliver such a piece by the next week. But that was a question for another day. "So where do I email it to?"

Katie slid a white embossed business card across the table. Susannah took it up and read it.

Katie Corrigan. Features Editor. Daily Post. And of course her twitter handle. Susannah knew about twitter handles only from half-heard conversations between Orlaith and Jess. Thank God Katie hadn't asked her about her non-existent social-media skills.

"Good." Katie glanced at the silver watch on her skinny wrist. "Now, I'd love to stay and chat but, as I said earlier, there's a bit of a crisis going on at the office." She smiled briefly. "So we have a deal?"

"We have a deal," Susannah said faintly.

She watched Katie sweep back out of the lobby and, when she'd disappeared from sight, she called the waiter over.

"A glass of white wine, please."

She took out her notebook and began to scribble down the story of how Rob had left her for a camper van.

CHAPTER 7

Susannah stared at her blank screen. It had taken her twenty-four hours before she could get the courage to open a new window in her computer and write down the title.

My Husband Left Me for a Camper Van. And that was as far as she'd got. She had never written a confessional piece of journalism before and every time she went to begin she'd become paralysed with fear. Now it was Friday morning and she had forced herself to go back to it because, if she didn't, she'd spend the weekend worrying.

Chewing on the end of her biro, she thought back to the five W's of journalism school: Who, What, Where, When and Why.

Who? Herself and Rob. She typed down their names.

What? Rob had gone off on their big adventure without her and she'd been so blindsided by this it had made her doubt everything she thought to be true about her life.

Where? Hippie trail in a fit of mid-life madness.

When? Five weeks ago.

Why? The last question floored her. She could guess – and had been guessing every spare minute she got. But she still had no answers. Maybe she never would have.

That last difficult week before he'd left, they'd had the same, circular conversation over and over again and it had always ended in one stubborn sentence from Rob: "It's something I have to do, Susannah."

She turned her attention back to the screen and started to type.

"Five weeks ago my husband of twenty-five years left me for a camper van. This is the year of our Silver Wedding, a time we're supposed to be celebrating all that went before and toasting what's to come. With our two daughters grown-up and gone, I was just coming to terms with the empty nest and ready to move on to our next chapter. I was even thinking – God help me – of date nights."

She paused, carried back in time again to when she'd been still trying to persuade Rob that there had to be another way. She'd actually suggested they start date nights, which only caused Rob to look at her with such bewilderment that she'd been mortified.

Her mobile rang and Susannah jumped on it, glad of the distraction.

It was Katie Corrigan.

"Hi, Susannah. Listen, can you file that column today? I know it's early but something else has fallen through for me."

Susannah looked at the bullet points and the short paragraph she'd written.

"Em – well, I don't know –" she began but Katie interrupted her.

"I don't need it until two. And it's only ten now. You'd be helping me out big-time. And it will go into tomorrow's paper which will be good for you because the Saturday edition is Mike's main priority at the moment."

Susannah massaged the bridge of her nose, trying to get up the courage to tell Katie she'd be lucky to make the original deadline, never mind this new one.

"How's it going anyway?" Katie spoke into the silence.

"Slow," Susannah admitted.

"Oh."

"I'm not used to writing personal stuff. That's not an excuse obviously but — you know — it's sort of still raw for me."

"That's when you do the best writing," Katie informed her. "Look, what if you used a pen name? I'm not a fan of them normally. But I'm really, really stuck — so if it helps you get the piece to me by this afternoon ..."

A pen name! Of course. Susannah wondered why she hadn't thought of that herself. It would mean she didn't have to let the world and its wife know what was happening between herself and Rob for one thing.

And she knew just what her pen name would be too: Elizabeth Castle. A vision floated into her mind of her very glamorous maternal grandmother. She had no memories of meeting her because she had died when Susannah was still a baby. But when she grew up, her mother had presented her with a box of diaries, all written in Elizabeth Castle's calligraphy-style handwriting on thick, cream-coloured paper. Susannah could still recall the hours she had spent reading them as a teenager. She had kept the journals all through the years and they were carefully stored now on top of her wardrobe in fancy boxes she'd bought specifically for them. She smiled. It was her grandmother's diaries that had got her interested in journalism in the first place!

"Okay," she told Katie. "I'll give it a go. I'll write it under my grandmother's name — Elizabeth Castle."

"Elizabeth Castle. Yeah, great, got it. Thanks for this — you're a lifesaver." And Katie put the phone down.

Susannah looked at the receiver for a few seconds. She couldn't get used to Katie's manner and how she always seemed to be in such a rush to be somewhere else. It struck her again how unlike her Olivia was with her gentle, grounded demeanour. Susannah would never have put them down as mother and daughter unless she'd been told beforehand.

She went into her bedroom and pulled down the box of journals, realising for the first time that she had never got around to showing them to Orlaith and Jess.

A photograph fluttered on to her lap. Yellow with age and curling at the corners, it nevertheless seemed to capture Elizabeth's spirit from across the generations.

She must have been about twenty-five when this photograph was taken, Susannah thought. She was breathtakingly beautiful, with lips like rosebuds and dark eyebrows shaped like wings over mysterious, sultry eyes. Her black hair was styled in a wave across one side of her perfect oval face. She wore pearl earrings with a matching pearl necklace and she had a fur stole draped around her shoulders.

Susannah wondered what her life was like when this image was taken. What was she thinking? What was she feeling?

She propped the photo against the noticeboard at the back of the desk and sat in silence for a while, trying to connect with the woman in it.

Susannah was a believer, in the sense that she'd always felt the spirit lived on after death. She'd felt the presence of her dad so many times after he'd died of a sudden heart attack when she was just sixteen. And she didn't know how she would have coped these past nine months if she hadn't felt her mother with her all the time.

But, even so, Susannah was taken aback when a surge of energy swept through her almost immediately and her fingers began to fly over the keyboard. It was uncanny but suddenly she knew exactly what to write.

As Elizabeth Castle, she was infected with a glorious sense of freedom, able to write from her heart – the sound of Rob and Cara and Olivia all putting their well-meaning oars in, telling her how silly she was to feel what she was feeling, or misguided to be doing what she was doing, muted down to nothing.

There was just her, writing it all out from her point of view. And how did any of them know what they would do, or feel anyway, unless they were standing in her shoes, she thought, as she wrote on, putting all her bewilderment and pain and confusion down on the page.

When she had finished she glanced at the clock. She'd just enough time to read over it quickly, run a spell-check on it and press 'send'.

She stood up with a sense of exhilaration. It was done.

She made herself a cup of tea and fixed herself a sandwich. Then she rang Olivia. She wanted to invite her to dinner as a thank-you for recommending her to Katie. Cara too for pushing her to face the truth about her situation. Both women were in a chatty mood and by the time she got off the phone Susannah knew exactly what she wanted to do.

She curled up on the sofa and spent the evening rereading her grandmother's journals, feeling peaceful and connected as she flicked through the pages, remembering the sense of purpose and ambition she'd got from them as a young teenager.

A middle-class girl, Elizabeth Castle had been brought up to become a well-to-do housewife and mother, and by all accounts had excelled at both. But she had poured all her intellect and lust for life into her journals. She had been fascinated by women like Clare Hollingsworth – the woman who was the first journalist to report the start of the Second World War, the American writer Dorothy Parker, and Constance Markievicz with her interests in Irish nationalism, socialism and the suffragette movement. All larger-than-life women who had lived lives full of adventure and achievement. Susannah got the sense that maybe Elizabeth had lived vicariously through them.

It made her sad, especially when she realised with a jolt that when her grandmother passed she had actually been only a year older than she herself was now.

She put down the last of the journals, lost in thought. She was grateful she didn't have the constraints on her life that Elizabeth Castle had. The world and society had moved on, and the only limitations on her now were of her own making.

So she was probably never going to become a famous writer or a fearless war correspondent, or even leave a bunch of beautifully written journals as a legacy. But she could do something.

That night she went to sleep with a long-forgotten sense of achievement and, when she awoke, the early spring sunshine was beaming bright, golden shapes into her bedroom, flooding it with light and warmth. Something had changed. She sensed it immediately. She lay there quietly, trying to figure out what it was. She had slept soundly – no nightmares, no nocturnal ramblings filled with anxiety about the future and grief about the past. But it was more than that.

Was she getting over Rob? For the first time since he'd left, her husband hadn't been the first thing on her mind when she woke up, nor had he been her last thought before she'd fallen asleep last night.

But it was more than that too. She couldn't be sure why, but it felt as if the universe had hit an energy-switch which had jumpstarted her life into full working-mode again and she was feeling enthusiastic about the day ahead for the first time in ages.

CHAPTER 8

She got up and dressed quickly, anxious to make the most of this new surge of energy and optimism, fearful that if she hesitated the old feeling of ennui would envelop her once again. She went down to the kitchen, had coffee and cereal and started planning what she could prepare for Cara and Olivia later on.

She was a talented cook and eventually opted for a complicated dish of roasted squash with pine nuts in filo pastry for a starter, a simple fish dish for the main, and her pièce de résistance for dessert: a fabulous confection of chocolate mousse, fresh raspberries and cream.

Feeling happy and motivated, she headed off for the supermarket. Online ordering had been fine when she'd wanted to hide away from the world but today she needed to be there in person, checking out the freshness of the food, and studying the wine aisle while she was at it.

But the first stop for her was the supermarket's newsagent section. The camper-van column would be her first published piece in years and Susannah felt as nervous as a rookie reporter this morning, checking to see if her story had made the grade.

She took a copy of the *Post* off the shelf and was about to open it when she became aware of someone watching her.

Actually, there were two people watching. Her neighbours,

Patsy and Joe Ambrose, were staring over from the fruit and vegetable aisle. When Susannah looked up Patsy waved at her brightly and Joe gave her a big grin and a wink. They started to come over, looking as if they wanted a big chat.

Susannah gave a feeble wave and swiftly steered her trolley in the opposite direction. While she was getting used to being on her own she wasn't ready for idle chitchat about where Rob was either. She'd have to wait until she got home to check out her column.

Back home she unpacked her groceries, looking forward to sitting down with a cup of coffee to check the paper. Would Katie have tucked her piece away in a corner or made it into a big splash?

But, just as she was sitting down, her mobile rang.

"Hey – I've just read your column." Cara sounded pleased. "It's great! Good for you, Susannah. It was brave of you to write it."

Brave? Susannah considered that. She supposed it might have been if she'd written it under her own name. Susannah Stevens would shy away completely from writing something that was akin to washing her dirty laundry in public, never mind publishing it in a national newspaper. But as Elizabeth Castle she'd felt no such compunction. In fact, now that she thought about it, it almost felt as if Elizabeth Castle had written the piece for her.

"I found it very cathartic to be honest."

Even though the column was written in a humorous, light-hearted style, Susannah knew the underlying pathos was clear in each and every line and she was so grateful now that Katie had given her the idea to use a pen name.

"Well, that's great," said Cara. "You're starting to seem like your old self again. I'm so proud of you." There was a pause. "So what do you think Rob will make of it?"

"I hope he'd see the funny side of it. But he won't see it, seeing as the *Post* isn't published in Southeast Asia." Her spirits dipped a little. Rob still hadn't been in touch. "And, even if he did, he probably wouldn't even remember who Elizabeth Castle was."

"What do you mean?"

"I don't think he'd connect the pen name Elizabeth Castle to me. He didn't even know her and I never spoke about her much to him."

"But the column doesn't say anything about Elizabeth Castle," asked Cara, puzzled.

Susannah laughed. "Look again! It's my pen name. Katie agreed that it would be published under that. That way I felt free to write what I wanted."

"But I have it right here in front of me. It says Susannah Stevens."

"What?" Susannah grabbed the newspaper and ripped through the pages until she found the features section. Her column was one of the main stories, with an interesting illustration accompanying it: a stock image of a dilapidated, rusty-looking camper van with a beefy, snowy-haired man leaning up against it, his white shirt straining against his belly.

Susannah silently thanked God that Rob was still in Thailand – hopefully deep in some jungle by now.

Because, sure enough, splashed on top of the column in big, bold print, for the entire world to see, was the headline and the byline.

How My Husband Left Me for a Camper Van
By Susannah Stevens

Susannah's grip on the paper tightened. Her heart speeded up as she scanned the page, as if she was going to see Elizabeth Castle's byline somewhere else.

A memory of her trip to the supermarket flashed through her

mind and the blood rushed to her face. No wonder the
Ambroses had been killing themselves trying to get around the
fruit and vegetable aisle to talk to her!

"Cara, I can't believe this. Katie promised. And I reminded her
of our agreement again when I was emailing the piece."

"It explains why you were so forthright anyway," Cara said
lightly. "You thought old Lizzie Castle was going to take the rap."

"It's not funny," Susannah snapped. "Everybody will see it. My
neighbours —" She briefly recounted seeing Patsy and Joe
Ambrose in the supermarket.

"They must have read it so." Cara took a deep breath. "What's
that saying? Worrying about what people think of you is a waste
of energy because they're usually not thinking about you at all.
They're thinking about themselves."

"The Ambroses were thinking of me," Susannah said flatly. "I
can't believe Katie could be so stupid," she added angrily.

"I don't think you could describe Katie Corrigan as stupid.
And I don't think you should describe anyone that way. What's
got into you, Susannah?"

"Well, incompetent then." Susannah was still furious. "It just
goes to show that appearances can lie. She looks like she's totally
together, as if she never made a mistake in her life."

"Well, now she has. And you'd better figure out how you're
going to deal with it since you have her mother coming over for
dinner tonight," Cara said sharply.

"I'll have to cancel it," Susannah said absentmindedly. She was
still staring at the feature article, her mind racing about who
could be reading it right now.

"You can't do that. You've already asked her. As a thank-you
for getting you the job. And you're going to have to face her at
some time so it may as well be tonight. Get it over with."

Susannah sighed. "I suppose you're right."

It would be beyond awkward to have to phone Olivia to

cancel the dinner party now anyway. And it was hardly her fault that her daughter had broken her promise.

She said goodbye to Cara and tried to concentrate on what she had to do to get ready for the night ahead.

But all day long she was preoccupied with the column. Maybe Katie had never intended to run it under a pen name at all, she brooded. Maybe she was one of those unscrupulous journalists who said anything to get what they wanted.

By early evening she was still brooding about it so she poured herself a glass of wine before starting on the dinner. The familiar ritual of chopping and slicing and stirring, testing the texture and the seasoning grounded her. The aroma of the garlic and onions frying made the house feel like home to her again.

By the time she had finished cooking she felt calm and relaxed – but the sound of her guests arriving led to all the mortification over the column flooding through her again.

If she'd been going to publish it under her own name, she wouldn't have been half as honest, she fretted, going out to answer the door. She would have made it funnier and shallower and the readers would probably still have liked it and she wouldn't be facing all this humiliation.

Cara was standing on the doorstep, the collar of her winter coat pulled up to her ears and a bottle of champagne clutched in her hands.

"I had already bought this to congratulate you on your reinvention. And I propose we celebrate that anyway – even if your debut feature went a little haywire."

Susannah saw Olivia's car pulling up the drive.

"Thank you." She took the champagne bottle from Cara. "Can you look after Olivia – I need to do something in the kitchen."

She stabbed at the oven switch to turn it off and took three champagne flutes out of the drinks cabinet. Maybe if she drank enough she wouldn't care any more.

When she went into the living room Olivia was looking at the newspaper.

"I'm just rereading your column," she said. "Well done. It is so raw and − well, authentic. I think it was very brave of you to write it actually."

There was that word again. Brave. It was beginning to get on Susannah's nerves. She took a deep breath.

"There was nothing brave about it actually. The column was supposed to be published under a pen name."

"Oh? Yes, I can see how that would be a good idea," Olivia said. "It would give you more freedom to write what you really felt, wouldn't it?" Her brow furrowed in puzzlement. "So what happened?"

"I don't know," Susannah said dully. "Katie promised me she'd publish the column under the name Elizabeth Castle."

"That was our grandmother's name." Cara explained.

"So why didn't she? Katie, I mean?"

Susannah shrugged. It would be rude to say exactly what she thought of Katie Corrigan right now. Especially to her mother.

"It's not like Katie, is it?" Cara put a hand on Olivia's arm. "Aren't you always saying how totally organised she is?"

"She is. Normally." Olivia looked worried. "But she's been all over the place for the last couple of weeks. I don't think she's getting on too well with the boyfriend." She looked at Susannah. "I'm so sorry."

"It's not your fault," Susannah said. "But this is a big problem for me. What will people think of me? My neighbours don't even know Rob is gone."

"But it's all true, isn't it, what you've written?" Olivia asked.

"Of course it's true! That's the whole reason I didn't want to write it under my own name!" Susannah snapped. She took a deep breath, trying to regain her composure.

Olivia was understandably looking deeply uncomfortable

now. Susannah had to remind herself again that she was here at her invitation.

Maybe Cara was right anyhow, she thought, trying to figure out how to change the subject. Maybe she was being too precious about the whole thing? The answer would have to wait until tomorrow.

"But I'd like to forget about it for tonight," she declared. "Let's be having that champagne, Cara."

As Cara poured the bubbly, Susannah forced herself to stay in the moment and it was the best decision she could have made because almost at once she began to relax.

By the time they were sitting down for dinner, Olivia was regaling them with the romantic adventures she'd had through a mature dating website and Susannah was positively enjoying herself. Cara, who was never short of a tale or two as a single air stewardess, seemed to be enjoying competing with Olivia for tales of derring-do.

As the wine flowed and the stories got funnier and more outrageous, Susannah decided that she'd never have the courage to go on a dating site.

"Well, that's the way it's done nowadays," Olivia said simply. "So if you want to meet someone you have to embrace it."

"Like if Rob makes another unilateral decision and decides not to come back from Southeast Asia?" Cara said, laughing. "You'd have to get on a dating site then!"

"Or I could learn to like my own company!" Susannah retorted.

And then the phone rang. Loud and unexpected, the tone shrill in the silence that fell over them. Susannah, with a forkful of chocolate mousse halfway to her mouth, dropped it and the fork fell with a clatter back on to the plate, the contents splattering all over the white tablecloth.

Cara checked the time on her phone. "It's eleven thirty," she said in a small voice.

Susannah rushed over to the phone and snatched up the receiver. "Hello?" She could hear her own voice, sounding panicked and scared.

"Mum?"

"Jess?" Susannah clutched her stomach. "What's happened?"

"We thought you could tell us that!" Orlaith snapped.

"Are you both on the same phone?" Susannah asked, confused.

"Yeah – miracle of technology and all that," said Orlaith. "But you'll already know that since you've obviously got over your tech phobia."

"Excuse me?" Susannah's head was more than a bit fuzzy after all the champagne and wine they'd consumed.

"My husband left me for a camper van? Seriously?" Orlaith sounded astonished.

"Oh … that." Susannah glanced over at the table and gesticulated for the others to listen in to her side of the conversation. Maybe they'd figure out a way to help her through it! "How did you find out about that?"

Cara came over, topped up Susannah's wineglass and stood close by.

"Well, there's this other, little-known technical invention. It's called the Internet!" Orlaith shouted.

"Mum, what the hell is happening over there?" Jess sounded as if she'd been crying.

"There's nothing to worry about," Susannah said firmly. "It's just your dad – well, he's gone on a bit of a sabbatical. That's all."

"When?" Jess asked.

"Well, that's not all according to this column you've written!" said Orlaith.

"That wasn't meant to be published under my real name," Susannah said.

"And yet here it is!" Orlaith snapped.

"So how long has he been gone?" Jess asked.

"Erm – a few weeks? Maybe four? About that."

"A month? Why didn't you tell us?" This time they spoke in unison, a mannerism she remembered from when they were little, when they wanted to get their own way about something.

"Your dad wanted to tell you himself at the beginning but I asked him to hold off until I got my head around it. And then I got a job offer and things were a bit hectic." Susannah knew that, as excuses went, it was lame. And not even true. She hadn't told them because she knew if she did, then she'd have to accept it herself. And she hadn't been ready to do that.

"But you found the time to write a column about it for the entire world to read?" Orlaith's voice was raised.

"Have you heard from him? Is he safe?" Jess asked, her voice high with anxiety.

"I heard he arrived safely. And I presume he's safe because as his next of kin I would have heard otherwise. Bad news travels fast as, you know."

"His next of kin?" Orlaith sounded astonished at her choice of words.

"Yeah, that. And his wife of course. So listen where – on the Internet – did you read my column? Just as a matter of interest?"

"Facebook," Jess said tragically.

"Facebook? How did it get on there?" Susannah wondered how her poor brain was ever going to catch up, and then keep up, with all this new technology.

"It's on Cara's page."

"Cara's page?" Susannah raised her eyebrows at Cara.

"I thought it was okay to post it," her sister defended herself. "I didn't know it was a secret. It's published in a national newspaper."

Susannah bit her lip. Cara was right. Another disturbing thought started to surface. "So does that mean your dad could read it on his Facebook page?"

"He'd have to have a Facebook page for that!" Orlaith was openly scathing now.

"Well, he does have one now. It's called The Intrepid Traveller. I haven't seen it yet. But – look, can I ring you back? It's almost midnight here."

"The Intrepid what? Listen, we need to know what is happening with you guys!" Orlaith was outraged now.

"I've just told you. Your dad's on a career break. I –"

She was interrupted by Cara, who suddenly snatched the phone out of her hand.

"Jess? Orlaith? This is Cara. Your dad, as you now know, is travelling. Somewhere in Thailand as we speak. Finding himself apparently. Susannah has enough going on without getting a hard time about it from you two. No, I didn't realise you didn't know about the column. Of course I wouldn't have put it on Facebook if I'd known. Yes, I'll take it down. Yes, right now." She stopped talking and held the receiver out so Susannah and Olivia could hear the beeps of the disconnected line. "They've hung up on me!"

"Well, you can't really blame them now, can you?" Susannah said. She walked over to the sink and emptied the rest of her glass of wine into it.

Olivia had already retrieved her coat and bag. "I've called a cab," she said, holding up her mobile phone. "Thank you so much for dinner, Susannah. It was a really nice evening."

"Thanks for coming," Susannah said automatically.

All her attention was now on fixing things with Orlaith and Jess, but she valiantly made small talk as she stood in the hall for the ten minutes it took for Olivia's taxi to arrive.

When she finally left, Susannah joined Cara in the kitchen.

Cara looked up from her iPad. "I've deleted the article from my page. I was so proud of you and I thought you'd be okay with it, as I've already explained. Especially since it was published in a national newspaper. And why the hell hadn't you told the girls about Rob yet?"

Susannah shrugged. The truth was that Cara's work with the airline meant she was away a lot. She and Susannah didn't get to see each other regularly so it had been easy for Susannah not to mention it to her.

"I just kept putting it off. I thought he'd be home by now, to be honest. Despite what you and Olivia said, I just thought it was something he needed to get out of his system and then he'd be back. I didn't want to worry the girls with it."

"You have to ring them back. But first you need to see what they're seeing. Here, let's have a look at Rob's page." She moved the iPad nearer Susannah so they could both look at the screen.

Rob looked exactly like The Intrepid Traveller he'd nicknamed himself. He looked thinner than when he'd left – almost scrawny now. He was sporting a goatee beard, designer-type shades and he was wearing the gigantic orange shorts which made his legs look as spindly as a fawn's.

There were a few photos of sunsets and one of him standing outside a beach restaurant. And a post about him getting up at some unearthly hour to visit wild monkeys.

"And this is where you're supposed to get your news about him?" Cara fumed. "Three posts in over a month?"

But Susannah was already dialling New York. The girls picked up on the first ring.

"So we're looking at it now. Dad's Facebook." Orlaith sounded shocked.

"Yeah – Cara has it up on her iPad so I can see it too."

"And what do you make of it?" Orlaith demanded.

"Well, there's not much to go on, is there? Pictures of sunsets. Trips to see wild monkeys. I guess that's what people do when they're on a sabbatical."

"I mean, what do you think of the fact that he's halfway

around the world on his own!" Orlaith was exasperated.

"Maybe he's having a breakdown or something. Have you thought of that?" Jess asked.

That's what she had thought too, in the beginning. But Rob looked tanned and rested. He had lost the grumpy face he had obviously reserved only for living with her.

"He looks pretty relaxed to me," she said quietly.

"Looks are deceiving," Orlaith said defiantly.

"Yes, and he could get rabies from the monkeys," Jess warned.

"Look," Orlaith said decisively, "we're coming home."

"No! Don't do that!" Susannah was shocked at how quickly the words left her mouth. Just a few short weeks ago, she'd have given anything to see them back. But not now. Now she felt like telling them they'd be better off going to Thailand if they were so worried about Rob. "There's nothing you can do here. And you have your internships to think of. Your dad would hate if his sabbatical were to interfere with that. He needs time out, not the third degree from you two." She hated defending him but if it stopped them heading for JFK airport then so be it.

"You shouldn't have let him go!" Jess wailed. "You should have made him go for counselling or something."

"I should have let him tell you straight away, like he wanted," Susannah said.

"Yes, you should have," Orlaith said. "Maybe we could have talked him out of it."

"Or got him help," Jess added sadly.

"But I thought he wouldn't go through with it," Susannah tried to explain. "And that, even if he did, he'd be back in a week. And when he wasn't – well, I suppose I should have told you myself then. I'm sorry."

There was a long silence, which Susannah deliberately didn't fill. She was exhausted from the turmoil of the evening and she knew she hadn't been able to give the girls any real comfort.

That bothered her. It was something she had done naturally all her life – given her family and friends friendly advice, whether they asked for it or not.

But now she didn't feel qualified to give advice to anyone.

Eventually Orlaith and Jess calmed down enough to say goodbye but only after they'd made Susannah promise she'd make contact with Rob to make sure he was okay.

"Why can't they phone him themselves?" Cara asked when she told her. "What are they – eleven?"

"Well, I'm sure they will," Susannah said distractedly.

She was still looking at The Intrepid Traveller Facebook page, a sense of unease curling around her stomach. She wouldn't break her promise to the girls but she wasn't looking forward to phoning Rob at all. Because she had a hunch that he wasn't going to appreciate the 'My Husband Left Me for a Camper Van' column one little bit.

CHAPTER 9

Katie opened up the planning diary in her computer and drummed her fingers lightly on the desk. She was feeling weird this morning.

After the strained Valentine's Night everything had become awkward between herself and Luke and then, just last week, he had announced that he needed "space" so he could think things through.

"I want us to be together, Katie, but I'm not sure what you want any more."

"I've told you what I want, for things to stay the way they are for now," she'd replied, but at some stage Luke had stopped listening to her. And now, for the first time in four years, she was single again.

On Saturday night she had poured herself a glass of wine and watched a movie she'd already seen. Halfway through it she realised she had become one of those women she used to despise, the ones who dropped their friends when they got a boyfriend. Or had her friends dropped her? They hadn't really got on with Luke, for no reason that she could fathom, and since they were all parts of couples her relationships with them had faded away. If she'd been the type of woman who needed to cry on someone's shoulder she couldn't think of one person she could call on.

But luckily she wasn't that sort of woman. She was angry with Luke for trying to blackmail her into doing something she didn't want to do, but another part of her felt relieved to be away from the tension that had crept into the relationship. She didn't like conflict. She remembered too much of the run-up to her parents' divorce to ever want to be in a difficult relationship.

So she'd spent the rest of the weekend at the gym, cooking up healthy meals for the week and catching up on her ironing.

And now she had a lot of work to keep her occupied. She turned her attention back to her to-do list. She needed to phone Susannah Stevens, to compliment her on the camper-van column. It was full of honesty, humour and bravery. And she was a good writer too. She was quite a find actually and Katie was definitely going to commission some more work from her.

When she'd first met her though she'd done nothing to inspire confidence. She'd been so precious about herself and her award-winning career that had happened back in the mists of time, and she appeared to have done little else since, apart from "rearing a family," even though the family consisted of three adults all living on different continents to her. It was only because of her mother's recommendation that she'd given her a chance. She dialled the number, still drumming her fingers. The phone was picked up on the third ring.

"Hello?" Susannah sounded quiet, subdued almost.

"Hi, Susannah – this is Katie."

"Oh. You."

Katie moved the receiver away from her ear a fraction. Did Susannah sound sullen or was it her imagination?

"Er – yes." She moved the phone closer again. "I wanted to compliment you on your column on Saturday."

"I want to talk to you about that actually."

And then Susannah launched into a complete rant. She was speaking so fast that Katie could only make out some of her words.

"Unprofessional," she heard. "Untrustworthy – everything bad I've ever heard about tabloids …"

What the –?

Katie finally managed to get a word in edgeways. "I don't know what you're talking about, Susannah."

"You know damn well! You used my real name after making a promise that you'd use a pen name!"

Katie slapped her hand against her forehead. She'd been so busy on Friday that by the time Susannah had sent her the column she'd totally forgotten that she was supposed to be writing under her granny's name.

"Oh yes. Elizabeth something, wasn't it?

"Elizabeth Castle."

"That's it. I totally forgot about it. I'm sorry."

"How could you forget?" Susannah was incredulous. "I emailed you!"

"Busyness, distraction, too much going on here. It happens."

"But you must realise how difficult this is for me! I've had my daughters on from New York. They didn't even know their dad had gone!"

Katie felt like saying that was hardly her fault. What sort of a person kept that kind of thing secret in the first place? But she stayed silent, zoning in and out of the monologue on the other end of the phone, waiting for Susannah to run out of steam. She had dealt with enough angry people in her time to know not to try to talk her out of her wrath.

Idly she picked one of the many brochures littering her desk. *Flow Your Life* was written on the top. There was a photograph of a man with dyed black hair and spectacularly tight blue jeans. The two top buttons of his dazzlingly white shirt were undone and there was a gold-coloured medallion nestling in his greying chest-hair.

Katie scanned the information, one ear still tuned in to Susannah's tirade. An international guru called Geraldo Laffite was coming to London, apparently to host a life-changing seminar and they wanted to invite someone from the *Post* to come along and report on it.

"So listen, Susannah, would you be up for going on a trip to London?"

"Excuse me?"

Katie smiled. That had stopped her in her tracks. Thank God. "There's this famous guru type coming over from America to host one of these super-expensive change-your-life seminars. It's a weekend thing. I'd expect a big feature. Two thousand words of your personal experience and also whether you think he's genuine or conning gullible people out of their money." She scanned the leaflet for more details. "Apparently it costs three grand sterling to go but he says that he'll change your life, raise your earning power, bring you the man or woman of your dreams, blah blah blah. Cheap at the price if that is really true but how can it be? Anyhow, someone must believe him because it's apparently booked out. They want us to do a feature because he's thinking of running a similar event here in Ireland later on in the year. So – can you do it? It's on next weekend."

Katie listened to the silence on the other end of the phone, doodling on a piece of paper, waiting for a response.

"Isn't there someone in the office who would want to go?" Susannah finally asked.

Yes, there definitely was, Katie thought.

Jennifer would probably try to kill her when she realised she'd given this gig to a freelancer but Katie hadn't forgotten the trouble Jennifer had caused by putting her big, careless feet into her life by proposing that stupid Valentine's column to Mike. It was her fault she'd broken up with Luke. So she could suck it up.

"Look, do you want to go or not? Because if you do I'll have to get on to the travel people here to get them to book your flight."

"Yes. Yes, I do. Of course I do. If you think I have the talent and –"

"Well, I don't know enough about you to know what you can deliver, Susannah. But you can write. And hopefully you can chat up this guru fella."

"I'll try."

"Good. And look, I really am sorry about messing up the pen-name thing. I know how difficult it must be for you. But this trip will take your mind off it. How about I courier out all the info to your house and you start getting ready?"

"Okay. I will. Thanks."

"My pleasure." Katie was smiling as she put the receiver down.

If only she could resolve the rest of her problems as easily as that.

She was having a well-earned cup of coffee when she noticed an email from Daniel Gilbert asking her to meet up for a drink later. On a Monday? That was weird. Still, after her home-alone weekend she was delighted. Luke breaking up with her had been so unexpected it had left a gap in her life that she wasn't entirely sure how to fill.

When she looked at Daniel's cool photographs of his holidays – he was just back from a surfing holiday in Fuerteventura – Katie felt as if life was somehow passing her by. She shook her head slightly, trying to dispel the uncharacteristic restlessness that had come over her. She'd always felt safe within herself – with her work and her life and her routine. But now she felt – what?

Katie stopped the thought right there, before it could lead her on a trail of more, equally useless thoughts. She didn't have the patience for introspection, which some people might have felt was ironic considering she was in charge of the MBS section of a national newspaper. But they would be people who didn't work on a national newspaper and didn't realise that you just did the work that came your way, regardless of how you felt about it. So all the deadlines would be reached, and the newspaper would be produced, and people would read it, and you started all over again and everything was on track.

But even though she stayed busy and was super-productive all day, by the time she was making her way to meet Daniel that evening she was still feeling edgy and off-balance, and puzzled by her state of mind. Maybe Luke breaking up with her had hurt her more than she wanted to admit?

She found Daniel sitting in a small snug in her favourite bar. He was dressed as if he were still on holiday, in cotton beige trousers and a khaki shirt. His brown hair was streaked fair from all the sunshine and, although she couldn't see him properly in the dim lighting of the bar, she knew his eyes would look even bluer against his tan. He was drinking a bottle of beer and had a vodka and tonic waiting for her.

She slipped into the chair opposite him, feeling like she always felt after nine hours cooped up in the office without a break – pale and tired and sadly deficient in Vitamin D.

"Hey there." She poured the mixer into her vodka and knocked half the glass back. "I'm delighted you suggested this. While you've been playing the cool surfer dude in a sunny country, I've been having the week from hell."

"Mike on your case again?" Daniel raised an eyebrow.

"Not Mike. Luke. We've broken up."

Daniel sat up in his seat. "What? Not the column?"

"Yes, the column. You were right. He took it all seriously. Asked me to move in. Told me I needed to be worrying about my deteriorating eggs."

Daniel's mouth twitched. "In fairness, you wrote that line yourself."

"I did. And I'm never breaking my rule of not writing personal

96

stuff again. Even tongue-in-cheek. Luckily I've found someone else to do it for me. Susannah Stevens writing about how her husband left her for a camper van."

"I read it! It was very entertaining. She could give *Footloose and Fancy-free* a run for its money."

"But it was meant to be written under a pen name and I made a mistake and let it go out under her own name. She tore strips off me today. I had to give her a trip to London to make up for it – which Jennifer will raise hell about when she finds out."

"Oh God. That's a bad week at the office all right." He paused. "So how do you feel about you and Luke? You've been together a long time."

Katie took another sip of her drink. "Four years. But look, I don't want to talk about him." She tossed back her hair. "Why don't you distract me instead, tell me about what's going on in your life?"

He traced the top of his beer bottle with his finger, the droplets causing it to squeal. "I do have some news actually."

"You've met someone!" Katie was disgusted. "Now that I'm single again and looking for someone to go out with. Typical. So who is it? Is it Lucy?"

"I haven't met anyone. It's to do with work actually."

"Oh?" Katie was disappointed. She didn't want to talk about work. She'd only just left the office.

"Yeah. I'm – er – leaving."

"Leaving? Leaving what?"

"Leaving work. The *Post*."

Katie sat bolt upright, spilling some of her drink on the table. She opened her mouth to ask him a question but closed it again because she didn't want to hear the answer.

Daniel dabbed at the spilt vodka with his beer-mat and said absently, "I'm not sure it's even what I want to do. But it's an opportunity I'd be a fool to turn down."

"But where are you going?" Katie frowned. The *Daily Post* was the best place for a writer in the country. There wasn't anywhere else for Daniel to go. Was there?

"London."

Katie's world suddenly took another tilt towards the dark side. "You're leaving the country?"

"I'm afraid so." He sounded as if he was finding the conversation as difficult as she was. "I've been head-hunted. *Footloose and Fancy-free* has come to the attention of a publisher in London. They have offices in New York. They want to publish the columns as a book on both sides of the Atlantic. And they want me to write another book – something similar. But they want me to work with their newspaper too, just doing one column a month, to promote myself for when the book comes out."

"Sounds like the best job in the world," Katie said quietly.

"Nothing you could turn down anyway."

"And why would you?" She knocked back what was left of her drink and put the empty glass back on the table. "So when are you going?"

He grimaced. "This is the kicker – they want me immediately. I've been in touch with Mike and he's agreed that I just need to work next week as my notice. Gave me a big lecture about disloyalty but then said he couldn't stand in my way. Pretty decent of him really – my contract stipulates a month's notice. I was surprised."

Katie wasn't. Daniel was the sort of person people went out of their way for – even grumpy old Mike.

"I'll miss you," he said softly.

"Me too." Katie was suddenly gripped by panic at how empty her life was starting to look. Terrified she was going to cry, she called a passing waiter over.

"Same again," she said, nodding at her empty glass and Daniel's beer bottle.

Daniel's phone buzzed and he squinted at the screen. "I have to take this. I'll be back in a bit."

Katie watched him move out to the smoking area to take the call and tried to manage her mounting terror. Everything was changing. First Luke had left her. Now Daniel was leaving the *Post*. And the country.

For the want of anything better to do, she checked her phone but there were no messages. Not one thing to distract her from all this stuff that she didn't want to think about.

Daniel must be hammering out his contract or something, she thought, irritated, as time went on. She was almost through her second drink when he finally reappeared.

"Fancy something stronger?" He nodded towards her glass.

She blinked. "Stronger than vodka?"

"Well, maybe not stronger. But different. How about a tequila slammer?"

"I've never felt more like a tequila slammer in my life," Katie said. "Whatever it is." She lifted her glass in Daniel's direction. "Here's to moving on. For everyone."

It felt more like she was being left behind than moving on. But she wasn't going to rain on his shiny new parade by admitting that.

So Daniel ordered the new drinks and they talked about work and surfing and new horizons until, around the third tequila slammer, Daniel finally brought up the proverbial elephant in the room again.

"So do you feel like talking about Luke now? How's life without him?"

She frowned. "Quiet. But I like quiet."

"What have you been doing to get over him?"

"Working mainly. It hasn't been long enough for me to think of anything more than that."

"Come over and see me in London. That will distract you."

"Maybe I will. I'll have to be quick though. Mr *Footloose and Fancy-free* won't survive long once he's a big-shot writer with a book deal in a city with a gazillion eligible young women."

"Well, what are you waiting for? Book your flight!"

A crowd of boisterous student types were setting up at the table next to them.

"Do you want to go for chips?" Katie asked suddenly.

"What?" Daniel put his hand to his ear, throwing the students an exasperated glance but they were oblivious to anyone beyond their own group.

"To soak up the alcohol!" Katie roared. That got their attention, she thought with satisfaction, as two of the group turned and stared at her.

Daniel leaned towards her and said, "I must be getting old because that actually seems like a good idea. Here, I'll lead the way."

She grabbed her bag and followed him out. She felt giddy when she stepped outside into the night air, the unaccustomed tequilas going to her head. The rain was coming down in sheets and she shivered. She looked down the road in the direction of the chipper – it was a good ten minutes' walk away and there was always a queue there.

Just across the road a fleet of taxis waited in the rank, yellow 'for hire' signs shining like beacons in the dark, blustery night.

"How about we go back to my place instead and I'll make us a snack?" she said.

"Excellent – at least we'll be warm and dry," Daniel agreed.

They slid into the back seat of the taxi and almost immediately Daniel engaged the driver in banter. Katie leaned her head back against the headrest, only half listening to them. Daniel was regaling him with stories of his surfing holiday and the taxi-driver was explaining how he never had a minute for hobbies or a spare cent for holidays because he had four kids to put through college.

By the time Katie opened her hall door she was glad to be getting away from the doom-and-gloom narrative. She needed positive, optimistic people around her right now. She turned on the table lamps and switched the radio to a mellow music station.

"I've no tequila but I can offer you wine?" She pulled a bottle of Pinot out of the fridge and planted it on the counter dividing the living room from her tiny kitchen. She handed Daniel two glasses and looked at what food she had. Chicken strips, ginger and garlic – the makings of the stir-fry she'd planned for her own dinner. It would make a snack for two.

"So." He looked around the apartment. "Do you miss having Luke here?"

"Of course I miss him. As you pointed out earlier, we were together for four years. But I didn't want us to move in together and he did. So there you have it. It's all very confusing, if you want to know. I thought my life was, like, on track. And now it isn't."

"I have no idea what an on-track life is like but it sounds painful." Daniel poured two glasses of wine and brought them over the coffee table. "I didn't know you could cook," he observed from the sofa.

"There's a lot of things you don't know about me."

"Really?" He raised his eyebrows.

"No," she grinned. "What you see is what you get actually. I like things being – orderly. Being on track with Luke wasn't painful for me. I like the feeling of being stable. You know that old saying: sane, sober and solvent? Now I'm only one of those things."

"You're definitely not sober," he smiled. "So are you sane or solvent?"

"Solvent. Always. But I don't feel sane. I stick to my routine as normal but I feel all at sea. I don't like it. Maybe I shouldn't have been so hasty telling Luke I didn't want to move in with him. What do you think?"

"I think it's easier not to let someone move in than it is to get them to move back out again."

"Really?" Her antennae were up. So Daniel hadn't always been footloose and fancy-free then. "You lived with someone? You seem so young."

He laughed. "Immature is what she said. I'm nearly thirty. But sure, I take life easy. I like being unpredictable." He gave her a look. "You should try it."

"I don't know, Daniel. I had a plan ..." Her voice trailed off mournfully.

He grinned. "Well, everyone has a plan until they get a punch in the face. I think Mike Tyson said that. Then all bets are off."

Her mouth twitched. He was so funny.

"Go on. Laugh. You know you want to."

She went over to join him on the sofa, and took a sip of her drink. "So tell me more about this new gig of yours then."

"I could do that." His placed his arm across the top of the sofa, brushing her hair as he did so. "Or."

"Or what?"

He looked at her. "You do know I'm attracted to you, don't you?"

No.

She hadn't known that.

He had always been very nice to her, taking up for her against Mike and Jennifer and making her laugh at his antics. But now that she thought about it, she guessed there weren't many women Daniel didn't find attractive.

She smiled. "I'm flattered but I'd never have guessed."

"That's because you were with Luke. But now you're not."

She laughed out loud at that. He was such a chancer. And so far from her type.

He was twenty-nine and acted as if he were twenty. He was a player. If even half of his *Footloose and Fancy-free* columns had any ring of truth about them – and, as a writer, Katie knew they probably did – he was most definitely the love 'em and leave 'em type.

But wasn't that exactly what you need right now? a little voice whispered to her. Not so much Mr Right as Mr Right Now?

She looked at him as if she were seeing him for the first time. The dark, tousled hair, the full lips that would have seemed girlish except he was such a macho sort of guy. The full-on charisma and the way he was looking at her as if she was the most amazing woman he had ever met.

This was a guy who wasn't going to whine about her deteriorating eggs, or moving the relationship to 'the next stage' as if it were a mortgage application.

Up until she'd met him this evening, she'd been having a bad day. A bad week really. And then he'd showed up, with his tequila slammers and his tales of derring-do – getting head-hunted and book deals and being asked to move to London – and, as usual, he'd brightened up her world.

She moved a little closer to him. The alcohol had taken the edge off her earlier panic because everyone was leaving her and now she was feeling kind of wonderful. Attractive and desirable.

He was looking at her quizzically, waiting for a response.

"No, I'm not with Luke," she agreed.

He looked at her. "So would it be all right if I kissed you?"

"What about the food?"

"What about it? You haven't even started it yet, have you?" He glanced across at the cooker. Then back at her. "So – should I kiss you?"

"You should definitely try. I'll tell you if I don't like it."

She liked it. A lot. And as the kiss deepened, she felt so relieved that she and Daniel weren't even work colleagues any more. Not technically, now that he'd given in his notice.

And soon enough he wouldn't be in her life any more. Her

days of living vicariously through Daniel Gilbert were coming to an end. No more daydreaming about what it might be like to live like one of the carefree people in *Footloose and Fancy-free*.

But didn't she have something far better than that now? She had the chance to actually be a *Footloose* character! A relaxed, one-night-stand girl, going to bed with a no-strings guy who was looking at her as if she were the sexiest woman in the world.

At the time, it felt like the easiest decision in the world to sleep with Daniel Gilbert.

CHAPTER 10

Susannah sat in the business section of the plane, too buzzed up to be tired, despite the fact she'd barely closed her eyes the night before. Even though she hadn't needed an alarm in years, she'd been nervous that somehow she'd sleep in and miss her flight to London.

The air steward offered her tea or coffee or wine. She opted for wine and then felt like an alcoholic when she noticed all the other passengers were barely looking up from their laptops to order coffee or water. She, as the newbie business type she was, couldn't help looking all around her, wondering where everyone was going and what sort of jobs they had, as wide-eyed as if she'd never been out of Ireland in her life.

But everyone was in their own zone, either tapping their phones or laptops, poring over notes or catnapping while the plane soared into the clouds. After a while, Susannah reckoned she might as well focus on her own work.

She fished her folder out of her briefcase and opened it up. Geraldo Laffite stared up at her out of an expensive-looking brochure. He was dressed in a sharp, dark suit, white shirt and a bright-pink tie. His teeth were improbably white, like teeth out of a toothpaste advertisement.

The brochure told her that the seminar in London was the

start of his European tour with other seminars lined up for Madrid and Paris and more to follow. Fans booked their places months in advance apparently.

Susannah rubbed her eyes. It sounded nice, having your life flow. The phrase made it sound like a river, with a destination and a certain momentum behind it.

Her own life had felt stuck for so long and, now that it was moving again, it wasn't so much flowing as bumping and jerking along and she didn't know where she was going to end up.

She was still mortified when she thought of how the column had been published under her own name. But going to London was a big consolation prize for her. It was by far the most exciting thing that had happened to her in years. She wondered what Rob would make of it. He'd have to be impressed, especially after the red-eye economy flights they were used to, courtesy of their perennially tight budget over the years.

She wondered if he was still living like he was skint. She sincerely hoped so. She wanted him to be staying in some flea-bitten hostel in the backend of nowhere, while she caught a cab on expenses to a stylish hotel near Westminster, where, according to their web page, you could see the Houses of Parliament from your window.

She must have dozed off and, when she opened her eyes again, the safety-belt signs were flashing for landing. She drained her wineglass and gathered up her stuff. The seminar was starting at five that evening and, while she'd intended to spend the previous night prepping, she'd found that looking over her notes was making her feel anxious so she'd put them away and picked up her novel instead.

So she'd have to spend the afternoon getting ready to meet the great Geraldo Laffite.

She was disappointed when she couldn't actually see the Houses of Parliament from her room after all. But it did have a small balcony and Susannah brought a cup of coffee out to the small table and chair and sat there, sipping her drink and savouring the experience of being eight storeys high over the city streets.

The tugboats were chugging up the river and she could smell the coffee from the hotel's café floors below her. She fleetingly heard a man raise his voice in the room beside her before the noise was drowned out by the blare of horns from the snarl of traffic below.

A gust of wind tugged at her dress and a fleeting sense of happiness stole up on her. It caught her by surprise, creeping up on her like an unexpected shaft of sunlight on a winter's day.

She looked down at her file. If she prepped for an hour that would still leave enough time to have a bite to eat and make use of the hotel's swimming pool before heading off to the seminar.

Susannah stared at the giant billboards dotted around the lavish lobby area of the hotel, trumpeting this, the first of Geraldo Laffite's European tours of the *Flow Your Life* seminars. There was a life-sized cutout of Geraldo himself, propped up just inside the door. He was sporting a deeply unhealthy tan and his face had an ironed look that suggested extensive plastic surgery. His eyebrows were like a pair of dark, furry caterpillars, giving him a permanently surprised look.

A small oblong table to the right of the entrance was covered with a white, linen tablecloth and held an array of name badges. Susannah found hers, signed in and made her way to a seat opposite the entrance, where she could study the people as they arrived for the seminar.

They were quite the mixed bunch – a few couples, a gaggle of women friends, and quite a few senior citizens. Possibly there were more women than men but not dramatically so. Everyone was very well dressed – presumably if you could afford a couple of grand for a weekend workshop you weren't short of a bob or two, Susannah mused.

As the crowd thickened, everyone became infused with an infectious excitement and when a tall blonde woman began to usher everyone into a huge, cavernous room to the side of the lobby they surged as one through the double doors.

Susannah got up and followed at a distance – trying to observe all the details that would make her article come to life. She saw the room was fitted with a sophisticated sound-and-light system and a huge makeshift stage made it seem more like a theatre space than a conference hall. She made her way to the top of the room where the first few rows were reserved for the media. She nodded a greeting at the woman beside her – twenty-something, funky red hair, black Doc Martens and a pale-purple lace dress. Her badge showed she was Harriet and hailed from a UK provincial paper.

"Hi," Susannah smiled at her. "So, what are you expecting from today then?"

"Oh, I'm just so excited to be here. I've followed Geraldo's vlog for, like, ever," she gushed.

"His vlog?"

"Video log – like blog only in video?" She peered at Susannah more closely, as if she was trying to ascertain how could anyone not know this.

"Right." Susannah felt sick thinking of all the technical stuff she needed to catch up on – and she got the feeling that while she was straining to learn one bit of it, some twelve-year-old was already working out a way to make her new skills obsolete.

She settled back in her chair while the last of the audience took their seats. The room was dim, interspersed with flashing red and yellow neon lights. The music started – a brash, aggressive sound that made Susannah instinctively shrink back in her chair.

But it was having the opposite effect on everyone else. The crowd began a slow handclap and started an insistent chant, "Geraldo! Geraldo! Geraldo!"

The yellow and red neon lights flashed faster now, on and off in time to the beat.

When the air of expectancy reached its zenith, Geraldo finally bounced out onto the stage.

Susannah sat up straighter to get a good look at him. He was smaller than she'd imagined – possibly no more than five feet six. He was dressed in a sharp, expensive black suit and had a cluster of black curls framing his head like a halo.

"So – people! Welcome to the *Flow Your Life* seminar!" he roared. He smiled, and his teeth, just like the picture on the life-sized hoardings of him in the lobby flashed supernaturally white at the audience. "If you pay attention you will learn to Flow your Lives and you will never again be at the mercy of your own small-minded, limiting thinking! Because – when you change your mind," he raised his voice to a roar, his body crackling with a ferocious energy that belied its insignificant size, "you change your –?"

"Life!" the audience shouted back obligingly.

Susannah blinked. Some of them at least, had obviously been here before. She glanced behind her and noticed they were staring up at the stage as if Geraldo were a rock star. And for the next hour the 'guru' acted exactly like that, pumping them up further with maxims and mantras flowing fluently off his tongue.

All of their problems, he proclaimed, were of their own making, fabricated by their own minds, a consequence of their failure to think positive thoughts and create feel-good emotions.

Susannah thought of Rob leaving her in the lurch and felt a stab of anger. Was Geraldo suggesting that she had in some way attracted that sort of betrayal when all she'd done was to be a good wife and mother her whole life?

"People wonder why they don't have enough energy, but they gloss over the fact that they are constantly poisoning their bodies with alcohol!" Geraldo continued, spitting out the word as if it were dirt. "And sugar. And fats. They sit on their lazy behinds and wonder why their lives aren't working. They have no goals, no motivation, they spend their time in their own heads, thinking their tiny, negative thoughts, when all they have to do is –?"

"Expand their minds!" shouted a woman at the back helpfully and was treated to a special, creepy smile just for her.

"But none of you are like that, are you? Because you are here! You have taken the first, important step of attending this seminar. And I am going to motivate you to take the next step, and the next and the next – all of the baby-steps you need to take until your life is transformed. I will show you the exact steps I've used to change my mind – and change my life! My exact experience of going from a bullied underachiever to someone who is now courted by kings and celebrities and sheikhs. They hire me personally to coach them. But am I going to confine my expertise to the rich man? No! Am I going to discriminate against people just because they can't afford to pay me a king's ransom! No!"

He paused to take a breath, moving lightly, as if he were walking on the balls of his feet, from one side of the stage to the other, never letting his gaze on the audience falter.

"This is why I do affordable seminars such as this one," he continued, "where, by the way, you can gain as much as you would if you were paying me to hold your hand. This is especially so if you buy some of my books which complement today's work perfectly. They are available today at a special discount. Just go and talk to one of my assistants if you want a book personally signed by me for yourself, or indeed that special someone in your life. We know the one, don't we?"

The audience giggled.

"The one who made fun of you coming to the seminar in the first place. The one who prefers to say 'Well, that's the way it is,' when you dare to suggest that you are not happy with your life!"

Susannah noticed the books – several titles all on the same topic of taking control of your destiny – were set out on trestle tables dotted around the room, guarded by tanned, glamorous assistants, male and female, all dressed in white jumpsuits.

She glanced at the rapt audience and couldn't believe they were swallowing this guff but they were. Geraldo soon had them on their feet, pumping with adrenaline and happy to follow the various exercises he shouted at them for the next hour and a half.

And then, as abruptly as he'd arrived, he disappeared again. The flashing lights dimmed and they were told to make their way through a pair of double doors for the next part of the seminar.

The assistants ushered them into a ballroom with a dome-shaped ceiling and several huge, ornate chandeliers glittering with dozens of tiny lights. Several circular tables had been laid out with stationery – big sheets of blank foolscap pages, pens and pencils, children's crayons, scissors, sticks of sticky glue and several piles of glossy magazines.

The assistants separated them from their companions, placing them in new groups at the various tables and, as soon as they were settled, Geraldo reappeared.

He had changed into a red-velvet jacket, a matching bow tie, white shirt and oddly, loose, dark-coloured harem-type trousers.

"So, welcome back!" he announced.

Susannah braced herself to be shouted at again, but the tempo had changed.

"In this part of the seminar," Geraldo said, all soft-toned now, "we will find out what our truest desires really are. Do we know the number-one reason people don't achieve their true desire?"

The crowd answered in unison, "Because they don't know what they want!"

"Exactly!" He rocked back on his heels. "You wouldn't set off on an important journey without first deciding on your destination, would you?" He began to prowl through the spaces between the tables.

"No!" shouted the crowd.

"Yet —" He came to abrupt halt behind Susannah's chair and rested his hands on her shoulders. She caught the strong, citrusy smell of his aftershave. "People go through their whole lives without engaging in the basic task of choosing their destination and consulting their maps."

He leaned his weight on her shoulders and Susannah twisted a little away, trying to dislodge his hands without being too obvious. She thought she'd like to invite Geraldo to a seminar on respecting other people's physical space.

Unperturbed, he moved on to the next table. "Those of you who are new to my seminars," he glanced back at Susannah, "may not realise the healing power of touch — a hug, a kiss, as we journey on our life's path. But — back to our maps. I want you all to choose the pictures here that call to your souls. When you find them, tear them out of the magazine as quickly as you can and stick them down into your pages. Remember you are like a child in a sweetshop now — you can pick and mix whatever it is you want in your life. By-pass your bossy inner critic who tells you that your happiness lies in slaving away for eight hours a day in a cubicle. Really? No way, Bossy Inner Critic! We want more than that. We —?"

"Deserve more than that!" the crowd responded with gusto.

"Good!" Geraldo was pleased. "So you know what to do. The timer is — on!"

As the people at her table began to grab at the stationery supplied, Susannah watched Geraldo making his way back to the top of the room, where one of his male assistants supplied him with a glass of sparkling water and a young, female assistant stood behind him, massaging his shoulders while he drank it.

She considered his words. Having been a homemaker for a quarter of a century, she quite liked the idea of being in a cubicle for eight hours a day. It meant your day was structured, you were earning money and when your sleeveen husband plotted stuff behind your back you had something to fall back on.

But all the others were completely focused on the task, their eyes glazed with concentration as they ripped out pictures and put them in a pile beside them. She turned to ask the man beside her a question but she was fiercely shushed by a tiny, birdlike woman on the other side of the table.

"Didn't you hear Geraldo? The clock is ticking," the woman hissed, pushing back a strand of grey hair out of her face and pointing furiously at her watch.

Susannah took a deep breath. She needed to get into the spirit of the day. She pulled over a pile of magazines and flicked through them. They were high-end glossies with lots of advertisements for luxury goods. The sunshine from outside was warm and cast a golden glow across the table. The only sound in the room was that of people cutting and pasting.

Susannah began to follow suit, tentatively at first, but then she relaxed into the task, the rhythm of the cutting and the pasting lulling her into the sense of security she remembered as a child when she was colouring pictures on her mother's kitchen table.

By the time Geraldo spoke again she was totally absorbed, only half aware of what pictures she had chosen and why.

"Time up! We can stop what we're doing now. Turn your pages over without looking at them," Geraldo instructed.

Everyone obeyed. They looked flushed, secretive, pleased with themselves.

"Later," Geraldo promised, "you will find out what your souls are truly yearning for."

After a fifteen-minute break, which Susannah used to have a

coffee and phone Cara back in Dublin to fill her in on how it was going, it was back to more motivational business.

Geraldo hit a switch on the music-centre and a mystical instrumental sound flooded the ballroom.

"It's time," he announced, "for the moment of truth! You can turn over your pages now."

Susannah looked at hers curiously.

She'd pasted a picture of a couple staring at their first house, full of pride at their achievement. There was a pink heart in the bottom left corner beside a baby in a wicker basket. A baby? Where had that come from, she wondered? There was a photograph of a designer kitchen with an island in the centre of it, where a teenager sat hunched over a magazine, earphones firmly stuck in her ears, and another adolescent was sprawled on a couch drinking a green smoothie.

And suddenly what seemed like jumble of random images took on meaning for her. Staring at the collage, Susannah was alarmed at the lump lodged in her throat and the tears pricking the back of her eyes. All this imagery represented her old life! When she and Rob and the girls were all together. When she had roles to play: a mother, a daughter, a wife. When she still knew who she was.

Even though she'd been so excited this morning on the plane over, she knew she'd swap the boutique hotel and the business-class flight and this stupid seminar in a heartbeat if she could have that life back again. The life that had gone by in a blink.

She could vaguely hear Geraldo telling the eager participants that the next step was learning how to manifest the images they had created on paper into their real lives.

But his advice was no good to her. It was gone – the time when the girls were at home and the old Rob was still in her life – not the one with the cold eyes and the selfish stubborn tilt to his chin, the one who had left her broken-hearted at Dublin airport without a backward glance.

No matter what happened now, Susannah had to accept that her future was not going to look like her past. She turned the page face down in front of her and huffed out a sigh. She was going to check out of the seminar early this evening.

For one thing, a wave of exhaustion had overcome her and all she wanted to do now was to sleep.

And really, she'd had enough of Geraldo Laffite for one day.

CHAPTER 11

Susannah arrived for day two of the seminar feeling tense and tired. Despite her exhaustion last evening, she'd slept badly again, tossing and turning in the overheated bedroom. But she'd been up since six, swimming fast lengths in the hotel's swimming pool to energise for the day ahead.

Geraldo was already on stage when she slipped into her seat beside Harriet, the redheaded journalist from the UK. He was prowling from one side of the stage to the other, yesterday's theatrical outfit replaced with skinny black denims and a ribbed, black polo neck.

After welcoming everybody back and explaining again that their hearts' desires were well within their reach, he stared into the crowd. "We have a lot to get through today, my people, so we are going to get straight to it. You!" He pointed a finger towards where Susannah was sitting.

Harriet was on her feet in seconds.

"Me?"

"Yes. Can you come on stage, please?" He waved at one of his white-robed assistants to welcome Harriet onto the stage and then swung his arm across the aisle and pointed at a man at the back of the room. "You!"

He continued until he had four people on the stage and then looked back at Susannah.

"And you, lady, you too." He waved his fingers in a beckoning movement at her.

Blue stage lights flashed intermittently as Susannah got up reluctantly and followed the others onto the stage. She looked curiously at the people on stage with her. Apart from Harriet, there was a middle-aged, overweight woman, who looked uncomfortable in a too-tight grey dress, a thirty-something man in a suit and an older man in his sixties with a crew-cut hairstyle and a military bearing.

"Now I want you all to close your eyes and visualise some way you want your life to change," Geraldo said.

Everybody did as he asked, except Susannah, who kept her eyes open, despite Geraldo's disapproving glare in her direction.

"Now imagine," Geraldo continued, "that your life has already changed in the way you want it to. You already have what you want. Really feel that it's happened."

Susannah noticed Harriet's hands balled into fists by her side. Everyone had their eyes squeezed shut, their features a study in concentration.

"Now open your eyes!" Geraldo said after a few minutes, snapping his fingers.

Before the participants got a chance to re-orient themselves on the stage, he stabbed a finger at the overweight woman.

"You there. What's your name?"

"Marianne."

Her voice was so soft Susannah had to strain to hear her.

"So, Marianne, I want you to come over here to me and my two assistants and tell us how you are now, now that you have already achieved your dream."

The woman looked like a rabbit caught in the proverbial headlights but she walked uncertainly over to Geraldo, who was flanked by two of the white-robed assistants Susannah remembered from yesterday – a blonde woman in her twenties, and a dark-haired, older man.

"I'm Marianne," she explained meekly. "I'm slim and fit and full of confidence. I wear amazing, stylish clothes. I have a great social life and I am following my passion of running a flower shop."

Her voice shook a bit at the end and Susannah held her breath, terrified that Geraldo was going to humiliate the woman in front of the audience.

But Geraldo took a step towards her and took one of her hands in his and looked at her sadly.

"I discern some resistance in you, Marianne, to getting what you want. Am I correct?"

Marianne looked at him in silence. Dumbstruck, Susannah presumed.

He nodded back at the assistants. "Are my spiritual aides in agreement?"

The pair of them nodded their heads mournfully and Geraldo turned back to Marianne.

"Go back and try again," he ordered.

Marianne did as she was bid, and this time the shake was even stronger in her voice and Susannah felt her stomach clenching with anger.

But, by the fourth effort, Marianne had managed to instill more belief into her voice and she was allowed to leave the stage. She heaved herself down the steps, looking no lighter, fitter or more confident than when she'd ascended. But when Geraldo and his advisors made a thumbs-up gesture to the crowd and they erupted into applause, roaring their approval with thunderous clapping and wolf-whistles, she went pink with pleasure.

Next up was Harriet, who didn't need any coaxing.

She stomped up to Geraldo in her Doc Marten boots.

"Hi, I'm Harriet and I live an amazing life. I have a big house in London, where I live with my three lovely children and my handsome, successful husband. I have a great job helping other people and feel totally supported in my creative, beautiful life."

This time there were no retakes. Harriet was convincing enough first time round to be allowed back to her seat, to more foot-stomping and handclapping from the excited crowd.

There were two more people to go before Susannah and, as she watched the man in the suit swagger up to Geraldo, she wondered how she could get herself out of this. Much as she wanted to experience the totality of the seminar, she didn't feel up to spouting a load of nonsense to Gerald and his "spiritual aides". She took a few tentative steps to exit the stage as unobtrusively as she could.

"Problem, Susannah?" Geraldo's voice was like the crack of a whip and she stopped, nonplussed that he'd put the spotlight on her.

"I'm –" She was about say she felt a bit sick. But why should she lie? She stiffened her spine and said, "I'm not comfortable doing this exercise." She'd intended for her voice to sound strong and clear but, to her mortification, the sentence came out in a whine.

"Susannah, Susannah, Susannah!" Geraldo left the man in the suit and strode across the stage towards her, shaking his head from side to side. "This is the fear talking! This is what the seminar is all about. Fear stopping you doing what you want. You mustn't let it win. Stay. Stay and complete the exercise."

"But I've just told you, I'm not comfortable," Susannah muttered, still intent on exiting stage left.

"You're not meant to be comfortable," Geraldo told her. He turned his attention towards the audience. "I am so glad this has happened here today. Because here in front of us, in this participant, we have a perfect example of what you can all expect to encounter in your own journeys." He nodded out at them earnestly. "This is how fear will try and control you as you take the necessary steps to change your life. This is how anxiety will try and stop you doing what you want to do. If you let it."

He gave Susannah a tragic look, as if she had let herself, him and the entire audience down by her cowardice.

She stopped, halfway down the stage steps. "You have someone perfectly willing to do the exercise in front of you," she told him, nodding in the direction of the thirty-something man who was waiting patiently for the mini-drama to be over so he could begin. "And I am not afraid. I just don't want to do it."

"Think that if you must." Geraldo heaved a heavy sigh. "But you need to practise bravery, Susannah, if you are to continue with your spiritual journey. And forgive yourself." Geraldo stared out at the audience meaningfully, as if Susannah had confided something to him earlier that she wouldn't want shared.

"Forgive myself?" She was outraged. "For what?"

"For not living your true life, Susannah."

"Er − okay − whatever."

Susannah descended the rest of the steps amidst a stony silence from the audience. By the time she slid back into her seat beside Harriet, her face was flaming, whether from embarrassment or rage she wasn't quite sure.

"It's hard when you do it the first time," Harriet whispered, and touched her arm in solidarity. "But it gets easier. I completely believe now that I'm living my ideal life. That took time and practice."

Susannah looked at her curiously. "So what you said up there? How much of it is true right now?"

She knew Harriet didn't live in London but maybe she had the handsome husband? Or even one of the three children?

Harriet pointed to her name badge. "I work for a small provincial paper. I've covered the local rose festivals and village fetes for five years now − and interviewed people who look like

I described on the stage. Healthy, happy, wealthy, with adorable children in tow." Her voice was wistful. "But I live by myself in a bed-sitter and the only handsome man in a twenty-mile radius is our gay doctor. That's why I want to change my life."

"And how is going up on stage saying stuff that's not true helping you to do that?" Susannah asked carefully. She didn't want to be judgmental but she was being paid to be curious here. But before Harriet could answer, Geraldo gave them such a baleful look that Harriet fell silent and didn't open her mouth to Susannah again for the rest of the session.

By the time the lunch-break came, Susannah felt too claustrophobic to lunch with the others in the hotel. Much as she needed to find out more about the motivation of the people who had paid a lot of money to humiliate themselves on a stage in front of Geraldo and their peer-group, she was unnerved by the intensity of the emotions Geraldo whipped up in the participants.

But at least they were passionate about something, she reflected as she walked along the Thames, taking in deep breaths of fresh air. She reckoned she could have been pro-active about her own life instead of mooning around Pine Close for so long.

She hadn't been happy for a long time, from even before Rob had left and she could see now there were a thousand tiny things she could have tried to improve her situation or her mood.

She bought herself a sandwich and a bottle of water from a kiosk and found a bench by the river. It was a bright, warm day in early summer and as she sat there, watching the world go by, she felt as if some frozen, hurt part of her was melting away in the sunshine.

Being in the vibrant city reminded her of how much she had been looking forward to visiting Orlaith and Jess in New York at the beginning of the year. And now she could see there was nothing stopping her going, except for her own rigid belief that she needed to put the plan on hold because Rob wasn't around. Which was total madness, she could see clearly now.

She smiled. Was it being in a strange city, doing new things that was helping her to feel more positive?

Or could it be that Geraldo Laffite's seminar was actually having a good effect on her despite herself?

By the end of the day, however, Susannah was revising her opinion yet again and once more looking at Geraldo with distrust and not a small degree of anger.

The main exercise of the afternoon was to see if you could break a wooden board with your bare hands. As Susannah learned more about it, she began to feel as if she'd entered some mad, down-the-rabbit-hole existence where everything sane and logical seemed ridiculous and vice versa.

First everyone had to be pumped up and Geraldo encouraged them to "dance, move, throw your arms up in the air, get the blood flowing," to a fast tempo of more loud music blaring and a zigzagging light display of electric blues and neon pinks turning the room into a disco.

They were to write their goals on one side of the thin piece of plywood and, on the other, all the reasons they felt would stop them achieving their dreams.

Harriet explained she had tried and failed at this exercise twice before. It all depended on how much she believed she could do it, she told Susannah earnestly.

She showed Susannah her board – fab house in London, handsome husband, three children all inked carefully in blue-felt pen on one side. On the other side of the board, she'd written down: *'Too hard'; 'Don't know where to begin'; 'Who do you think you are, looking for all that?'*

When the time came for Harriet to go up on stage, Susannah squeezed her eyes shut, not wanting to see the young woman disappointed. She heard an odd sound, and it took her a few seconds to figure out that the loud, guttural roar was coming from the diminutive Hannah. She opened her eyes in time to see her raising her hand high in the air only to bring it down again, smashing the block apart.

The assistants hit the sound-deck and a triumphal march filled the room as the spectators jumped to their feet, clapping their hands and drumming their feet, and Susannah found her heart swelling with hope for Harriet, that she would get the life she wanted.

Geraldo enveloped Harriet in a bear hug.

"I told you you could do it!" he roared after her as she left the stage, pink-faced with pride, as if she had actually achieved all she'd wanted, instead of breaking a bit of plywood. He then turned his attention to the rapt audience. "We don't believe what we're capable of. Before Roger Bannister broke the four-minute mile in the fifties experts said it was impossible. Yet the year afterwards, four more runners had managed to achieve the 'impossible'. You must believe and you must be prepared to break your own barriers."

His eye fell on Susannah.

"What about you? Are you prepared to break your limiting beliefs?"

She thought about refusing again, but she knew she couldn't keep on ducking out of the exercises, no matter how much she hated them. It wouldn't be fair on Katie, who had given her the opportunity to come here today, or to readers of the *Daily Post*. So she made her way gingerly on to the stage again, acutely aware that the audience was still angry with her because she hadn't attempted the earlier exercise.

She held her block in her hand. It was lighter and thinner than she had imagined but that didn't mean she had a clue as to how she was supposed to break it.

She didn't even know what to write on it.

Her wish for Rob to come home didn't fit in here. For one thing, she understood from Geraldo that the goal had to be something she could at least influence in some way. But it also seemed very pedestrian compared to Marianne's romantic dream of running a flower shop or Harriet who wanted it all.

She bit her lip as she looked at the block. Then she quickly wrote, '*Find a new direction and purpose in life*' on one side and on the other, '*Too old, too de-skilled, too heartbroken over Rob*'.

Geraldo smiled at her in that eerie way of his before explaining to her and the audience that the board would break if she used speed, energy and focus as he had instructed them. And, of course, if she believed with every fibre of her being that she could do it.

Could she break her mental blocks? She could try anyway. Susannah brought her hand up and then down again, as forcibly as she could. As her hand made contact with the wood, she felt a sharp pain shooting up her arm and a sense of mortifying failure overwhelmed her as she looked at the block – stubbornly, solidly unbroken.

"Not to worry!" Geraldo was all over her, rubbing her shoulder sympathetically. He looked at the goal she had written down.

"Not specific enough, I'm afraid," he told her blandly.

Susannah felt a stab of rage. Couldn't he have told her that before now? But he was already turning the plywood over.

"And this limiting belief you've written down – 'too heartbroken over Rob'?" He glanced at her wedding ring. "Is he your husband, dear? Is he dead?"

"No!" She was raging she had unwittingly revealed something so personal to this fake. "Well, yes. He is my husband. But he's not dead. He's –"

But Geraldo put his palm up to stop her talking. "You don't

have to share, Susannah, unless you want to. It's nobody's business."

She returned to her seat, again to no applause, and scribbled a reminder in her notebook to look up the science of breaking blocks when she got back to the hotel. She tried to concentrate on what was happening around her but, just like yesterday, there were a lot of strong, unexplained emotions churning up inside her.

She thought the day would never end and by the time it did she had developed a splitting headache.

"You look very pale," Harriet said, all concerned. "Are you still worrying about breaking the board? Just forget about it." She smiled excitedly. "Just think. Tomorrow, we'll be walking on hot coals."

"We will?" Susannah was only half-listening. She was looking at the people filing through the double-doors of the conference room. The people who had broken their boards, like Harriet, had faces wreathed in smiles and a purposeful look about them, while those who had failed, like her, looked dejected and worried.

She herself didn't give a fig about failing to break her board. And she would have walked on hot coals right then if it could save her from the next item on her itinerary.

Interviewing Geraldo Laffite.

CHAPTER 12

Back at the hotel, the piercing pain behind her right eye had escalated so much that if felt like someone was stabbing at it with a knife. She'd tried to look over her notes but the words were zigzagging in front of her eyes.

Great, just when I need to be on top of my game I get a monster migraine, she thought.

She knew if she didn't stop it in its tracks she was in for a couple of days of pain and discomfort. She swallowed her migraine medication, drank a litre of water and lay back on the bed and closed her eyes. She had to interview Geraldo, no matter how she felt. The entire feature would hinge on that.

She would fall back on an old journalistic trick – she would start by asking him the three main turning-points in his life – that usually got interviewees away from idle chatter and into something deeper.

By the time her taxi arrived to take her back to Geraldo's hotel she was feeling marginally better.

She was met by the woman who had been playing the "spiritual aide" role on stage earlier. She had changed from her white jumpsuit into a clinging red-jersey dress and she smiled at Susannah, showing white, even teeth. "Geraldo is ready for you. I'm Greta by the way."

Susannah smoothed down her cream skirt – it seemed that linen didn't travel well, even in business class – and stuck out her hand in greeting.

"Nice to meet you, Greta."

She followed Greta to the lifts, trying to keep up with the young woman's long-legged stride.

You've interviewed presidents and prime ministers, she told herself sternly as the elevator whisked them up seventeen floors. You can handle a celebrity guru.

Greta remained aloof as the doors slid open and they stepped out onto a small landing with direct access to Geraldo's suite of rooms.

The rooms themselves were high-end luxury – thick-piled, pale-yellow carpet, good pieces of dark, wooden furniture, a chaise longue upholstered in yellow and gold stripes.

Greta ushered her through a patio door and onto a spacious roof garden, an oasis of greenery and exotic plants – bird-of-paradise, cacti and orange-coloured lilies that filled the air with their distinctive scent.

Geraldo was sitting cross-legged on the black-and-white tiled floor, his back ramrod straight and supported by the wall. He was dressed in a navy-blue silk robe and matching harem pants, and his feet were stuck into blue flip-flops studded with crystals.

He was giving her the dazzling smile, beaming the full force of his personality up at her and she noticed his eyes were a peculiar shade of blue. Coloured contacts, she assumed, used for effect. The scent of his citrus cologne fought with the aroma of the lilies and Susannah's stomach, sensitive from the still-lurking migraine, heaved. Geraldo reminded her of a snake charmer, she decided, and she felt distinctly like the snake.

"Geraldo." She smiled down at him, keen to make a connection.

"Susannah. I am pleased to see you again." He unfurled himself sleekly off the floor and enveloped her in a bear hug as if she were a long-lost friend. Then he placed one hand firmly on the small of her back and steered her back into his suite of rooms.

"You can set yourself up there." He pointed to the small, square dining table and flung himself onto the chaise longue.

Susannah sat down and took out her notebook and pen.

"Don't you have a recorder?" He seemed put out by this.

"No. I like written notes."

"Seems like a lot of work." He interlinked his hands behind his head and observed her from afar. "You seem nervous."

"I'm not," Susannah lied.

She cleared her throat to begin but Geraldo suddenly jumped to his feet again and disappeared into the bedroom. When he returned, he was holding a small snow mobile. He shook it vigorously, and held it out for her to see the fake flakes of snow building into a storm inside the little glass bubble.

She raised her eyebrows. "What's this for?"

He dropped onto his hunkers and stared at her with his electric-blue eyes. "You cannot conduct the interview while your thoughts are flying all over the place like these snowflakes. You need to take some time to relax, let yourself settle. Like the snowflakes are settling – see? Perhaps we need to meditate together?"

"No. I don't meditate."

Geraldo put the glass sphere down and glanced at her wedding ring. "Are you thinking of Rob? The man you mentioned on your board? The one who broke your heart?"

"I'm the one who's supposed to be asking the questions," Susannah reminded him.

But he continued as if she hadn't spoken. "You've had big changes in your life, Susannah, and you don't like change, do you? Nobody does really. But it is only when you embrace change that your life really begins to fizz. Wouldn't you like your life to fizz, Susannah?"

"Erm," Susannah began but Geraldo didn't require an answer.

He jumped up to his feet again and began to stride around the room in a circle. "You need to let go of this man's betrayal of you and forgive him. Otherwise your resentment against him will drain all the energy out of your spirit, leaving you no room for the fizz. Is that enough? Are you prepared to spend your one and only life just getting by? Telling yourself you don't deserve to have the fizz? While people around you are living their lives, feeling their fizz every day?"

Susannah gave up. How was she supposed to interview him when he wouldn't shut up for five seconds?

"Do you know, I think we'd get on better if we did this interview in the bar, Mr Laffite." She took up her stuff. "I'll meet you there."

He looked as if he was about to protest, but then he shrugged. "If that's what you want."

"It is," she said firmly.

He left her waiting for so long she reckoned he must have taken umbrage at her changing locations, but when he finally reappeared he was all smiles.

He'd swapped the harem pants and jewelled flip-flops for an expensive navy suit and blue striped shirt. He sat beside her and snapped his fingers at the waiter.

"Gin and tonic for me – and for the good lady?"

"Champagne," Susannah said on a whim. Geraldo was right. She did need some fizz in her life.

"Excellent choice." He seemed impressed. "So," he turned to her. "You must be wondering why so many people come to my seminars. And the answer is that many come because they want to be rich and successful. They think money will bring them happiness but I always tell them that some of the richest people in the world are the most miserable. Why? Because they're afraid of losing all their money! Isn't that hilarious?"

Susannah didn't think so but she smiled at him encouragingly, determined to build an empathy with him. "We'll get to the kind of people who come to your seminars in a moment," she said. "But I'm interested in hearing more about you. For example, what were the three major turning-points in your life so far?"

He creased up his forehead as if he was thinking deeply about it. But then he shrugged.

"Haven't a clue. Being born? Becoming a multi-millionaire? Becoming an international guru?"

"Yes, so maybe we can talk about them. Not being born, obviously. But the others."

"I'd rather talk about what I can do for others."

He leaned in closer so his shoulder was touching hers.

"Like for you. I sense there is something missing from your life, Susannah. Something big."

Oh Lord, he was impossible! Susannah was grateful when the waiter returned with their drinks. She downed a glass of champagne in one go and poured another.

"So, go on then. Tell me about this big thing I'm missing in my life." She nodded at him encouragingly.

"The Big Thing." He nodded at her meaningfully.

"The – Big – Thing?" Susannah searched his face for clues. It was like playing charades but without the gestures. Just random words which meant nothing.

"Sex. The Big Thing." He nodded down to his nether regions.

Susannah's mouthful of drink went down the wrong way and she would have choked if she hadn't spluttered most of it all over her lap.

He grabbed a napkin from the table and dabbed forcefully at the wet stain, taking the opportunity to move closer to her.

"I can take you up the Hindu Kush," he whispered. "And I can guarantee you won't be disappointed. I have written testimonials to my expertise in that department."

Susannah pushed his hand away. The man was a madman.

"I think it's time I left," she said, standing up. From this height, she could see he had a bald patch on the crown of his head which for some irrational reason pleased her.

"Fine!" Geraldo shrugged. "It's no big deal. But it might help you relax. You don't meditate. You don't make love. What do you do for fun?"

She noticed the waiter was standing within earshot, pretending to be saying something into his earpiece, blatantly eavesdropping. He caught her eye as she passed him by and he fell into step beside her.

"Our concierge can get you a cab, madam. It's raining outside." He glanced back at Geraldo and raised his eyes to heaven. "I overheard some of that," he added sympathetically.

"No, thanks – no need for a cab." She flashed him a smile. "I could do with washing him out of my hair."

As she stepped out into the teeming rain, Susannah wondered what she was supposed to do now. She had no interview with Geraldo. She'd have to come and try and walk on hot coals after all.

CHAPTER 13

Katie's mobile rang and her stomach lurched when she saw Daniel's face filling the screen. She pressed the reject button. She didn't want to see him again. In a week he would be in London and she could forget she ever knew him.

A bleep announced an incoming text.

We need to talk. Answer your phone! Dx

Katie sighed. What was there to talk about?

She switched her mobile off and put on her headphones, turning up the music, trying to forget about the monumental mistake she'd made in sleeping with Daniel Gilbert.

The excellent sex they'd had was providing surprisingly scant comfort against the onslaught of anger and self-recrimination she had put herself through since it happened. She had veered from blaming herself, to blaming Daniel, to blaming the tequila slammers she had merrily downed.

Fail to plan, plan to fail, she thought grimly now. She'd allowed herself to get too lonely without Luke. She'd been too proud to ring him or to even get in touch with some of the old friends she'd lost touch with since her big work promotion.

She had hoped the bed-to-work twilight zone she'd entered after she took up the new position would be temporary, and that she'd pick up the threads of her social life as soon as she got on top of the job.

But that had never happened. Being features editor had been a steeper learning curve than she'd envisaged. Every time she thought she had the hang of it, Mike piled something like the Mind, Body and Spirit pages on it and she was back to square one.

Now, without Luke in her life, she had very little going on apart from work. She'd been thinking of going to a yoga class with her mother tonight but, when she phoned her earlier, Olivia was still harping on about Katie's mistake over the pen name for Susannah Stevens.

"The poor woman, her daughters had to find out about it on Facebook!"

"Well, that's a barometer of her spectacularly dysfunctional family in fairness," Katie defended herself. "She must tell those girls nothing."

That's what she got for trying to do people favours, she thought, shoving a frozen ready-meal into the microwave. Mixing business with your private life never worked. Not with her mother and her friends and certainly not with Daniel Gilbert.

She mooched around the kitchen, thinking about Luke. They'd never have broken up if it hadn't been for that stupid column. He'd be here and she'd be cooking something decent to eat and telling him about the blunder she'd made about using Susannah's real name and how she'd solved it by offering her the trip to London, and he'd be telling her again how great her job was.

But he wasn't here. In fact, there hadn't been so much as a text from him. She fleetingly thought of ringing him, just to see how he was doing, but it would be too awkward now, after the Daniel incident.

She brought her microwaved meal into the living room and propped the tray on her lap while she watched an American soap about four fabulously wealthy female friends who all had great jobs they could leave at a moment's notice if one of them got as much as a broken fingernail.

Katie loved it. She loved the clothes and the make-up and the cars and the way one minute they were wrapping up mega-deals at work and the next they were all in someone's kitchen commiserating over a love-gone-wrong situation, even when it was the middle of the day.

If one of these women had been dumped, the others would all have been over, cooing and cooking and commiserating. Katie knew it was only fiction, but tonight it made her feel all alone and in need of a shoulder to cry on.

But the only one available was the shoulder she had to avoid. Her phone beeped again just as the closing credits were rolling. Another text from Daniel.

I need to see you. I'll be gone by Friday.

And another one.

Please?

God, he was persistent.

She was about to finally text him back when the doorbell went.

Even more persistent again!

She got up and flung open the hall door.

Daniel, there's nothing to talk about, she was about to tell him. But the words died on her lips as the man outside pulled a peaked cap off.

"Luke!" She flushed. "Come in."

She stood aside and he walked into living room, shrugging off his tweed jacket and hanging it with his peaked cap in the hall.

"I'm sorry I haven't been in touch," he said, flopping down on her sofa. "I've been in England. My grandmother died."

"Oh." Katie felt stung that he hadn't told her.

"Yes, it was sudden. She had a heart attack. And I stayed on a bit after the funeral. I spoke to my aunt about you and she said I needed to come talk to you – to clear the air between us."

Katie had never met Luke's aunt but she knew they were as close as people can be when they live in different countries. His mother had died when he was small and he had no sisters, so she was the main female influence in his life.

"Can I get you a drink? Tea? Something stronger?"

He reached into his briefcase. "I've brought some wine."

Katie took the bottle from him and went out to the kitchen for a corkscrew and a couple of glasses.

They talked about his grandmother and the funeral and what a shock the death had been for the family. It was only when they were halfway through the bottle that he brought up the rift between them.

"I guess I need to say this. I was going to propose to you on Valentine's Night. I had the whole thing planned – well, I didn't have a ring because I thought you'd want to choose your own – and then when I read the column I thought maybe you were going to propose to me."

"I know. It was a mistake to write the column. I can see that now. It led to a lot of – miscommunication, I suppose. But I don't want to get married, Luke."

Despite her confusion, on this at least Katie was now very clear.

"Of course I know that now. But then? I felt so disappointed. And then the night was ruined and, by the time I'd got my feelings sorted, my grandmother had died and I had to go away. I didn't get in touch with you because I thought we both needed time to think things over."

Oh, it had given her time to do a lot more than that, Katie thought.

"So." He looked at her closely. "What have you been up to?"

"Oh, this and that."

"How's work?"

136

"Okay, I guess. Eh, Daniel Gilbert's leaving." Thank God. "He's got a new job in London."

"You'll miss him," Luke said.

"I'll miss his column because I'll need to find something to replace it. He's left me in the lurch because he's barely working his notice." She swallowed. She needed to change the subject. "Look, Luke, I may not want to get married. Not just yet anyhow. But I have missed you. A lot."

"And have you thought any more about us moving in together?"

She swallowed. She'd had one grotty flat-share since she'd moved out of home and then she'd bought her own place. She was practically an only child, because her half-brother Seán had never been part of her life, so she certainly wasn't used to compromising.

But did she want to live alone forever?

"Look, I'll be up front with you," Luke said. "My flat-mate is moving in with his girlfriend and so I'll be looking for a lodger anyway. Do you want to apply?"

"God, no!"

Katie couldn't think of anything worse. Luke's house, a small bungalow at the foot of the Dublin Mountains, would mean a long drive into work instead of the fast train journey she had now. And the house was situated in the shadow of a mountain which Katie had always found oppressive and vaguely threatening. She couldn't imagine living there ever.

"I need to be here – closer to work."

"So what if I moved in here? You could probably do with the rent?"

Katie didn't need his rent. She had a good salary and she was good with money, always had been. But she did want him back.

"We could do it as a trial," he suggested. "And if it doesn't work out I'll move out. No problem."

Katie remembered Daniel saying it was easier to stop someone moving in than to get them to move out. But she was sick of being cautious. Luke was right. It was time for them to take the relationship to another level.

"Okay," she said.

He made a face. "Just okay?"

She sloshed more wine into their glasses. "Better than okay." She leaned over to clink his glass. "Much better."

He smiled. "You won't regret it, Katie Corrigan. This is going to be great."

But by the end of the week Katie was doing exactly that – regretting her decision. He had returned the next day with so much stuff. She was shocked to discover how much space it took up in her apartment. How much space he took up.

It had been one thing when he slept over at the weekends but now his man-things were permanently cluttering up her neat, tiny bathroom, his clothes were stuffed into her wardrobe, his big boots parked under the stairs.

When she came home from work exhausted, there was no lovely space for her to do her own thing before she met him. He was there first thing in the morning and last thing at night, cooking or talking or sprawled on her couch watching television with the volume too loud, his legs taking up half the floor space.

She'd never realised just how long his legs were, she thought balefully one night after she'd tripped over them not once, but twice.

It's what comes from living alone for so long, she tried to reassure herself one evening after work. It was the night of Daniel's going-away party and it was a relief to be going out straight from work. She'd changed out of her office clothes into a maxi dress she'd bought in her lunch-hour and she'd even managed to get her hair done in the afternoon.

Finally she was getting on top of her job, she thought. And she was with Luke again. Her life was back on track. Which would make it easier to face Daniel tonight.

He'd hired a room in the local pub. Katie arrived early deliberately. She wanted to say goodbye to him privately, before everyone else arrived. She stood in the doorway, taking in the scene. Multicoloured strobe lights flashed around the room, reminding her of how much younger Daniel was, decades it sometimes seemed, in spirit if not in actual years.

He was standing with his back to her, talking to the DJ. He had blue jeans on and a tight navy T-shirt, which rode up on his back, leaving an expanse of brown skin. Katie closed her eyes briefly, wishing their night together had never happened, that she was arriving here to give her good friend and colleague a great send-off, instead of having to perform this damage-limitation exercise.

She took a deep breath, pushed back her shoulders and strode across the expanse of empty dance floor.

"Hey there!" She tipped him on the shoulder.

He swung around and she couldn't help noticing the way his face lit up at the sight of her.

"Katie! You came!"

She put her arms around him in an awkward hug. "I told you I would."

"Still, I wasn't sure. You've been ignoring all my phone calls. Texts and emails too."

"Yeah, I'm sorry about that. Here, let me get you a drink."

They walked over to the bar and Katie sat on one of the high stools. Daniel tried to drape an arm around her shoulders but she moved back a fraction so his hand missed its target.

They both ordered beers and Katie took a large swig of hers before announcing baldly, "I'm back with Luke."

"I see." He had his face turned away from her slightly and she couldn't see his expression.

"Yeah – he called around during the week and said – well, you don't really need to know what he said, but we're back together anyway." She glanced towards the doorway. "He's coming to meet me here later so I just wanted to tell you that he doesn't know anything about us." She swallowed. "Just so you don't let anything slip."

Daniel gave her a behave look.

"So you're back 'on track'." He grinned, hooking the air with his fingers, putting quotations marks around the phrase. "I'm happy for you."

"Me too," she said. But of course that wasn't entirely true. Part of her did feel more comfortable being back with Luke. But, on the other hand, she'd started to feel as if she wasn't able to catch a full breath. And sometimes she was gripped by a faint foreboding she didn't quite understand. It was like something was going to go wrong again, sooner or later – that it was inevitable and she herself would cause it.

"I'm not sure how long it will last, mind you."

Daniel turned to face her and she could see the concern now in his eyes. "Really? Why's that?"

"Well, if he finds out what happened with us – like, if I told him – I don't know how he'd take it."

Daniel gave a short laugh. "I do. Your happy, fuzzy, 'back on track' vibe would be over in jig-time."

She felt anxiety curl around her stomach. "Do you think so?"

"I know so." Daniel took a swig from his bottle of beer. "Please tell me you're not thinking of telling him about us?"

"You needn't worry about any fallout. If I do tell him, I'll make sure you're in London first."

"I'm not worried about the fallout for me. I'm worried about the fallout for you. Look, you and Luke weren't together when it happened, so technically it's nothing to do with him."

"That's not really true," she said. "And what if he finds out some other way?"

"How's he going to find out? There's only two people who know about it and one of them is leaving the country on a big jet plane."

"True." She bit her lip. "Don't you think honesty is important in a relationship?"

He smiled. "I think you're forgetting I make my living writing about how I can't make relationships last. I'm not the one you should be talking to about this. But I don't think Luke is the type to forgive you for sleeping with another man."

"Some men would, though, don't you think?" She raised her eyebrows.

"It would be a hard to come to terms with it. Of course it would. But I'd like to think my priority would be saving the relationship. I'd want to sit down and figure out why it happened. Generally, I think both people have a responsibility when things go wrong."

"And you think Luke wouldn't do any of that?" Katie was defensive. "You don't like him, do you?"

"It's what you think of him that counts." He nodded towards the door. "Hey up! People are arriving. So here – take care, Katie Corrigan. And remember, you can come and stay with me in London any time." Then he added, seeing her expression, "On my couch." He gave her a big hug and then he was gone, across the room to greet Mike and his coterie of ambitious staff hanging on his every word. Laughing at his unfunny jokes and buying him drink in the hope of a promotion down the road.

She should probably get over there herself, Katie thought.

But then she spotted Susannah Stevens standing uncertainly at the door. She was wearing a blue coat that looked a bit tight and was fiddling with a silver wristwatch. Katie had invited her, explaining it would be a chance for her to get to know some of the other people working on the paper. She beckoned for her to join her.

Susannah came over to the bar, relieved to find a familiar face.

She looked around the room, starting to fill up with various people from Daniel's life, not just the *Post* staff. "This looks like it's going to be a fun evening. You'll have to introduce me to Daniel so I can wish him good luck in his new job."

"Of course. And Mike. He's just arrived." Katie nodded over at the boss. "But let's give them both a chance to chat together first. What can I get you to drink?"

Susannah asked for a white wine and Katie got herself another beer.

"So you'll have to tell me all about London. But first – did the column cause all the repercussions you feared?"

"The girls aren't speaking to me. And I still don't know if Rob has read it." Susannah shrugged out of her coat.

"But they're off in New York living their lives, and Rob is in the Far East doing the same thing, so I don't see that it has that much to do with them."

"It's because I didn't tell them the column was going in. I hadn't even told them their dad was in Thailand."

"Why didn't you? And how?"

"I thought Rob would be back after a few weeks – that he'd get whatever was going on with him out of his system and come home. And I figured that while I was waiting I could protect the girls from worrying about it if I just said nothing. It was a stupid decision because in the end I had to explain it all anyway. Telling the truth in the first place would have been easier."

Katie remembered her mother saying that. When she found out from a friend that her husband had been cheating on her, she said if he'd had the decency to be honest with her it would have been much easier to come to terms with. So did that mean that she should come clean with Luke about her and Daniel? Olivia would say yes. She would declare that relationships can't thrive on a foundation of lies. And Daniel had said the opposite – that the truth would spell the end for her and Luke.

She didn't know what she thought herself so she was glad to put it to the back of her mind when Mike arrived at the bar. His face was flushed and his shirt was straining against this belly. Sweat stains had formed under his arms and he pulled out a dotted hanky to wipe his brow.

"Hot in here, isn't it? Who's your friend?"

"It's Susannah Stevens, the author of –"

"My Husband Left Me for a Camper Van!" Mike finished for her. He gripped Susannah's hand in his big paw-like grasp. "I've been looking forward to meeting you."

Susannah looked a little nervous to be meeting the editor but Katie knew she'd be fine. Mike had been very keen to meet her and, in all her time of working for him, Katie had never seen that happen before. She left them chatting and made her way to the bathroom to freshen up. When she came out she saw Luke had arrived. He was standing by the door, looking uncertain.

She weaved through the crowd to greet him. The DJ had started up, which would make any meaningful conversation impossible. And Katie wasn't in the mood for dancing.

"Not much going on around here. Just boring work stuff. Do you want to head home?" she shouted over the music.

"Shouldn't I say hello to Daniel?" he shouted back.

"I doubt you'll get near him. He's surrounded by well-wishers. He won't even notice if we slip away."

She took Luke's arm and gently propelled him back through the exit door. She'd done what she'd come here to do. She'd said goodbye to Daniel Gilbert.

CHAPTER 14

Katie sat on the sofa in her living room, watching the Liffey wind its way towards the Dublin docks. The days were getting brighter and she enjoyed watching the boats and the people and the activity of city life that she loved. Watching the river always made her feel as if she was washing away the tensions of the working day, like a welcome bridge between work and leisure.

Now, though, she felt all keyed up. Luke had been up until three writing his thriller. He had to work when the muse struck him, he'd explained when she asked why he wasn't coming to bed. Katie, who before becoming features editor had churned out stories all day long, had to bite back the sarcastic comment on the tip of her tongue – and when he'd finally come to bed, trying to interest her in some plot point in his story, she'd pretended she was asleep.

But it had actually taken her ages to nod off and she felt as if she'd barely shut her eyes when the alarm went off at six o'clock. She'd been grumpy all day and when her phone beeped and she saw it was a text from Luke to say he was working late, she felt guilty at the relief that washed over her.

Great. See you later, she texted back.

What was wrong with her anyhow? Was it just a case of getting used to living with Luke or did she, as Olivia had often told her, have "issues" she needed to resolve?

Katie stared out at the river but she was lost in thought now. Her parents' marriage had been tumultuous even before her dad had left. And, as often was the case with warring couples, her parents appeared to think their only child was deaf simply because she pretended she couldn't hear their frequent arguments. But that made her no different from half the population, Katie reasoned.

And then there was all the travel.

Des Corrigan had been a foreign-affairs journalist who had travelled to wherever his next assignment was and had dragged his family right along after him. Other parents in the same situation put their children into boarding school, but her parents didn't approve of that and never bothered to find out what Katie wanted.

It meant that each time they moved she had to start her life all over again. She had hated it. Her stomach still contracted when she remembered how the house would become festooned with her mother's yellow post-it notes and long to-do lists – a clear sign that yet another unwanted new home and school were on the horizon.

Olivia, who loved the itinerant life and had a knack for making friends wherever they landed, thrived on it, but Katie had been bullied at every school she'd started, a new gang of mean girls materialising with such regularity that eventually she started to believe there must be something in her which attracted them.

And the people her parents socialised with were all like themselves, corporate families living in big, rented houses in some foreign country or other. They would move on sooner or later, just like the Corrigans, and Katie had worked out early on there was no point in trying to make friends that way.

Instead she had taken refuge in reading and writing down her thoughts in her journal – which had at least given her a career she loved, she reflected.

In college she'd forced herself to get along with others, recognising it was a skill she'd need for her career.

But she'd never made any lasting connections there either.

Except for Jolie. Katie smiled at the thought of her best friend, living in County Wexford now, with a couple of curly-haired toddlers in tow and a part-time job as a small-town solicitor. They'd met at Fresher's Week at Dublin City University and oddly enough it was with the kooky Jolie, with her hair dyed a different colour every week and her devil-may-care attitude, that Katie finally felt someone 'got' her.

Now their lives were so different they barely managed to see each once or twice a year but a big part of Katie wanted what Jolie took so much for granted – the house, the kids anyway. She couldn't have a part-time job, not if she was going to be editor of the *Post* one day. But another part of her doubted very much that relationships could weather the trouble and storms of life.

Because no matter how confident Katie looked on the outside there were still times when she was catapulted straight back to that screwed-up little girl she had once been, the gang of mean girls existing now only in her own head, but just as cruel with their comments.

Unsettled by the memories, she got up and washed her cup in the sink. She'd always strenuously resisted Olivia's suggestion that she should go to counselling to talk about her childhood. Because, unlike her mother, she didn't believe it was good to talk. She liked action, as much of it as possible.

She was more like her dad in that way. He was always busy too, and seemed confident on the outside, but Katie always got the sense he was battling some inner demons too. And now, she reflected, she had something else in common with Des Corrigan. He'd been a cheater – something she had hated him for since the day she'd first heard about it. It was the reason she'd refused to get to know his second wife or her half-brother Seán and why she felt pretty much estranged from him now.

And now she was a cheater too.

She grabbed her sports bag and headed out to the city gym where she trained six days a week. She changed quickly and put the treadmill at 7k an hour and stuck in her earphones, ready to outrun her thoughts of a turbulent past and her own cheating present.

She always had the radio tuned to a talk station in case there was anything she needed to hear for work. This evening, they had a psychologist on saying the world had become a more isolated place even though more people were living in urban areas.

"We live in our bubble of digital distraction, apart from the real-life people in our vicinity."

Katie realised she hadn't exchanged any small talk with the other people in the changing room − she had barely looked at them in fact. And when she looked around her now she could see that all of them had headphones on and were totally focused on their workouts. Nobody had even looked up when she'd arrived.

"But social interaction is vital to our happiness and if we could be more mindful of what is going around us and be kinder to the people we meet − the young mother struggling with the pushchair or an elderly person crossing the road − we would reap just as many benefits as the people we're helping."

Katie slowed down the treadmill. This could be a good feature for the MBS pages, so she wanted to catch the psychologist's name so she could pass it on to Susannah.

"And it can help in other ways too," the psychologist continued. *"Suppose there's someone in your life you're holding a grudge against or someone you've wronged in some way. You may not want to make amends face to face. You may not be able to do that − if, for example, the person has passed on. But by doing random acts of kindness for others, you can make spiritual amends to that person which will in turn help you to find the peace of mind you're seeking."*

Like doing penance, Katie thought, remembering her

Catholic education. Admit your sins, do your penance and you will be forgiven.

Do your penance and you will be forgiven.

She slowed the treadmill to practically a standstill as the significance of that thought hit her. What if she'd been overthinking everything, her head full of Olivia's psychology bullshit about commitment issues, when the truth of why she couldn't settle with Luke was staring her in the face.

They had started living together with a big lie between them – one that was all her fault. But what if she did penance for it? What if she tried these random acts of kindness the psychologist was going on about?

What if she was nicer to everyone, not just Luke, until the awful guilt left her and she could relax again? It would be far less risky than taking a chance on telling Luke what was really bothering her.

She wasn't even in contact with Daniel any more. She'd had one email from him since he'd left and she'd deleted it without opening it. She wondered fleetingly what he'd make of her new plan. She could see him in her mind's eye, his face arranged in mock outrage. "You're doing penance for sleeping with me? Really?"

She smiled. Daniel had always taken her side – against Mike, against Jennifer, against the world, if that's what he thought she needed.

But in this case he would be wrong to do so. Katie had made a big error of judgement and she needed to put it right. And in the absence of any brighter ideas, what harm could a few random acts of kindness do?

As it happened, she got a chance to do her first one the very next morning.

On her way to work she spotted a homeless man in a doorway. He was sitting on a sleeping bag, tying the laces of his ancient boots. She hadn't noticed him before, but then she wasn't normally the most observant soul at this hour of the morning. She was usually living in her own head, thinking about her to-do list.

She stopped, debating whether she should give him money or buy him a breakfast from the fast-food café two doors down. She was late for work and she reckoned he'd prefer the cash but what if he spent it on drink or drugs instead of food? And did throwing a fiver at another human being even qualify as a random act of kindness?

She decided not and walked past him and into the café. Queues of commuters snaked out from all the cash registers. Katie got in line, trying not to think about how much she hated being late.

Hopefully the inconvenience might make this particular random act of kindness worth even more, she mused as she watched the servers take their own sweet time pouring coffees as if they were baristas.

By the time she'd grabbed an egg-and-bacon muffin and coffee she knew she was going to have to work though her lunchtime again to make up for the lost time. As she made her way out of the café she wondered briefly how the homeless man would react to her buying him breakfast. Maybe he'd think she was a nosey do-gooder and tell her to eff off with her fiver breakfast. Well, there was only one way to find out. She took a deep breath as she reached the doorway, her arm outstretched with her offering.

But all that was there was an empty sleeping bag.

She looked up and down the road, prepared to run after the man if she had to. But there was no sign of him.

Disappointed, she walked the three blocks to her office at a fast clip.

She was nearly at her desk when she tripped, sending half the coffee flying through the air.

"Oh, for God's sake!" she yelled to nobody in particular as the hot liquid scalded her hand.

"You should be more careful," Jennifer said, looking up with a disagreeable expression. She had evidently not forgiven Katie yet for sending Susannah to the *Flow Your Life* seminar.

"Here – it's for you, a gift." Katie held out the cardboard box with the bacon-and-egg muffin and the half-cup of coffee.

Jennifer glanced down at her skinny body and back to Katie. "What would I want with that?"

"Never mind." Katie took it back. "I'll give it to Mike." Somebody was going to avail of her first random act of kindness. She pulled some tissues out of her bag and mopped up the mess before striding off down the corridor.

"Mike!" Katie smiled broadly at her boss. "Good morning. I've brought you breakfast."

"Hmmm? Oh. thanks. Leave it there, will you?"

Katie placed the muffin and coffee onto his desk and waited expectantly. For what she wasn't sure, maybe a word of thanks. But Mike had barely looked up – taking the breakfast as if it was no more than his due. Katie eyed him suspiciously. Maybe Jennifer did this every morning? Brought him in homemade healthy muffins to get in his good books? Why else would he take it for granted?

She shrugged and tried to get back into the spirit of what she was trying to do. She had a vague recollection that you were meant to do the random acts of kindness in a humble way, so she'd better stop fretting about what thanks she got for them.

Still, a bit of gratitude wouldn't have gone astray, she thought as she sat down at her desk. She powered up her computer and tapped 'penance' into the search engine.

"So. Did Mike appreciate his breakfast?" asked Jennifer.

Katie looked up to see the older woman scooting herself into her cubicle. She wondered how Jennifer managed to stay so thin when she barely moved a muscle unless it was utterly impossible not to. She rolled herself around on that office chair as if it was stuck to her bum, got taxis on the newspaper's account to absolutely everywhere while the rest of them had to arrange their own transport.

Once, when Katie was still a feature writer, she was stuck in a hot, hired car behind an articulated truck on the motorway when she saw Jennifer in a taxi swanning past in the bus lane. It was a metaphor for Jennifer's life really. Things came easily to her. And when they didn't, she wanted to know why.

"Yes. I think he appreciated it." She smiled brightly at her colleague.

"What's going on?" Jennifer's green eyes were narrowed with suspicion.

"Excuse me?" Katie looked back at her screen, trying to look busy. Because no matter where this conversation started, if Jennifer had her way it would end up with Katie having to explain why she hadn't sent her to cover the *Flow Your Life* seminar.

"What are you doing, offering myself and Mike a heart-attack breakfast? Are you trying to clog up our arteries? Get rid of us?"

"I was trying to do a random act of kindness actually."

She swivelled her chair back and showed Jennifer the list of penance sites listed on her screen. "Did you ever do Croagh Patrick by any chance? You know, that mountain in County Mayo which pilgrims climb as a form of penance?"

Jennifer frowned. "Why would I want to do penance? Or you for that matter? What have you been getting up to behind our backs?"

"Nothing." Katie shook her head. But a note of warning stirred. If Jennifer assumed she'd something to hide, it stood to reason Luke might too so she'd better cut him out of her kind deeds altogether.

152

And Jennifer too. She was far too cynical to understand something as spiritual as a kindness project.

The phone rang and Katie grabbed it, giving Jennifer an 'I'm up to my eyes here' look.

"Hello, Katie Corrigan here. Oh, hello, Susannah."

She huffed out her breath. She'd arranged to meet Susannah to talk about the London feature but she hadn't expected her for another half an hour.

She glanced across at Jennifer, who was still sitting in front of her, determined to while away an hour or four talking about why Katie hadn't sent her to London.

"You got here early? No, it's no problem – I can meet you right now in fact. Do you see the café on the corner? I'll see you there." She hung up and gave Jennifer a triumphant smile. "Have to dash. Byeeee!"

CHAPTER 15

Katie spotted Susannah sitting at the back of the café, staring at the spiral notebook in her hand.

"What's up?" She slipped into the seat opposite her. "You look worried."

"No, I'm fine. Well, maybe a little worried."

"So how is the feature for *Flow Your Life* coming along?"

"Good. It was – interesting."

In fact, Susannah wasn't at sure what she was going to write for the feature. When she'd turned up for the hot-coals day she'd learned that the final part of the programme had been cancelled because of "unforeseen circumstances". The participants had been offered a refund or else entry to the full weekend again at one of his European dates.

Probably suffering from a raging hangover, Susannah fumed, as she left the hotel. She was disappointed she couldn't see Harriet anywhere – she should have taken her number so she could check out how she felt about the seminar in a week or two, when all the deliberately pumped-up adrenaline had died down. And she hadn't managed to interview Geraldo properly either.

Still, she'd made good use of the unexpected free time. She took a riverboat from Westminster down the Thames to see the world-famous Kew and spent the morning exploring the beautiful botanical gardens. Basking in the scents and sights there, Susannah forgot about Geraldo and Rob and her anxiety about where her life was going and managed to enjoy a glorious, carefree couple of hours before she needed to head back to the hotel to check out.

She'd managed to get an outline down on the plane home but she remembered how specific Katie had been about what she wanted for the MBS pages – "Bright, sexy prose, include case histories, never miss a deadline" – and she knew it needed a lot of work.

"And what about Geraldo Laffite? What was he like?"

"He was – an experience. He offered to show me his Big Thing."

"His next big thing? Great. Which is what? Another seminar?"

"No, his actual big thing." Susannah widened her eyes meaningfully. "Well, not that I'd know if it was big or not, because obviously I declined but I –"

"Hold it! Back up a bit there. He asked you to look at his –?" Katie stared at her.

"His penis. Yes. That's what he called it. His Big Thing. Said he'd take me halfway up the Hindu Kush with it."

Katie burst out laughing. "And you said?"

"I'm not sure it was funny – although I admit I might have laughed at the time. I almost choked on my drink actually, so I didn't say a whole lot. But when I thought about it later, back at the hotel, I wondered if it might have been sexual harassment?"

"He asked you if you wanted to see his Big Thing and you declined and he left the matter there. That's not sexual harassment. That's a straightforward request for sex. He's not your boss. He has no power over you and you're both adults. A kind of bizarre and unexpected request granted, but who knows what people are like? Some other woman might have been delighted to see his Big Thing." Katie couldn't wipe the smile from her face. This was reminding her of her coffee meetings with Daniel when he used to regale her with his adventures.

But Susannah still looked doubtful.

"So am I supposed to write about it?"

"Is it relevant to the seminar?"

"Not exactly. But people trust this guy. He goes on stage saying you need to be pure of mind and body and there he was knocking back gin and tonics and offering perfect strangers a look at his Big Thing. It seems wrong."

"Let's not complicate things," Katie advised. "Just stick to the facts of the seminar. Leave the private stuff out. And if you feel you have to mention something, just be careful about how you write it. We don't want to be sued."

The waitress arrived and while Susannah put in an order for coffees and muffins, Katie looked at her thoughtfully. She needed a sounding board about this 'random act of kindness' project and whether it could help improve her relationship with Luke.

Jolie would have been perfect – she was kooky enough to actually believe in all that stuff and she would also want what was best for Katie. But Jolie was in the South of France sunning herself right now. Whereas Susannah was here, in front of her. And she'd been very open about the creepy-sounding Geraldo Laffite.

"Now can I ask your advice about something?"

"Me give you advice?" Susannah looked terrified.

"Yes. I'm assuming it won't get back to Olivia?"

"It won't get back to anyone," Susannah said and something in her steady grey eyes made Katie believe her.

"Okay so." She took a deep breath. "Do you know my boyfriend Luke and I broke up a while ago?"

"Yes. Olivia said something about it." Susannah remembered her saying how cut-up Katie had been about it the night she'd had her and Cara over for dinner.

"Well, we're back together now. We've even moved in together."

"Well, that's great. Isn't it?"

"I think so. Apart from a few teething problems I think it's working out. But the thing is – while we were still split up I did something I shouldn't have done. And now I don't know whether I should tell Luke about it or not."

Susannah looked confused. "And I can help you – how?"

"I just need a listening ear, that's all. The thing is, I feel guilty – about the thing I shouldn't have done – and I think that's affecting my relationship with Luke. He irritates me a lot more than he used to when we didn't live together."

"Maybe you just need time to adjust?" Susannah ventured. "Living together is a big step."

"Maybe. But what if it's this issue between us? I'm thinking if I could sort that out, everything would improve between us."

"It should do. In theory. But I guess it depends on what the thing you shouldn't have done was."

Of course it did. Katie cursed herself for starting this conversation. But now that she had, she was determined to continue.

"Look – I had a one-night stand with someone," Katie said flatly, watching Susannah's face carefully for a reaction. If Susannah was going to be judgmental then she'd only added to her woes, but she had a hunch she wouldn't be. She'd been understanding enough about the errant husband, God knows.

"While you were broken up or together?"

"Oh, broken up! Definitely broken up. And when we got back together I intended to tell Luke about it, get it out of the way, so we didn't have secrets between us. But then the guy I was involved with said it would be a mistake and I started doubting myself and I put it off. And now I think too much time has passed."

"It can't be that much time if it only happened when you broke up," Susannah pointed out.

"Look, just hear me out. I was listening to a radio show last night – it was about us all being kinder to each other – I thought it might be good for the MBS pages." She rooted in her bag and took out a yellow post-it note and handed it to Susannah. "This is the guy's name maybe you can look him up sometime and see if you can get a feature out of it. According to him, you can make amends to someone without dealing directly with the person involved."

"How? And why?" Susannah sounded totally bewildered now.

Katie shrugged. "The example he used was if someone had died. But in my case it would be just easier for me to do it that way. I could atone for cheating on Luke by doing kind things for other people, by becoming a nicer person."

"You're a nice person already," Susannah interrupted. "And you weren't cheating if you were broken up at the time."

"That's what the guy I was involved with said. So why do I feel so guilty about it?"

"I can't tell you that, Katie." Susannah looked at the post-it note. "Did this guy have any evidence that it works?"

Katie shrugged. "I didn't catch the whole interview. But people who believe all this woo-woo stuff are not renowned for providing scientific evidence, are they now? Maybe it works through karma? Or helping me to feel better about myself. I don't really care about proof, or why it works. I just want the problem sorted."

"Maybe it would be easier in the long run to just tell Luke? Rob had been planning his trip in secret for years – three years to be exact – and that made everything worse to me. So if Luke were to find out about you and this other guy …"

"But how would he?" Katie cut in. "There's nobody else who knows. Apart from the guy and me. And now you."

Susannah smiled. "Well, I can guarantee he won't hear it from me." She pushed the crumbs of her muffin around the plate. "But are you sure you won't change your mind one day? Because as I said, if you do, the lie might seem worse than what actually happened."

"I never change my mind once I make it up." Katie tilted her chin. "Look, I've only just got Luke back. I'm not going to risk losing him again. So that's my answer, I guess. I don't tell him. See, I told you I just needed a sounding board. Thanks, Susannah."

"You're welcome."

"And I can be your case history when you're writing the feature – using a different name and disguising any identifying details of course."

"Of course," Susannah smiled. "Unless I was to use your real name by accident?"

"Very funny!" Katie nodded at the waitress who had come over to give them both refills of coffee. She looked back at Susannah. "So how is Robgate now anyway?"

Susannah's face clouded. "I need to phone him actually, to find out. I promised the girls I'd do it last week but then the London trip came up and I put if off again. Queen of Procrastination, that's me, I'm afraid."

"So when was he last in touch with you?"

"He hasn't been. He wanted us to stay in touch through Facebook – even though I don't have a Facebook page. And neither did he," she added, "until he decided to take off."

Katie shook her head. "You should have told him to take a hike!"

"He is taking a hike – in Thailand."

"So what's he been getting up to on his Facebook page then?"

"There wasn't a lot on it, to be honest, when Cara showed it to me. I haven't looked at it since. I'm not too clued in on all the new technology."

She bit her lip. She hadn't meant to advertise her skills-shortage at this point.

Katie raised her eyebrows. "Facebook is not new technology. It's over ten years old. You're going to have to change your attitude to the modern world if you're serious about rebuilding your career, Susannah. Here – let's have a look."

She reached down into her briefcase and pulled out a silver laptop, opened it up and started clicking the keys. "So his name is – Rob Stevens?"

"The Intrepid Traveller," Susannah said faintly.

Katie continued clicking her keyboard. "Yup, here he is. Relationship status: it's complicated."

"It's that all right," Susannah agreed.

"But did you know that's what he has down on his page?"

"What?" Susannah jumped up and came across to lean over Katie's shoulder. "Where does it say that?"

"There." Katie pointed at the screen.

Relationship status: It's complicated.

Occupation: Banker on sabbatical at the University of Life.

Favourite quote: "To Thine Own Self Be True."

Dear God, thought Susannah.

"Let's see who his friends are." Katie grinned and clicked on another part of the screen. "Here, sit down." She indicated the empty chair beside her and Susannah sat down, her face glued to the computer. A parade of Rob's friends with photos attached appeared. They were different ages, different sexes, but they all seemed to have the same smug, self-satisfied smile on their faces.

"I don't know any of them," Susannah said slowly.

Katie looked up and noticed the look of anguish on her face. She closed own the laptop. "I'm sorry," she said quietly. "I probably shouldn't have done that."

Susannah got up and returned to her seat opposite Katie, twisting a paper napkin between her fingers. "I had to see it sometime. You've done me a favour."

"I got a bit carried away."

"He was paler when he left," Susannah said bleakly. "And fatter. He seems happy now."

"Maybe. Maybe not. Most people put up only the edited highlights of their lives on social media. He's not going to put up about the homesickness or the fact that he's made a big mistake …" Katie's voice trailed off as she realised that Susannah wasn't listening to her.

She was staring off into space, as if she were in a trance.

"Olivia would say you should see someone – a counsellor," Katie offered.

"What good would that do? Telling a total stranger about my private life?" Susannah snapped.

"I don't agree with her about the value of counselling as it happens. I think you should just face the facts and move on. The fact that your marriage is over is up there on Facebook for the world to see."

"My marriage isn't over," Susannah said stubbornly.

"Wake up, Susannah, and smell the coffee. 'It's complicated' means it's not complicated at all. It means the person has bailed on one relationship but is too much of a coward to admit it because he's afraid he won't find something better out there." She clapped a hand over her mouth. "There I go again! Pontificating. Listen, how would you like a trip to Croagh Patrick?"

"What?" Susannah did a double take, disorientated at the sudden change of subject.

"I was looking it up this morning – it's a mountain in Mayo – pilgrims climb it as a penance." Katie was determined not to say another word about the subject of the Stevens' marriage.

"I've heard of it," Susannah said. "And this is part of your becoming a better person, is it? Earning karma kudos?"

"Yes. And that'll make a great headline! We could do it

together and you can write the feature about it. I think the readers would love it. What do you think?"

"Sure. I'll look into it."

But Katie knew Susannah was only half-listening to her. She felt so sorry for her, sitting there, looking as bewildered as the first day she'd come along for the job interview and agreed to write the camper van column that had caused her so much trouble.

Katie pressed her lips together. Whatever happened with Susannah and the run-away Rob, it was none of her business. She had enough troubles in her own life to worry about.

CHAPTER 16

Susannah sat in the conservatory, staring through the window. The sky was streaked with puffy white clouds, the flowering shrubs were wreathed with pink blossom and the robins and blue-tits were still flocking around the bird-feeder. Normally their antics cheered her up but this evening all she could see was Rob and his Facebook page. It's complicated. It wasn't as if she could argue with that. But there was something so impersonal and hurtful about it the way it was laid out on a social media page for anyone to see. What was it Katie had said about it yesterday? "It's complicated means the person has bailed on the relationship but is too much of a coward to admit it." Something like that anyway.

Was she right? Was she being naïve in believing her marriage wasn't over? She glanced at the clock. She needed to contact him. But it would be 2am in Thailand now. Rob was an early riser, so it was likely he'd be asleep now. But if she waited until it was Rob's morning, it would be – oh, who knew what time it would be? She was sick of trying to figure out the time zones between Dublin, Thailand and New York.

She dialled Rob's mobile. She could leave a message for him to call her back whenever it was convenient for him.

She was waiting for the foreign ringtone to switch to Rob's

mailbox when he answered the phone.

"Hello?" He sounded wide awake.

"Hi. It's Susannah."

"Oh." The alert tone faded. "What's happened?"

Susannah scrunched up her face, sick of hearing the hostility in his voice. She felt like asking him when the hell she had become his enemy, the handy scapegoat for whatever it was he felt was missing from his life. "Well, lots of stuff has happened actually."

"Is it the girls? Is one of them sick?"

"No. Nothing like that at all. I was going to leave a message – I presumed you'd be asleep and I'd get your voice-mail."

"So no emergency then?"

"No emergency. But we need to talk."

"But why would you phone me in the middle of the night if there's no emergency?" he asked plaintively.

"It's not the middle of the night here." A thought occurred to her. "Why are you awake at this hour of the night anyway?"

"I've just got in."

"From where?"

Silence. And then a sigh, a deep long-suffering sound that put Susannah's teeth on edge.

"That hardly matters, Susannah. This is why I said you were to phone only if there was an emergency. Because I knew otherwise I'd be getting all these questions, the third degree. I explained how I can't be in touch with you during my break. My therapist said …"

"You're seeing a therapist?"

"Was. When I was in Dublin."

Susannah blinked. "About what? Oh sorry, another impertinent question."

"I don't want to discuss it over the phone. But that's why I suggested using the Facebook page to stay in touch casually."

"Ah, yes. Your Facebook page. I've seen it."

"So why didn't you get in touch with me via that? Like, private-message me?"

Like? Susannah felt like Alice down the rabbit hole. She shook her head, trying to focus on why she was phoning him at all.

"I need to discuss something with you directly. Orlaith and Jess have found out you're away, and they're pretty upset about it."

"Well, if you'd let me tell them from the beginning that wouldn't have happened. If you're only getting around to telling them now it's no wonder they're upset."

"I didn't tell them. They found out through a column I wrote about you going on a career break. It wasn't the best way for them to find out, I'll give you that. But, in my own defence, I didn't think they would. The column was meant to be published under a pen name. My grandmother's name. Elizabeth Castle. You remember she left me her journals?"

There were a few beats of silence from the other side of the world. Then, "You wrote a column. About me? Where?"

"Um – I was actually writing about me. But yeah, you featured in it. I wrote it for the *Daily Post*." She registered his intake of breath with satisfaction. The *Post* had a wide readership in Ireland.

"And how did the girls come across that in New York?"

"They – um – saw it on Cara's Facebook page."

"Your column about me is on Facebook? What did you write? Where can I – here, let me log on and find it …"

"Cara has taken it down. But you could try the *Daily Post*'s on-line edition."

"What's it called? The column?"

Susannah swallowed. "My Husband Left Me for a Camper Van."

There was a longer silence and then an expletive from Rob.

"What the –? Really?"

"Well, that's the headline. But it's about more than that – you'd have to read it really. Look, I didn't ring you to argue. But the girls asked me to find out how you're doing. I know they could have contacted you directly but they were upset so I offered to do it, just so I can call them back and say you're okay. Put their minds at rest."

"But why did you write that I left you for a camper van?" He sounded genuinely bewildered.

"I saw it on your screen saver. A camper van with loads of slogans on it. The Journey Begins Here. Stupid stuff like that," she couldn't help adding, even though she'd just told him she hadn't called to argue.

"Seriously? You've told the whole world – and my daughters – that I left you for a camper van because you saw it on a screen saver?"

"And because that's the way it felt from where I was standing."

"Ah, I see. It's the world according to Susannah again."

"Actually, yes, in this case. That's exactly what it is." Susannah gripped the phone a bit more tightly, trying to figure out how Rob had somehow managed to twist everything around so that he got to be angry with her. "While we're talking about Facebook – you have your relationship status down as 'It's complicated'?"

"Well, it is. But I put it up as a joke."

"What's funny about it?"

"You'd need a sense of humour to understand."

"I see. It's lucky you've regained yours because I'm writing regularly for the *Post* now. You might even get to feature in one of my columns again."

"You can't do that!"

"What, have a point of view?"

"I'm a private citizen."

"And the last time I checked the libel laws it would appear I have nothing to worry about."

"I forbid you to write about my private business. I have a career to go back to there."

A career, Susannah thought. Not a wife. Not a family. "Well, I guess I have one of them now too. So you'd better get used to it. At a *Flow Your Life* seminar I went to recently —"

"Excuse me?" he interrupted her. "*Flow Your Life* with Geraldo Laffite?"

"Yes, that's the one."

"You've been? You've met him?" Rob's bewilderment would have been funny if she wasn't so annoyed with him.

"Yes, I have. Why?"

"I've wanted to do that seminar for so long. But I couldn't afford it."

Susannah thought about the money he was spending on his skite to the other side of the world, the money he'd spent on a therapist when he could have been talking to her.

"Well, neither could I, obviously, out of my own money. But the paper sent me. They flew me business class to London, actually, to do it. The third day was cancelled — just as well really because it had something to do with walking on fire."

"What was Geraldo like?" Suddenly he was hanging on her every word.

"Wonderful. He offered to show me his Big Thing."

"Oh. What was that?"

"It was his private member."

"That's disgusting."

Susannah stifled a giggle.

"How could you make up that stuff?" he asked, aggrieved.

"It's true. Anyhow, I'll tell girls we've cleared the air and they can get in touch with you directly. I'm not comfortable about being the go-between."

He sighed. "And they're not happy with me?"

Susannah thought of their last hysterical last phone call. "No. They're not."

"But then, who's ever been happy with me? I keep hearing on this trip about 'The Bank of Mam and Dad'. But in our house it was just 'The Bank of Dad' and when I finally do one thing for myself after years of —"

"I think I know where this monologue is going, Rob, so I think I'll skip it this time around."

And Susannah put the phone down. She stared at the receiver in the cradle for ages, as if it could still connect her to Rob, the husband she had loved with all her heart, and who had inexplicably turned into a stranger. He still hadn't managed to tell her their marriage was over but she had finally got the message, loud and clear. She couldn't believe she'd been waiting all these months for him to walk in the door and declare it was all a mistake.

Part of her felt like crying for all she had lost, all they had lost. But the image of his Facebook page and his stranger Facebook friends floated into her mind and anger won over the grief. She had been dumped on Facebook! At fifty-three. Well, at least she'd get a column out of it.

She took a deep, inward breath. If Rob wanted over, she'd give him over.

But later that night she woke up with a jolt. The nightmares were back. She lay there, disorientated and terrified, halfway between sleep and wakening.

She'd been running down a dark alley. Someone was chasing her, but she wasn't sure who it was. Ahead she could see bright lights of the main street and she could hear the roar of city traffic and knew if she could just get out of the laneway she'd be safe. She kept her eyes on her goal and her focus on putting one foot in front of the other. She could outrun whoever it was giving pursuit.

But then, out of nowhere, a giant rat appeared and stood in the centre of the alley, facing her and blocking her way. Instinctively she sidestepped it and pressed on, her breath coming now in hard, fast rasps. Another rat, bigger than the first one, huge, rose up to block her way. She kept running. She was almost there.

And then she knew she couldn't make it. Thousands of rats materialised out of nowhere, staring up at her, blocking her path, baring their teeth. She couldn't get past them. It was impossible. She screamed, just before she woke up.

Her skin was drenched with sweat, her muscles rigid with tension, her heart thumping at what felt like twice its normal speed.

She fumbled for her phone. 4.00am. Of course it was. It was nearly always the same time she woke up out of these dreams. She knew the unpleasant long-distance call with Rob must have triggered it but she wasn't thinking about him now.

She was catapulted back to the year she was sixteen. All over that summer, her stalker had been lurking about, at the bus stop or when she'd walked back home from school. She'd felt uneasy about him. He was older, but he was a neighbour so she ignored her misgivings.

Until the evening she walking through the local park when she caught sight of him up ahead, hiding behind some bushes. She was wondering whether she should turn back the way she'd come or just walk past him when he suddenly made the decision for her. He jumped out of the bushes, flashing himself at her, masturbating. For a moment she froze, and then turned and fled, back the way she had come, out through the park, back towards the house of the friend she had been visiting.

She rang her dad to pick her up, making an excuse about

feeling sick. It was three more months before she could bring herself to tell her parents and when she finally plucked up the courage to do that, there had been uproar. Her dad had gone and almost banged the man's door down and when he got no answer he frog-marched her to the police station to make a statement.

And then, three weeks after that, her dad had dropped dead from a heart attack. Everything had changed in an instant. They'd moved house, Susannah and Cara and their mother – and the stalking episode and the police report had never been mentioned again.

Even Susannah didn't think about it very much now. When she'd been younger the nightmares had come so often she'd been scared to close her eyes at night but now they only occurred when she was overtired or overstressed.

She sighed and went out the bathroom to splash cold water on her face. The remnants of the dreams were still with her – the fear when the thousands of rats popped up out of nowhere, the feeling that she wasn't going to escape, but most of all the running. In the dreams she was always running.

She stared at her reflection in the mirror. Was this the way it was always going to be – with her being persecuted with these nightmares every time life didn't go the way she wanted it to?

She guessed it was, unless she found a way to stop running. She would have to face up to each and every one of her fears from now on. She would make a plan and no matter how scared it made her she would do it anyway.

And then, she decided, the nightmares would disappear for good – and she'd feel in control of her own life.

She started with the tiniest step she could think of. One of her fears was technology so she bought herself a new laptop with all the bells and whistles and taught herself how to use it. It meant she could now work anywhere, didn't need to wait for minutes while Rob's ancient computer powered up and then have to look at his stupid screensaver when it did.

It was ridiculous the amount of pleasure she got, just looking at her laptop.

The first thing she'd done was to learn how to skype and she'd been pleasantly surprised to find out it wasn't harder than rocket-science after all. She'd had a terrifying moment when she couldn't conjure up what they looked like – their eyes, the expressions on their faces. The way Jess's brow furrowed when she got anxious, the distinctive cornflower-blue of Orlaith's eyes.

But now she was skyping, all dressed up for the occasion, with full make-up and the string of pearls the twins had bought for her birthday. She was shocked to see that Orlaith was still in her pyjamas while Jess was dressed in a big, baggy blue sweatshirt. But then she remembered it was 9.00am on a Saturday in New York.

"So," she started brightly, "it's so good to see you both."

Orlaith scowled back at her. Her face looked a little puffy and Susannah wasn't sure if the camera had a distorting effect or if she'd been crying.

"Dad's been on to us," she said.

Of course he had. Why was she even surprised that he hadn't bothered to tell her he was going to get in touch with them himself?

"So he's explained everything to you? How he needed to get away on his own?"

"He was saying weird stuff," Jess muttered.

"He said the magic was gone out of the marriage." Orlaith's face was a mask of anger. "Like, T.M.I!"

"T M what?"

"Too Much Information," Jess said helpfully.

Susannah had to agree. It was bizarre that Rob would be sharing this stuff with his daughters.

"He sounded very strange – not like Dad at all." Orlaith still

173

had that accusatory tone in her voice, as if it was all somehow Susannah's fault.

"He just needs space for a while, that's all," Susannah said. "From me, that is, not you two."

"But it affects us too," Jess announced. "It's not the same living in New York without you two being together."

"Yeah, the whole point of a gap year is you can go off and fly your kite knowing you have your home to go back to," Orlaith agreed. "Now, who knows whether you'll even be there by the time the year is up?"

"What, like the house could be sold?" Jess looked across at her twin, panicked.

"Of course," Orlaith told her.

"That's not going to happen," Susannah said quickly. But then she thought maybe it might. The future looked extremely uncertain and she didn't want to mislead them any more. "Not without us discussing it with you first anyway."

"Yeah, like you discussed the situation with Dad with us." Orlaith stared at her. "Maybe we should come home now while we still have a home to go to."

"Or I could come visit you?" Susannah said quickly.

"On your own?"

"Without Dad?"

"Well, of course without Dad." Susannah tried to hide her irritation. "He's in Thailand!"

"I think you should come," Jess, the peacemaker, broke in. "It would be nice if we could all talk about it properly."

"Of course," Susannah agreed. But privately she decided there was no way she was going to spend all her time in New York talking about Rob. She made a mental note to create an itinerary for herself before she went so she didn't get sucked into the Robgate drama again. She'd wasted enough of her life on it already.

"So will I get online and check the fares then?" Orlaith asked, switching from surly to helpful in an instant.

"That would be great, Orlaith. Thanks."

Suddenly Susannah could see that behind all the anger, Orlaith was scared. Both girls were. She could understand that, because it was exactly how she'd felt too.

Up until now the fear had won, hands down. It had paralysed her with inertia and gave her the feeling of being completely powerless in her own life.

But now that she'd made a decision that she'd at least put up a fight, she felt better about herself.

And when she disconnected the call she realised she was actually looking forward to the weekend. She was meeting Cara this evening and tomorrow she was going to work on writing up the feature on Geraldo Laffite.

Thinking back to that weekend, she wondered if the *Flow Your Life* seminar had affected her on some level after all? Because while she'd failed to break the wooden block on stage it felt as if she'd broken a few mental blocks over the last couple of days.

She felt different. Lighter, almost as if a weight had literally been lifted off her shoulders. It was like the surge of energy she'd got from looking at Elizabeth Castle's photograph was filling her up again, making her feel grounded and centred.

Finally ready to start her new chapter.

CHAPTER 17

Susannah sat at her desk, sifting through the piles of brochures that arrived daily from the *Post*. She had boxed up the last of Rob's travel paraphernalia and got rid of the ancient computer to make more room but the desk still felt disorganized and untidy.

She scanned through the leaflets, trying to figure out where to begin. *Ayurveda. Reflexology. Cranial-sacral Therapy. Empowerment Within. Healing with Your Angels. Personal Empowerment. Emotional Freedom Technique. Reiki. Energy Psychology. Transcendental Meditation. Rebirthing. Rolfing. Money consciousness. Mindfulness.*

She shook her head in disbelief. She'd lived her whole life without knowing anything about this whole other world. The good news was that she now seemed to be the go-to freelance MBS correspondent with the *Post*. Their rates were good and, if the trip to London was anything to go by, there were exiting opportunities to be had.

The bad news was that she wasn't finding it easy to come up with feature ideas of her own.

She'd filed her story about the *Flow Your Life* seminar, but she'd found it tricky to write. She tried to steer a path between being as truthful as she could about Geraldo Laffite, while at the same time being careful not to write anything that might get herself, Katie, or the newspaper into trouble.

Reading over the feature before hitting the 'send' button, she wasn't one hundred per cent happy with it. But since she couldn't put her finger on what was wrong with it and the deadline was looming, she had to let it go. This, at least, was familiar to her from her job two decades ago.

But that was where the similarities ended.

Previously her work had been connected to a fairly predictable news cycle and she had provided information and analysis of events that were clear and tangible.

Now it felt as if she had to come up with ideas out of the clear blue sky.

She couldn't rely on Katie to give her assignments all the time. She'd have to come up with something. She leaned back in the chair, linking her hands behind her head. She needed to get out and find people, she realised.

Katie was right. Talking to these practitioners without case histories just wouldn't work – her features would read like advertorials. But where could she find the people she needed?

Her mind came back with a blank so she went downstairs for a break, idling around the kitchen for a while before making herself a cup of coffee and wandering out to the conservatory. The garden, which had once been manicured to within an inch of its life – all Rob's handiwork – was now a jungle of weeds and flowering shrubs jostling for space. Springtime had seen the plants erupt into new growth and now there were bushes that needed to be trimmed, borders to be weeded, and the lawn, in particular, needed to be mowed before it got so high the mower wouldn't cut through it.

But, instead of doing any of those things, she watched a blackbird pecking at the fertile black soil for a while and then allowed her attention to drift to a plane streaking across the blue sky above her. She watched the plume of cloudy-white smoke it left in its wake and thought about Rob again.

When he'd left, she hadn't known how to fill the hours between getting up and going back to bed. The days had stretched out in a terrifying vista of emptiness before her.

Now she had too much to do. The book club was in a few days and she wasn't anywhere near finishing the nominated novel. The book was still open on the wicker table where she'd left it in her rush to get ready for the London trip.

She sat down and started to read, trying to remember the story. Ironically it was about a woman whose husband had left her, in this case, to join a cult. She'd hunted him down and killed him and made it look like a suicide. She was a kick-ass sort of heroine, Susannah mused, but how realistic was she as a character?

When Rob had left, she'd felt more like a walking, talking cliché of an abandoned wife and she reckoned that was the way most women who found themselves in that position felt too.

She was just getting absorbed in the story when a bookmark fell on to her lap. It was an advertisement for the bookshop where Phil, their new book-club member, worked. Susannah looked at it thoughtfully. The bookshop he worked in must have a substantial Mind, Body and Spirit section. Maybe she could pay him a visit, see what sort of people were looking at the shelves. Granted, she could hardly tap them on the shoulder and invite them to tell their personal life stories to a national newspaper. But anything would be more productive than staring into space.

She went back into the kitchen and glanced at the train timetable. It was still pinned to the fridge from when the girls used to take the train across the city to college. If she hurried she'd be at the bookshop in an hour.

She ran upstairs to change, switching her trainers for smart black courts, then pulled on her trench coat and set off for the station.

As she walked through the village to the station, she remembered when she and Rob had come to this neighbourhood as newly weds, full of hope for the future. It was still a charming place, with gourmet food cafés and bars and shop-windows stuffed with colourful flowers, and Susannah had made some good friends here.

But now it felt as if she didn't belong any more. Not on her own. Other people must have felt the same way she did because those whose marriages had ended through death or divorce had tended to move away, downsizing or whatever it was people did when they had to start a new phase of their lives. Olivia Corrigan had sold her house as soon as Katie left home and booked herself into a lodging house near the college where she'd studied to get her psychology degree. Then she bought her tiny city apartment. She really only used that as a base because her freelance work contracts took her throughout the country and beyond, and since her marriage had broken down she'd developed an insatiable appetite for learning new things and seeing new places.

People found ways of moving on, Susannah told herself, scanning her ticket and, as the train pulled out of the station, she wondered whether this familiar journey would soon be just another part of her past too.

She found the bookshop easily with the help of the satnav on her phone. Between the Covers was set in a narrow alleyway off the main road. It was one of the few independent bookshops which had survived the changes in the publishing industry and Susannah could see why as soon as she pushed through the doors. Mismatched sofas were placed strategically around the room for the browsers and the aroma of strong coffee wafted from an area at the back of the shop. It had a strong, welcoming energy and Susannah felt her shoulders dropping away from her ears as soon as she stepped over the threshold. There had been a time in her life when losing an afternoon in a shop like this had been one of her greatest pleasures.

But that had stopped when her mother got sick. Everything

had stopped then, everything apart from trying to take care of her at home for as long as possible. It had meant putting her own life on hold to an extent. Cara had done as much as she could, but her hours with the airline didn't give her an awful lot of spare time so most of the responsibility had fallen to Susannah.

Moseying around bookshops had become a luxury she couldn't afford, along with regular hairdresser appointments or anything really that wasn't essential. But it had all been worth it. It was time she'd never get back, she reminded herself, and she'd never regret it, even if it had somehow contributed to the fact that she and Rob were now separated.

She brushed away the memories, picked up a wire basket and strolled around, looking for a Mind, Body and Spirit section. She found it upstairs, four wall-to-ceiling shelves packed with self-help titles. *The Journey. The Secret. Your Energetic Field Force. Are You Living Your Best Life?*

Susannah pulled that one off the shelf. She flicked it over to read the blurb on the back. The book promised to show her tactics to find a perfect partner and career, how to attract the wealth she deserved and how to improve her relationships with everybody, including herself. What wasn't to like, she thought, dropping the book into her basket. She scanned the shelves again and saw *He's Just Not That Into You* which made her smile, given her circumstances, so she dropped that and a *Social Media for Dummies*, which was just to the right of the MBS shelves, into her basket too.

"Can I help you, Susannah?"

She recognised Phil's voice. He was taller than she remembered, his features harder than they had appeared in the soft light of her living-room lamps. She noticed now he had a ruddy hue to his complexion and from the tiny broken red veins around his nose, she reckoned he might like a drink or two.

He gestured towards her basket. "A lot of time on your hands for reading with the hubby gone?"

"Er no, it's ..." Susannah took a step back. He was standing too close to her. "It's just some stuff for work."

He raised his eyebrows. "You got the job with Olivia's daughter?"

"I did." She attempted a friendly smile. "Keeping busy, you know."

"So did you find everything you need?" He put a proprietorial hand on her shoulder.

"I'm good now. Thanks."

Susannah tossed a few more titles she liked the look of into her basket and looked around for where to pay. She'd changed her mind about asking Phil for help. He was acting way too familiar for someone she'd only met once before and there was still something about him that made her feel vaguely uncomfortable.

He trailed after her, steering her towards the cash desk.

"James," he announced jovially, "this is a friend of mine, Susannah. Susannah, This is my boss, James Moran."

"Pleased to meet you." James was tall too, taller than Phil, and older. He wore wire-rimmed glasses and his silver hair had started to recede.

Susannah gave him a half-smile and put her basket on the counter.

"Self-development fan?" he asked chattily, as he started to scan the books through the register.

"Not really." Susannah handed over her credit card. "It's for work."

"Oh?" He was intrigued.

"I've just started working for the *Daily Post*. Freelancing." She gave a wry smile. "I'm their Mind, Body and Spirit correspondent for my trouble. I probably need more books but –" she waved a helpless hand at her basket, "it's a bit overwhelming. To be honest, I wasn't a fan before I got this job. I can't believe how much there is to choose from."

"They're massively popular. Lots of bestsellers in that category." He looked at her. "If you want I can talk to you about the genre and the type of customers who like it?"

"Would you?" A wave of relief came over her. "That would be so helpful."

"It's a bit of a passion of mine so it's no problem. And of course it's good for business! Feel free to quote anything I say!" He smiled. "The *Post* has a big readership."

"So – are you free now?" Susannah asked. James was right. This could be a win–win situation for both of them.

"Sure, it's quiet enough at this time. We can have a coffee and see what it is you're looking for. Phil, can you take over here for a bit?"

Phil reluctantly swapped places with James and placed Susannah's purchases into a big carrier bag. "I'll keep these here until you're ready to collect them if you like?"

"No. I'll take them now."

"Fine." Phil sighed as he handed over the bag, as if Susannah had done something wrong. "So will I see you at the book club on Wednesday?"

"You will." Susannah wasn't looking forward to it. The book club was in Olivia's this month and the thought of sharing the tiny apartment with Phil wasn't that appealing.

"Great." He smiled thinly. "I'll see you there so."

She followed James into the coffee-shop area. He was at the counter, ordering coffees. Susannah rummaged in her bag for her reporter's notebook and pen. She was pretty sure he was a busy man and she needed to get as much as possible out of him in the shortest time possible.

"I wasn't sure if you wanted something to eat?" James put two mugs of coffee on the table. "We have cake, scones, sandwiches?"

"No, coffee is fine. Thanks."

He pulled out a chair and sat down opposite her.

"So where will I start?" he mused, opening a sugar sachet and tipping its contents into his mug.

"I'm looking for some background into the whole Mind, Body, Spirit area – how self-help has become so popular, that sort of thing. And whether you feel these books actually help anyone." Of course he was bound to say they helped, seeing as he earned his living selling them, so she added, "And why, of course."

"Well, I can answer one of your questions straight away. It was books like these that helped me turn my life around at a time when I found it difficult to get up in the morning. So yes. I believe they can help."

"Really?" She couldn't keep the surprise out of her voice. She hadn't been expecting this level of candour.

"Really." He smiled. "In the past – in another life, it sometimes seems now – I was your typical stressed-out IT professional with so little time for my family I didn't realise anything was even wrong with my personal life until it all blew up in my face."

"I see." She chewed the top of her pen. "Do you mind if I take notes?"

"Not at all."

Susannah started scribbling down random words and phrases – a narrative that would be unintelligible to anyone but her – and continued with the questions.

"And how did the books help?"

"I was in a lot of pain, and I wanted to feel better. I started reading anything that looked as if it might vaguely help. Some of them didn't resonate with me, but others did. And soon I was hooked, getting through a couple of books a week, trying to put my life back together."

"And did you?" she prompted. "Put your life back together?"

A shadow passed across his face. "It's a very long story. I changed careers for one thing."

"You swapped IT for running a bookshop?"

"I own this place actually. I have other business interests too so this is a bit of a labour of love for me. Phil does the actual day-to day management." He looked across at the counter. "Is he a friend of yours?"

She shook her head. "I met him once at a book club I go to, that's all. My sister introduced him."

She paused. She needed to know more about James' story. So far it sounded a lot like Geraldo Laffite's guff, if she was honest. She tried to keep the cynical note out of her voice as she pushed on with the interview.

"So now you're doing something you love and your family has been put back together and it's all because you read some of these books? How did that work exactly?"

"Yes, I'm doing something I love. But no, my family wasn't put back together."

"Oh. I'm sorry."

"There's no need to be." He smiled ruefully.

She swallowed. She knew it would be a bit of a cheek, considering she'd only just met him, but she was starting to see that James Moran might make a good case history. He'd said his story was a long one. And it would be good publicity for his shop, as he'd pointed out himself.

"Look, I have no idea how you'd feel about this," she began tentatively, "but would you be interested in talking to me about your own story? For the paper?" Then, noticing his brow furrowing, she added quickly, "I'd make sure Between the Covers gets a very good mention."

"Shouldn't you wait to see if the case history is worth publishing before you go making rash promises?" He raised his eyebrows, but he was smiling.

"I think it will be. Call it a hunch." Or a desperate reporter with zero other ideas.

"I don't know," he said slowly.

Back to square one. Susannah felt her spirits slump again.

"But I will think about it, I promise. Tell me a little more about yourself. Where can I read your work? Oh, and give me a business card so I can contact you."

Susannah scribbled out her mobile number on a page of her jotter, ripped it out and handed it to him. "Sorry. I'm just getting started at the *Post*, so no business cards yet."

He raised his eyebrows. "Did you change jobs recently?"

"I was at home for a long time, rearing my twin girls. They're grown up now – and they're both living in New York. I got a chance to go back to work and – here I am."

It sounded great when she left out all the details about Robgate.

"You must miss them."

"I do. But I'm planning on visiting them soon so it's not as bad as it was when they went first. And I'm busy now which helps. It's not good to have too much time on your hands."

"It sounds as if you might have a story of your own to share with your readers," James observed.

She grinned. "Oh, I do. And I did share it."

Susannah knew the first thing he would do when she left him would be to Google her name and find the camper-van column so she told him where he could find it, leaving out the part about the pen-name mix-up.

"So – you were going to fill me in on the general background to all this wellbeing stuff?" she prompted.

"Yes. I was." He folded the page she'd given him in two and tucked it into his shirt pocket and started to talk.

"Some people say the popularity of these books is because

people have lost faith in the religion they were brought up in but they still want to have a spiritual basis in their lives. Others feel these authors offer an affordable education in living more effectively. One way or the other, I don't think they can do any harm."

Susannah thought of Harriet, dreaming up her perfect life in London and spending a lot of money to be convinced it was all a matter of time before she'd turn it into reality. But it wasn't the time or the place to voice her doubts and, besides, James was looking at his watch.

"I need be getting back to work," he said. "It was nice meeting you, Susannah. And I will be in touch about the case history. I'll let you know what I decide, one way or the other."

Susannah stuffed her notebook and pen into her bag, stood up and reached out to shake his hand.

"Thank you." She couldn't believe how she'd lucked into meeting him. In half an hour he had given her so much material and he might be her case-history himself. She felt far more optimistic than when she'd walked into his bookshop.

He was an intriguing character, she thought to herself on the train home. Very centred and composed for someone whose life appeared to have crash-landed at some point. She hoped he'd call, and not just because he might be her next feature for the *Post*.

James Moran appeared to have reinvented his life pretty successfully – which was exactly what she was going to have to do now too.

CHAPTER 18

Susannah drove towards Olivia's apartment, aware of an odd fluttering in the pit of her stomach. It was the same sense of unease she'd felt when she'd met Phil at the bookshop, when he'd stood too close to her and put his hand on her shoulder. She had to admit she wasn't looking forward to the evening the way she normally did.

She wouldn't be able to tell Olivia and Cara about the weekend in London, or her plans to go to New York soon to see Orlaith and Jess or that she had met James – not with Phil sitting there.

Part of her wished now they'd made a rule that everyone had to agree before someone new could join. But, as she steered her car onto a steep downward slope to get to the underground car park, she reminded herself it was a book club. New members brought new life and opinions. It saved them from getting into a rut of reading in the same genres and hearing similar viewpoints. It was more stimulating when someone new joined and she guessed that Phil, as the manager of Between the Covers, must be widely read. She could keep the social chitchat for another night, she told herself as she walked the five blocks to Olivia's.

She was the first to arrive. As she entered the small hallway she could hear jazz playing in the background and catch the aroma of lavender-scented candles. The atmosphere was mellow and inviting.

She shrugged out of her coat and handed it over to Olivia to hang up.

In the small living room she sank down into the sofa.

"Let me get you a drink," said Olivia.

"Just coffee for me," Susannah said. "I'm driving."

Phil was next to arrive. He was dressed in black jeans, a green army-type jacket and he had a rucksack over his shoulder. He had a well-thumbed copy of the book they were reading in his hands. He dumped the rucksack on the ground, took off his jacket, and sat down next to Susannah.

She tensed, despite her good intentions to try to get know him a bit better. Was it her imagination or was he sitting a fraction too close to her?

She smiled at him, trying to shake off a feeling of claustrophobia, the sense that Olivia's living room wasn't big enough, even though she'd never felt like that about it before.

"So?" she asked him. "What did you think of the book?"

He shrugged. "It was interesting. I was disappointed in the ending though. You?"

"I felt the heroine was a bit of a rock star going off to take revenge the way she did. I found myself wishing I had some of her chutzpah actually."

"I thought you were very dignified the way you behaved when your husband ran off on you," Phil told her.

"Oh listen, the bell. That must be Cara." Susannah took the opportunity to get up and answer the door. She didn't want Phil talking to her as if he was a close friend or confidant. It only deepened her sense of unease about him. When she came back she sat on the armchair opposite and listened while Cara regaled them with news of her day with her usual enthusiasm.

"So." She paused for breath. "So how has everyone else been?"

"I've had a good week," Olivia arrived from the kitchen with a bottle of wine and some glasses.

"As has Susannah. She interviewed my boss, James Moran, for the *Post*," Phil announced. "Didn't you, Susannah?"

"I did," Susannah replied but she was determined to turn the conversation back onto books. "You should choose our book for next month, Phil. You must have a lot of titles you'd like to put forward."

"Yes, I do. Even some which don't glamorise evil female killers."

"What?" Cara stopped, one of Olivia's neatly cut sandwiches halfway to her mouth.

Phil leaned back in the sofa and folded his arms behind his head.

"Susannah was saying earlier she thinks the heroine of our novel is a bit of a rock star."

"Yeah, I can see that." Cara continued eating.

"But if it was a man who'd killed his wife we'd all be calling him a monster," he said, "and calling for him to be packed off to prison for life. Or worse."

"I didn't think of it like that," Susannah murmured. She couldn't figure out if there was a thin veil of hostility in Phil's tone or if she was just being hypersensitive.

"Well, maybe you should. Think." He was smiling when he said it but this time there was no mistaking the put-down.

Susannah flushed, feeling as if she'd been caught in a trap of her own making.

Olivia looked up sharply. "That's sounded a bit disrespectful," she told Phil bluntly.

"Did it? I'm sorry, Susannah. I didn't mean to offend you. But you said you didn't think and isn't that what we're meant to be doing here – thinking?"

"Is there something wrong, Phil?" Cara was puzzled, as if she'd sensed the air of tension that had crept into the room but couldn't figure out the cause.

"No." He shook his head. "Forget I spoke."

"I see where you're coming from," Susannah offered, but only because she wanted to get the evening back to some level of congeniality.

"Thank you, Susannah. I just think it's an important point to discuss. The way women killers are portrayed compared to male killers – in life and in fiction." He drank his glass of wine, very fast, and filled it up again from the bottle on the coffee table. Now that he'd got his way he seemed to have lost interest in the topic he'd been determined they would talk about, and was only interested in what was in his wineglass.

Susannah was about to bring up the rather unorthodox ending of the book, when Olivia cleared her throat.

"I'm uncomfortable with the way the evening is going," she said baldly. She looked at Phil. "You seem upset and you're drinking very fast."

"So? That's what the wine is here for, isn't it? To drink?"

Olivia took the bottle off the coffee table and brought it out the kitchen. Susannah and Cara looked at each other, both confused and unsure as to how they should handle the situation.

Suddenly Phil got to his feet and bent down to retrieve his rucksack.

"I think I know when I'm not wanted," he snapped. He grabbed his jacket and marched down the hallway, slamming the hall door so loudly that the glass in the side-panels shook.

Olivia came back and stared at the empty space on the sofa. "What just happened?"

"He left. Said he knows when he's not wanted," Cara said, her face wrinkled up in a frown.

"No, I meant what happened overall tonight? Why was Phil so hostile?"

Susannah turned to her sister. "How well do you know him, Cara?"

"Not very. I was in the bookshop where he works and he

started chatting to me about what I liked to read and I told him I was in a book club and he said he'd always wanted to be in one. So I invited him along."

That was so like Cara, Susannah thought. She was always inviting home strays when they were younger and her job as an air stewardess meant she was used to chatting to strangers as if they were her friends. Susannah was much more circumspect in that regard.

"I see. Well, maybe we should vet new members in the future," Olivia said, echoing what Susannah had been thinking earlier.

Phil's outburst had clearly upset her and after a while Susannah decided to excuse herself.

"I could do with an early night anyway," she said.

"I'll stay and finish this," Cara gestured towards her wineglass and her sandwich. "I'll call you tomorrow."

"Take care, Susannah," Olivia said as she accompanied her to the door.

Susannah was still feeling upset as she walked towards the car park. She was about to descend the steep slope into the underground area when she sensed someone was behind her. Automatically she pulled her bag closer. She turned back and saw a man walking fast to close the gap between them. Phil.

She tried to hide the fact that he'd startled her. "I thought you went home?" It made her uncomfortable to think of Phil lurking outside Olivia's for the last half hour. Had he been waiting for one of them to come out?

"I had an errand to run," Phil said vaguely. "But you shouldn't be walking on your own." He looked up and down the deserted streets. "It's not safe around here."

Susannah had felt perfectly comfortable up until he'd appeared but she didn't say anything. The less she said to Phil the better, she reckoned. He fell into step beside her.

"I'll walk you to your car. A friend of mine got mugged around here not too long ago."

"It's not necessary, really," Susannah protested.

But it didn't make any difference. Phil kept right on walking alongside her. She pointed her key-fob at her car and felt reassured by the yellow lights flashing on, indicating her doors were now open.

But he surprised again when he asked suddenly, "You wouldn't mind dropping me home, would you? It's on your way."

Susannah bit her lip. She wished she were the type of person who could just say "no" without having an excuse. She tried to think of one, but before she could say anything at all, Phil had opened up the passenger seat door, dumped his rucksack across the back seat and folded himself into the front.

She got into the driver's seat warily.

"So what's your address?" she asked him as she switched on her sat nav.

"Here, let me put it in."

He punched in his details and Susannah saw with relief that he lived only a ten-minute drive away.

"Listen, I'm sorry I got a bit stroppy in there," he said as Susannah turned the car into the street.

"No need to apologise to me," Susannah said. It was Olivia's night, she felt like adding, she's the person you should be saying sorry to.

"I was having a bad day and took it out on you," he added.

"It happens," Susannah said casually, keeping her eyes on the road.

Phil then proceeded to tell her about how his wife had somehow managed to stay in the family home with their daughter even though she'd been the one to break up the relationship by having an affair, as if that were an excuse for his behavior earlier. He sounded deeply disturbed by it all and Susannah thought she'd never get him out of her car.

Finally she pulled up at his address: a big, bay-windowed

house, with different types of curtains on the windows and a general air of neglect about it.

"See that attic window?" Phil tapped on the glass. "That's my bedsitter."

"Right." Susannah kept her engine running. "Well, goodnight then."

He leaned into the back of the car to get his rucksack and Susannah shrank back a little.

"Thanks for the lift."

"You're welcome." She revved her engine.

"And Susannah?"

"Yes?"

"I really felt as if you understood where I was coming from earlier. That meant a lot to me. I find it hard to keep in control of my emotions since my marriage broke down." He looked at her meaningfully. "But you can probably understand that too. Can't you?"

When she didn't reply, he nodded, as if she had just agreed with him anyway, and finally got out of the car.

Susannah put on all the child-locks and switched on the heater, because even though it was still warm outside, she was shivering. She turned into the main road and accelerated, barely managing to stick to the speed limit until she got home. All she wanted now was to put as much distance as possible between her and the unpredictable Phil.

CHAPTER 19

Just when she was giving up hope that he would, James got back in touch. Susannah had been working on a lot of promising stories in the intervening time but she still hadn't figured out how to get case histories to accompany them so she was more than happy to hear his voice.

"I'm sorry it's taken so long," he began. "I needed to think about it a lot. But the good news is that my answer is yes – I'll do the interview with you."

"That is fantastic. Thank you so much." She sent up a prayer of gratitude to the heavens. "So when can we met?"

"I've a pretty busy week ahead of me actually. But I have some time early tomorrow morning. Could you manage breakfast?"

"Sure. Where? What time?"

James mentioned an exclusive boutique hotel on the southside of the city that apparently catered for business breakfast meetings. "Can you be there for eight fifteen?"

"Of course." Susannah noted the precise timing.

"There's one thing I need to clear up first though – there's a condition to my doing the interview."

Susannah's spirits dropped. What was the saying – if it seems too good to be true, then it is too good to be true?

"I want to read the piece first before it's published. Before it's even submitted to the paper."

Susannah hesitated. She knew it wasn't best journalistic practice and she wasn't sure the newspaper would approve.

"Look, I've only just met you," James pointed out. "And it is my personal life – and other people's lives – we're talking about here. I'm only agreeing to be interviewed because my story might help other people who are in a bad place right now. I don't want anything getting lost in translation."

Susannah thought of the camper-van column and the confusion that had come in its wake and came to a decision. "Fine. I'll let you read it."

"Great. See you tomorrow so."

She had made arrangements to go to Cara's for dinner that night so she wouldn't have time to prepare for the interview. But the train journey in to meet James in the morning would take almost an hour so she could do it then.

That night she and Cara talked about Phil again – how oddly he'd behaved at Olivia's. He had phoned Susannah the next day, apologising again for his behavior and confirming that he wouldn't be attending the book club any more. They were all relieved but Susannah was alarmed when he'd taken to phoning her out of the blue, asking about how she was getting on and whether Rob had come home yet. She tried to be as evasive as she could but the phone calls were a worry to her, although she didn't tell Cara that, because her sister felt so guilty for introducing him to the group in the first place.

As she waited to board the train to Pearse Station the next morning she reminded herself to see if James could cast any light on Phil's character. She stood on the platform, looking at the scrum of other early-morning commuters beside her. Everybody was looking at their phones, or reading on their devices or lip-synching to whatever they were listening to on their headphones. But once the train pulled into the platform, they all pushed forward in one, big movement. It seemed to be a case of squeeze onto the overcrowded train somehow or be left on the platform and Susannah found herself being carried along with them. She ended up wedged between a woman with a briefcase and a suited and booted man who was so close that her nose was actually touching the back of his tweed jacket.

So much for using the time to prepare for the interview, she fretted, trying to keep her balance as the train gathered pace. About fifteen minutes into the journey, they stopped between stations. Susannah waited for an explanation over the tannoy system but there was nothing forthcoming. She looked around at the other passengers, but nobody looked up from their electronic gadgets. Susannah figured the unscheduled stop must be a regular occurrence and, sure enough, after about ten minutes, the train took off again without warning.

Suddenly Susannah remembered this was the train Rob caught each morning to work, the commute he had been ranting about that last week before he left for Thailand. She could see first-hand now how doing this every single week morning for two decades might well take its toll on you. But, she thought as she finally escaped from the stuffy carriage, it was a pity he hadn't discussed it with her like a normal person instead of using it as an excuse to break up their marriage.

When she reached the hotel she could see straightaway it was all discreet luxury: fine furnishings, a thick plush blue carpet, ornate paintings hanging on the wall.

As she made her way to the restaurant where the meeting was to take place, she did a double take.

"I've just seen a Paris Hilton look-alike," she told James when she found him. He was sitting sipping coffee with a newspaper on the table.

"Not a lookalike. It's her!" He laughed at the star-struck

expression on Susannah's face. "I saw her earlier. I suppose she has to stay somewhere where she's in town."

Susannah took in her surroundings. The restaurant was a splendid room with ceiling-to-floor windows looking onto beautiful, manicured gardens to the rear of the hotel.

Despite the fact James had told her he had an exceptionally busy week on, hence the breakfast meeting, he looked as if he had all the time in the world.

He was smartly dressed in navy chinos and a crew-neck sweater, his silver hair neatly brushed back, literally not a hair out of place.

"I'm sorry I'm late. The train ..." Susannah started, but he waved her apologies away. Thank God, she thought – the train broke down had to be the lamest excuse ever.

He filled her glass with water from a terracotta jug on the table and handed her a menu. "Croissant? Muffins? Bacon and eggs?"

"Just coffee for me, please." She'd missed breakfast but she didn't like to eat when she was working.

He poured the coffee and gave her time to settle in before looking at her expectantly.

"So. How do we start?" he said with a smile. "I've never talked to a newspaper person before."

Susannah reckoned she'd have to go with the same tactic she'd used in London. And if it didn't work out again, she still didn't have a Plan B so she'd have to wing it.

She took a deep breath. "I thought we could start by asking you about the three major turning-points in your life?"

"That's easy. Falling in love with my ex-wife Marjorie. Divorcing my ex-wife Marjorie. And my son committing suicide." He looked at her levelly. "The last two, as you might have guessed, were not unrelated."

Susannah was nonplussed. For several seconds she literally didn't have a clue as to how she was supposed to respond. She sat there, listening to the sound of the summer shower that had blown up as it spattered the glass roof of the restaurant, wondering what to say next. I'm sorry? How awful? Everything she thought of sounded woefully inadequate in view of what he'd just told her. But if Geraldo Laffite had been a nightmare interviewee, James was just the opposite.

He launched into his story with the sort of fluency that made Susannah think that he'd told it before, many times, and she guessed that he had probably done a lot of therapy. On the other hand, people had always opened up to her. It was part of what had made her a good journalist back in the day and she was relieved to know she hadn't lost her touch. She started to relax and the words 'You can do this!' flashed into her mind.

It was the encouraging voice of her dad echoing down the years – his stock phrase for whenever she'd been afraid to try something new, or to face down a challenge. That was who James reminded her of, she realised. Her kind-hearted, twinkly-eyed father who had been the sun around which they'd all revolved.

James went on to explain how his son's death had derailed his life and how he had felt he would never recover but that somehow with good grace and the help of professional therapy and, yes, the self-help books, he had made it to the other side. Now he was living life in a way he could never have imagined, and had emerged from the turmoil with a newfound sense of purpose.

"It was a long, hard road to travel and if someone reading this interview finds any little thing in it which will help them get their lives into a better place, then I would see that as my way of giving back some of what's been given to me."

"I see. And this was the beginning of your interest in the Mind, Body, Spirit stuff?"

Susannah was genuinely interested now. Up until today she had been thinking of MBS as the domain of pampered, dissatisfied professionals who didn't know how to be grateful for what they had. Or alternatively gullible people like Harriet, ripe to be taken advantage of by the likes of Geraldo Laffite. She'd never considered these books and therapies might be a lifeline for people going through genuine hardship and heartbreak.

"Yes. I tried everything. And everything helped – a little. But then it would stop working, or I would stop working it, I was never sure. And then one day I met someone and that someone changed my life."

A woman, Susannah thought instantly. Perhaps even a second wife, she reckoned, her eyes flitting down to his left hand, but he wore no jewellery at all.

James took up the thread of his story again. The person he had met had been a friend of his son's, but he hadn't known anything about her beforehand. "As I said, there was so much I didn't know about his life." He was silent for a time, someplace inside himself, and Susannah maintained a respectful distance.

After a while, he explained how the young woman had got in touch with him on the first anniversary of his son's death and asked if she could meet up with him and Marjorie.

"What was his name – your son?" Susannah asked softly.

"Tony. His name was Tony. He was nineteen years old, his first year in college. He was studying art – I don't know much about it, but apparently his paintings showed major promise."

"And the woman who got in contact with you. How did she know Tony?"

"They were friends – Maria was an art student too. She seemed to know more about Tony than I did. My wife didn't go to the meeting – at the time she was barely getting through the days, didn't see the point. So I went by myself – I saw the girl as a connection to Tony, you know?"

Susannah nodded.

"And she told me Tony would want me to be happy. He'd struggled so hard to be happy himself, that was the best thing I could for him: find it within myself to be as happy as it was possible for me to be. She was a very enlightened young woman." He sighed, lost in memories for a few moments. Then he continued. "Anyhow she said I had to make my own healing a priority, that I had to learn to be selfish. It's funny, all the time I had spent in therapy nobody had ever said that to me. I didn't understand what she meant at first but it kept going round and round in my head, and then one day everything she said made sense to me. So I learned to be selfish."

"And then what happened?" Susannah asked.

"Then my life totally fell apart." He grinned ruefully. "Things got worse – a lot worse. But when I started practising being selfish I realised I despised my job as an IT consultant – that all the hours I had worked at it had made me bitter and absent from my wife, my family, myself. My son." He looked immeasurably sad. "That Marjorie and I had changed from who we were when we'd met first, and that the tragedy of Tony's death had taken a heavy toll on us. Well, on Marjorie more than me – she'd been the one who'd been more involved with his care – he'd suffered with clinical depression from his early teens. I didn't know how to cope with it, so I just left it to her, I suppose." James traced the rim of his water glass with his index finger. "Anyhow I didn't know what to do next so I took a career break and did some soul-searching."

Disappointment washed over Susannah, followed by a quick flash of anger. He was starting to sound more like Rob than her dad now – another selfish man looking out for number one. What about poor Marjorie? Where was she in all this? Suddenly she wanted to wrap up the interview as quickly as possible.

"Are you okay?" he asked, instantly picking up on the change in her attitude.

All the years indulging in his self-help whinge-fest must have sharpened his intuition at least, Susannah thought darkly.

"I'm fine." She raised her eyebrows. "Please. Go on."

She had to force herself to keep her personal feelings under wraps. This was her job now, and she needed to maintain her professionalism.

She concentrated hard while James explained how he'd rebuilt his life, brick by painful brick, until one day he'd realised he had built up a positive momentum and had actually begun to enjoy life again. They talked about what therapies he had found most useful and how personal development had become a way of life for him.

"It helped me fight a whole new set of demons when Marjorie left me."

"She left you?" Susannah tried to keep the surprise out her voice.

"Yes. She'd had enough by that stage. I don't blame her either – although I didn't think so at the time. I was still full of self-pity then."

"I know what that feels like," Susanna said. And then, to her own surprise, and despite her earlier determination to be professional, she found herself telling him all about Rob. She knew it was wrong of course, even as she was yabbering on.

And on. It felt like the time she'd channelled the spirit of Elizabeth Castle into writing the camper-van column. Once she'd started, she couldn't stop. She explained about her husband's unilateral decision to go off on a career break without her, the secret savings stash, the travel forums she'd come across.

"I thought Rob was working for us, you know? The family unit. But it turns out he was just interested in himself." She still couldn't believe how hurt she felt about it, all these months later.

"I know what it's like to wake up one day and discover that the job you hated but did anyway because it provided for your family turned out to be the thing that destroyed the same family, because it made you so miserable to be with," James said quietly. "Sorry," he added, taking in her look of annoyance.

"There's no need to be." Susannah thought of her healthy daughters and suddenly felt ashamed at the way she was going on, as if Rob leaving was the end of the world. James had gone through unimaginable grief and yet, here he was, willing to bare his soul in the hope that it might help someone else.

It was time to get a grip, she decided.

"I guess if Rob hadn't gone I wouldn't be here sitting with you now, getting paid for something that frankly I would do for nothing. I wouldn't have gone to London. I'd probably be putting in another wash and counting off the calendar to when the girls would be home and moaning about my mid-life crisis. So if I'm looking for a silver lining, there's certainly one to be had." She smiled ruefully.

"What took you to London?" James asked.

Susannah explained about the *Flow Your Life* seminar, how the walking-on-fire element had been cancelled, and how she'd found the first couple of days slightly bizarre.

"I've heard of Geraldo Laffite. I was considering doing a seminar with him myself actually. It's on in different European countries each year. I think it's in Barcelona later this year."

"And maybe Dublin," Susannah told him. "That's why the *Post* was there. Although you could save your money. I thought Geraldo was a bit creepy to be honest – all fake tan and gold chains."

"Yes, I've heard he's very theatrical. But that's okay if what he's offering helps. And I've read his books and I liked them." He drummed his fingers lightly on the table. "I like to keep an open mind."

Susannah realised this should be her speech. After hearing James' story, she saw now she couldn't approach this MBS subject as the political journalist she'd once been, constantly on the alert for empty promises and posturing.

She still thought Geraldo Laffite was probably a charlatan but she guessed she'd need to be more sensitive about sharing that viewpoint in the future. What mattered most were the opinions of the people who'd paid to be there. She'd need to find a way to get in touch with Harriet again, she realised, and find out if the seminar had made any actual difference to her life.

"Thank you very much for agreeing to meet me," she said.

He smiled weakly. He seemed exhausted and Susannah recognised how emotional he must be feeling after reliving his story for her.

"Are you okay?" she asked uncertainly. "You look a bit pale."

He rubbed his face with both hands.

"It never gets easier, telling that story," he confessed.

"Would you like more coffee?" She felt way out of her depth but it didn't seem right for her to just stand up and leave now, as she would in the course of a normal interview.

"If you have time, that would be lovely." He seemed relieved at her suggestion. "But let's talk about something else, shall we?"

CHAPTER 20

Katie sat at her desk, flicking through the MBS pages. She had made the *Flow Your Life* story into a double-page spread. There was a photo of Geraldo and some of the participants, including Susannah grinning out of the page, sent on by the PR company handling the event.

She wondered what the errant husband would think of her now. Susannah had told Katie how he'd tried to forbid her to include anything about him in any of her future columns. The arrogance of the man. Susannah deserved a medal for having put up with him all those years.

She didn't think herself and Luke would last that long. Unless it got better, and so far, it hadn't. The random acts of kindness weren't working. Well, specifically the one random act of kindness hadn't worked. She hadn't dreamed up any more yet. She'd enough to do to look after herself without looking for people to be kind to, in fairness.

It was starting to dawn on her that she didn't know Luke as well as she'd thought. She could never have predicted how his voice would grate on her nerves as he told her how lucky she was, again, for having such a creative job, while he complained – again – about how hard it was to find the time to write his thriller while he had a full-time job. A bit of discipline would have gone a long way, she'd wanted to tell him. Like going to bed and getting up at roughly the same time instead of the erratic hours he kept.

She'd had a moment of sheer panic during the week when for a mad minute she thought he was actually going to suggest he give up his job to concentrate on writing full-time. The thought of Luke in her apartment all day long – even if she wasn't there – filled her with horror and that was before she'd even got around to wondering about what he would do for money.

She became aware of a shadow hovering over her and sighed when she looked up to see Jennifer. It was nearly going-home time and she wasn't in the mood for idle chatter.

"Mike wants to see you." Jennifer tapped her fingers on the double-page spread of the *Flow Your Life* seminar. "And I must warn you, he's on the warpath – he's not happy with this at all."

Katie shrugged. Jennifer would say that. She didn't expect her to forgive her any time soon for sending Susannah to London instead of her.

"Thanks," she muttered and returned her attention to the newspaper, scanning through the story again. There was no doubt about it, Susannah was a very good writer.

The phone rang and when she picked it up it was Mike, snapping something about them needing a chat, pronto.

Katie grabbed her notebook and pen and walked down to his office in some trepidation. She had no idea what could be wrong with Susannah's feature. But Mike was staring at the newspaper spread out on the desk in front of him with a great big frown on his face.

"You wanted to see me?" She hovered at the door.

"Yes, I did. Stop lurking over there. Come in and sit down." He waved an imperious hand in the direction of the chair in front of his desk.

"Is there something wrong? Jennifer thought that maybe –"

"Yes. This is what's wrong." He placed his elbows on the desk, interlinked his fingers together, laid his chin on his hands and stared at her. "Geraldo Laffite – is that even a real name? – is threatening to sue me, you, her." He stabbed a knobby finger at the photo-byline of Susannah smiling up at him.

"For what?" Katie leaned forward to inspect the piece, as if she could figure out if there was something she had missed by scanning it upside down. "There's nothing defamatory there."

Mike snorted. "I sincerely hope you are correct because I don't have the time right now to go through it with a fine-tooth comb. I won't get home until nine as it is and I have back-to-back meetings tomorrow. I have enough on my plate without having to deal with this geezer. What do you think his problem might be?"

"Er …" Katie thought hard. Susannah had written a robust account of the seminar, including her own substantial reservations about whether gullible people could be tricked into parting with large amounts of money in vain – but she was entitled to do that.

"Er …?" Mike was at his most bullish this evening. "That's your answer? If I'd known I was going to have to be doing all this hand-holding, I wouldn't have made you features editor, Katie."

Katie bit her lip. "He made an advance to Susannah – asked her did she want to see his Big Thing and she refused. Maybe he's angry that he was spurned and he's trying to make trouble for her now by threatening to sue?"

"That is disgusting!" The boss took a handkerchief out of his trouser pocket and rubbed it across his mouth, as if the incident was making him nauseous.

"But he can't have consulted lawyers because they would have told him there's nothing he can sue us for." Katie crossed her fingers in her lap. She hoped she was right. She'd need, as Mike had suggested, to study it with a fine-tooth comb.

"I don't think I want to hear any more. I'll forward on his email on to you. And Katie?"

"Yes?"

"Find a way to make this go away."

As soon as she got back to her desk, Katie reread the feature carefully, one eye on the content and the other on Geraldo's email. His alleged problem was that Susannah had been unsympathetic and portrayed him in an unfair light. The first part of the sentence was fair enough, but that was tough on Geraldo. They had promised to cover the seminar, not to write an advertisement for it. The second part – about portraying him in an unfair light – might cause them problems.

"Geraldo Laffite provides little proof that his unorthodox methods work in the long-term," Susannah had written. *"He uses theatrics and adrenaline-boosting exercises at his seminars to make the participants feel they can do much, much more with their lives. Break out of their comfort zones, achieve goals that may seem impossible. But how do we know what the real results are? We don't know what happens when these people go back to their real lives. And call me cynical, but a few glowing testimonials on publicity material is not enough."*

In his email he'd argued that Susannah had made no effort to contact any of the participants herself to find out how effective his seminars were in the long term or otherwise. It was a legitimate criticism.

She rubbed her eyes. She was exhausted. She'd had a bad start to the day and it hadn't got any better. This morning when she'd jumped into her shower – she still thought of it as 'her' shower – the water had been cold. Luke had gone out early – to write his novel in the office for an hour or two before work started apparently – and he'd obviously used all the hot water. She'd have to get one of those electric ones with instant hot water installed. She sighed. She could add that to her list of things she needed to do to make her apartment more couple-friendly.

She closed the newspaper. She'd have to be in the whole of her health before she could bring herself to ring Geraldo Laffite. In fact, she mused, maybe she didn't need to ring him at all. Susannah herself should probably call him in the first instance.

Sometimes that was all that was needed – people just wanted to feel some love from whomever they felt had misunderstood them. Then they'd let go of whatever it was that was bothering them. She picked up the phone.

"Susannah? We need to talk. We may have a problem with Geraldo Laffite."

"Oh no! Did I screw up?" Susannah sounded terrified.

"Hopefully not. But we need to discuss it in person." Mike was right. This was just the sort of thing that could blow up in your face if you ignored it. "Would now be convenient?"

"Yes. For me. But aren't you finished for the day? It's after six."

Katie ignored the anxiety in the other woman's voice. Technically it could wait until tomorrow but if she could delegate it to Susannah this evening it meant she could tell Mike first thing in the morning that it was sorted and he'd know she was back on her game.

And besides, it would be a break between the office and home because she knew if Luke did one more little thing to aggravate her this evening there was every chance they'd have a very bad argument.

"I can call out to you if you like?"

"To my house? Do you know it can take up to an hour to get here from the city?"

Katie brushed off Susannah's surprise. She'd evidently forgotten that journalism wasn't a nine-to-five job. "That's no problem. What's your address?"

She scribbled down the details, hung up the phone, and grabbed her stuff.

In the car, she punched Susannah's address into her satnav, switched the radio to a country station she liked and relaxed into the drive.

The traffic was busy but not deadlocked and she enjoyed watching the passers-by jogging along the coast, or having a beer outside the bars that lined the route. It was a glorious summer's evening, something she hadn't appreciated when she'd been chained to her desk all day. By the time she was pulling into Susannah's cobble-locked drive, Katie was feeling a lot better.

She rang the bell and, while she waited for an answer, she stood back and inspected the house. It was far too big for one person. Detached in a street of other detached family homes in an affluent area. Katie could understand how Susannah would feel all at sea here, now that the daughters had left home and the husband had done a runner.

Susannah opened the door, her face a mask of anxiety, one hand balled into a fist by her side.

"Come in," she said tightly and gestured for Katie to follow her.

The distinctive scent of the tiger lilies stuffed into a vase in the hallway wafted through the air and there was classical music playing at a low volume in the background.

Katie followed Susannah out to the kitchen, a spotless, minimalist space that could have featured in a lifestyle feature. There were framed photographs of the Stevens family on every wall and the house still felt solidly like a family home.

"Sit down." Susannah pulled out a kitchen chair for her. "Tell me what's wrong."

"There's no need to panic. It will probably just take a phone call, that's all. But it's best we deal with it as quickly as possible. If we go through it this evening you could phone Laffite first thing in the morning."

"Me phone him?" Susannah sounded shocked.

"Yes, I think that might be the best idea."

"But what's it about?"

"He says in his email that you didn't bother to follow up with any of the participants to find out what sort of long-term effect the seminars had on their lives. But this was an area you sought to criticise in your article."

"That's true. But I was going to talk to people on the day he cancelled the seminar."

"So he'll probably say you should have got the contact numbers from him and conducted some telephone interviews."

"I never thought of that." Susannah frowned. "And I can see his point now."

"Yes, but there's nothing to sue us with. You have to make him see that. We can't have him bothering Mike. So you need to ease troubled waters."

"And how do I do that?"

"Phone him. Try to find out more about where he's coming from. If you can't calm him down, then I'll take it over. But I don't want to give his petty complaint a level of seriousness it doesn't deserve unless I really have to."

Susannah looked worried. "What do you suggest I say? It's a long time since I've done anything like this."

"Listen to him. Say you hear where he's coming from. Explain how the feature is really good publicity for him and his seminars. I see in his email he's all 'get your people to call my people' so you'll probably get through to one of his minions first."

"Okay. Hopefully I can sort it out." Susannah sounded as if she was being asked to broker a peace deal for the Middle East but Katie reckoned she could figure it out as she went along.

The sun had disappeared behind a cloud and Susannah lit a table lamp, the yellow glow brightening up the room.

"Have you eaten?"

"Not since lunchtime. I could do with a cup of coffee."

"I was just about to eat myself when you called and I held off. I can make a couple of sandwiches."

Susannah busied herself with the kettle and plates and Katie stood up and wandered into the conservatory. The light was beautiful at this time of evening and sometimes she missed having a garden. This one though was overgrown and neglected and she reckoned hers would be the same if she had one.

Susannah arrived with a tray of pastrami, salad and rye sandwiches and two mugs of coffee and asked Katie to move a book on the wicker table out of her way.

"I'm reading that for my book club," she said. "It's good. I'll keep it for you when I'm finished if you like. Are you a reader?"

"I don't have time for reading." Katie put the book on to the cane sofa and sat down at the table.

"I love reading. I've always been in some sort of a reading group, although my current book club has become a bit controversial. One of the new members took umbrage at something that came up in the discussion."

Susannah sounded upset, confirming Katie's suspicion that she would hate to be in a book club, having to listen to people project all their own prejudices onto the story. Or maybe she just didn't like being with people all that much, she thought darkly, thinking of her problem with Luke again.

"Listen – d'you think there's anything in this spiritual atonement malarkey?" Katie asked. "I've been thinking of Croagh Patrick again." Thinking she didn't want to spend hours on the side of a mountain if there wasn't a point to it – if it wasn't going to fix her and Luke.

"To be honest, when you mentioned it to me first, I didn't. But recently I met someone and he reminded me that I need to be more open-minded about these things. How much do we know really about something we haven't experienced? So I'll reserve judgment for the time being."

"That's true enough. So will we do it? Climb the mountain. Me for penance and you for the feature? I could do with a weekend away anyway. My apartment is a bit bijoux for two people living in it. I can find a hotel with a spa and a decent restaurant so we can recover from all the climbing. When can you go?"

Susannah explained about James and that he was part of her next feature. "I need to go through some things with him again. And I've to get back to Orlaith – she's going to book my flight to New York. But apart from those two things, I'm free."

It had been a productive evening, Katie mused, as she drove back home. She had delegated Geraldo Laffite and his problems and the Croagh Patrick weekend had the green light. Maybe time away from Luke would help her figure out what was really wrong between them.

But no sooner had she turned the key in the door of the apartment than all the tension returned. Rock music was blaring out of the living room and Luke was sprawled on the couch. He was staring at his laptop, one hand on the keyboard the other in a bag of popcorn. How could he expect to write a book with that racket going on, Katie thought irritably, going over to snap off the music.

"Hello, Gorgeous," he said, half looking up from his laptop.

She frowned. Hello, Gorgeous. That's what Daniel Gilbert used to say to her. And Luke never had. Weird.

"So what are we having for dinner?" she asked, noticing there was no sign of any cooking going on.

"Um –" he looked at her vaguely, as if dinner was a strange, abstract subject – "take-away?"

"Take-away is unhealthy."

"Not once a week." He finally looked up from his laptop and looked at her properly. "Are you okay? You look a bit pale."

"I'm hungry," she lied.

"Hangry more like," he grinned. "You know when hunger is making you angry?"

Jesus. Katie stomped out to her kitchen and took down the dinner-making rota she'd pinned to the fridge. She came back and stood over Luke, waving it in front of him.

"Oh, for God's sake! You're not seriously wanting to have this conversation now, are you?" he said. "I've finally got back into my book, I've got that knotty plot problem solved and I'm motoring. I can't waste my creative time on cooking dinner."

"I don't think cooking healthy food is a waste of time." Katie wasn't going to tell him that she'd eaten already in Susannah's — not when she'd made dinner for the past three nights. There was a principle here to defend.

"Well, I do." He stood up, grabbed the rota sheet and stared at it. "And for the record, I never agreed to be part of this."

"You didn't?" Katie's voice came out in a squeak.

"No. You assumed I'd want to be part of it. I don't live like that, Katie. I can't."

"So why didn't you tell me that when I was pinning this onto the fridge?" she snapped.

Suddenly she felt really upset. She hardly ever argued with anyone.

"Because —"

He took a step towards her and she flinched. An old memory had risen up out of nowhere. Her dad shouting at her mother — her face pale and bewildered. What was it about? The woman he'd left them for?

"Katie? Are you even listening to me?"

Luke's voice sounded angry. And loud. Had he just shouted at her? He was towering over her, in any case, his face a mask of frustration.

She took a step back.

"Get out of my space, Luke."

"Your space?" He was exasperated now and that just added to Katie's mounting distress.

This row (because that's what it had developed into, in an unexpected flash) and the other, half-remembered one from years ago somehow merged into one and crowded out all rational thought for Katie.

She turned away, grabbed the bag and coat she'd just put down and moved towards the front door. Outside, she ran down the four flights of stairs she'd just climbed, trying to stop the panic that was rising in her chest. Outside in the street, she stopped, wondering where she thought she was going or what had just come over her.

"Katie!"

She looked up to see that Luke had his head out the window of the apartment.

"Come back!" he shouted. "We need to sort this out!"

Oh, lovely. Now he was drawing attention to himself. And her. She ducked her head and walked away, her shoes barely touching the pavement until she'd turned the corner at the end of the street and she could no longer hear Luke's voice pleading with her to come back.

She stopped and stood beside a bus stop, waiting for her heart to stop thumping. How in hell had this happened?

Had Luke had a personality change since he'd moved in? Had she?

She didn't know the answers but the problem with Geraldo Laffite threatening to sue the paper now seemed like a minor hurdle compared to her personal problems.

In fact, she felt like getting back on to Susannah and offering to ring Geraldo herself after all. She could eat the head off him, direct some of this inexplicable rage she didn't know what to do with at him.

Which wouldn't be the wisest thing to do, she realised, but it made her wonder why she wasn't afraid of facing a top international guru with a possible army of lawyers in his employ and yet she had just run away from what should have been a minor disagreement with Luke?

She knew Olivia would give her some psychobabble about mixing up the present with the past and she'd point out, once again, that she had issues she needed to work through. But Katie wasn't about to sit in a therapist's office bleating about abandonment no matter how many times Olivia told her that.

That wasn't who she was. She was independent. And strong. She knew how to find solutions. She would go back, right now, and sort everything out with Luke.

But when she went to retrace her steps, she found she couldn't. It was like her legs wouldn't work the way she wanted them to. She knew she was too uptight to have a rational conversation right now anyhow. If she did go home, it was highly likely she'd tell Luke about Daniel Gilbert, just to give them something meaningful to fight about it. But where else could she go?

She thought of the evening she'd just spent in Susannah Stevens' house. The scent of lilies, the family photographs, how she'd somehow managed to create a sense of safety and security in the house that everyone had left, bar her.

On impulse she took out her mobile and punched in her number.

"Susannah? It's me again. Katie. I know this sounds ridiculous but something's come up. Could you possibly put me up for tonight?"

CHAPTER 21

The next morning, Susannah was standing in her kitchen, trying to puzzle out what had happened to drive Katie Corrigan back out to her house last night. It was bizarre enough that she'd insisted on coming out the first time. The problem with Geraldo, aggravating as it was, could clearly have waited until today.

She must have used it as an excuse not to go home. She had looked pale and distressed when she returned and not inclined to talk so Susannah hadn't asked any questions. She put her in the twins' old room – delighted she'd taken the time earlier in the year to do her massive clear-out.

And then this morning Katie was up, showered and gone without as much as a cup of coffee.

"I'll pick up something on the way to the office," she'd muttered, when Susannah offered to make her breakfast.

Susannah frowned, wondering if Orlaith and Jess had such hectic days at work that they didn't have time to eat. Probably – seeing as it was New York they were working in. And why hadn't Katie phoned Olivia instead of her? It was worrying but Susannah didn't see what she could do about it. Katie was a grown woman. And her boss. And she had work to do herself today.

She had this morning earmarked to write the feature about

219

James but first she needed to make the call she was dreading. Geraldo Laffite. She called the number on the email and, as Katie had predicted, an assistant picked up the phone.

"Mr Laffite is otherwise engaged at this time," she said. She'd get him to call her back "a.s.a.p."

But by early afternoon he still hadn't returned the call. Susannah read through the draft of the story she'd written about James critically, pinpointing places where the manuscript would need to be edited and tidied up, wondering what parts James might veto.

It would be better if he could approve it now, she realised – before she did any more work on it. It would save her having to restructure the whole piece, if James objected to something fundamental in it.

She opened up her email and typed 'feature for approval' into the subject line but then she thought it would be better if she could talk to him in person. She could gauge his reaction more accurately if she was there when he was reading it and they could discuss any potential problems he might have. She tapped out his mobile number and he picked up immediately.

"Hi. It's Susannah Stevens here. I have the first draft of the feature done and I was wondering …"

"Already?"

"Yes." She hoped he didn't think she'd just dashed something off. "But it's not finished. I wanted to discuss it with you first."

"Still – you're a fast worker. I saw your story on the *Flow Your Life* seminar today. I liked it. Well done."

Susannah couldn't allow herself to be happy about that – not with Geraldo threatening to sue her.

"Thanks. So listen, you were saying you wanted to read over it. If you could take a look at it, see if I'm on the right track, it might save a lot of rewriting down the line for me. And I could come by the shop this afternoon, if you're free?"

"I'm in Belfast. I'll be here until late afternoon at a meeting. But I can meet you this evening on my way home?"

"That would be fantastic. There are a lot of coffee shops in my neighbourhood."

"Great. I'll give you a ring when I'm approaching Dublin." There was a pause. "But I could call by your house if that would be easier?"

"If you're sure it's no trouble." Susannah was delighted. She hadn't got used to this personal sort of writing and she felt very unsure about it. It would be helpful if there weren't any casual eavesdroppers close by if James decided he hated the piece.

She gave him the directions to her house, then printed off the article so it would be ready when he arrived. She spent an hour in the garden, digging away at the weeds, her mobile on the ground beside her in case Geraldo Laffite called back. When the rain started she came back in, showered and changed. Then she started cooking.

By the time the doorbell rang she had a beef stew simmering away on the stove, filling the house with the aroma of home-made food: garlic, beef, onions, potatoes and the good red wine she insisted on using for this dish. Rob used to insist good wine was wasted in food because the heat burned all the alcohol off and had been unimpressed by her conviction that it added to the overall taste of the food.

She opened the hall door to James, who was looking a bit wan and tired in the fading light of the day.

"Come in." She pulled the door open wider and, as he stepped inside, added automatically, "Will you have a cup of tea? Or coffee?"

"Coffee would be good, thanks." He pulled his tie loose and shoved it into the pocket of his black suit jacket. "I was on the road at five thirty this morning and I've had meetings all day."

She led him into the kitchen and looked at him speculatively.

"Have you eaten?" She gestured towards the stove. "I make a ton of food in one go because I never feel it's worth cooking for one. I'm happy to share."

"I'm starving. Haven't had a thing to eat. And the only way I get to eat anything that smells as good as whatever you have on that stove is if I go to a fine-dining restaurant."

"Great." Susannah handed him the printout of the article. "Wait until we've eaten before you read this. Everything seems better on a full stomach."

He glanced at the pages then laid them to one side on the table while Susannah bustled around setting up the table for two.

As they sat down to eat, she was struck again at how comfortable she felt with him. She told him about her plans to go to New York, about finding ways to move on and having to accept her marriage was over.

"Are you sure about that?" James asked gently. "Rob sounds as if he was in a really difficult place."

"He looks a lot happier now all right. On his Facebook page anyway. And why wouldn't he be? He's in a sunny country with no responsibilities."

She knew that sounded bitter and she didn't want every single evening to be hijacked by the subject of Rob so she asked James about something that had been bothering her.

"How long has Phil worked for you?" she asked casually.

"Oh, about two years. I don't know him that well though. He's always on time, loves reading, loves books. He's a good manager. Why?"

She told him about the book-club meeting and how Phil had been so edgy, but she didn't say anything about driving him home or how he'd taken to ringing her at odd times ever since.

"He seemed to have a lot of pent-up anger and when I asked Cara – that's my sister – how well she knew him – it turned out she didn't."

"If he's angry he goes out of his way to hide it, and it's certainly never caused any trouble at work. Maybe it's something to do with the way his marriage broke up?"

That's what Olivia had said.

"It's hard to be the one left behind," James added. "I know I was very angry when Marjorie left me."

The anger hadn't come for Susannah for a long time after Rob left. All she'd felt was fear. Fear of being on her own, of not being part of a couple, of not having a role in life or any personal goals of her own. She felt sick now when she thought back to how she'd begged him not to go.

After dinner, they brought their drinks into the living room – red wine for Susannah, coffee for her guest. James put on his glasses and started to read the piece and Susannah found herself knocking back more wine than she'd intended to while she watched him carefully. But his features remained inscrutable as his eyes flicked over the pages. By the time he finished and looked up at her, she was a nervous wreck, clutching the stem of her wineglass far too tightly.

"It's perfect," he said simply.

"Oh thank goodness!" She breathed out a huge sigh of relief. "I wasn't sure at all what your reaction was going to be. And I couldn't make anything out from your expression. You'd make a good poker player."

He smiled. "I have no concerns at all about this going into the paper. You are a fine writer, Susannah. I know you said you sort of fell into this job, but portraying sensitive human-interest stories in a way that's interesting and respectful at the same time – not everybody has that. It's a gift – and one the world needs."

"Well, I'm flattered. Actually, I'm in a bit of bother with the *Flow Your Life* feature. Geraldo has a problem with it." She bit her lip, wondering why he still hadn't called. "If I get a better footing in the paper I might try and diversify into something easier. Like politics."

223

"What's his problem? I'm no lawyer but it didn't seem in any way contentious to me."

"I didn't follow up on something I should have. But, quite apart from that, he's a very strange man." After half a bottle of wine it seemed easy to relate the Big Thing incident to James. "Katie – she's my editor – said it was just a straightforward pass that I turned down so it was all no big deal. I thought it was extremely unprofessional but I've been out of the workplace for a long time ... and ..." She felt flustered suddenly. She looked at James. "What do you think?"

"I can't blame him for making a pass at you, if that's what he was doing. But you were the one who was there, so I'd say trust your own instincts."

I can't blame him for making a pass at you. Did that mean James found her attractive? Susannah realised she hadn't felt attractive for a long time. Long before Rob had taken himself off, first to the box-room and then to Thailand. Now, she had no idea if James was just being kind to her or if he meant something more. She had that sense again that the world had gone on without her and she didn't know how to behave in it any more.

Not that it made any difference, she thought gloomily. She was hardly going to do a Katie Corrigan and have a one-night stand with a perfect stranger, no matter what he thought of her.

Her eyes fell on the framed photograph of Elizabeth Castle and for a moment she felt she was staring straight at her. Really? she seemed to be saying. You do realise that nobody lives forever, don't you? And how bad would it be if you were to do something out of character for once? Or if something good and joyful happened in Pine Close after so much misery?

Alarmed at where her thoughts – or rather, Elizabeth Castle's thoughts – were taking her, especially because James didn't seem in the slightest bit interested in anything other than finishing his coffee, Susannah was relieved when the sound of her phone interrupted them.

"Excuse me," she said, "I have to take this." She looked at the screen. "It's Geraldo!" she said in a stage-whisper.

She answered the call.

"Yes, this is Susannah Stevens. Thanks for calling back."

Her dread at having to talk to Geraldo was considerably lessened now by the fact that the call had stopped her potentially making an awful fool of herself with James.

James stood up to leave.

"Geraldo, can you hold for a moment?"

She led James to the hall door, the phone still stuck at her ear. "Thank you for calling by – and I'll let you know when the article is going to be in the paper."

He smiled and left and Susannah took a deep breath and prepared to tackle Geraldo Laffite.

"I believe you've a problem with the feature I wrote," she said lightly.

"I felt it was very unfair. You wrote it as if I were a charlatan. You didn't do me any favours, Susannah."

She felt like saying that wasn't what she was being paid for, but she had to focus on the fact that she was supposed to be persuading him to call off his legal watchdogs.

"I'm sorry you feel like that. But I wasn't writing an advertorial and you knew that. People pay a lot of money for your seminars and my obligation was to any of our readers thinking of doing that."

"But you didn't interview anybody at the seminar. Lots of people there were return visitors. If it didn't have a good long-term effect on their lives they wouldn't have been there, would they?"

Susannah thought that was debatable. Harriet had graduated from not breaking a block to breaking a block. She still had the same life, longing to find love while working in a village with no eligible men. If she had spent her time and money looking for another job with people in the same situation as herself, she could have got better results for a lot less money.

"I'd intended to interview people the day we were supposed to be walking on fire but you cancelled the seminar," she reminded him.

"So why didn't you call me? I can get lots of people to speak to you."

She had no intention of calling Geraldo's hand-picked posse. Probably the same ones who'd written the testimonials on his website.

"Look, the feature I wrote generated a lot of interest with our readers. I tried to give my honest opinion and I think that resonated with people."

That was true enough. Katie had said that Geraldo Laffite could fill several seminars in Dublin if her inbox was anything to go by. She'd said they might even do a follow-up on Geraldo at a later stage.

"How about you get me Harriet's number and I'll call her?" she suggested. "You remember she was the young journalist who broke the block?"

"Of course I remember. She wrote an article I was very pleased with as a matter of fact. I will send it on to you."

"And her telephone number. I might even do a follow-up on the seminar."

"Okay then." That pleased him. And then: "So how have you been, Susannah?"

"Fine." Susannah figured the less she said the better.

It was hard for her to reconcile this mild-mannered man with the one who'd wanted to show her his Big Thing and had written an angry email about her to her employers.

Geraldo seemed to have a bit of a Dr Jekyll/Mr Hyde going

on with his personality. It could be down to anything – too much drink or drugs – or maybe it was just who he was. Either way she could never know which version of him she was going to meet. She was just glad she had Dr Jekyll for now. A Dr Jekyll who was pacified by the possibility of a follow-up feature which meant she had only good things to report to Katie tomorrow.

She finished up the conversation before he could switch back again and congratulated herself on the successful outcome.

Later that night, when she was lying in bed, Susannah found herself replaying the evening in her mind. She'd handled Geraldo Laffite better than she'd anticipated. And she'd really enjoyed having dinner with James.

She felt he liked her and, even though it was probably a throwaway remark when he said he could understand it if Geraldo found her attractive, it was nice of him to say it. He was a sensitive man and would have sensed her self-esteem had taken a battering after Robgate.

Even if she never saw him again, she would always be glad they'd met. Having to write his story had helped get her own problems into perspective and made her see that she had so much to look forward to.

After she filed the story on James she was going to finalise her New York trip and then she had Croagh Patrick with Katie coming up too. She smiled to herself. Somewhere along the way her life had started to work again and she fell asleep feeling more relaxed than she had for a long time.

So when she awoke with a start, all the old feelings of gloom back again, she was bitterly disappointed. She fumbled for her phone and squinted at the time. 4.00am. Again. How could her mood have changed so dramatically in such a short space of time?

Maybe she'd had another nightmare. There were flashes of a dream all right. Something she couldn't quite remember – to do with the row with Phil. An image of him flashed through her mind – the tall, six-foot build, the closely cropped haircut, the rugged complexion. And then she realised what it was about him that bothered her: he reminded her of her stalker from all those years ago.

Her heart started to speed up again as she compared their images in her head. There was no doubting the resemblance. But her stalker would be twenty years older than Phil. Had she been projecting her negative feelings onto him because she hadn't resolved something from her past? Maybe she had, but there was no doubt that Phil was weird in any case, with his own admission that he couldn't always control his temper, and the unpredictable phone calls to her at odd times of the day and night.

Maybe she'd ask Olivia to refer her to someone after all, she thought, and put that whole episode from the past back into the past, where it belonged. She had turned on her side, trying to get comfortable, when a strange, rattling noise made her freeze.

Suddenly the remnants of a half-remembered nightmare or even a stalker from decades ago were the least of her worries. She sat up slowly, all her senses alert, trying to figure out where the sound had come from. Downstairs, she thought.

She tried to calm herself down – think of a logical explanation for what she'd heard. A wind had blown up – maybe it was rattling the windows now. She'd been in the garden earlier – had she forgotten to close the conservatory door properly?

What had Geraldo said at the seminar? Fear is only what you make it in your head. He was right. She was just frightening herself. She'd go down and investigate, put her mind at ease, instead of lying here paralysed with terror. She slipped out of bed and pulled on her dressing gown, tightening the belt protectively around her. She tiptoed down the stairs and stopped in the hallway, glancing towards the rear of the house.

The conservatory door seemed to be shut tight. She looked at her hall door. Maybe she hadn't closed it properly when James was leaving? She'd been distracted by the phone call with Geraldo. Could James have forgotten his phone and was trying to retrieve it without waking her? It seemed an unlikely scenario but Susannah didn't want to consider the alternative.

And then she heard it again. It was a scuffling noise. The sound of someone moving. And it was coming from her living room. Someone was in the house! She stayed very quiet, rooted to the spot, but her mind was racing.

She just needed to — what?

The kitchen door was maybe twenty steps away. She could creep towards it and lock herself in. There'd be knives there if she needed a weapon. Or that heavy crystal vase that had been a gift from her aunt for the 25th wedding anniversary she and Rob had never celebrated. But she didn't feel she'd be able to knife someone or batter them over the head all that easily either.

"James?" she called hopefully, her voice so soft it was barely audible. But it brought a fresh flurry of movement from inside the living room and the door was flung open. Susannah's throat tightened as a man emerged and stood in the doorway. It certainly wasn't James in his good black business suit.

The intruder was wearing dark baggy jeans and had a black hoody pulled up over his head. A shabby green knapsack was hoisted over one shoulder. It was bulging with objects and Susannah could see he'd got a sizeable haul from the living room already.

Why had she come down? She should have locked herself in her bedroom and pretended to be asleep She cursed the insanity she'd called bravery earlier, cursed Geraldo Laffite even more for brainwashing her into not heeding her own instincts.

Face Your Fear indeed, she thought. Her throat was dry and her muscles were rigid with tension, ready to flee.

But could she outrun him? Would it be better instead to try

and talk him around? She could tell him to take his haul and leave now and in return she wouldn't even ring the police.

He moved again and Susannah caught sight of his shoes, scuffed black sneakers with dirty laces. Something registered at the back of her mind. There was something familiar about them. In fact, she was sure she'd seen them before.

"Phil?" she asked.

A noise gurgled in the back of his throat and the man lunged at her, pulling back his hood at the same time.

Adrenaline surged through her and she darted towards the kitchen.

"Susannah?"

She stopped dead at the sound of a voice as familiar to her as her own.

She turned around slowly, a sob stifled in her throat.

"Rob?"

CHAPTER 22

"What the —?" Susannah didn't know whether she was more surprised that Rob was home or at the state of him. "What the hell happened to you?"

He rubbed a weary hand over his face. "Twenty-hour flight with stop-overs. Haven't had much to eat. Is there anything for a sandwich?"

"I'm sure there is." Susannah was still recovering from the fright he'd just given her. "What were you doing in the living room?"

"I sat down for a rest. And then got up again. Why are you making such a big deal about it?"

"I thought you were a burglar."

He gave her an odd look. "A burglar named James? Or Phil?"

She raised her eyes to heaven and moved towards the kitchen. Rob remained where he was, standing in the same spot, as if he didn't have the energy to take a step forward or back.

She looked back at him, still shocked to see him. "Put down your rucksack at least."

Rob hoisted the rucksack off his shoulder and it fell with a thud onto the hall carpet. He followed her into the kitchen, pulled out a chair and sat down. In the bright light he looked even more bedraggled. Susannah could see that his skin was yellowish rather than tanned. The dark circles etched under his eyes had a blue tinge, like a faint bruise.

"What happened to you?" she asked again. "Your clothes are filthy."

"As I said, it was a long journey." He pulled at the neck of his T-shirt as if it were too tight.

She rooted around in the fridge for a portion of the beef stew she'd made earlier and stuck it in the microwave. The kettle clicked to boiling and she poured it over a teabag, adding the milk and one sugar as she'd done for years. She placed the mug in front of him and eyed him speculatively.

"Thank you." For a few minutes he just sipped his tea in silence.

The microwave pinged and she put the bowl of stew and a spoon in front of him and then made herself a coffee, using the time to process the fact that Rob was home again and, just like when he'd left, she'd found out at the last possible minute.

She sat down to join him.

"So how are you?" he asked, as casually as if he'd just got in from work.

"That's a very long story." Susannah eyed him curiously. "What has you home so early? You're meant to be gone for a year."

"My plans changed." A shadow passed over his face. "I decided to come back on impulse. That's why I didn't tell you. So what have you been up to, really? Having a romance with James or Phil. Or both maybe?"

She bit back a retort. Maybe he thought she'd had a personality transplant similar to his own.

"I'll give you a pass on that because you're clearly still jet-lagged."

She got up to leave but heard him coughing, a peculiar, wracking sound that sent a chill through her. When she swirled around to look at him she could see he was shivering.

"Are you sick? Is that why you're home early?"

"I don't feel great, but I'll be fine."

"Wait a second." She turned, ran upstairs, and pulled a blanket out of the airing cupboard.

But by the time she came back Rob had moved into the conservatory and was lying on the cane two-seater, his knees pulled up to his chest, his eyes closed, dinner forgotten. At first she thought he was asleep but then he started coughing again and the shivering had begun again too.

She threw the blanket over him but after a few seconds he threw it off. "It's very hot in here. Have you got the heat on?"

"No. I haven't." She put one hand on the radiator to check it was cold. "I thought you were starving? You haven't touched the stew."

"I thought I was hungry too but I don't want it now."

Susannah frowned. "Should I call a doctor?"

"No! I told you – I just need to sleep for a bit." He got up and made his way towards the stairs.

"The bed in the box-bedroom is made-up," she called after him. God forbid he should think he could jump back into the marital bed now without a conversation or a moment's notice. Not that he'd probably want to, she remembered.

Watching his slow, plodding pace, a picture of Orlaith and Jess flashed through Susannah's mind. How angry they had been with him, at both of them! What would they say if they could see their dad now?

She hoped he was right, and that all he needed was a good night's sleep, a shower and a hot meal. She poured the tea he hadn't finished down the sink and scraped the stew into the bin.

She felt totally disorientated, and had a sinking sense that her life was descending back into chaos. There was so much she needed to know. But she didn't want to know it either, didn't want to have the inevitable conversations she and Rob needed to have now, conversations that would spell further change for her, just when she'd started to feel she getting some stability back in her life.

She switched off the lights and climbed the stairs to bed, convinced she wouldn't sleep a wink. But no sooner had she pulled the duvet over her than a wave of exhaustion came over her. Everything will have to wait until morning, was her last thought before she fell into a deep sleep.

She woke to the smell of frying bacon and the sound of the radio on. She glanced at the clock. She'd slept for hours! Astonished she'd slept so long and so deeply, she lay in bed, piecing the events of last night together. One minute she'd been harbouring romantic thoughts towards James – totally unreciprocated of course, but still – and the next she'd been making Rob a meal. She shook her head to try and dispel the feeling she'd fallen down a rabbit hole again, pulled on her dressing gown and went downstairs.

Rob was in the kitchen, shoving rashers around the frying pan, humming. Dressed in the customary navy jumper and blue jeans that had been pretty much his weekend uniform, he looked so much like his old self that the raggedy wraith who had frightened the hell out of her last night could well have been a mirage.

Except she could see his jeans were hanging around his hips – he'd obviously lost a lot of weight.

"You're up," she said warily.

"Amazing what a comfortable bed and a hot shower can do – never thought I'd appreciate home comforts so much."

He set a plate in front of her – rashers and eggs, tomatoes and orange juice.

Then he sat and started to eat his breakfast with such enthusiasm her worries about his health faded.

"You need to let the girls know you're home," she said.

"I'll phone them, no worries."

"They'll be relieved you're back." She pushed the food around her plate. "I'm going to visit them soon."

"To New York? Really? On your own?"

"No, with James and Phil," she deadpanned. "Yes, on my own."

He grinned and for a moment Susannah got a glimpse of the Rob she used to know. He pushed his hand through his hair and it stuck up like a fork and Susannah had to fight back an old muscle-memory impulse to smooth it down.

"So – how have you been? Really?" He tried again.

She shrugged. "Up and down. Down at the beginning. Up now. You?"

"The opposite. Up at the start of my big adventure. Down now." He smiled ruefully. "We're haven't been on the same page for a long time, have we?"

She didn't answer that.

"So tell me about your work," he said.

She couldn't stop herself from smiling. "I love it. It's challenging but I can handle it. Really, it's been the best thing in the world for me – especially after everything that's happened – Mum dying, the girls leaving, you ..." Her voice trailed away. "You know, if I'd known that going back to work would have made me feel this alive I would have done it years ago."

"Why didn't you?" he asked curiously. "Do it earlier, I mean?"

"You always put me off – said things had changed since I'd been in the workplace. That it was horrible."

He gave her a sceptical look. "That wouldn't have stopped you – not if it was what you really wanted."

"Maybe. I guess I'd got used to thinking about myself in a certain way for such a long time that I couldn't see anything different for me. I didn't realise all of that until I went to the *Flow*

Your Life seminar." Susannah reflected how unlikely it was that it had been Geraldo Laffite who had made her see that she'd been living in the past.

"We should have talked to each other more," Rob observed.

"You weren't even here most of the time though." Susannah twisted a paper napkin between her fingers.

He raised his eyebrows, indignant again. "I was never anywhere else. The train in and out to work was as far as I got. I used to think on that commute that men in prison must have had more freedom than me."

She raised her eyebrows, thrown as much by the sudden change in his mood as by the extreme sentiment.

"I'm sorry you felt like that. But I meant you weren't here emotionally."

"That sounds like Olivia's pop psychology," he said dismissively. "Although now that I think about it I could say the same – you weren't there emotionally either. Grieving after your mother. Mooning about the girls. There was nothing left over for me."

"Yeah, cos it's always about you, isn't it, Rob?"

The minute the words were out of her mouth, Susannah wished she could take them back. Rob wasn't back in the house twenty-four hours and they were back where they'd left off, bickering and arguing.

He must have felt the same because he pushed himself up off the chair. "I think I'll go back to bed for a while."

"You haven't finished your breakfast."

Most of the food he'd attacked with such gusto at the beginning was still on his plate.

"I'm not as hungry as I thought I was." He coughed again, and the grey pallor was back on his face. "Jet lag," he said, noticing the concern on her face.

But Susannah was starting to wonder if it was more than that.

She was wondering again if she should phone the doctor when her mobile went.

It was Katie, checking on her progress with the feature on James Moran.

Susannah could hardly believe it was just last night he'd been in her house. It seemed like weeks ago. In fact, with the shock of seeing Rob back she had completely forgotten she had work to do.

"I need to do some editing but I'll get it to you by the end of the day," Susannah promised.

She would take herself off to one of the local cafés and work on it there – it would get her out of the house at least.

"Listen, how would you be fixed to go to Croagh Patrick soon – like, tomorrow morning?"

"It's not very much notice, is it?"

"How much notice do you need to throw a few things into an overnight bag, though?" Katie demanded.

Susannah realised Katie probably needed to leave home again for a bit. She wanted to tell her that running away from her problems was never going to work, not in her experience. But then she thought of Rob and how she felt as if the weight of the world was back on her shoulders and reckoned that's exactly what she wanted to do too – run away.

"You're right," she said. "I'll come"

"Great. I was thinking of two nights. One day on the mountain and one chilling out in the spa, with a nice meal and a few drinks."

Susannah grinned at Katie's notion of penance.

"I'm going to have to pull a double shift here to clear my work," Katie went on, "but we can do all our background research on the journey down. You just concentrate on getting me in the feature on James Moran."

As Susannah hung up the phone, she heard Rob coughing

again – that peculiar rasping sound that gave her the shivers – and wondered whether it was wise to leave him when he was obviously ill.

But she had to do her job, she reminded herself. For the first time in a long time she felt a sense of who she was again. She loved her work and was good at it.

She was earning good money, planning to go to New York on a mini-adventure of her own. She wasn't going to give all that up, no matter how strong the pull was to go back to playing the role of Rob's wife.

She made tea and toast, put it on a tray and made her way up to the box-bedroom. Rob was awake, slumped against the pillow, the dark circles under his eyes more noticeable than ever.

"I'm off on a job tomorrow – to Westport. I'll be gone for two nights. So you'll have the house to yourself at least."

She handed him the tray and he balanced it awkwardly on his lap. The single bed seemed too small for his long frame.

"Thanks for this." He nodded at the tray as he picked up a piece of toast. He went to eat but the cough returned and he had to put it back on the plate. When the coughing fit subsided, he leaned his head back against the headboard wearily.

"Don't know what's after happening to me," he mumbled.

Susannah had to fight the impulse to cook up two days' dinners and leave them in the freezer.

"And you're sure you don't need a doctor?" she asked again.

"No. If I get any worse I'll call him myself. But thanks anyway." He flopped his head back on the pillow, his eyes already closed.

She decided to leave the tray there. He might eat later on and cold toast was better than nothing.

She left, closing the bedroom door quietly behind her.

She got ready and walked down to her favourite café in the village. As she waited for the waitress to bring her coffee, she switched on her computer and started to scan down through the feature. But she found it hard to concentrate on the task.

Everything keeps changing, she thought unhappily. She sighed. She could hardly believe she'd spent so much time pining for Rob to come back to her. And, now that he had, she couldn't bear to be under the same roof as him.

CHAPTER 23

Katie yawned. It had been a long hard day and she still had to finish her double shift by reading Susannah's feature on James Moran. She didn't mind the work because it took her mind off her personal problems. But she was exhausted now and she had an early start in the morning. She had hardly slept in Susannah's house and had decided to book herself into a hotel near the office while she organised the trip to Croagh Patrick.

As far as Luke knew, she was away for work already. She had slipped home during her lunch break, when she knew he would be at work. She'd packed her weekend case and left him a note, explaining she was sorry she'd left the way she had, that she was away for work for a few days and they could talk about everything when she got back.

She wasn't looking forward to that, but she realised it had to be done. She wasn't ready to face him yet – his concern, his questions, his demands for an explanation of why she'd run out of the apartment.

She was still puzzled herself by her behaviour, so she wouldn't have any answers for him. She was particularly ashamed of how she'd deliberately set out to have an argument with him and then run away from it. This was not what she did. It was not who she was.

If she'd been thinking rationally she would have booked into the hotel in the first place instead of going back out to Susannah Stevens' house. The fact that Susannah knew Olivia meant she had put her in a difficult position by asking her to put her up, especially when she was so obviously upset.

But, to her credit, Susannah had asked no questions and Katie felt pretty sure she could trust her not to say anything about it to Olivia. She probably had enough problems of her own anyway, without concerning herself about other people's, Katie thought.

She made herself one last cup of coffee while she settled down to read the feature Susannah had filed. It was, as usual, well-written and imbued with the author's particular brand of empathy but Katie was surprised to find her eyes welling with tears as she read about the tragedy of the father and his lost son and how he had made his journey back to wellness again.

She dabbed at her face with a paper tissue, trying to compose herself. During the course of her career she had reported on all sorts of tragedies herself and, if she were honest, they'd rarely had much effect on her. Like anyone working on the frontline she had been trained to put a wall between herself and what she was reporting on, to maintain her journalistic objectivity and not get emotionally involved.

But sitting here in the empty office, with everyone, even Jennifer, gone home for the evening, Katie suddenly found herself thinking of the dad she was estranged from and the brother she hardly knew. What if something was to happen to one of them and her chance to change things between them was lost forever? What if she didn't decide to forgive her dad until it was too late? Until now she had somehow fancied she had endless time to deal with all this stuff, and that she would probably do it sometime in the future, when the time felt right, when she was good and ready.

But as she reflected on how fragile life was, she wondered if she'd made a mistake in keeping her dad at arm's length. It wasn't as if he hadn't tried to reach out to her over the years. But Katie had always given the excuse that she was too busy whenever he'd called and eventually he'd given up. Which up until now had suited her just fine. She stretched, turned off the computer and gave herself a mental shake.

These thoughts were just adding to the confusion she felt about Luke. She gathered up her things and switched off the lights in the office. Two nights in Westport were just what she needed, to get herself back on track again.

Back at the hotel she ran a warm bath and had a chamomile tea but she couldn't wind down enough to sleep and she spent the night tossing and turning, thinking about James Moran and all the feelings his story had triggered in her.

By the time Katie arrived at Houston Station next morning she felt shattered. She had big bags under her eyes and she'd had to cake on the make-up to make herself look even half-awake.

Susannah had already arrived and was standing in the middle of the busy railway station clutching take-away coffees and a bag from the early-morning bakery. She looked lost in thought but she brightened up when she spotted Katie.

"Here –" She handed her a polystyrene cup. "Hot coffee, strong caffeine. I'm still not used to early starts."

"Thanks." Katie inhaled the strong coffee aroma as they strolled along the platform to board the train. "I need this! I was editing your feature on James Moran last thing before I left the office last night and it kept me awake half the night."

"It was such a tragedy, wasn't it?" Susannah said. "It must be the worst thing to happen to anyone and yet he is such a lovely, generous man still. I think I would be very bitter."

Katie thought again of her dad and her brother as she stowed her coat overhead and settled into her seat.

She looked at Susannah. "You look tired yourself. Did the story keep you awake too?"

"No, it didn't because I was too busy trying to craft it into a narrative to be that affected by it. But I remember the first afternoon I interviewed him I was very moved." Susannah's mouth twisted in a rueful smile. "But I do have a very good reason for looking tired right now. Rob is home."

"What?" Katie nearly spilled her coffee with shock. "When did that happen? Were you expecting him? You never said."

Susannah raised her eyebrows. "I wasn't expecting him, no. I thought he was a burglar! James had called in to me – we needed to go through a few more things about the feature and after that I went to bed. When I heard someone in the house I didn't think for a moment it might be Rob. I came downstairs, intent on facing my fears, breaking my internal blocks like the Geraldo Laffite school of self-development had recommended." She shook her head. "If he had been a burglar he could have killed me. As it was, the shock nearly did anyway."

"But why didn't Rob tell you he was coming back?" Not for the first time Katie was fascinated with what passed for a relationship between Susannah and her husband. "He wasn't due back for months, was he?"

"No, not until the end of the year. He said his plans changed. He didn't seem to be well actually. He was exhausted and running a temperature, I think. I felt a bit guilty leaving him on his own actually."

"Come on!" Katie scoffed. "If he was big enough to get himself to the Southeast Asia on his own I'm sure he'll be able to muster up the energy to call a doctor if he needs one." She looked at Susannah curiously. "So how do you feel about him being back?"

"You know – I honestly have no idea." Susannah looked out the window as the train started to pull out of the station. "I guess those fun and games will start when I get back home. I was delighted when you rang to say we should do Croagh Patrick today actually. It gave me a chance to remove myself from a very awkward situation."

You and me both, Katie thought. But she wasn't about to exchange any more confidences with Susannah Stevens. She needed to work out the stuff she had going on with Luke on her own. Susannah opened the brown-paper bag, fished out a buttery croissant and handed the bag to Katie.

"Here's to a weekend of penance!" Katie grinned.

Once they'd finished their breakfast, they connected their laptops up to the train's Wi-Fi system and began their research.

"'Croagh Patrick, which overlooks Clew Bay in County Mayo, is considered to be the holiest mountain in Ireland,'" Katie read out loud. "'Almost 30,000 pilgrims make the trek on the last Sunday in July, known as 'Reek Sunday'. For most Catholics the pilgrimage to the top of the sacred mountain is an act of penance. Accordingly, some take the journey barefoot or even on their knees.' What?"

Susannah burst out laughing. "The look on your face! I am certainly not trekking up a mountain in my bare feet. Or on my knees. I've brought my sturdiest walking boots. Do you have to be part of the pilgrimage for it to count as penance?"

"I don't have a clue." Katie squinted at the screen, then started tapping away at her keyboard again. "I'll try a travel forum. Here's something. 'On Reek Sunday, about 30,000 visitors do a special pilgrimage in honour of St. Patrick, who is said to have fasted there for 40 days in 441 AD. Driving rain, freezing winds and rockiness of the trail drove us back to the comfort of our hotel. Enough with the penance already!'"

Both women looked out the window. The sun was shining out of a clear blue sky, with very few clouds on the horizon.

"Well, the weather is fine today," Katie said. "It's a pity we didn't do it on Reek Sunday though. We could have talked to loads of people for the feature."

"Except you didn't know you needed to do penance back then," Susannah reminded her with a smile.

Katie, in fact, was already beginning to have doubts about the whole trip. The penance part, which had seemed sort of whimsical when she'd conceived of the notion of making things up to Luke through good-deeds karma, seemed frankly ridiculous now that she was practically living in a hotel. She felt that should be penance enough for any misdemeanours on her part. But she'd committed to the Croagh Patrick climb and she'd see it through because, whatever her faults were, she wasn't a quitter.

She decided they should get Croagh Patrick over and done with so they could avail of the spa, fancy restaurant and funky bar afterwards. She was still feeling highly strung and nervy and she was looking forward to some down-time where she could chill out and forget her problems.

By the time they got to Westport, they hadn't managed to get much research done despite the fact they had been on the train for over three hours. Susannah had fallen asleep and Katie had spent the time staring out the window, brooding about Luke, love and the universe.

Still, how hard could it be, she asked herself as she handed over her company credit card to the hotel's reception, to trek up a mountain and come back down again? If they set off straight after check-in they could have the whole thing done and dusted and be back at the hotel in time for dinner.

She ordered a taxi to arrive in thirty minutes and arranged to meet Susannah back in the lobby. Upstairs she dumped her bags, changed into her hiking boots, squashed a raincoat into her small backpack. Checking she had enough battery left on her phone to last the afternoon, she saw several missed calls from Luke but she ignored them and went downstairs to wait for Susannah.

Susannah arrived a few minutes late and looked worried. "I've left my phone up in the room," she fretted. "Can you wait and

I'll go back ..."

"The taxi's here. Besides," Katie held up her smartphone. "I have one." It was a good thing Susannah wouldn't have her phone with her, she thought privately. She'd probably be checking up on the prodigal husband every five minutes with it. She didn't seem to be able to help herself from wanting to baby-sit him, even after he'd dumped her without any explanation.

They settled into the cab, happy the driver was chatty and full of information about Croagh Patrick. It shouldn't be too busy because it was a weekday, he explained, and because the weather had been very unpredictable this past week.

He advised them to buy walking sticks at the visitor centre, stick to the path and, if they were doing it for penance, to find out about the prayers they needed to say before they set out. Katie exchanged glances with Susannah. This was the first they'd heard of prayers.

"I hope you both have proper shoes and warm clothing because it can be cold at the top," he warned. "Especially if the mist comes in. Or if it starts to rain."

Looking out at the clear blue sky, still only a few puffy white clouds on the horizon, Katie thought that visitors must wonder why everyone seemed to mention rain in the same breath as Croagh Patrick. Still, it was Ireland after all. She was glad she'd packed her fold-up rain-jacket.

"So do you want me to collect you and take you back to your hotel later?" the taxi-man asked when they reached their destination.

Katie could see Croagh Patrick in front of them, a bit brooding-looking, but not particularly high, with the visitor centre to their right.

"That would be great – thanks." Katie took the white business card he gave her and scrutinised it before shoving it into her jeans pocket.

"So I'll come back for you then – say in four hours?"

"What? Four hours?" Katie was horrified. She'd been thinking an hour would give them time enough to do the trek and have a cup of coffee afterwards.

"Yes. It takes over two hours on the journey up and one and a half down. More if you're not fit," he added, looking at Susannah.

Dear God, thought Katie. "But if we phone you earlier than that – if we finished earlier for example – you'd come out, right?"

"Sure." He caught her eye in the mirror and warned, "But if you want to say you climbed Croagh Patrick, dearie – then that's the time it takes."

CHAPTER 24

Susannah began walking, all her doubts made worse by the information they'd gleaned from the taxi driver. She cursed herself for not doing her own research, but between James Moran calling in, Rob arriving home so unexpectedly and then Katie bringing the trip forward without any notice whatsoever, she reckoned maybe she was being too hard on herself. She'd just have to make the most of things, she thought stoutly.

She looked at Katie striding along ahead of her, looking young, fit and athletic, anxious to get the journey out of the way. Susannah was making much slower progress, carefully picking her way across the uneven ground with the help of a stick she'd purchased at the visitors centre, concerned she might trip on the uneven ground beneath her.

She had never been an outdoors sort of person so this was a brand-new experience for her. She was also unfit, despite the many failed promises she'd made to herself to join a gym to while away the hours after Orlaith and Jess had left home.

Still, she was here primarily to write a feature and that was working out well so far. She had picked up some literature at the visitor centre and she intended to do more research from her desk. This afternoon was about adding colour to the story, using her personal experience of the mountain, and Katie's, to bring the feature to life.

She looked around her. The scenery was stunning and as time passed she forgot about catching up with Katie and settled into a pleasant rhythm of her own. She might as well have been on her own and after a while her thoughts inevitably returned to Rob. What would his unexpected return mean for both of them, she wondered. She didn't think that even Rob could expect that they would just pick up where they'd left off at the beginning of the year. And he probably wouldn't want to. But where did that leave them? Would they sell the house? And, if so, where would she live? Where would Rob live for that matter, or the girls when their internship was up?

Despite how far she'd come since he'd left, these questions were still too big for Susannah and she turned her attention back to the present moment. She smelled the scent of heather on the air, heard a bird caw-cawing in the sky above her. While she was tracking its movement in the sky she noticed the terrain ahead was much steeper.

Her legs were already starting to ache and she began to panic about the challenge she'd taken on so blithely.

She stopped and rested for a bit. She should have done more research, she told herself again. And put herself on a fitness regime before she agreed to come. And she shouldn't have listened to Katie when she told her to leave her phone behind her.

But there was no point in berating herself. Even though she felt like turning back, she remembered the promise she'd made to herself. She was done with running away from things she didn't like.

Katie stopped and shouted back at her. "Are you okay?

"I'm good." Susannah hoisted herself up and started to walk again. After a while, she began to see that if she just concentrated on putting one foot in front of the other, and stopped looking ahead to see how far she had to go, she could cope. In fact, after a while she was surprised to find she was doing better than just coping – she was actually starting to enjoy herself.

So this was why all those fitness addicts took on extreme challenges, she thought. For the endorphin rush.

And by the time she finally got to the top she too was euphoric. She breathed in great lungfuls of fresh air and looked around her. The view was spectacular, with Clew Bay and the surrounding countryside presenting a perfect panorama for her. She sat just staring at it, in awe of the wild, natural beauty. But it was the fact that she'd accomplished what she'd set out to do, not turning back midway, that was the real buzz for Susannah.

Katie was standing at a picturesque white church, talking to a group of other walkers gathered there.

"Well, if you wanted penance, Katie Corrigan, you've certainly got it," Susannah called over to her.

Katie grinned and came over to her. "Did you say the prayers?" she asked.

Susannah raised her eyebrows. She'd passed the pilgrim stations on the way up and she knew from her brochures that pilgrims were encouraged to stop and pray. But she'd barely even looked at them, so focused had she been on her task of completing the climb.

"If I'd stopped to say seven Our Fathers, seven Hail Marys and whatever else it was, I'd never have got here. What about you?"

"I don't pray," Katie said.

"Well, St Patrick fasted and prayed here for the Irish people for forty days." Susannah informed her. She pulled out one of the brochures she'd taken from the visitor centre and scrutinised it. "And then he banished the snakes from Ireland. But even before he came it was a sacred site. People came to worship the Celtic sun god, Lugh – that's why the big pilgrimage is on the last Sunday in July – because it's the nearest Sunday to the original pagan festival of Lughnasa."

Katie looked deeply unimpressed, but Susannah was enjoying

learning about the history of the place.

"Also," she added, "this is supposed to be at the centre of a number of cosmological alignments."

"Whatever they are," Katie said. "No, don't tell me!" she said, alarmed as Susannah started rustling through more brochures. "I'll wait and read all about it in the paper."

"Right." Susannah sounded disappointed. "So what do we do now?"

"Dunno." Katie shrugged. "Go back down?"

"But we've only just got here. Or I have anyway. I'll have to have a rest before I tackle the descent."

"Okay. We'll take half an hour," Katie agreed.

They found a flat piece of stone and sat down side by side, each lost in her own thoughts for a while.

Then Katie said, "I'm beginning to think that maybe I didn't need to do this climb after all. Because to be honest, living with Luke feels like penance enough."

Susannah grinned. "I'm presuming you two had a row the night you stayed at my place?"

"We did. But it was my fault. I'm not used to living with someone. He uses up the hot water, doesn't keep to the dinner rota – small things like that."

"Is that all?" It sounded as if Katie just needed to give herself time to adjust to living with someone else.

"I'm not sure what it was about, to be honest. I know we were arguing about the dinner rota but of course it was about more than that. It was a build-up of tension from all the things I just mentioned and things got a bit heated. Luke stood up and raised his voice and I think I had a kind of panic attack. I got a flashback to a big row at home when I was a child. Before my dad left us for the woman he's with now, there were a lot of rows." She shrugged. "I don't know why it came back to me at that particular moment. It's just stuff from my past. Nothing really."

"I'm not sure that stuff from your past is ever nothing," Susannah said slowly. "When I was younger I had a stalker and I thought I'd forgotten him. I got the odd bad dream when I was under stress but that was all. Then, when Rob left, it was as if the whole trauma was retriggered in me."

"What do you mean the whole trauma was retriggered?" Katie was curious.

"Well, there was this new guy in my book club who looked a bit like my stalker, although I didn't see that at first. I felt uneasy around him all the time and, although in fairness he is a little strange, I think the fact that he reminded me of the stalker magnified everything about him for me. In fact, when Rob came home I thought it might be this guy who was after breaking into my house."

"So what are you saying?" Katie asked.

"I'm saying you shouldn't discount your feelings. Maybe this row with Luke did remind you of your dad's rows with Olivia. But you need to deal with that because it sounds like it's having an effect on you still."

"You sound like my mother," Katie grumbled. She looked at Susannah curiously. "Did you know her back then? When she and my dad broke up?"

Susannah shook her head. "No. I only got to know her through Cara in the last few years. Why do you ask?"

"I can't remember a lot of it. I thought you might be able to help me fill in the blanks."

"Why don't you ask Olivia about it?"

"Because, like you, she'll give me some psychological bullshit about having issues. And she'll harp on at me to do something about it even though she knows I don't want to do that. I don't buy into this dealing-with-the-past stuff. I have enough to cope with, with all that's going on in my life right now, thanks very much." She shifted on her rock, trying to get more comfortable.

"So what's stopping you settling down with Luke, do you think?" Susannah asked.

"I don't like having someone else in my space," Katie said gloomily.

"That could be a problem all right." Susannah grinned. "But look, maybe you're overthinking all this. Maybe it's just a case of Luke not being the man for you."

"Why do you say that?" Katie asked curiously.

"Don't you think it's a bit of a red flag if you don't like having him in your space? This is supposed to be the honeymoon period, isn't it?"

"But you're forgetting I slept with someone else, which I think is what's causing all the problems in the first place."

"Well, maybe you should think about why you did that," Susannah said tentatively. She was half-expecting Katie to tell her to mind her own business.

"Tequila slammers were the reason I did it."

"And you've never had the equivalent of tequila slammers in the four years you were with Luke and never slept with anyone else?"

"Of course I had. But there were other things going on. Luke and myself had broken up and I was missing him. And then Daniel told me he was leaving the *Post* and I realised I was never going to see him again. What can I say, it seemed like a good idea at the — oh!" Katie broke off as she realised she'd revealed the identity of her mystery man.

"The writer of the *Footloose and Fancy-free* columns?" Susannah asked. "That was the guy you slept with?"

"The very same."

"He's handsome. And he was very charming when Mike introduced me to him at the going-away party," Susannah remembered. "So are you still in touch with him?"

Katie shook her head. "He emailed me once but I deleted it.

He's out of my life now."

"Do you miss him?"

Katie shrugged. "Work isn't the same without him. He always had my back in the office. And he was such fun! He leads such an interesting life and he used to tell me all about it. Everything is duller without him."

"It sounds as if you were living vicariously through him if you don't mind me saying. Maybe you're not missing Daniel so much as actual fun? As far as I can see you seem to work an awful lot, you're with a boyfriend you're not sure about and you've not much else going on in your life. No wonder you were lonely when you and Luke split up."

"Look at you. Sounding all Mind, Body and Spirit!" Katie grinned.

They began to talk about MBS issues and it was some time after that Susannah looked up and saw that the white fluffy clouds had disappeared and a soft, grey mist was gathering.

"It looks like the weather is about to change," she told Katie. "We'd better head back."

Katie didn't need any encouragement. They were on their way immediately and were making good progress when Katie suddenly lost her footing. She was a bit ahead of Susannah.

Susannah inched her way towards her, terrified that she'd slip too.

By the time she reached her, Katie was sitting on a rock, looking forlorn, with one foot out in front of her.

"Are you okay?" Susannah asked fearfully.

Katie winced with pain. "It's my ankle. I don't think I can manage to continue without help. I'm going to phone back to the hotel and ask for advice. They must have loads of guests who come out to this mountain and fall. I have their number on the emails we exchanged."

She rooted in her rucksack and pulled out her phone.

"No signal," she then said in disgust. She threw the phone back into her bag impatiently. "Try yours, will you?"

"Mine is in the hotel room, in the charger," Susannah reminded her.

The two women stared at each other, neither knowing what to do next.

"Can you walk?" Susannah asked fearfully. She had no clue what she was going to say or do if Katie couldn't.

"Of course. I just turned my ankle, that's all. I'm fine." Katie got up to show how fine she was but she had a bad limp.

Seeing as she got most of her medical knowledge from medical dramas on the television, Susannah refrained from making any rash diagnosis.

"The taxi will be waiting for us," Katie said. "When we don't turn up he'll phone someone to come for us. They must have a procedure for this sort of thing."

Susannah didn't have the heart to point out that they had both sounded so unenthusiastic about Croagh Patrick that the taxi man would probably presume they were sitting in the hotel Jacuzzi if they didn't show up at the appointed time.

Katie pulled her raincoat out of her rucksack and sat back down again. Susannah sat nearby. The mist was getting thicker, shrouding the mountain from their sight.

"What if it doesn't clear?" Katie asked quietly.

"It will," Susannah tried to sound confident.

"But what if it doesn't? We can't stay here all night. We'd freeze."

There was no answer to that so Susannah started talking, trying to distract herself as well as Katie from their predicament. She went into greater details about her stalker and the nightmares she'd struggled with when Rob had left. She told Katie how nervous she'd been going for the interview with her, and how she'd been terrified when her real name appeared under the column.

She was probably boring Katie to death but it was the only way she knew to stop both of them from freaking out at the possibility that they would be left out in the elements for the night.

"I know I said that meeting James Moran made me want to be more open-minded about all things spiritual but I've had it with all this palaver about penance," she announced. "It's ridiculous when you think about it. It would be like Rob deciding to dig the garden for six Saturdays in a row in order for me to forgive him for doing a runner."

"Forgiveness is a funny thing though," Katie mused. "Up until now I've wanted Luke to forgive me for something he doesn't even know I did. But, when I was reading your feature on James Moran, I realised I haven't been that good at forgiving people in my own life. My dad for example. I've been harbouring resentment against him for years. I always thought I'd get over it someday, in my own sweet time. But when I read about James's son taking his own life I thought maybe I wouldn't always have the luxury of time. Maybe I need to do whatever it is I have to do to forgive him right now."

"And maybe I don't have that much to forgive Rob for. I thought he was off having the time of his life on his big adventure but when he came back he was in bits – sick and as miserable as when he left." A thought occurred to her. "Maybe he'd been feeling ill before he went? That would explain all the moody behaviour, the personality transplant he seemed to have."

"I thought you said he'd been planning it for three years?"

"So I did." Susannah had forgotten that. Another theory busted. She'd been thinking Rob had showed up in her life again, ready finally to talk to her. But had he really? Or was he just back for a comfortable bed and board because things had gone against him when he'd been abroad? He'd said nothing about missing her, she remembered. She sighed. "I guess I'm still looking for excuses for his behaviour. But it's kind of exhausting harbouring ill-will against someone, don't you think?"

"That's what Olivia always says. She wants me to meet my dad again and his son – my half-brother Seán. I've only seen him a few times ever."

"I think you should talk to Olivia more. I'm certainly going to be talking to my girls a lot more in the future."

Susannah was only realising now that life might not be the bed of roses she imagined it was for her daughters. Because they were doing something she had never done, living on their own, in an exciting city like New York, she had painted a picture of them as having an ideal life with no worries or problems. She'd imagined them as footloose and fancy-free as the characters in Daniel Gilbert's columns. But was that really true for anyone? Even Daniel Gilbert?

For the first time she realised she had been in a trap entirely of her own making, continuing to play the dutiful wife-and-mother roles when everyone, except her, had long outgrown them. There was nothing to stop her doing the things she'd wanted to do years ago, the things she'd shelved for family life. She just needed to be brave about it. But first she had to put the past behind her.

Actually, that was the second thing she had to do. First she had to get off this mountain. They were both chilled to the bone now and getting more frightened with each moment that passed. She looked around her, trying to think up a plan, but in the face of the weather and Katie's injury her mind came up blank.

It was another endless hour before the mist started to clear and, with that, salvation from an unexpected source.

"Shush!" Katie said suddenly. "Did you hear something?" She looked behind her, up towards the summit of the mountain.

"Voices!" Susannah hoisted herself off the rock, just as a trio of walkers appeared.

It was the group Katie had been talking to at the summit,

outside the church. It turned out they were experienced trekkers from Norway, two men and a woman who were more than happy to help the tired and inexperienced Irishwomen.

One of the men took Katie's rucksack and the other lent her his arm and they all started their tentative journey back down the mountain. Even with the help, it seemed to take an age to get back down to ground level.

When she spotted the taxi man, waiting patiently for them in the same spot he'd left them off, Susannah wanted to cry with relief.

He was keen to hear about their experience but they barely answered his questions and finally he got the hint and fell silent.

By the time they got to the hotel all Susannah wanted to do was to put her head on the big, white fluffy pillows she'd got a glimpse of when she'd been in the room so briefly earlier in the day. And by the look on Katie's face, she felt the same. They parted company in the hotel corridor and Susannah let herself into her room, filled with gratitude they'd got off the mountain safely. The first thing she did was to unplug her phone to put in back into her handbag. She glanced at the screen and noticed four missed calls.

All of them from Rob.

The panic she'd felt on the mountain returned with force and she held her breath as she clicked into her voicemail to listen to her messages.

"Susannah?" Rob sounded agitated and distracted. *"I wasn't feeling any better after you left so I phoned the doctor. He sent me to the hospital. They're keeping me in."*

CHAPTER 25

As the train got nearer to Dublin, Katie put her head back against the seat and closed her eyes. She felt drained by the events of the last couple of days – being trapped on the mountain and the fear of what would have happened if help hadn't arrived when it did was still preying on her mind.

When they'd finally arrived safely at the hotel, all she'd wanted was to sink into a hot bath and had been about to do so when she heard someone banging on her door. It was Susannah, freaking out because Rob had been admitted to hospital, and saying she'd have to go home early.

But it was too late to catch the last train to Dublin and they'd spent a miserable couple of hours in the bar, Susannah still trying in vain to connect with Rob.

Katie felt a bit guilty that she'd been so glib about his illness, and her efforts to reassure Susannah were useless. Finally she'd given up and they'd both returned to their rooms. She pulled out the plug on her now freezing bathwater, had a quick shower and ordered a room-service dinner she hadn't been able to eat.

This morning, Susannah was a nervous wreck, and Katie said an awkward goodbye to her at the station, making her promise to call as soon as she knew how Rob was.

By the time she got to turn the key in her own hall door Katie felt exhausted. She'd hardly slept the previous night, and all the drama had left her feeling strung-out.

She threw her overnight bag and laptop into the bedroom and stepped straight into the shower, hoping the hot water would wake her up. She dressed in tracksuit pants and a sweatshirt and ran the dryer over her hair. Her ankle was still sore and she swallowed a couple of painkillers before limping over to flop down on the sofa.

The river was murky-looking today and rain was starting to spit at the windows. It was a grey cold day, more like winter. Weather to fit her mood, she thought sadly.

She had decided on the train home that today was the day she was going to break up with Luke, and this time it would be for good. And, while she was dreading having to tell him this, she couldn't help feeling relieved that she'd soon have her apartment to herself again.

There was no sense in trying to make something work that was obviously broken, she thought as she poured herself a glass of wine.

Now that she had made up her mind about Luke she was surprised at how much other stuff was crowding her thoughts today – thoughts about her dad in particular.

She'd felt abandoned by him when he walked out on them and, later on, felt replaced by Seán. She'd refused to have anything to do with him in the beginning out of loyalty to her mother. But even after her mother had moved on, Katie had hugged her hurt to her through the years, taking comfort in feeling hard done by him.

Susannah had more or less called her a workaholic on the mountain. She preferred to call it a strong work ethic but it was true she had kept herself eternally busy – too busy for anything like having to try and fix her relationship with her dad. And that's what she'd been doing with Luke. Keeping herself so busy she didn't have to deal with the problems staring her in the face.

Except they weren't going to go away on their own. She could see that now. They would always be there, until she found a solution to them.

And, of course, she was no longer the frightened and powerless child she'd been when her dad had left – she was an adult now and this evening she was going to act like one.

By the time Luke got home, she had rehearsed her speech until she knew it by heart. She was determined she wasn't going to be sidetracked – although her resolve almost faltered when she saw the way his face lit up when he saw her there.

"Katie! Thank God. Are you okay? I phoned and texted you." He put down his briefcase, loosened his tie and sat down beside her on the sofa.

"I'm sorry. I was busy, and out of coverage for a lot of the time."

"I was so worried about you, especially after the way you left." He kissed the top of her head.

"Luke, we need to talk."

"We definitely do," he agreed. "You need to tell me why you ran away the way you did. And where have you been? I even called your office but all they would tell me was that you were away for work."

"Well, that's true. But look, I need to tell you something."

He sighed. "Something tells me I'm not going to like this."

He tried to put his arm around her, but she stood up, trying not to limp on her injured foot as she walked over to the window.

"Are you limping?"

"I turned my ankle – it's a bit sore, but I'm fine."

"So. What do you want to talk about? It's about me saying I was going to propose on Valentine's Night, isn't it? But I meant it when I told you I'm prepared to wait. You do believe me, don't you?"

"Of course," she said. "But the thing is, I don't need time,

Luke. I thought there were things I needed to do first – my career …" she waved her hand vaguely. "It sounds ridiculous in hindsight."

"That's because it is!" He was on his feet, encouraged. "There's absolutely nothing to stop you getting ahead in your career and being married at the same time. We're not living in – whatever age women had to make those choices. I'd be nothing but supportive of your choices, you know that, Katie."

"That's not it!" She was alarmed at how the conversation had taken a wrong turning.

"What then?" He stopped midway over to her, wary now.

She swallowed. "The reason I didn't want to marry you was because I don't want to spend the rest of my life with you, Luke."

There. It was out. She'd said it. She breathed a huge sigh of relief.

Luke was staring at her, his forehead furrowed, his face a mask of shock and bewilderment.

"But – I don't understand. Why did you agree that we'd get back together if you felt like that?"

"I didn't know how I felt then. But I've been doing a lot of thinking over the last few days and –"

"And you're panicking," he interrupted her. "It's okay to be afraid, Katie." He was speaking to her now as if she were a small child. "You've said it yourself so many times – your parents' break-up affected you. Made you wary of commitment. That's understandable. But you and me – we're not your parents! We're us. And we can work through this."

"I don't want to work through it," she said, but Luke wasn't listening.

"We can slow things down. I can move out of this apartment while we work things out. It's tiny anyhow – far too small for a couple. And maybe we could find someone to talk to – a counsellor or –"

"No!" Katie put her hand over her mouth. She hadn't meant to sound so emphatic. But when were people going to stop getting on her case about counselling?

This whole conversation was going wrong. She hadn't predicted that Luke would want to fight for her.

She began again, "There's something else that's been getting in the way of me not being happy living with you, Luke." She hesitated. She hadn't wanted to go here but it looked like she was going to have to give him a good reason to go.

"See? I knew there was something. Tell me what it is – and we can deal with it together."

"I slept with someone else." Then she added hastily, noticing how stricken he looked, "But not when we were together."

"What do you mean when we weren't together? We've been together for the last four years." His face was a picture of bewilderment.

"It was when we broke up that time …" She tried to explain but he stopped her.

"A few weeks ago? When we had the tiff?" A thought occurred to him. "But it was after that you agreed to move in with me!" He frowned, trying to make sense of it.

Katie bit her lip. The whole scenario sounded a lot worse when she heard it from Luke's perspective. The two people she had talked to about this – Daniel and Susannah – had been all like 'Well, you were broken up. Don't be too hard on yourself'. She had allowed them to lull her into a false sense of entitlement but Luke was now looking at her as if she was a monster.

"Who was it?" he asked finally.

"That doesn't matter." Katie shook her head.

"It matters to me," he said coldly.

She gave a tiny sigh. "It was just Daniel. From work."

Luke laughed into her face. "Just Daniel? Daniel 'I-met-him-today-for-lunch-and-he-was-hilarious'?" he mimicked her voice. "Daniel as in 'He lives such an interesting life, Luke'? Daniel. Daniel. Daniel. And all the time you were sleeping with him and I didn't see it. He must think I'm a right idiot. And so must you. How could I have been so stupid?" He ran his hand through his hair, distracted by all the information coming at him.

"I wasn't sleeping with him 'all the time'! It was just the once."

He stared at her. "Yeah, because that's what Daniel Gilbert is all about, isn't it? So you added yourself to the list of the one-night conquests of the *Footloose and Fancy-free* Lothario himself."

"It wasn't a conquest. We're not living in the Middle Ages."

"Why did you do it?"

She shrugged. Because she wanted to? "It just happened. I was lonely and he was there and he –"

"I'll stop you right there if you don't mind," Luke cut in. "On second thoughts, I don't need the details." His face changed as another thought occurred to him. "So that's why you got back with me? Because Daniel dumped you for his big job in London? For the next shiny thing?"

"No! I told him I'd made a mistake. That I shouldn't have done it."

"But it wasn't a mistake for him, was it? He was going to London and you were someone to keep him amused for one night only. Seems to me he got exactly what he wanted."

Katie thought Luke probably had a point there – but she'd got what she wanted too. She thought it best to keep quiet about that though, in the circumstances.

"And you ruined what we had for that?" he asked bitterly. "We were together four years, Katie. Four years. Weren't you happy with me?"

"I was happy. For most of it. But at the end? I'm not sure," she said bravely. "On Valentine's Night the only thing I knew was that I didn't want to marry you. And then, when you moved in,

I couldn't get used to living with you. And I put it down to us both having to adjust, but it was more than that."

"You can say that again," he said bitterly. "It was about you cheating on me with Daniel Gilbert the week before we moved in together."

"I'm sorry," she said forlornly. "I did try to make it better." She reckoned Luke didn't need to know the details of how – her mad plan to make it up to him by doing secret penance and random acts of kindness. Well, one random act of kindness.

"And when did you stop?" he asked. "Trying to make it better? When did you decide that it was over – that you didn't want to be with me any more?"

"Truthfully? It was when Susannah said that maybe you weren't the man for me."

He looked at her in astonishment. "This is Susannah 'My Husband Left Me for a Camper Van' we're talking about? This is who you're taking advice from now about relationships? About our relationship?"

"It was when we were stuck on the mountain and –"

"What? Wait. You were stuck on a mountain? When? Why didn't you phone me?"

"I told you – I was out of coverage. It was Croagh Patrick. In Mayo. That's where I hurt my ankle. These experienced walkers had to help us get down safely. And then when we finally got back to the hotel Susannah had all these messages on her phone to say her husband had been taken to hospital. And everything went a bit crazy because she was trying to get to see him."

"In Thailand?"

"No. He was in Thailand but he came home unexpectedly and –"

"And you never thought to ring me even once to tell me any of this? You were more concerned with Susannah's idiot husband? Do you know something, Katie? You've made it easy for me. I'll call back for my stuff tomorrow while you're at work. I'll leave my key on the table."

And he walked away from her, leaving her wondering if the conversation could possibly have gone any worse. She could hear him in the bedroom, throwing his stuff into a bag. He must have only taken a change of clothes because he was back within minutes, clutching an overnight case. He grabbed up his briefcase from where he'd dumped it at the side of the sofa.

"Goodbye, Katie," he said tersely. And he left.

She didn't sit down until she heard the hall door bang behind him. A tiny sigh escaped her as she heard the bell ring for the lift. Another wrecked relationship, she thought sadly.

CHAPTER 26

Susannah rushed down the corridor of the hospital, hearing the sound of her own heels clicking loudly against the tiles. The last time she'd been in a hospital was when her mother died, she realised.

She had phoned Rob from the hotel and for what felt like a million times on the train journey back to Dublin. But each time the phone had gone to voicemail. His recording was one he'd evidently adopted for his career break – a cheesy message in the same tone as the slogans she'd discovered on his computer all those months ago. *"Hi – it's Rob Stevens here. You might have noticed I'm not at the office – yay! – so, if it's to do with fun, leave a message and I'll get back to you. If it's to do with work I certainly won't. Ciao!"*

Eventually, she'd phoned their family doctor to find what hospital Rob was in. The hospital switchboard connected her to his ward but the nurse who picked up the phone would only say he was comfortable and that he'd been asking for her.

"He's asleep now, and I don't want to wake him. Call back later," she advised, "or better still, pop in to see him."

Susannah gritted her teeth at her tone, as if she were at home peeling grapes instead of trapped on a packed train. The journey back felt far longer than when she and Katie had been gleefully running away from the problems in their lives.

269

She picked up a taxi outside Heuston, deciding not to call Cara yet. Her sister didn't even know that Rob was home yet, and Susannah didn't want to have to deal with the drama of her reaction to that until she found out what was wrong with him.

As the taxi stopped and started, picking its way through the city traffic, she tried to prevent her mind from descending into a whirl of fearful what-if's and concentrated instead on what was going on right now. She deliberately watched the huge, white seagulls hovering over the Liffey, listened to the sound of the engine as the car idled at yet another set of traffic lights, felt her heart thumping in her chest cavity as she tried to work out why Rob hadn't returned any of her messages.

Now she was finally here she just wanted to find out why, but when she turned into the ward she'd been directed to she discovered he'd been moved to an isolation ward on another floor.

As she retraced her steps, she tried to be positive, telling herself that whatever was wrong with Rob it was bound to be something that could be fixed quickly.

But when she opened the door into the tiny isolation room, he was surrounded by a posse of concerned-looking medics.

"What's wrong with him?" she asked the doctors, taking one of Rob's hands in hers. It was hot and clammy. His eyes were closed and he looked flushed, with tiny beads of sweat glistening on his forehead.

A young man in a white coat came around to her side of the bed.

"Are you next of kin?"

"I'm his wife."

"Good. You can fill us in on your husband's medical history."

He put his hand under Susannah's elbow and steered her back out of the room, down the corridor and into a tiny, overcrowded office. He sat behind a desk and opened up a computer window.

"Your husband was referred here by his family doctor," he explained, "but he appears to have taken a turn for the worse since he arrived and we haven't been able to get the information we need from him. So I need to ask you some questions Has he been abroad recently?"

"Yes." Susannah nodded. "Thailand."

"Thailand," He wrote something on the form attached to the clipboard in front of him. "What part? Cities or rural areas?"

"Cities. Bangkok for sure. But I can't be sure where else he might have been."

"You weren't with him?"

She shook her head, fear making her go very quiet inside.

"How long has he been away?"

"Since January."

"And how long has he been back?"

"Just a couple of days."

"Was he travelling for work or leisure?"

"Leisure," she said, wondering what the hell the doctor would make of that.

"Okay. So, Mrs Stevens, we think your husband may have a tropical disease. But we're waiting on lab results before we can confirm." He then started firing off questions at her, about allergies, and general health and previous illnesses. When he'd finished, he smiled absently, "We're expecting some results this afternoon, so we should have more information for you then."

"But he'll be okay, won't he? There has to be medication for tropical diseases – how long do you think before he'll be able to come home?"

"It's best to wait for the results," he said. He was clicking on the computer keyboard now, already disengaged from her.

Susannah made her way back to Rob's bedside, feeling very lonely and afraid. He was wearing a hospital gown and she realised she'd need to bring in his pajamas and toiletries.

It was time to ring Cara. Her sister picked up straight away and Susannah thanked her lucky stars when Cara confirmed she had just finished work.

"I've been working extra shifts so I have five days off. I was just about to ring you, see if you wanted to meet up for coffee?"

Steeling herself for a thousand questions she wouldn't know the answers to, Susannah told her briefly that Rob was home from Thailand and had been admitted to hospital.

But to her credit Cara only registered her surprise with a quick, audible intake of breath.

"So what's the matter with him?" she asked.

"They think it's some sort of tropical disease. They're waiting on test results."

"Okay, I'm coming in. Is there anything you need me to bring? Or do?"

"I'm not sure what he needs," Susannah said. "I've only just got here myself. He needs pyjamas and toiletries but I'd need to go home for them. And I need to let Orlaith and Jess know."

"I can do that for you," Cara said briskly. "What will I say is wrong with Rob?"

"Well, that it's not been diagnosed yet. They said they should have some more information this afternoon."

"Yeah, and we don't want to frighten the hearts out of them, not until we know what we're dealing with. I'll come to the hospital first, shall I? And when we have some concrete information I can phone New York."

"Thanks, Cara. Rob was going to ring them to tell them he was home but I don't know if he ever got around it. I can't ask him anything at the moment because he's a bit out of it." Susannah stared at her husband as she spoke. He looked very vulnerable in his hospital gown, his complexion waxy against the stark white of the bed linen.

"Don't worry. We can figure it out as we go along," Cara said.

But when she arrived, her face was set in lines of worry and confusion.

Susannah filled her in on the little she knew – how she was away for work and had got stuck on the mountain without her mobile and missed Rob's calls to say he'd been admitted to hospital.

"You could have been killed," Cara said soberly.

"But I wasn't." Susannah was determined to be optimistic. "And Rob is going to get better."

But an hour later when Susannah arrived home to pick up some of Rob's essentials, she wasn't so sure. She took the time to have a shower and change her clothes because she couldn't be sure when she'd get home again. She packed an overnight bag for Rob and shoved a magazine, a few bags of nuts and some travel toiletries into her bag.

She noticed Rob's glasses on the table in the conservatory and went out to fetch them. She stared out the window at the overgrown garden. The late summer sunshine was bathing it in a glorious glow, accenting the wonderful blue of the lobelias, the perfect red of the roses, and the breathless white of the baby's breath, which must have self-seeded from last year, because there had been no planting in Pine Close this year.

She stepped outside onto the cobblestones, breathing in the scented air, trying to block the upsetting scene of Rob's hospital room out of her mind.

She noticed a big yellow-headed dandelion beneath the roses and absent-mindedly picked up a nearby trowel and dug it up. Then she spotted a weed a few feet away and, almost as an automatic reflex, dug that out too. It was the task real gardeners hated, Susannah thought. Weeding. But Susannah had never been the real gardener of the family. She'd always found weeding therapeutic, however, and for a short time as she crumbled the black soil between her fingers she felt a momentary sense of peace.

But when she crushed a sprig of lavender between her finger and thumb and inhaled its heady scent, her defenses broke and she burst into tears.

She recalled how cold and frightened she'd been on the mountain and how lucky she and Katie had been when the group of climbers had come along to help them. She remembered her mother at the hospital, so very sick. And she pictured Rob, clammy and feverish and sleeping so deeply she'd been afraid to ask if he was even conscious.

She thought of Orlaith and Jess, on the other side of the Atlantic, oblivious to what was going on. She'd been loath to ruin their year of freedom by telling them about their dad's decision to go travelling, but she couldn't protect them from this. She couldn't protect them from anything any more, she realised with a jolt.

What had happened to her family, she wondered, drying her tears. She hadn't even been able to answer the doctors about Rob's exact whereabouts. How the hell had she ever allowed that to happen? Why had she been so passive when Rob had come up with his stupid plan that they would stay in touch on Facebook? He must have infected her with his own madness, she thought grimly.

Well, that was now over. She was going to have to take control of things from now on. She grabbed up the bags, locked up and drove back to the hospital.

When she returned, Rob had a drip attached to his right arm, and transparent liquid dripped from a suspended medical bag into his vein.

"Have they just put that in?" she asked Cara, dumping Rob's bag on the floor.

"I went out to the ladies' and it was in when I came back," Cara said. "Sorry."

She was about to go and find out when the door to the room was pushed open and a doctor she hadn't met before stepped inside.

"Mrs Stevens?" He looked from her to Cara.

"That's me." Susannah stepped forward and briefly shook his hand.

"I'm Doctor Mason. Your husband has pneumonia, and we are treating him with antibiotics. We expect him to respond quite quickly. We're wondering also, though, if something else is going on." He looked at the clipboard he was carrying. "I see he was travelling for some months. Was he anywhere else, apart from Thailand?"

"I've already explained to the other doctor — I'm not sure." She felt frustrated at having to answer the awkward question again. But the fact was that Rob could have been in Timbuktu for all she knew.

"There's a very low risk of malaria in Thailand, especially in the cities. But if he ventured into the very rural parts near the border, particularly into dense jungle, there's a small chance he could have picked it up."

Susannah remembered something about Rob going to see monkeys and the girls being afraid he'd get rabies. She thought it was to a monkey refuge, but maybe it was in a jungle? She frowned, trying to remember.

"I know he'd planned to see wild monkeys but I'm not sure where it was."

"Would anybody else know?"

Susannah shook her head mutely.

When the doctor left, his face fixed in a frown, Cara glanced at her watch.

"I'm going to ring the girls. I know I won't have all the answers they want but I don't think it's a good idea to delay this any longer, do you?"

"No. Go," Susannah agreed. "And Cara?" She looked after her sister. "Try not to alarm them too much, will you?"

She sat down in the hard plastic chair by Rob's bedside to wait. She knew the girls would be home on the next available flight and for a mad moment she felt wistful that she wouldn't get to visit them in New York after all. She'd been looking forward to it so much. But then she looked at Rob and guessed that was the least of her worries right now.

CHAPTER 27

After a while, and restless from waiting, Susannah did what everyone is told not to do but does anyway, and consulted Doctor Google. Flicking through the most reputable medical websites she could find, she discovered that malaria, particularly certain strains, could be life-threatening, and that pneumonia, while treatable, can be dangerous in someone with a compromised immune system. Which Rob probably had, considering the state of him when he'd arrived back home. He probably hadn't been looking after himself properly, she fretted, clicking on the various links to find out more about both illnesses.

When Cara returned, she was frowning. "I just talked to Orlaith. She's very upset – and angry. She thought Rob was still in Thailand and said you'd promised that you'd be honest with them from now on."

Susannah raised her eyes to heaven. She could do without the complication of the twins getting irate and irrational again.

"They're making arrangements to come home anyway." Cara pulled out a second plastic chair and sat opposite Susannah. "I didn't try to dissuade them – was that the right thing to do?"

"Of course. They should be with their dad." Susannah thought of Doctor Google's bleak prognosis and hoped there might be good news by the time the girls arrived. She opened the top button of her shirt. It felt as if there wasn't enough oxygen to go around in the small, sterile, hospital room.

"I have to get out for a breath of fresh air. Can I get you a coffee?"

Cara looked as if she could do with something stronger after her conversation with her nieces but it was all Susannah could offer.

"No, I'm fine. I'll go out myself when you come back." Cara pulled a magazine out of her bag and began to listlessly turn the pages.

Susannah hurried out of the hospital, through the corridors, down the elevator, through the swing doors at the entrance. She found a café on a corner two streets away. Pushing the door open, she could see it was busy but she found a seat at the back and slumped down in the chair. She took in her surroundings. People here were doing ordinary things – checking their phones, having conversations with their companions, laughing out loud on occasion. Not tip-toeing around in a hushed, horrible atmosphere, waiting on news about their loved one's illness.

The normality of it all helped her to ground herself and she took a deep breath in. She had to figure out what she needed to do next. She ordered a double-strength espresso and thought about her daughters. She hoped they wouldn't take out all their fears on her again, like they had when they'd first heard Rob was in Thailand. Blaming the victim, she thought bitterly.

But was that really true? The thought came out of nowhere and took her by surprise. Up until now, everyone, apart from Orlaith and Jess, had agreed that the breakdown of her marriage had been entirely Rob's fault. But, by the time he'd left, he and Susannah hadn't had much to say to each other for a long time. And while it was a hard thing to admit to herself now, she'd known that, and she'd chosen to ignore it. Rob had become obsessed with his troublesome work situation and, as she now knew, plotting his grand escape. She had become over-involved in her daughters' lives until they'd left home. And by the time there was just the two them again, the rift between her and Rob had turned into a chasm they hadn't been able to bridge. Would they ever?

The waitress arrived back with her coffee and Susannah sipped the strong, aromatic brew gratefully. But she was interrupted by the sound of her mobile ringing.

Cara, she thought, fishing it out of her bag. Or Jess, looking for reassurance. Or Orlaith, to eat the head off her. But the screen was flashing an unknown number at her. It must be the hospital. Fear twisted Susannah's stomach into a hard knot.

"Hello," she asked, her voice high and shrill.

"Susannah Stevens?"

"Yes?" She tried to place the voice, to figure out which of the doctors she'd spoken to was calling her.

"It's Geraldo. Geraldo Laffite."

Susannah felt all the breath leave her body in one, huge sigh of relief. Geraldo! Funny how not so long ago this was a call she had been dreading. Now, once it wasn't someone phoning with more bad news about Rob, she didn't care who it was.

"What can I do for you?" she asked in a professional voice, willing her heart to stop racing and her pulse to return to normal.

"I sent you Harriet's contact number. But you haven't been in touch with her yet."

"I'm sorry but I've been busy with other things and I haven't got around to it yet."

"I understand. Listen, I have a proposition for you."

Another one! Susannah gripped her phone a little tighter.

"Yes," Geraldo continued smoothly, "I would like to offer you one-to-one training with me so we can heal your heart."

Despite everything she was going through, Susannah felt her mouth twitch into a smile. He really was incorrigible.

"So let me get this straight," she said. "Instead of suing me you want to help heal my heart?"

"Not help. Actually heal it. Look, I've been thinking about the tone of my email to your paper and I see now that I was not practising my own principles of love to all when I wrote it. So I am trying to live my values by making amends to you with this offer. Which, as you know, would cost thousands if you were to pay for it."

"Mr Laffite, my husband is ill at the moment, so while I am flattered that you want to help me, I'm afraid I can't take you up on your kind offer at this time."

"So he's back? From his travels?" Geraldo sounded fascinated.

"He is." She figured the less said the better. Besides she needed to get Geraldo off the phone is case the hospital rang.

"Be careful, Susannah."

"Excuse me?"

"You've been hurt and made bitter by this man's treatment of you. That's why you didn't approach my work with an open heart – I can see that now. And now he's back you need to ask yourself – has his wanderlust been truly sated?"

"Well, he's in an isolation ward in a semi-conscious state with a drip attached to his arm at the moment so for now I'd say the answer to that is an unequivocal yes." Susannah tried to keep her voice even. "And now I need to free up this phone in case the hospital is calling. If you contact the paper, my editor Katie Corrigan will talk to you about any other concerns you may have."

"So I won't see you again?" he said sadly. "You were a challenge to me, with your sceptical outlook. I have so much to teach you."

"I'm sure. Goodbye, Mr Laffite." Susannah hung up the phone.

He was as mad as a brush, she thought ruefully.

But his phone call had reminded her that she had work to juggle now as well as her family. She'd totally forgotten that she still had to write the article on Croagh Patrick. And the feature on James Moran would be published soon too. She hoped it would help people in a dark place, as James had wanted it to.

She knew now, for the first time, what he'd meant when he'd said that. Because if Rob were to die, she didn't know what she'd do.

She finished her coffee, left some change on the table and slung her bag over her shoulder. She needed to get back to the hospital. She wanted to be there when Rob woke up.

But she was too late. As she approached his room she could hear voices inside and, when she pushed the door open, she saw he was half sitting up, propped up on the pillows and talking to Cara.

"You're awake!" She strode over to his bedside. "You gave me such a fright. Are you feeling okay? The girls are on their way home. Have you spoken to the doctors?"

He raised his hand weakly to stop the onslaught of questions. "I've only just woken up. I don't remember anything after the last phone call I made to you. I must have spaced out or collapsed. I did try to let you know what was happening."

"I was stuck on a mountain," Susannah told him. "And I'd left my phone charging up in the hotel so I didn't get your messages for hours after you'd left them."

"You were stuck on a mountain?" He frowned, as if the thought was too much for him to figure out.

"It's a story for another day." Susannah brushed it off.

"He was just saying before you came back that he travelled near enough to the border of Thailand and Myanmar," Cara cut in.

"We'd better get this information to the doctors so." Susannah moved back towards the door.

"Why?" Rob looked puzzled.

"Because they think you may have malaria."

"Really? Thailand's a very low-risk country for malaria. I did my research."

"You did." Susannah had a flashback to the overflow of books

281

and documents she'd discovered in the box-room. "But low risk is not no risk. And they said if you were in a rural place near the borders there's a chance you could have picked it up."

"I went to see wild monkeys. It was jungly enough there, now that I think of it."

"So why didn't you take medication or whatever it is you're supposed to do when you're going to these places?"

"It was an 'impromptu' trip."

Dr Mason arrived back at that moment, looking as if he were in a hurry to be somewhere else.

"Ah, you're awake," he said when he saw Rob. He consulted his chart. "You're on antibiotics for pneumonia, Mr Stevens. And we're still waiting on lab results to make sure you don't have a tropical disease as well."

Rob told him about the monkeys and he scribbled something on his notes before smiling briefly and hurrying out of the room again.

Cara's phone beeped. "That's a text from Orlaith. They'll be arriving on an early flight in the morning. I can collect them at the airport." She stood up and looked from Susannah to Rob and back again. "And I think I'll leave you two alone now."

After Cara left, they sat in silence for a while, until Rob said finally, "You must think I'm a right idiot." He reached out to hold her hand and Susannah didn't know whether to snatch hers away or squeeze his tight as if she never wanted to let it go. Damn it, the man could still confuse her.

"So you got sick in Thailand. That's why you came home early?"

He sighed. "Yeah. Mostly that." He closed his eyes as if it was an effort to keep them open. "But the novelty was wearing off too. Once I got over the buzz of doing something totally out of character for me, of being impulsive, I started to realise that most of my problems were in my head. And my head, unfortunately, was still stuck on the top of my body and causing me the same old problems."

He opened his eyes again and grinned at her, and for a moment Susannah got a glimpse of the old Rob. There was so much she wanted to say to him. But she didn't know where to begin and the window of possibility closed almost immediately when he murmured, "I'm exhausted."

And then he fell asleep again. Susannah flicked through the magazine Cara had left until Dr Mason returned.

"The medication is likely to have him out of it," he said, observing the sleeping Rob. He looked at Susannah speculatively. "You might want to go home and get some sleep yourself. Your husband is a little better today but he's still a very sick man. You'll need to keep up your strength – no point in both of you being sick."

He was right. Sitting here all night made no sense. It would be a better use of her time if she went and got the beds ready for Orlaith and Jess – they'd be exhausted after their flight.

"I'll leave a message at the desk for someone to phone you if he's in any distress," the doctor promised.

"Thanks." Susannah gave him brief smile and squeezed Rob's hand briefly. There was nothing she could do here.

Once she got home, however, Susannah barely had the energy to brush her teeth, never mind change bedclothes. The trauma of the last few days crashed over her like a tidal wave and she fell, fully clothed, on to her bed and closed her eyes.

When she woke up it was six in the morning, she was freezing and her phone was ringing.

"It's Cara. The flight has landed. We should be home within the hour."

They descended on the house in a flurry of luggage, duty-free bags, and a barrage of questions. What happened this time? Had she been on to the hospital yet? When could they see their dad?

"Whoa!" Susannah put her hand up to slow them down. "Let's have a cup of tea first. You both look as if you could do with one."

Reluctantly they joined Cara at the kitchen table and Susannah busied herself with putting on the kettle and the toaster, all the while sneaking glances at her daughters to see how they were doing.

Jess had lost weight, she noticed at once. She was pale and withdrawn, barely eating her toast and ignoring the eggs Susannah had boiled.

Orlaith, on the other hand, looked glowing, her vibrant russet hair framing her beautiful face like a picture. But Susannah noticed she kept picking at her nails, and every so often she would sigh as if she couldn't quite catch her breath.

Over breakfast she filled them in on the details as quickly as she could. Rob had intended to let them know he was home but he'd ended up in hospital before he got the chance.

She steeled herself for their reaction, waiting for the interrogation about how she could have gone away for the weekend when their dad had been sick because, in truth, she'd been asking herself the same question.

But Jess didn't say anything at all and Orlaith just asked, "So he might still have malaria? And that's dangerous, yeah?"

"It depends on what strain you get apparently. And he might not have it at all."

Nobody seemed to have anything to say after that and so they all piled back into Cara's car and made their way back to the hospital.

CHAPTER 28

Katie was in work, looking at the feature on James Moran. It was a double-page spread with accompanying photos of James and his late son, a gorgeous young man with a shock of fair hair and a strong, athletic build. She couldn't take her eyes off him, trying to figure out what had gone so wrong in his life that he'd made such a catastrophic choice.

Katie knew the piece was going to create a strong resonance in her readers. James seemed to be an unusual soul, full of joy and gratitude despite having experienced despair and hopelessness, and Susannah's article, despite its dark narrative, was an uplifting one.

It was James's story, Katie reflected, that had started her re-evaluating her life. That and the time she had spent on Croagh Patrick with Susannah. They had both been all serene in the taxi going back to the hotel, but that hadn't lasted long for either of them. Katie's last conversation with Luke was still playing on her mind. And Susannah now had the husband back home, so ill apparently that the daughters had been summoned back from New York. Katie felt a stab of guilt again at the way she'd made light of his illness. What was it she'd said? If he's big enough to go to Southeast Asia on his own, he's big enough to call a doctor.

Susannah had phoned yesterday with an update.

Katie had been delighted to hear from her, especially when she said she'd send her the Croagh Patrick article as soon as possible. She'd been afraid Susannah would get drawn back into taking care of everybody else but herself again and that she might even quit the *Post*. Katie didn't want to lose someone who had turned out to be one of her best writers now that Daniel Gilbert was gone. But her concern was more than just professional. Somewhere along the line, she had started to feel like she'd found a kindred spirit in the older woman. Despite the fact they were so different from each other, both in age and temperament, Susannah seemed to get who Katie was, which was an unusual enough event. Now Katie desperately wanted a happy outcome for her new-found friend. Which she wasn't going to get if she went straight back into the arms of the sneak-off husband who'd probably only come home because he was too ill to stay away, she brooded.

But then she copped herself on and smiled ruefully. She was doing it again. She was getting caught up in what she imagined to be Susannah's awful problems instead of attempting to solve her own.

Katie folded over the paper and went to get herself a coffee. She had been at work since seven, and she was still nursing a sore ankle. She limped to the café she used to meet Daniel in, ordered a coffee and a pastry and tried to make sense of her life now.

Luke had kept his promise and arrived during the day when she was at work and removed all his possessions from her apartment. The first thing she noticed were his keys, placed like an accusation on the hall table.

She tossed them into the drawer, overwhelmed by a range of emotions. Sorrow of course, not only because the relationship was over but because it had ended so badly.

But there had been relief too – relief that she was free again. And that she had her apartment back to herself.

And now she had to admit the relief was the strongest emotion by far. She finished her coffee and went back to the office, intent on getting ready for the afternoon news conference.

But she was only back five minutes when Jennifer Leslie scooted her chair into her cubicle, bristling with importance and holding out one of the British newspapers. She must have news – probably some celebrity gossip that Katie couldn't care less about. But she'd made a resolution to try to get on better with people, so she smiled pleasantly.

"Jennifer. What can I do for you?"

"See your old pal has got a big media award for himself?" Jennifer smirked.

"What old pal?"

"How many old pals do you have in the media then? Here, have a look. Daniel Gilbert. Awarded best humorous writer for his *Footloose and Fancy-free* column. Some big blog award. They say papers will be irrelevant soon," she added darkly. "Everything will be online."

"Well, we'll have to cross that bridge when we come to it," Katie said. She was used to Jennifer's doomsday predictions and while she was sure she had a point, she didn't feel like discussing it with her right now. Or ever.

She took the newspaper from Jennifer and saw Daniel staring up at her, clutching a gong and standing in a line-up of other award-winners. She smiled. His hair was still long and tousled, he still had that beaming, impish grin she remembered and – oh God, she wished she could see him again.

"Are you still in contact with him?" Jennifer was watching her curiously.

"Not since he left." Katie recalled the email Daniel had sent her from London and how she'd deleted it because she was committing to her future with Luke. She wondered if it was still in her trash file, which is where her relationship with Luke had ended up.

"He's written his very last *Footloose* column too, so I'm glad he got the award for it."

Katie frowned. "Wasn't the whole point of him moving that the bosses loved the *Footloose and Fancy-free* stuff?"

Jennifer shrugged. "Maybe he's met someone, moved on. Everyone has to eventually. Even Daniel. You'd miss him around the office, wouldn't you?"

"You would," Katie said, trying to keep her voice neutral. But as soon as Jennifer went back to her own desk, she snatched up the newspaper again to read the article more carefully. Jennifer was right. Daniel had written his last *Footloose and Fancy-free* column some time back and she hadn't even known about it. She turned to her computer and clicked on various links until she found the article online. **Why I'm Giving Up Being Footloose and Fancy-free.**

She settled down to read it, expecting to be as entertained as she'd always been by Daniel's columns. But moments later, she was feeling flat and despondent. Daniel was giving up the column because, as he wrote, **"There comes a time when we all have to finally decide what it is we want to be when we grow up and that time for me is now. It happens when something – or someone – comes along and changes our point of view, makes us see things differently. Now the allure of the unknown just isn't as attractive to me any more. I've stopped wondering if there's someone better out there because I know I've already met the best."**

And on it went, for another five hundred words. Katie gave up on the article halfway through. She didn't find Daniel's witticisms funny any more, and besides, she'd got his point in the first line. Daniel Gilbert hadn't grown up – she wasn't sure he could, even if he wanted to. But he'd met someone who made him want to.

And it was too late for Katie to do anything about it. Her *Footloose and Fancy-free* guy was all settled down now.

That evening, Katie made tea and grimaced as she threw a ready-made meal into the microwave. It hadn't taken her long to forget about the benefits of healthy meals she'd been preaching to Luke about.

When the doorbell rang she opened it to find her mother standing there, wearing a stylish belted trench coat and colourful flats.

Katie looked down at her tracksuit and wondered how come her mother was more stylish that she was. That was something she could spend her spare time doing – developing a decent wardrobe.

She made a pot of tea, put out her cups, transferred her dinner from its plastic tray onto a plate.

"You want anything to eat?"

Olivia shook her head. "Any more word from Luke?"

"Nope. There's no reason for us to talk. It's over for good this time."

When she'd first told her mother how the relationship had ended so badly she'd been worried she'd be judgemental but she'd only been concerned about how Katie was.

Now she looked at Katie speculatively and asked again, "And how do you feel about it now?"

"It was the right thing to do. I know that. But," Katie shrugged, "I feel guilty all the time."

"About Daniel?"

Katie nodded.

"But you were broken up with Luke when that happened. And then you decided you didn't want to be with Luke after all. There's no law against it."

"But we were together for four years!" Katie said passionately. "He thought we were getting married. He took that stupid Valentine's column as a message from me."

"Well, that's for him to work out. You're not married. You don't have children together or even a shared property to sell.

There's nothing complicated about it. You don't even appear to be that heartbroken about it if I'm not mistaken. Am I wrong?'

"No, you're not," Katie admitted. "I'm relieved to be honest. But I'm worried too. What if I didn't want to get married because I don't want to run the risk of it all falling apart – making the same mistake as you and Dad did?"

Olivia took a small packet of sweeteners out of her bag and stirred one into her tea.

"Is that what you were afraid of? When you were living with Luke?"

"It was something I worried about. And now we're split up all I can see is another wrecked relationship behind me – just like with Dad and Seán."

"Well, they are very different situations, Katie, and it's dangerous to get them mixed up. Anyhow why all the angst about your dad and Seán now? You never wanted to meet them – or even talk about them."

"It was a feature Susannah Stevens wrote. It's about a guy whose son took his own life when he was only a teenager. And I got to thinking back to my teenage years and how difficult I found life then. But it also made me realise that we don't have all the time we think we might have to put things right with someone."

"So why wait? Meet your dad and Seán now if that's what you want to do. Stop putting obstacles in your own way, Katie. People often have very different viewpoints of the same situation. You've always known what mine was about my marriage breakdown. Maybe it might help you if you found out about your dad's now?"

"Maybe," Katie murmured. "I'll think about it."

They finished their tea and were watching one of their favourite long-running TV dramas when Olivia announced that she had some news of her own.

"I've got a work contract in Surrey for six months – so I'll be moving to England in a few weeks' time."

"Seriously?" Katie felt like crying. She was used to her mother's nomadic ways, but this time it just felt like someone else was leaving her.

"You can come and visit me," Olivia told her.

That's what Daniel had said to her, the last time she'd talked to him, Katie remembered. And of course she hadn't, and now it was all too late.

"How do you get used to all the moving?" She shook her head. "We did so much of it when I was little that all I want now is stability."

"We did move a lot," Olivia said thoughtfully. "But inside I wasn't moving, inside I was stagnating because I'd stayed in a failed marriage for too long. I didn't like that feeling then and I like it less now. So, if I start to feel like I'm in a rut, I know it's time for me to make changes. And I've set up my life so that is possible."

"You are the exact opposite of me," Katie told her. "My life is set up so that as little change as possible can come my way."

"Change is happening all the time anyway." Olivia looked at her daughter closely. "Sometimes it's important to believe that you can be the agent of that change instead of leaving it all to the vagaries of fate and nature."

"I'm not sure I'd know how to do that," Katie said sadly.

"Well, don't wait on a big message to be written in the sky," Olivia advised. "Think about something you'd like to change and take one small step in that direction. And see where it takes you. That's all."

"Maybe I will," she smiled.

After her mother left, Katie thought about what she'd said. What was a tiny thing she could do to change the way she felt? Now, tonight?

The answer was instantaneous. Read the email from Daniel. But what was the point in that, Katie argued with herself. He'd moved on now – had found what he was looking for with someone else. And what was it Susannah had said? That maybe she wasn't missing Daniel so much as the fact that she had no fun in her own life. It would serve her better to concentrate on that instead of attempting to live vicariously through Daniel Gilbert again.

But the thoughts wouldn't leave her alone. What harm could it do to just read it? And wasn't she curious to find out what he'd wanted to say to her back then anyway?

She was. So she opened up her laptop and searched her trash box until she found what she was looking for.

Hi Katie,

I hope you are well and your life is back on track. No, that's a lie. I don't wish that for you because you deserve so much more. I know our night together complicated things for you and I'm sorry about that. But I don't regret it – and I never will.

I don't want to come between you and Luke, though, so I am afraid I have to withdraw my offer to let you couch-surf in London with me any time you want.

I miss you so much. I never thought I would, so I guess that saying about not missing someone until they're gone is true. Even though it sounds like a terrible country and western song.

I know you will probably laugh out loud at this but I want you to know that you have influenced me in so many ways.

So much so that I want to change – I want to be more responsible so if I meet someone like you again – someone who wants an actual life instead of the series of

who-cares days I've been stringing together for so long now – well, then I might have something to offer her.

And, Katie – I know you always said I made you laugh and I loved that because it's what I like to do most in the world – make people laugh.

But I never told you that the reverse was true too. Nobody brightened up my day like you did.

Love, Daniel x.

Katie shut down the email and stared into space.

So he'd found his elusive someone, someone like her.

But he couldn't have. It was the same voice that had insisted she open up the email.

Because there was nobody else like her.

And whoever it was, she would be second best. The same way as anyone she met wouldn't compare to him.

She took a deep breath. Her mother had said to take one small step and see what direction it would take her in. And that direction was clear as crystal to her now.

She had to see Daniel Gilbert again.

CHAPTER 29

Susannah was in the kitchen, putting the final touches to a big family dinner.

She steamed the potatoes and put them in the top oven to keep them hot while she carved the rosemary chicken she'd just roasted. The room was steamy and she felt flustered. Rob had been home a week and there had been no mention of the girls going back to New York.

Pine Close was full again, the scenario she had fantasised about for so long. But when Susannah had imagined a day like this, back at the beginning of the year, they had all been living happy and productive lives, the chaos of family life a small price to pay for the love and closeness connecting them all.

Instead the girls were nervy and highly strung and, while Susannah had not forgotten how untidy they were, she had not predicted how irritable she would feel to see every room in the house littered with their personal effects.

They appeared to have brought every possession they had in New York back home with them and, apart from the fact that the clutter made her anxious, it also led her to wonder if they were home for good. If they had quit the internships, it left them with uncertain futures. Just like the rest of the Stevens family.

She hadn't brought it up with them yet because she felt she

was walking on eggshells as they came to terms with the fact that their dad could have died.

They had been devastated at the sight of Rob, weak and pale in the isolation room, with the drip still in his arm, the fever not yet abated. And then Orlaith had transformed into someone Susannah barely recognised, charming the enigmatic Dr Mason within minutes of meeting him.

"I'm just in from New York," she told him meaningfully, as she pressed her hand into his, as if reassuring him that Rob had one responsible member of the family in his corner now.

"I'm so pleased to meet you both," he said, shaking both her and Jessie's hands. "I'm a tropical disease specialist and I can assure you we are doing everything we can for your dad. It looks pretty definite he has malaria. We're checking out what the strain is right now."

Susannah looked at him properly for the first time. He had blond hair and dark, definite eyebrows. He looked as if he was barely out of school and she marvelled that Rob's life might lie in his youthful hands.

But he had many years of experience, he explained to Orlaith and seemed keen to pass on every relevant piece of information at his disposal to her daughter.

"Don't worry, we have this," he told Orlaith finally, putting his hand on her shoulder.

Orlaith rewarded him with a look of adoration and after that, any time they needed to know anything at all about Rob, Orlaith was sent off to find out from Doctor Mason. Susannah would place bets that she left the hospital with his telephone number when Rob was discharged.

With the dinner finally prepared she called everyone to the table but they hardly spoke to each other, beyond asking someone else to pass the salt. Soon enough Susannah was scraping most of the food into the bin, Rob had gone back to bed and the girls had disappeared after him.

They had spent the last week fussing over him as if he was a newborn baby and in fairness he probably needed all the help he could get. He was weak as a kitten and the doctors had said that while they felt they had treated him on time, it would be a while before he was back to full health. There was also a chance that the malaria could recur in the future.

Susannah didn't want to wait for an indeterminate time before she and Rob figured out a way forward, nor did she want the girls putting their whole lives on hold either. But right now she was trying to keep everyone happy until they'd all had the chance to calm down.

She finished tidying the kitchen and escaped to the relative peace of the conservatory. She was meeting Katie that afternoon and she needed to work on story ideas.

Miraculously a whole hour went by without interruption and when her phone rang she answered it absent-mindedly, her eyes still on her computer screen.

"Hello?"

"Susannah? It's James Moran."

"James!" She was taken aback to hear from him. Katie had told her that the feature had been published but it felt as if it belonged to another part of her life, a life that was now over. Hearing his voice jarred with her new reality and left her feeling disorientated.

"I see the feature is in the paper." He sounded pleased.

"Yes, I heard. I would have called you but I haven't been at work for a while because ..." She was about to explain about Rob but she changed her mind. James had hardly phoned to hear about her personal problems. "Were you happy with it?" she asked instead and held her breath as she waited for an answer. It wasn't beyond the realms of possibility that Katie or someone else had tinkered with the article at the last minute, unbeknownst to her. They might have changed the tenor or the tone or put an inappropriate headline over it. She so wanted it be right for him.

"More than happy," he said and Susannah let out a tiny sigh of relief.

"So much so," James continued, "that I would like to take you out for lunch if I may?"

She hesitated.

"It's a beautiful day," he prompted.

She looked out the window. The sun was shining from a clear, blue sky. Susannah knew it couldn't be long before it was winter again and days like this would be a rarity.

And, apart from all of that, someone had just switched on rock music at an ear-shattering volume.

"I wouldn't have time for a full lunch," she said, "but I do have to meet my editor today so I'll be in the city. How about meeting in Stephen's Green for a takeaway coffee?"

The park at the top of Grafton Street was one of Susannah's favourite places in the city. Years ago she used to go there in her lunch-break and she still remembered how she loved watching the way the changing seasons showed on the trees and the plants. And it was near enough to the café where she was meeting Katie.

"Great. I'll bring the coffees so."

Susannah remembered how she'd felt attracted to James when he'd come to her house, and even though it had been unreciprocated, she wondered about the wisdom of meeting him again, especially now. But he sounded so pleased about meeting up that she couldn't help looking forward to seeing him too.

She grabbed her bag and coat.

Jess was sitting at the kitchen table, poring over an Internet article on rare tropical diseases.

"That's not going to do anyone any good," Susannah said, but Jess just glowered at her. "I'm off to meet my editor —" she began but Orlaith suddenly appeared in the kitchen.

"Do you think that's wise?" she demanded. "Look what happened the last time you went off to work when Dad was sick. He almost died."

The accusatory tone was heavy and Susannah knew she was going to have to sit both of her daughters down soon and have a chat with them about all that had happened.

"Well, you're both here now," she pointed out.

"That's a heavy burden to put on us. What if he gets sick again?" Jess looked terrified.

"All the numbers are on the fridge." Susannah nodded to the neatly typed contact numbers of the hospital.

"And what if Dad needs you?" Orlaith demanded.

Susannah sighed. She didn't want to fight with either of them, not when she hadn't seen them in so long. And not when they were all under such strain. But this couldn't go on. She took a deep breath.

"You're right. Me being busy with work probably isn't what your dad needs right now. Or what you two need either. But it's what I need. And what I want. So I'll keep my phone beside me at all times but unless there's an emergency," she looked at them meaningfully, "you're all going to have to work it out for yourselves."

And she swept out of the house.

Despite the sunshine, there was a chill in the air and Susannah shivered in her thin jacket as she sat on a wooden bench waiting for James. The park was busy today, the clear day bringing in hordes of shoppers and tourists to enjoy the beauty of the gardens.

A family of four, two toddlers and their parents, were busy feeding the ducks in front of her.

A little bit away, two young tourists were taking photos of each other, delighting in each other's company. The woman had a dark, pixie haircut and was wearing a light black coat with biker boots. She was leaning against the low wall of the bridge over the lake, her back arched as she looked laughingly into the man's face as he took her photograph. He was a head taller than she was, blond, in a denim jacket and blue jeans. His head was bent towards her, engrossed in getting the best shot.

Susannah's mind suddenly catapulted back through the years to a memory, sharp as the crisp blue of the sky above her, to an evening when she and Rob were coming home from a concert and had cut through here on their way to meet up with some friends for dinner.

She frowned, trying to remember the details. They were married, but they weren't parents yet. There had been just the two of them, and they had been everything to each other. Comparing that happy time to now, and all the confusion and chaos back at Pine Close, she felt as if her heart would break.

She spotted James sauntering towards her and she shook off the memories. He was carrying take-away coffees and a brown-paper bag from one of the delis on Grafton Street and she couldn't help noticing that sense of ease he had about himself. He had come through worse than this, she reminded herself, far worse. And he had found happiness again. And she would too.

They spent a happy forty minutes sitting in the sunshine. Susannah fed most of her sandwich to the ducks, since she was meeting Katie straight afterwards for lunch. James had brought a copy of the newspaper and it was the first chance Susannah had to see how her article looked published.

She was pleased with it – nobody seemed to have altered her copy, the headline was respectful and, most of all, James was happy with it. They finished their coffees and sat in companionable silence for a while.

Then James said out of the blue, "Remember you bought a *Social Media for Dummies* book when you called to the shop that day?"

"I do." Susannah smiled at the memory. She hadn't even opened it yet. Social-media mastery seemed a long way down her list of priorities right now, whatever Katie felt about it being an essential career skill for her. But then James said something that made her change her mind.

"I still do some IT consultancy work – as much to keep up my own skills as anything – and I'd be happy to help you out. No charge of course – unless you wanted to cook me dinner the odd time in return?"

Susannah thought of bringing James back home to Pine Close for dinner and hid a smile. That wasn't going to happen for the foreseeable future. But she didn't have to go into that right now.

"I'd be delighted if you would do that," she said at once and she meant it. Because being in his company made her feel more relaxed than she had in weeks.

She wasn't going to give up on the chance to feel like this again and soon, just because Rob had deigned to rock back up in her life.

CHAPTER 30

Katie sat in her hotel room looking at a street map of London. She had already phoned Daniel to tell him she was here for business – a small white lie. The truth was she didn't know what she was hoping to achieve by coming. She was acting out of a compulsion, listening to a gut instinct she didn't understand and which was making her feel crazy right now. This wasn't who she was, she fretted – acting impulsively, chasing after guys who were with someone else.

She took out the printout of his email, the one she had tucked away in her purse and read it yet again. **'I miss you so much.' 'Nobody brightened up my day like you did.'** These were phrases that were imprinted on her brain, the ones that had led to her being here today. Going for what she wanted. To see him again. It was something she did in her work all the time – so why did she find it so scary when it was her personal life?

Daniel had seemed to be his usual cheerful self when she'd phoned him, but she felt he was a bit wary too. They talked about work and he said he was busy all the time with the new job. They'd arranged to meet today during his lunch hour and he'd invited her to his home for dinner that evening. She presumed it would be a take-away but she didn't mind. She just wanted to see him and she was looking forward to seeing where he lived.

She looked at her reflection in the mirror. Her hair was nice, she supposed. It was blonde, newly highlighted and fell in soft waves past her shoulders. But she didn't look her best. The changes she was trying to bring into her life – to be spontaneous, embrace change, and face up to the past – they had all brought plenty of anxiety with them, and she had a pinched look about her. Without her usual highly controlled routine, she felt like she was walking on a high wire without a safety net. But she had plenty of make-up on, a funky new jacket that was a departure from her usual style and a determination to get on with things.

It was all about finishing, she reflected, sitting in the back of the cab as it drove through the London streets. She was sick of relationships ending awkwardly, leaving her with a residue of anxiety about them. She wanted to break that pattern now. She was hoping to resolve her unsatisfactory ending with Daniel and to get to keep him as a friend at least.

Luke was already lost to her in that capacity. They had met again, at Katie's request, and she had tried her best to connect with him. But he'd been so cold and angry that she knew almost immediately it was a lost cause. She'd probably never see him again, she realised, and to be honest she didn't much mind. That made her wonder about the four years they'd spent together. How real could it have been if the relationship could be ditched so easily?

And then there was her dad. When she told Olivia about the flashback she'd had when she and Luke were arguing, her mother had suggested again that she needed to sort out her feelings about the past, and that maybe it was time to forgive her father.

She peered out the window as the cab pulled up outside the address she'd given the driver. The café where she was meeting Daniel reminded her of a bistro she'd eaten in once in New York. There was a blackboard on the pavement, with the day's menu written up in different-coloured chalks. Window-boxes stuffed with late summer flowers adorned the windowsills and two big bay trees stood like sentries on either side of the entrance. She paid the driver and went inside. It had big oval mirrors on the walls, steel furniture and a lot of baristas busy making very aromatic coffee.

She found Daniel sitting in an alcove towards the back of the room. A dark-haired woman was sitting beside him, her head almost touching his as she leaned in to look at something on his phone. Katie's spirits dipped. Was this her? The woman who'd made Daniel want to settle down? She hadn't bargained on meeting her quite so soon. Or at all, if she was honest. But here they were, all together. She pushed back her shoulders and approached the table.

"Katie!" Daniel greeted her like a long-lost friend, standing up and wrapping his arms around her in a huge bear hug. She wanted to freeze time in that moment, and just stay there, with her head buried in his chest. But it was only seconds before he was letting her go, eager to introduce her to his friend.

"This is Lauren. And Lauren – this, finally, is Katie."

Lauren stood up too and extended her hand in greeting. "Daniel's told me a lot about you, Katie. I'm so pleased to meet you at last."

Katie shook hands and tried to look pleased to meet her too. Lauren was petite, with black shiny hair cut in a feathery bob. She had a heart-shaped face and her clothes were casual for a workday – a white floaty top over black leggings and cowboy boots and a lot of silver jewellery, including rings on almost all her fingers.

They all ordered coffee and cakes and sat and chatted about inconsequential things. Katie learned that Lauren was a journalist too. She wrote about health and fitness and Katie found herself telling her about the *Post's* MBS pages and how popular they were with her readers.

She was easy company, very like Daniel in that respect actually

– relaxed, friendly, optimistic. Katie couldn't help liking her and in different circumstances she would have been enjoying herself here.

They got around to talking about Daniel's blog award.

"It was well deserved," Lauren said. "But I have to say I do miss reading the *Footloose* column. But I suppose it wouldn't have worked once you'd given up the chase."

Katie wondered if it was her imagination or whether a private look passed between them. Either way, she felt like an outsider now.

She took up the bill. "I'll get this," she smiled. "I need to be getting back. It was nice meeting you, Lauren."

"You too," Lauren said.

"I'll see you tonight." Daniel got up to accompany her to the cash desk but Katie waved him away. She went up to the cash register and, while she was waiting for her change, she took a surreptitious look back at them. Lauren was laughing at something he'd just said and he was smiling down at her. And they looked so comfortable and happy together that Katie just wanted to cry.

She'd planned to catch a double-decker bus back to her hotel, with the intention of taking in her surroundings from the top deck as she travelled back through the city. But she spent the whole journey staring unseeingly out through the window, playing back the scene in the café in her mind. Lauren's head leaning in towards Daniel's. How they both shared the same sense of humour, had laughed at the same things.

She was glad he'd met someone nice, she thought bravely. Daniel deserved to be happy – and if that left Katie feeling sad and broken because she'd missed the boat with him then so be it.

Later, lying on the hotel bed, staring at the ceiling, she found herself again doubting the wisdom of embracing change. Right now, she wished she were back at work, editing the pages of the *Post*. She felt busy and safe there and, if she felt a bit stuck sometimes, well, it wasn't a bad trade-off. Instead she was here, on her own in an anonymous hotel room in London, worried about how tonight was going to go and feeling adrift on a high sea of dangerous emotions she had no idea how to handle.

When she couldn't stand her own thoughts any more she pulled on her jacket and took the lift down to the hotel lobby. She bought herself a very fancy journal and pen from the shop and went into the bar and ordered herself a large coffee.

Then she sat down and thought hard. She had wanted this trip to be spontaneous and free but she couldn't bring herself to just arrive at Daniel's home with no idea of why exactly she was there. What exactly am I trying to achieve, she asked herself.

She scribbled down the answers as they came to her.

I want to tell Daniel I'm happy that he's met someone as cool as Lauren.

I want him to know I've broken up with Luke again and that this time I know it's the right thing.

I want to tell him I miss him and, now that he's with someone else, that I'd love for us to be friends again.

That was it. She felt happier as she looked at what she'd written. If she could achieve these three things tonight, then she could go home tomorrow without feeling that the whole trip had been a wasted journey. She closed the journal and felt relief that at last she felt a tiny bit more in control of her day.

And while she was feeling this way, there was something else she could do. She scrolled through the photos on her phone until she found what she was looking for. The latest pictures she had of her dad. There were half a dozen of them, all taken on the same day one Christmas, at a perfunctory lunch that Katie had begrudgingly attended and then spent the time being annoyed because her dad had dragged Seán along too.

Her half-brother had even less to say to Katie than she had to say to him, so her dad had spent the time taking a bunch of photos, no doubting trying to ignore the mounting tension between the three of them.

But then, how could that lunch have turned out any other way? Katie asked herself. Seán was like a stranger to her and she had shut her dad out of her heart a very long time ago. She didn't know how to begin letting him back in now – even if he was still interested in her after all this time.

But she was still on her mission to be a better person, even if she didn't have to make amends to Luke any more, so she fired off a text, asking her dad if he wanted to meet up at the weekend. It would be something to do at least, she told herself. And it might help her sort out some stuff, like Olivia had said.

That evening, Katie arrived at the Notting Hill neighbourhood Daniel lived in. She was deliberately early, keen to explore a neighbourhood she had been fascinated with since she'd seen the movie of the same name. And she was delighted to see it was everything she'd imagined.

It was full of bookshops and cafés and curio shops, lending the area a bohemian air that she loved. It had cobblestoned alleyways, pastel Victorian townhouses, and big white mansion-sized houses. Buoyed up by the atmosphere of the funky neighbourhood she forgot the time and it was some time before she realised she needed to get a move on.

She pulled out her street map, trying to reorient herself and figure out which direction she should go in now to get to Daniel's flat. But just at that moment, wet raindrops fell, spattering her map. She looked up to see thunderclouds racing through the darkening evening sky and soon the rain was coming down in sheets.

Within minutes she was soaked, her hair plastered to her head, her dress flapping damply against her bare legs. She was forced to slow down in case she slipped again in her heels and by the time she found Daniel's flat she was fifteen minutes late.

He lived in a flat in one of the big white houses she had been admiring earlier and, as she waited for him to answer the doorbell, she couldn't help comparing it to her own bland two-bedroom apartment back in Dublin. And once again she felt a stab of envy at Daniel's life.

His flat was on the third floor, a steep climb that left her breathless. Daniel was waiting for her on the landing.

"You're soaked!" He pulled her into the flat. "Let me get you a towel."

She waited for him, looking around her in astonishment. The flat was simply stunning. It had white walls and exotic artwork, floorboards the colour of the sun and a window dressed with pristine navy curtains, framing a picture-postcard view of a small park facing the flat.

Two grey sofas flanked a black iron fireplace where a small fire was building. A slate-grey dining-room table was set for dinner with candles and flowers and a blue jug of mint water in the middle. Soul music was streaming through a white speaker and there was the aroma of something delicious being cooked in the kitchen.

It like stepping into a movie set, an oasis of colour and artistry and beauty. Why had she thought Daniel would be living like a student, with unwashed dishes and microwaved food?

"This is so beautiful," she breathed.

"Thank you." He handed her a white towel and rubbed a tendril of her hair between his thumb and two fingers. "The water's hot if you want to take a shower while I'm putting the finishing touches to dinner. You can wear one of my tracksuits and put your clothes in the dryer."

309

"You shouldn't have gone to so much trouble." She indicated the beautifully set table. "I thought we'd have takeaway tonight."

"Spicy butterbean and red-lentil dhal with fresh spinach actually. Superfoods."

She burst out laughing. "When were you ever into superfoods?"

"Always." He looked surprised. "The panini lunch I used to have with you was a once-a-week treat only."

She hadn't known that. She'd made assumptions about him based on absolutely nothing and she guessed now there were probably a lot of things she didn't know about Daniel. They had only ever met in a work setting until the tequila-slammer night.

She took him up on his offer of a shower, taking her time there in the en-suite of his bedroom, checking for any signs of Lauren while she was at it. She didn't find anything.

She wandered back out into the living room in the borrowed oversize tracksuit. "I couldn't find a hairdryer," she said.

"Yeah, I have one somewhere, but it's nothing fancy. I can check in Lauren's room for something better if you like."

Katie tried to hide her surprise. Lauren lived here? In a different bedroom? What the hell could that mean?

"No. Don't. I can towel-dry it." She wrapped a towel turban-style around her head.

Daniel served the dhal with mini naan breads and a big green salad. When he was pouring the wine she thought briefly of their tequila-slammer night but her mind was preoccupied with Lauren. She was about to ask him about her when her phone rang.

It was a text from her dad saying he was on holiday with "the family" at the moment but, when he got back, they'd definitely meet up. The way he used "the family" brought up all the old feelings of abandonment for her. She was his family too, she thought angrily, shoving the phone back into her bag.

"What was that?" Daniel asked, noticing her change in mood.

"I'm trying to arrange a meet-up with my semi-estranged dad. We don't have a very good relationship but when I was stuck on Croagh Patrick I was thinking what if I died out here and I never got around to trying to fix things with him?"

"Wait a minute! What if you died on Croagh Patrick? What's all that about?"

"Oh." She'd forgotten he didn't know anything about her life any more. "Myself and Susannah did it together and I sprained my ankle on the way back and couldn't walk. It was misty and the stones were slippery. We had to wait for over an hour for help to come along and for the want of something better to do, I got to thinking about life, love and the universe."

"But what made you want to climb Croagh Patrick in the first place? I didn't have you down as the outdoor type?"

"I'm not. Susannah was writing a feature for the *Post* – and I," she grinned, "I was doing penance for cheating on Luke."

He burst out laughing. "You cannot be serious! You are. Go on, tell me. Did it work?"

"We broke up the day I came home."

"You and Luke are broken up?"

He was surprised, she thought, but not jumping up and down with joy.

"Yes. I told him about us. And you were right. It was a deal-breaker for him."

He raised his glass at her. "Good decision. If Luke couldn't cope then he wasn't good enough for you."

"I'm happy it's over this time. Here's to better times." She clinked her glass against his and they both took a sip of wine.

"So how have you been, apart from breaking up with Luke and getting stranded on mountains. As soon as I turn my back too."

"Well, I'm trying to change."

"Why do you need to change? There's nothing wrong with you."

She told him about Olivia saying people needed to embrace

change and how reading Susannah's feature on James Moran had made her think more deeply about her own life. She explained about her chaotic childhood and the scars left by her parents fighting over their divorce and the constant moving about. It had all left her, she told him, with the feeling that she was only ever safe if she kept to a very predictable routine.

He looked at her thoughtfully. "I think we all make decisions when we are young but they are not always good ones. I've figured out that the reason I never have goals and plans is because of something that happened to me. I had a sister – but – well, she died when we were children. She was drowned at sea – a freak wave overturned our boat. She was two years younger than me. It was then I decided I'd just deal with each day as it came and not expect too much in the way of fulfilling ambitions. It seemed enough that I got to live and she didn't. And I guess I wanted to really enjoy my life – as a way of honouring her, you know?"

"I think I do," Katie said slowly. "I am so sorry that happened to you. It's a very sad story."

"It was a long time ago now. And, to be honest, I'm starting to wonder if I went too far with the no-planning rule. Sometimes I think it might be good to have something to aim for – but then I think life can't be bossed about like that so why bother?"

"But things are working out for you, aren't they? You've met Lauren now and – well, I just wanted to say I like her. She's nice." Katie was remembering what she'd come here for.

He raised his eyebrows. "You think myself and Lauren are together?"

"Yes. Aren't you?"

"With separate bedrooms?"

She shrugged. "Maybe she snores."

That got her a smile. "She doesn't snore. Not so loud that I'd hear her anyway."

"So who have you met?" Kate persisted. "You wrote in your last *Footloose* column that you'd met someone who made you want to grow up?"

"That would have been you, Katie." He watched closely for a reaction.

"Me? But I —"

"Was with Luke. Or so I thought when I was writing it. But I figured that if I were to meet someone I loved, then she'd probably be like you. So I thought I'd start getting my act together so I'd be ready." His eyes softened. "It was always you, Katie. From the very first day I saw you at the *Post*."

"It was?" Her eyes were filling up. "By how come you didn't tell me at the beginning?" She was frustrated with all the crossed wires, terrified at how close she had come to never hearing any of this.

"You were with Luke for all the time I've known you. And, for the short time you weren't, I lost no time as I remember."

She smiled. That was true enough.

"But, to be honest, there was something else."

"What?" she was full of fear again, trying to imagine what obstacle he had now that would stop them being together.

"I thought I'd be punching above my weight with you," he said simply. "You always seemed so together and responsible. A grown-up. And I just lived from day to day – no plans, no commitments. Nothing to be 'on track' for."

"I'm starting to think being on track might be overrated," she said slowly.

"Seriously? Because I have been trying so hard to train myself in that direction. To be responsible. Get my act together. Have something to offer."

She looked around at his gorgeous flat, and the lovely meal he'd surprised her with and the way she felt so happy just being here with him.

"You know, Daniel, I can do responsible – with one hand tied behind my back if needs be. So maybe you could concentrate on the fun? We could play to our strengths instead of killing ourselves trying to be someone we're not?"

That earned her one of the heart-melting smiles she remembered so well from the *Post*. "I can do fun."

They both had big smiles now, hardly able to believe they were on the same page at last.

"Katie Corrigan, I believe we have here what you corporate types call a win–win situation!" Daniel got up and came around to her side of the table. He stood behind her, untwisted the towel and began to weave his fingers through her still damp hair.

She let out a tiny sigh – with relief or happiness, she wasn't quite sure. All she knew was that for the first time in her life she felt like she'd come home.

"Nothing wrong with win–win, Daniel."

"I love win–win. And I love you, Katie. I always have."

CHAPTER 31

Susannah was running late by the time she got to the café. Katie was already there, seated at a table near the back, fanning herself absent-mindedly with the menu. There was something different about her, Susannah noticed immediately, something softer she'd never noticed before.

"Susannah! How's Rob?"

Concern and guilt were etched on Katie's face and Susannah knew she was regretting how dismissive she had been of Rob's illness.

"Well, it was malaria in the end, but the doctors think they caught it in time. It will take him a while to recover though. And, apparently, it can recur. The girls are watching him like hawks. It's a bit tense at home at the moment."

Susannah sat down and they both placed their lunch order and talked about work while they waited.

"So did Geraldo call you?" Susannah asked. "I was waiting on a call from the hospital and I had to direct him to you."

"He did, yeah. He's dropping his threat to sue us – it wasn't aligned to his values apparently." She shook her head. "He's a colourful character all right."

Susannah smiled. "He offered to work with me for free – help me to heal my heart. Did he mention that to you?"

"He didn't get a chance to say much. I was busy and said we'd consider doing a follow-up if he's coming to Dublin and he seemed happy enough with that. By the way, he gave me a phone number for you – Harriet, I think the name was."

"Ah yes, Harriet." Susannah was definitely going to ring her. She really wanted to find out if she was any closer to her ideal life. And despite Susannah's continuing distrust of Geraldo Laffite she really hoped that Harriet was making progress.

"The piece with James Moran is getting great feedback," Katie remarked. "It seems to have touched something in people. I get the impression he's a special sort of person."

"He does have something special about him," Susannah agreed. "You know he was an IT expert in another life? Well, he's offered to give me a crash course in social media. So I'm taking your advice."

Katie grinned. "Nothing like a crash course in social media for getting a woman all red and flustered."

"I like him," Susannah admitted. "But I don't think I'd inflict myself and my emotional baggage on him even if he was interested. I need to sort my head out first." She wasn't joking. She was no closer to figuring out what she and Rob were supposed to do now and the fact was there was a very big elephant living in Pine Close that everyone was busy ignoring.

The waiter returned with their order and Susannah took the chance to change the subject. "So what's been going on with you then?"

Katie pulled a face. "Well, Luke's moved out."

"It's over? Again?"

"Again and for good this time. It's for the best."

"Did you tell him in the end? About you and Daniel?"

Katie's eyes clouded over. "I did. It was awful. I wish it could have ended differently, you know? Better. So I took your advice and spoke to my mother. She said I shouldn't be so scared of changes because change happens anyway. And sometimes we need to help it along instead of running away from it. And if I didn't know how to do that, then all I needed to do was to start by taking one, tiny step."

"And what tiny step did you pick?" Susannah was curious. Maybe this was an approach she could use to resolve her difficulties with Rob.

"I went to London to find Daniel Gilbert."

"You what?" Susannah dropped her dessertspoon into her lemon mousse.

"Well, that was a big step." Katie grinned. "The tiny one was where I read the email he'd sent me after he first left for London. The one where he said that he really missed me and that nobody brightened up his day like I did."

"Oh my! And to think you might have never read that. That would have been tragic."

"That's what I thought. And I just felt the next step after that had to be to talk to him. So I took a very big chance, which you know doesn't come easily to me, and just went. I even thought he was with someone else – he'd said as much in his last *Footloose and Fancy-free* column. But even that didn't stop me. As I said, it was like someone else had taken over my body."

Susannah remembered feeling like that with Elizabeth Castle. "So. What happened?" she demanded. "Had he met someone?"

"As it turned out, no. But it took a while for me to figure that out. And even if he had, it would still have been the right thing for me to do – to go and see him." She stopped, her face radiant. "But look. We're together now!"

"What? Seriously?" Susannah was amazed.

"Yes, seriously. We are so different from each other and it's a long-distance relationship but it feels right for me. And I'm having fun again – which you might remember was part of your prescription for me!"

"I do remember." Susannah smiled. Anything that made Katie this happy had to be a good thing.

"And there's more. Because I'm going to need time for all these fun weekends with Daniel I figured out I need more time for a personal life. So I went in and played hardball with Mike. I insisted I needed an assistant and hell's bells, when I convinced him that I was serious, it turned out that he didn't want to lose me." Katie shook her head, a bit nonplussed at how well that had turned out.

"That is fantastic, Katie. Well done, you!"

"Thanks." Katie hesitated. "So it's yours if you want it."

"What is?"

"The assistant position."

"Me?" She was astonished at Katie's offer. "I'm flattered. But well, don't you need someone younger? Someone who knows her Snapchat from her Instagram? I'm sure you could get an intern —"

"An intern is the last thing I want," Katie interrupted her. "I want you. You'll still be writing, but there'll be some editorial duties too. You handled Geraldo Laffite very well, so Mike was happy to give me the green light to hire you, if you want it."

Susannah was momentarily speechless.

"Do you need time?" Katie asked.

"No."

"No, you don't want the job?" Katie asked.

"No, I don't want time. So what I really mean is yes. I want the job. Thank you for asking me."

"Oh, wow!" Katie was beaming. "Okay, there's one more thing." She hesitated again. "I don't know if you've heard this already but my mum is moving to England for six months. She's got a job contract in Surrey."

"No, I hadn't heard. I've been out of the loop for a while. You'll miss her, I'm sure. I know I will."

"You won't have time to miss her, you'll be so busy," Katie deadpanned. "But look, forgive me if I'm out of line here, but she's looking for a short-term tenant for her apartment. It's near enough to the office – just in case you were interested." She picked up the bill. "I have to go now. Think about it, but don't leave it too long. I'd say her place will get snapped up."

Susannah watched her go, letting the implications of their meeting sink in. A new, full-time job. In a way it couldn't have come at a worse time, with Rob being sick and the girls back home.

But in another way, it was the best time because it would mean she couldn't get sucked back into organising everybody's life. Not if she wasn't there. She drummed her fingers on the table, trying to work out what exactly she was feeling. Scared but excited too, she decided.

As if another new chapter had just started for her.

CHAPTER 32

Susannah was enjoying a rare night on her own in Pine Close. The girls and Rob had gone to a show at the National Concert Hall, and, partly as a treat and partly because he tired so easily, they were staying overnight in a nearby hotel. The lamp in the living room was turned down low and she was enjoying a large mug of tea. At some stage in the last year, she realised, she had learned to like her own company.

But now everything was about to change again. She had agreed a rent with Olivia and soon she'd be moving out of this house. She tried to picture herself living in Olivia's one-bedroom apartment after the space of Pine Close and couldn't. She'd be a liar if she didn't admit to being nervous about her decision but she'd made up her mind. It would give her time and space to get to grips with her new job without the complications of family life. And it would also mean that she and Rob weren't living under the same roof.

Susannah bit her lip. She hadn't told him yet. But she knew she couldn't go back to the person she had been, when the pinnacle of her ambition had been minibreaks with a man who didn't even see her any more, even though he had been her husband for a quarter of a century.

That should have made her feel old, she reflected, but actually she couldn't remember a time when she'd felt so invigorated.

She seized her opportunity the very next day when Rob returned home alone. Orlaith and Jess had appointments with recruitment agencies all day. The girls had decided not to go back to New York – it turned out they hadn't been that happy there after all and Susannah was hoping they'd be keen to keep an eye on their dad while they were at home.

"We need to talk," she said to Rob, bringing two cups of coffee out to the conservatory.

"I know we do." He followed her out and sank into the seat beside her. "Look, Susannah, I can't tell you how sorry I am for the way things have turned out. When I started planning my trip I only ever considered it to be a fantasy. It was a way of dealing with the stress at work, and the way I felt my life was slipping away from me. And then the bank started offering career breaks and it all suddenly seemed possible. Doable. I know you wanted to come," he added, "and I know I hurt you and I'm sorry about that. But I was in such a bad place at that stage I felt you'd be better off without me for a while."

He looked exhausted, so Susannah bit back the retort that it should have been a decision for both of them to make, not just him.

"It's water under the bridge now," she murmured.

"But is it?" He searched her face. "Can it ever be? I'd give anything to go back to the beginning of this year and make different choices. But I can't do that." He gazed out into the back garden, still overgrown because he hadn't regained enough strength to tackle it yet. "So the question now is, I guess, where do we go from here?"

She saw her opening and took it. "I'm moving out, Rob."

"What? Why? Where?" He twisted his head back to look at her.

He definitely hadn't seen that coming, Susannah thought,

looking at his stricken expression.

But then, neither had she, until she'd spoken to Katie.

She explained to him about the new job offer, and how she decided to rent Olivia's apartment for six months.

"So it will give us space to figure out what we want to do next."

"I know what I want," he said and she felt herself tensing up, bracing for what he'd say next, aware that, at this stage, she felt he could say anything at all.

"I want you to forgive me – so we can go back to being a couple again."

"Just like that?" She raised her eyebrows. She was amazed, all over again, at his sense of entitlement that life should rearrange itself to whatever he happened to want at the time.

"We need to work on our relationship – of course we do," he said, as if she'd just agreed with him in some way. "But I've figured out now why I was feeling the way I did a few months back."

"Why?" she asked, intrigued despite herself.

"It was empty-nest syndrome," he said solemnly.

"You were suffering from empty-nest syndrome?" Susannah couldn't keep the astonishment out of her voice.

"Yes," he said. "The girls were gone, and you were going through their stuff – dumping it. It filled me with terror, Susannah, I don't mind telling you."

"But you didn't tell me," she reminded him. "And isn't empty-nest syndrome when you feel you've been made redundant from your role as a parent?" It was exactly how she'd felt, now that she thought about it, but she hadn't skipped off to Bangkok to find herself because of it.

"Yeah, well, I felt that too – redundant parent. And my therapist thought the reason I was angry at you all the time was because I was subconsciously jealous of all the years you spent with Orlaith and Jess while I had to work."

"Chose to work," she reminded him. That had been a decision they'd both agreed on — that he'd be the one who would work at a career while she looked after the family.

"Yeah, well, the point is, I was working. A lot. And seeing the house being emptied out, first of the girls and then of all their possessions — it reminded me of the years I couldn't get back — years when I didn't follow my dreams."

"What dreams?"

"I didn't even know what they were then," he admitted. "That's why I went to Thailand. And you know what I discovered there? That my dreams were right here all along — right in front of me. With you."

"No. That's not going to happen, Rob." Susannah, who up until that moment had only ever been thinking of moving out temporarily, was suddenly filled with clarity. This speech of Rob's, touching as she might have found it one time, sounded false to her ears now. It was all about him and what he wanted, she realised, and filled with the presumption that Susannah would squeeze herself into whatever shape she had to, just to make what he wanted happen.

"You don't mean that," he told her, his voice deep and persuasive. "You're angry with me and I understand why. But when I was in Thailand —"

"Will you shut up about Thailand for two minutes and listen to me?" Susannah's voice cut through the air like a whip and Rob reeled back, stunned both by the words and the tone of her voice. "I do mean it, Rob," she said, her voice calmer now. "It's too late for us. Maybe it was too late even before you went away. But we'll never know that now — because you took that choice away from me. You broke us up and now you want it all put back together because things didn't work out the way you wanted them to. But choices have consequences, Rob. And this is one of the consequences of yours. I am moving out at the end of the week. And at some point we are going to have to sell this house so we can both move on with our lives properly."

He had no answer, but Susannah didn't get any pleasure out of that. She saw how very quiet and pale he'd become and she very nearly changed her mind.

Part of her – the old Susannah – wanted so badly to withdraw everything she'd just said, to tell him that she was sorry, and that of course they could work things out between them.

But she couldn't because it just wasn't true. Rob had travelled continents to find himself but, by staying at home and connecting closely with her own heart, Susannah knew who she was again. She'd had the most amazing Big Adventure of her own, one she wouldn't have dreamed she was capable of creating.

She thought of all the lessons she had learned and the helpers who had appeared along the way. Olivia, Katie, Cara and James had all influenced her. She even had Rob to thank, because he had forced her out of the rut she'd been in.

But ironically it had been Geraldo Laffite who'd had the most effect on her. He had made her see the world differently, introduced her to people who thought in a different way, people who understood instinctively that if they wanted a different result then it was up to them to figure out how to get it. Even it meant walking on fire and breaking blocks and paying a small fortune to a guru with questionable credentials – at least they were willing to try something new, and she could see the benefits of that now.

The picture collage she'd made at the *Flow Your Life* seminar flashed through her mind. Hers had shown that she wanted Rob and the girls home again. And, in fact, that was now a reality, something Geraldo would probably claim as proof of the effectiveness of his methods.

But they weren't home in the way she'd imagined back then,

because life, of course, had moved on for all of them now. It had a habit of doing that, she reflected soberly, whether you were ready or not.

And even if Geraldo were to give her a magic wand to conjure up that old vision into being she knew now that she wouldn't wave it.

Because even though she hadn't got what she wanted, she'd got what she needed. She had got a life back.

Not Rob's – although she would be forever grateful her husband had survived his illness.

But her life. And no matter what happened in the future, she wasn't giving it up again. Ever.

The End

If you enjoyed *Reinventing Susannah*
you may also enjoy *The Cinderella Reflex.*

Here's a chapter sample as a taster . . .

THE
CINDERELLA
REFLEX

JOAN BRADY

CHAPTER 1

The Cinderella Reflex

There were days when Tess Morgan wished she was back in Bali. Like today. Her boss, Helene Harper, was standing behind her, hands on hips, the pointy toe of one red shoe tapping impatiently on the floor. In front of her, Ollie Andrews, presenter of *This Morning with Ollie Andrews*, Atlantic 1FM's prime-time radio programme glowered out at her from behind the soundproofed glass window of his studio.

"Are you asleep or what?" Helene's voice cracked through the room. "Ollie has just got his facts wrong!"

Tess peered in at Ollie. His popularity – such as it was, considering his plummeting listenership – was a bit of a mystery to her. He had dark bushy eyebrows dominating a pale, almost waxen complexion, a mouth curved downwards in perpetual disappointment and thin hair dyed black in a ludicrous attempt to hold back the years. He managed to look somewhere between forty and forty-five but Tess happened to know he was actually nearer to fifty. She had googled him one day when he had been particularly vile to her and discovered from an old gossip column that he customarily shaved years off his age. She could understand why he was trying to look young though. '*Youth Audience*' seemed to be the mantra for the media industry. And while Atlantic 1FM had once been tipped to get a national licence and put everyone working there on the map, today it held only the faint whiff of desperation as people sensed their careers sliding silently down the drain.

Tess leaned forward, trying to catch up with the conversation between Ollie and his telephone guest. They were perfectly audible but with all the other things she had to do in studio – making sure she had another guest lined up, checking the ad breaks were ready to go, and always having to keep an eye on the clock to make sure the programme fit into the time allotted – it was easy to forget you were supposed to be listening to them as well.

In fact, when Helene had burst in behind her a few minutes before, Tess had been in a pleasant daydream of how different her life had been this time last year. Beach in Bali. Blissed out and suntanned. No responsibility.

She dragged herself back to the present. They seemed to be trying to unravel the complex labyrinth of the banking crisis and the fact that the country was now up to its neck in hock for generations to come. At least that's what Tess thought they were doing.

"Eh, Ollie, go easy there, will you? We wouldn't want to libel anyone!"

Ollie Andrews flicked a switch on his mike so the listeners couldn't hear him.

"I can't get any more out of this numbskull!"

Tess sighed. She had tried to put Ollie off this particular item but he had insisted that the banking crisis was still hot among the trendy young business-heads. Tess wasn't sure she followed his logic. As far as she knew, the banks were now a complete bore to everyone. But she was still relatively new to the job and had assumed he must know something she didn't.

But now it seemed that even Ollie was getting bored. Tess clenched her fists as she watched the telltale signs. He was sighing and pushing his hands through his hair and muttering. But if he finished this item too early it was going to leave her with a gaping big hole to fill. In a show that was going out live. Not to too many people, if the programme's figures were anything to go by. But still. Dead air was the cardinal sin of the radio producer.

And Tess couldn't afford any more mistakes. She needed this job. She flipped the talkback button.

"Ask him ..." She looked down at her notes, trying to frame a question which would enable Ollie to prolong the interview. But she was too late. Of course she was! Ollie Andrews was on-air again.

"So thank you so much for that insightful if controversial analysis of the situation. Of course we could talk about this subject all day, but time, I'm afraid, has run away with us again. So let's take a break!"

As the ad-break jingle filled the room, Tess heard Helene Harper sighing dramatically. Tess's eyes flicked to the wall clock. Her next item up was about a gangland killing in Dublin. But the eyewitness Tess had talked to earlier was nervous and she couldn't rely on Ollie to draw him out – not when he was throwing her dagger looks through the glass.

"Sara!" Tess turned to her assistant who was busy examining her nails – long oval talons, varnished carefully in thin red and black stripes. "Ring Mandy Foley – she's a councillor in that neighbourhood. Maybe she can add something to prolong the discussion."

Tess jumped as Helene gave one more theatrical sigh and barged back out of the studio, slamming the door behind her.

Sara raised a perfectly plucked eyebrow. "We tried Mandy earlier. She's not available this morning. Like, have you forgotten?"

Tess stifled a sigh. She had forgotten. She was thirty years old, and the fresh-out-of-college, super-confident Sara could make her feel ancient. And incompetent. And not too well groomed either. She put the eyewitness through to Ollie, consulting her dog-eared address book at the same time. Tess didn't trust electronic gadgets, not since her computer had caught a virus two weeks before and wiped out all her contacts.

"Try Adam Ellington then." Tess scribbled a telephone number on a scrap of paper and pushed it across the desk. She jiggled her foot, mentally urging Sara to hurry as she leisurely pressed out the number with one perfectly painted finger.

Ollie's interview about the gangland killing was a disaster. The man was giving monosyllabic answers and Ollie was doing nothing to save the item. If he finished up this one early too …

"Hi, Atlantic 1FM here," said Sara. "Mr Adam Ellington, please? Oh hello, Mr Ellington!"

Tess felt herself relaxing slightly as she realised Sara had got her man. Ellington was a well-known human rights lawyer who liked nothing better than the sound of his own voice, preferably on the airways. He'd definitely take a call.

"Streptococcal throat? Right … yeah … we understand. You need to go to bed and get yourself a hot drink and an aspirin … right …"

Tess resisted the urge to reach over and slam down the phone. 'Like', could Sara read the clock?

"Sara!" Her voice rose semi-hysterically and Sara replaced the receiver with a dramatic sigh.

She followed Tess's glance at the studio clock. "I'll try Simon Prenderville." She was already punching out his number before Tess could protest.

Tess's shoulders slumped. Ollie would hate it! Prenderville was a local politician who was on the warpath about making pooper scoopers mandatory for dog-walkers. It would sound ridiculous coming after the gangland killing, but she was up against the clock and she didn't have an alternative. She listened tensely as Sara went through the drill.

"Hi, Mr Prenderville, you will be on-air in just a minute, okay? No, we won't be covering any other topics. Only pooper scoopers, yeah."

Tess took a deep breath and pulled back the talkback button.

"Ollie? Er ... Simon Prenderville is on the line for you. He wants to talk about his plan for more pooper scoopers for Killty."

"What?" Ollie's features flushed scarlet. "We had him on only last week!"

Actually it was two weeks ago, Tess thought. But luckily she didn't have to reply. The red light was shining and they were back on-air. She leaned back slightly while Ollie and Simon Prenderville talked about pooper scoopers. Ollie would make her pay for this of course. But the main thing now was that the item would bring them to the end of today's programme. And tomorrow, in the immortal words of Scarlett O'Hara, was Another Day.

And finally, there it was. The sweet sound of Ollie wrapping up the programme.

"So okay, Councillor Prenderville, thank you for that scoop, *ha ha ha*! And that's all we have for you today, listeners. Until tomorrow then, when you can tune in to *This Morning* again and hear more of the stories you *really* want to hear ... Bye-bye now!"

As the music faded away the smile drained from Ollie's face. Sometimes, Tess mused, he seemed so angry she thought his head might do a 360-degree-turn rotation like a scene out of *The Exorcist*. She stood up, swooping up her pile of manila work files and clutching them to her chest like a shield. She had to get out of here before Ollie stumbled out of his little glass box.

She nodded at Sara. "Er ... I have stuff I need to do. Can you tell Ollie I'll talk to him later?"

Sara gave her a disapproving look. "He'll want to talk to you about the show," she reminded her.

Tess shrugged. She'd have to listen to him soon enough about the bloody show. This afternoon to be precise. At the post-mortem meeting where everyone would put in his or her tuppence-worth about what had worked and what hadn't worked.

But, for now, she needed a break.

Ten minutes later Tess was staring at her reflection in the cracked mirror above the sink in the cramped Ladies' room. Her skin was flushed red and two stains of damp showed darkly under the arms of her white shirt. She pushed her hair out of her eyes, blowing out a sigh. Maybe she'd train for something else. She was good at sketching. And she'd always enjoyed taking photographs. But that only made her thoughts turn to her sister, the super-successful designer in London. While Verity had been busy turning the dream she'd had since she was eleven into a reality, Tess had been drifting from one temporary job to another and from one country to another until finally she'd ended up back in Ireland again.

And now she was in a job that made her feel like a square peg in a round hole. Or a fish out of water. Or some other metaphor that she couldn't think of right now. She winced. She could hear her parents already. "You have to settle at something, Tess. You're *thirty*. Look at Verity, and how well she's doing. That's because she stuck at something."

Tess's mobile bleeped and she pulled it out of her bag, her stomach twisting in case it was Ollie or Helene summoning her.

U free for lunch? Zelda's in ten? A.

Tess brightened. Andrea McAdams, her friend from college, was the reason she was working at Atlantic 1FM in the first place. She had been at home living with her parents for exactly three weeks when Andrea had emailed her about this job. Three weeks in which she had felt as if she'd never left home. So, when Andrea had told her there was an opening at the radio station where she was working as a reporter, Tess had grasped at the offer like a starving person, convinced she could make a success of it. She had a journalism degree and a few freelance bits and pieces on her CV – stuff she'd done in between the beach-bar jobs and the office jobs and the looking-after-children jobs that had paid for her travels around the world. How hard could the gig be?

Only a living nightmare, she had to concede now.

She was supposed to be Ollie's boss but, unfortunately, Ollie thought he was the boss of everyone. And Tess couldn't help wondering if Ollie sensed how scared she was of displeasing him.

Travelling like an itinerant had given her amazing experiences she'd remember forever but had also left her with an alarming financial situation, an overwhelming impulse to 'catch up' with her peers, and a major crisis of confidence when things went against her. Which they seemed to do on an almost daily basis since she'd arrived here six months ago.

Already she'd overheard Ollie complaining about her to Helene.

"She doesn't have what it takes, Helene. Face it!" he'd barked, his face taking on that puce hue that appeared whenever he was even angrier than normal.

"You'll just have to suffer on, Ollie," Helene said flatly. "I don't have time to find someone else right now. Besides, Andrea recommended her – and she does have a journalism degree."

"Journalism degree? She doesn't have a clue!" Ollie exclaimed.

"Well, she's bound to get better. She just needs more experience."

"She's thirty! She should have experience. Can't you get me someone better?"

"I've told you. I don't have time. Give her another three months and I'll reconsider then."

After that, Tess seemed to make one mistake after another. Now with the post-mortem meeting looming she knew lunch was a luxury she couldn't afford. Regretfully, she tapped out her reply.

Working through. Too much of a backlog. See you this afternoon.

She hit send and went off to unpack her plastic box of sandwiches and fruit and settle down to figure out how she was going to defend herself this afternoon.

As soon as she pushed open the door to Helene Harper's office Tess knew that lunch had done nothing to improve Ollie's temper. Several chairs were clustered around the battered brown table that Helene persisted in calling a conference table. Helene hadn't arrived yet but Ollie was sprawled on the chair just inside the door.

"Afternoon," he muttered, barely looking up from his newspaper.

Tess gave him a cursory nod and picked a chair at the opposite end of the table. She flicked her notebook open and started doodling, trying to ignore Ollie ignoring her.

The door opened and Helene arrived. She flung her purple pashmina on the back of a chair and dumped a mountain of newspaper cuttings and press releases onto the table. "Are we the only ones here?" She pursed her lips and glanced at the wall clock just as Andrea arrived.

"Sorry I'm late." Andrea sat down beside Tess. She looked flustered. Her normally perfect auburn bob was dishevelled and her trademark red lipstick smudged, as if she had attempted to touch it up and then realised it was just too late to bother. "Unforeseen circumstances," she added breathlessly to Helene.

Helene sighed. "More domestic drama, I presume? Well, you're here now at least. So, Ollie, what did you think of this morning's programme?"

Ollie glanced down to where Tess was trying to make herself invisible. "It was not our finest hour, Helene."

"No. It wasn't. But this afternoon I'd like us to talk about improvement. Improving our listenership, improving our programmes, improving *ourselves.*" Helene looked around the table. "You all know from the latest figures that we need to – we *must* – come up with better ideas. Tess, you'll be glad to know I intend to put this morning's programme behind us. So – going forward – what are your thoughts?"

Tess swallowed. She had spent the entire lunch hour thinking up ways to justify this morning and now Helene was springing something completely different on her. She looked down at her file. She had spent a large part of Sunday swotting over a pile of newspapers the size of a small country, trying to come up with ideas. But every time she'd notice a story she thought might be worth following up she would remember Ollie and what he'd said about her to Helene and start to question her own judgement. Now she had very little to choose from but she had to try, at least.

She slid a cutting out of the yellow folder in front of her. "I was thinking about doing a slot on how important pets are to people," she said. "This Sunday supplement feature is all about how some people feel just as bereaved by the loss of a pet as they do with a family member and how they can have them buried in a pet cemetery and ..."

Ollie and Helene stared at her in stony silence.

"It would be very popular," she continued uncertainly. "I mean, pets are very in. All the celebrities have dogs they can fit in their handbags ..."

"I wonder if they have pooper scoopers, too?" Ollie asked.

Tess ignored him. "I just think people's pets are important to them – I mean my auntie says her dog is half-human and –"

Andrea kicked her under the table. They both knew that once Ollie or Helene didn't like your idea, it was toast. And, sure enough, Helene was raising her hand imperiously – an unmistakeable signal for Tess to stop.

"I don't think pet bereavement is really us. But I have a great idea myself as it happens. It's a slot on how to look ten years younger!"

"Now *that* is a great idea!" Ollie Andrews banged his thigh with satisfaction.

"It is, isn't it?" Helene beamed at him. "I mean, I know *Ten Years Younger* isn't exactly a new or novel idea, what with every TV programme doing it for years now. But it hasn't been done on radio!"

And that would be because no one will be able to see the makeover on radio, Tess thought.

"It would," Helene continued, "be extreme makeover meets positive thinking meets brand-new future!" She looked expectantly around the table for reaction. "Andrea? What do you think?"

"Em … I suppose …" Andrea was momentarily lost for words.

"What do you think?" Helene repeated impatiently. "About extreme makeovers?"

"I suppose it depends on just how extreme you were thinking," Andrea said cautiously. "I mean, I wouldn't be prepared to go under the knife or anything like that. Maybe Botox."

"And who said you would be going under anything?" Helene interrupted her.

"Oh! I thought you meant I should do a personal-experience report."

"Why?" Helene's voice was brusque.

"W-w-well, I am the reporter for *This Morning*." Andrea stammered a bit, uncharacteristically unsure of herself in the face of Helene's hostility.

"*W-w-well*, we need new voices," Helene mimicked her. "Your reports haven't exactly been setting the world on fire lately, if I may say so. No, I thought I could do the *Ten Years Younger* slot myself actually."

Tess and Andrea exchanged sceptical looks. New voices, my arse. It was obvious Helene had just had some big freebie offered to her in return for a big plug on Atlantic 1FM. But Helene was a disaster on-air.

Tess had seen cases where people walked into the studio appearing to be really coy and shy, and then, as soon as the red light came on, they suddenly became charged with adrenaline and performed to perfection. Helene was the opposite of those people. On the few occasions she insisted on doing a broadcast her face had glowed as red as the on-air light, with a nervous rash spreading all over her face and neck. She'd stumbled through her scripts, her normal acerbic fluency deserting her as she *ummed* and *ahhed* and rambled down all sorts of blind alleys without ever really getting her point across. Nobody ever told her this, of course. Everyone simply tried to discourage her from ideas that would involve her going on-air.

But today, she was fired up with enthusiasm and would not be deterred. She was rummaging through the enormous pile of papers she had dumped on the table, her voice getting higher as she spoke.

"Let me explain. The Spa Fantastic is keen to get more publicity and they've offered us a weekend of *Ten Years Younger* treatments! Now where did I leave their brochure? Ah yes, here it is!" Helene pulled a pink brochure from the pile in front of her and began to read: " '*The Spa Fantastic Experience can make you feel ten years younger. In this oasis of Me Time you can take a break from the stress of day-to-day living. Take the time to be pampered with our fully trained therapists. Have a four-handed hot stone massage . . .* '"

Four hands? What the hell does that mean, thought Tess.

Helene glanced on down the page, "*Blah blah blah* . . . well, we get the idea anyway." She looked around the room for reaction.

"How is it going to work on radio?" Tess ventured. "I mean, nobody will be able to see the result of the makeover."

No one answered, so Tess tossed out an idea.

"Maybe we could run a competition? We could ask the listeners to email us as to why they feel they need to look ten years younger in the first place? We could get a very interesting debate going about why our society is so obsessed with youth. It would be great material for us and the contestants would feel rewarded for listening to *This Morning*."

"Excuse me?" Ollie sat up straighter in his seat. "Since when did listeners need a reward to listen to me?" he asked icily.

"I meant a bonus," Tess amended hastily.

"I'm sure you did!" Ollie turned to Helene. "I think it would be best if I did the *Ten Years Younger* slot myself, Helene."

"And how would that work?" Helene raised an eyebrow. "You interviewing yourself about your experience at the spa? I think not, Ollie."

"It's me the listeners are interested in!" Ollie persisted. "Maybe we could go together, Helene?"

Helene threw the Spa Fantastic Experience brochure down on the table with considerable force. "I am going to do it, Ollie. By myself. That's the end of the discussion. Tess! Can you get on the case and set it all up for me? The weekend at the Spa Fantastic will be just the start. For instance, Botox. Does anyone know if it hurts much?" She looked directly at Ollie's suspiciously smooth forehead.

Ollie narrowed his eyes, but didn't respond.

Helene shrugged. "Tess, find out if Botox is painful!"

Andrea wrote '*Get Sara to do it*,' on her notepad and leaned in towards Tess so she could read it. Tess hid a smile. Sara, who still hadn't shown up, would have the beauty industry thinking their product name was being heard by hundreds of thousands of listeners instead of simply hundreds, purely by virtue of her snooty attitude.

At that moment, the door opened and Sara burst in. Helene went through the same routine she had with Andrea, looking at the wall clock with a pained expression. But Sara just put on her most stuck-up impression.

"Bloody traffic. I simply couldn't get parking. You'd want to be driving, like, a Smart car to get parking in this town. And Daddy wouldn't put up with that at all – he says it would make him the laughing stock of the golf club if he bought me one of those!" She slipped into one of the seats and looked expectantly around the room. Her pale-blonde hair fell in an expensive cut around her exquisite, heart-shaped face, and her outfit, Tess calculated, probably cost the equivalent of six months' wages.

Helene muttered something under her breath, but she seemed almost embarrassed to be chastising Sara. Yet she'd practically bitten the head off Andrea earlier. Tess sighed. No matter what treatments they drummed up for Helene, none of them were going to make her ten times nicer. When was someone going to come up with a serum for that, she wondered.

Helene turned to Sara. "We're thinking of doing an item on *Ten Years Younger*. Do you have any ideas about that, Sara?"

"Me?" A bewildered look passed over Sara's beautiful face. "Why would I want to know anything about looking ten years younger? I mean, if I looked ten years younger, I'd only look about twelve. I already have trouble getting served drink unless I have ID with me. Of course," she looked around the room thoughtfully, "it's probably a good idea for the rest of you." Then she asked kindly, "Would you like me to do some research on it, Helene?"

"You can give Tess a hand," Helene muttered. "Now. Can we have your ideas for the week please, Andrea?"

Andrea looked panicked. "I don't have anything nailed down at the moment. But," she added hurriedly as Helene's features darkened, "I do have a few ideas floating around in the ether ..."

"The ether?" Ollie cut in. "That's the place to have them all right!"

"There's no need to be sarcastic, Ollie!" Helene admonished him. "We must all be positive together now! We are losing listeners but we can turn it around! Can't we, people?" She looked challengingly from face to face.

Nobody said a word.

Then Ollie spoke. Or rather shouted. "*How* can we turn it

around? *How?*" His face was flushed and his brown eyes were bulging. "Will we get more listeners with Andrea's ideas – out in the ether? Or with Tess's stories about pooper scoopers? As for your idea, Helene! How to look ten years younger! That is just a ruse to get a freeloading weekend and I am so stressed right now I could do with one of those myself. But how is it going to improve my figures?"

"Your figures are not my only problem, Ollie," Helene said coolly.

"You can say that again, lady!" Ollie jumped to his feet. "And trying to look ten years younger won't help your problems either! Try ten decades. Ten decades of the Rosary, that is!" And with that Ollie stormed out, nearly taking the door off its hinges as he slammed it behind him.

Inside the room there was complete silence. All Tess could hear was the ticking of the wall clock. She focussed hard on her notebook, pretending to be reading over her notes.

Finally Helene broke the silence. "So!" she beamed around the room. "That was a frank exchange of ideas! Lots of creative tension – that's good! That's what we need to turn this station around, folks. And now I have another meeting to attend. You can all go now."

As Tess stood up to leave she could hear Helene clicking and unclicking the top of her biro compulsively – the only outward sign that Ollie's tantrum had rattled her in any way whatsoever.

Did you enjoy this chapter sample from
The Cinderella Reflex?

See the full book online at poolbeg.com